A PLUME BOOK

BECOMING JOS...

Angie Parkinson

HEATHER WEBB is a contributor to the popular writing blog *Romance University*, and she manages her own blog, *Between the Sheets*. When not writing, she flexes her foodie skills, or looks for excuses to head to the other side of the world. She is a member of the Historical Novel Society and lives in Connecticut with her family. Connect online at www .HeatherWebb.net, Twitter/@msheatherwebb, or Facebook/Heather Webb, Author.

Praise for *Becoming Josephine*

"With vivid characters and rich historical detail, Heather Webb has portrayed in Josephine a true heroine of great heart, admirable strength, and inspiring courage whose quest is that of women everywhere: to find, and claim, oneself."

—Sherry Jones, bestselling author of *The Jewel of the Medina* and *Four Sisters All Queens*

"Heather Webb's epic novel captivates from its opening in a turbulent plantation society in the Caribbean, to the dramatic rise of one of France's most fascinating women: Josephine Bonaparte. Perfectly balancing history and story, character and setting, detail and pathos, *Becoming Josephine* marks a debut as bewitching as its protagonist."

—Erika Robuck, author of *Hemingway's Girl*

"A fast-paced, riveting journey, *Becoming Josephine* captures the volatile mood of one of the most intense periods of history—libertine France, Caribbean slave revolts, the French Revolution, and the Napoleonic Wars—from the point of view of one of its key witnesses, Josephine Bonaparte." —Dana Gynther, author of *Crossing on the Paris*

"Vivid and passionate, *Becoming Josephine* captures the fiery spirit of the woman who stole Napoleon's heart and enchanted an empire."
—Susan Spann, author of *The Shinobi Mysteries*

"Spellbinding . . . Heather Webb's novel takes us behind the mask of the Josephine we thought we knew."
—Christy English, author of *How to Tame a Willful Wife* and *To Be Queen*

"Enchanting prose takes the reader on an unforgettable journey. . . . Captivating young Rose springs from the lush beauty of her family's sugar plantation in Martinique to shine in the eighteenth-century elegance of Parisian salon society. When France is torn by revolution, not even the blood-bathed terror of imprisonment can break her spirit." —Marci Jefferson, author of *Girl on the Gold Coin*

Becoming Josephine

A NOVEL

Heather Webb

A PLUME BOOK

PLUME
Published by the Penguin Group
Penguin Group (USA) LLC
375 Hudson Street
New York, New York 10014

USA | Canada | UK | Ireland | Australia | New Zealand | India | South Africa | China
penguin.com
A Penguin Random House Company

First published by Plume, a member of Penguin Group (USA) LLC, 2014

ℙ REGISTERED TRADEMARK—MARCA REGISTRADA

LIBRARY OF CONGRESS CATALOGING-IN-PUBLICATION DATA
Webb, Heather, 1976 December 30–
     Becoming Josephine : a novel / Heather Webb.
       pages cm
     ISBN 978-0-14-218065-5
     1. Josephine, Empress, consort of Napoleon I, Emperor of the French, 1763–1814—
Fiction. 2. Self-realization in women—Fiction. 3. France—History—Revolution, 1789–
1799—Fiction. 4. Biographical fiction. 5. Historical fiction. I. Title.
     PS3623.E3917B43 2014
     813'.6—dc23
                                        2013022719

Printed in the United States of America
10 9 8 7 6 5 4 3 2 1

Set in Baskerville MT Std
Designed by Eve L. Kirch

For Christopher

)

On ne naît pas femme: on le devient.
—Simone de Beauvoir

One is not born woman; one becomes woman.

Malmaison
Paris, 1814

The missive arrived in the night. I paced from bed to bureau and back again, finally pausing to open the velvet drapes. The moon cast a ghostly glow on the dogwood blooms and barren rose gardens. My gardens of paradise. Others had intended it to be my prison, but I found it a hard-earned refuge. A place of safety after a lifetime of flight, a heavy crown, and the deaths of so many I held dear.

I covered my face with my hands. My benefactor, my greatest love, had been arrested. What would become of him?

At one time, I could have summoned answers, but those days and the Rose I was were long since buried, consumed by the powerful woman I'd created. Still, I thought, perhaps I yet possessed my Creole heart.

I dashed to the vanity and found the dusty white pouch with my cards. One by one, I placed black candles in a ring on the floor. Match to wick, and their flames sparked to life in the stillness.

What would the future hold?

I drew the tarot from its pouch and lay a spread. My eyes blurred at the message. The ancient drawings danced. First the Empress, a nurturer of her people. Six of Cups—nostalgia for long ago. And finally the Judgment card, an angel calling lost souls home.

My pulse quickened as a draft blew through the room. To understand my future, I must revisit my past.

The candles went out.

Leaving Home

Martinique, 1779

We wandered along a darkened trail, farther from the house than Papa ever allowed.

"This way." I pushed through a web of tangled vines. "We're almost home."

My younger sister peered up at the sky. "We'll get lashings if we don't hurry." Silvery twilight filtered through the thick canopy of jungle trees and the trill of a lone bird warned us to proceed with caution.

"I wouldn't have made you come if I didn't have to. And it was worth it." I put my fingertips to my lips. Guillaume had kissed me after losing three straight hands of brelan. Payment, he had said. I always outplayed him at cards.

"Papa will be furious if he finds out."

"You're not going to tell him?" I asked.

She looked at me with an innocent expression. "That depends."

"You can use my new drawing pencils."

"I don't know. . . ."

"You can wear my earrings to town next week." I looked at her for confirmation.

"Done." A thorned vine attached to the skirt of Catherine's gown and she tugged it away. "Why do you insist on meeting the blacksmith's boy anyway?"

"Why not? He's handsome and he makes me laugh."

"You'll spoil yourself, you know. If you're not careful. Who will marry you then?" she asked.

"I don't wish for marriage at all if it is like our parents'." I had no intention of leading a life like Maman's. I would escape to France, to the adventure of Paris and the grand court life of Papa's tales. The elegant gowns and intrigue, the handsome men. And love without bounds.

"I may not wed, even if I wish to." I swatted at a winged insect hovering about my face. "Papa invites suitors to the house for you, not me." A twinge of envy darkened my mood. "He favors you."

"He doesn't favor me, Rose."

I threw her a doubtful look. "You know it's true. He said to me yesterday that I'll never capture a man's affection."

A flash of lightning illuminated the thicket; a rumbling followed.

"Time to go." I grabbed Catherine by the hand.

The sky split open. Rain soaked the verdant landscape, turning the forest floor to a soup of mud and rotted vegetation. We leapt over holes filled with water and waxen leaves and darted through the underbrush. When at last the sugar mill—our home since the Great Hurricane—came into view, Mimi threw open the door.

"Best get inside," she scolded. "Your *maman*'s right upset." My maid bundled us in dry blankets. "Catherine, you're pale as death."

My sister coughed and shivered as Maman stormed into the room.

"Rose!" She clutched my arm and dragged me toward my bedroom. "Your sister doesn't disobey without your prodding. I swear you'll be the death of you both! Learn to follow the rules of this house or you'll spend a week in the cellar! Do you understand?"

She pushed me into the room and slammed the door.

As it happened, I was only the death of one of us.

Catherine contracted a fever and by morning she could not get out of bed. Within the fortnight, she was gone.

The afternoon of her funeral, we trudged silently back to the house through the rain. Rain like the day I had led my sister to her death.

Banana trees bowed beneath the weight of water driving from the swollen sky. Palm fronds waved in the wind like arms desperate for attention. Maman and my youngest sister, Manette, linked their arms with mine. I stared ahead, ignoring my soaked skirts and the desperate grip of Maman's hand. Regret throbbed in my chest.

I remembered Catherine limp in bed with blood trickling from her pasty lips. My stomach turned. I stopped by the edge of the path and retched.

"If you hadn't been up to mischief, she wouldn't be ill," Papa had said when Catherine's condition worsened. He blamed me.

We had played in the rain so often. It was always raining on the island. How could I have known that day would be different?

The throbbing grew—hammered at my head, my insides, my heart. My sister was gone, as if she had never been. And it was my fault. I choked back a sob. Maman patted my shoulder with a light hand.

We entered our humble salon and handed our dripping cloaks to Mimi. I moved to the window, numbly avoiding conversation.

The rain ceased as suddenly as it had begun. Sun blazed around the edges of the clouds.

"I'll fetch some tea," Mimi said, her brown eyes sad. She had loved our Catherine, too. "And, monsieur, there's a letter come in the post from your sister."

"Read it for me?" Papa handed the missive to Maman and blotted his sodden wig with a cloth.

She read the letter aloud.

> As you know, dear brother, I aim to secure my position with the Marquis.
>
> Despite our constant love, his wife refuses to sever ties with him.

Maman paused. "The Marquis hasn't divorced his wife yet?" She didn't hide her disdain.

Papa made an exasperated sound. "You know very well a divorce would scandalize the Beauharnais name. The Marquis would sooner wait for his wife to die and marry Désirée after."

"I love your sister, but cannot abide her living with another woman's husband." Maman's thin lips stretched into a line. Her nostrils flared. "It's immoral."

I knew Papa disagreed. He bedded every willing lady in Fort-Royal and all the prettiest slaves on our plantation, willing or not, a sickening situation and a never-ending embarrassment for Maman. I eyed Mimi while she tended to the mud tracked across the rug. She was the result of one of his affairs with a slave.

Papa threw his hands in the air. "Don't question Désirée's morals. Marriage is not about love."

I cringed at his words. I would not, could not endure a marriage like theirs. My future husband would cherish me. If I had one at all.

"I married you for love, you *con*," Maman seethed. "But your philandering and drinking ruined everything! And don't get me started on your gambling! If I didn't manage this plantation, we'd live in huts with the slaves. As it is, we live in tatters and you do nothing!"

Manette cowered on the faded divan. I moved to comfort her. We both detested their arguments.

"Don't take that tone with me! You forget your place, wife!"

A long silence followed.

At last Maman smoothed the crinkled letter and began again.

> I would also like to ensure the financial assistance you desire. Please send your daughter Catherine to Paris at once. I will arrange her marriage to the Marquis's son, Alexandre. Their union will join our families, and Alexandre's inheritance may save your plantation from ruin. Make haste. We are all anxious to enact this plan.

"Catherine would have made a perfect bride," Maman said, voice thick with sorrow. "Enchanting to Désirée and Alexandre alike."

I gritted my teeth in jealousy. Catherine had been no better than I and yet my parents always compared my flaws to her perfections. A sudden pang of guilt left me ashamed. My darling sister, ill and now stone cold in the ground, how could I be jealous of you?

"Manette is too young." Papa's expression darkened. "And Rose is too old and would offer little to Alexandre."

His words hit me like a blow. I recovered quickly and stood. "*Parfait*, Papa. As I have no wish to marry any man you choose for me." I raised my chin. "I will marry for love or not at all!"

Papa gripped my shoulders. "You will marry when I say!"

I wrenched free and bolted through the front door to the garden, beneath the frangipani trees and into the dense foliage. Tears streamed down my face. I possessed no control, even over my own life. I ran to outpace my thoughts, to push the hurt from my limbs. Oh, Catherine! How could you leave me?

I climbed the longest path, the one Papa forbade even on the best of days. The path that led to the most feared woman on the island, the voodoo priestess. The slaves bartered for her potions despite their fear, as would I to learn my fate. Catherine had sworn she would visit her with me, but spooked when we started on the path. This time I would not turn back.

There had to be more for me, more than this life.

I sucked in the steamy air, heart thundering in my ears. A screech sounded from the shadows. The familiar shapes of the wood grew grotesque in the fading light. I ran faster. Serpents slid from their holes when the heat of the day faded, seeking victims for their poison. I had witnessed bitten men convulse with frothing lips and blue-black swelling beneath their skin. I shook my head to dispel the images. I couldn't think of that now.

I had to know.

I pushed deeper into the forest until a clearing came into view— and her house, a small thatched hut and fire pit.

I wiped my face with the back of my hand and moved beyond the cover of the jungle.

"I've been waiting for you." A woman stepped through the doorway into the clearing. Silver hair sprang from her head in unruly waves. Layers of wooden beads encircled her neck and a fetish of an Ibo god dangled between her drooping breasts.

"I don't have coins," I began, "but—"

"Sit." She motioned toward a ring of uneven stumps near the fire.

I chose the seat farthest from her and sat down, uncomfortable in my black mourning gown now slick with sweat.

The old woman chanted, lips moving in rhythm as she rocked. She tossed dried herbs and entrails into the fire. My throat tightened at the stench.

As suddenly as she had begun chanting, the priestess stopped. She fixed her probing eyes on mine. My breath halted in my lungs.

"You will travel a great distance and be married." Her eyes rolled back in their sockets.

My heart quickened. To France? I longed for adventure and love.

Let there be true love. I said a silent prayer.

"Beware, child." The priestess paused. "This union will come to a violent end. A dark stranger without fortune will become your husband." The priestess leaned forward, her eyes reflecting the flashing light of the fire. "And you will become more than queen."

I frowned. "No woman is greater than a queen."

The priestess's eyes fluttered. Her throat gurgled. She fell to the ground in a seizing fit, limbs flailing.

I gasped and knelt over her.

"Go!" She shoved me away.

I leapt to my feet and flew through the jungle, thrashing against the dark undergrowth. My lungs burned and my shoes grew heavy with mud. I dared not look back.

Evening shadows reached home before I did. I burst through the side door, tripped on the threshold, and fell to the floor.

At Papa's feet.

"You're filthy." He glared down at me. "Change at once and meet me in the salon. I have news for you."

Étrangère

Brest, France, 1779

The priestess's voice vibrated in my soul, her black magic as real as flesh. I could not make sense of her words and dreamt of her most nights at sea, or those I managed to sleep. Papa sent me in Catherine's stead. A marriage in a distant land, as the old woman had promised.

I rubbed my chilled arms. The journey had ended, *merci au bon Dieu.*

My feet touched solid ground. Not the salty gray sands I had expected of the Brittany coast, but rather an enormous port crammed with all manner of vessels. Boats bobbed in a gentle procession over the wake, creaking as the water slapped their sides. Sailors and soldiers, boat hands and passengers scurried in every direction as bells announced the incoming fog. Brest was grander than Fort-Royal in every way but color. Slate blue, charcoal, and lifeless gray dominated the sky, the land, and everything between.

I would miss my vibrant home. But at least there would be no more blasted ship, no more hurtling through the sea. I gathered my filthy skirts and stumbled up the walk on wobbly legs. My pink shoes stood out like pearls against the jet of the dock and the black water below.

A familiar nausea rolled in my belly and crept up my throat. I clutched my midsection.

"You ill?" Mimi called as she dragged our trunks behind her. Clumps of her crimped hair stuck out from beneath the colorful scarf tied over her head.

"Still a bit seasick. A proper bed will be heaven. *Mon Dieu*, Mimi, I thought we'd never make it." I descended the dock stair and stepped onto the dirt path. It led to several boathouses and a tavern with fogged windowpanes. The next row of buildings faced the harbor, lit doorways open, inviting. Women in vermillion corsets and netted stockings lounged within, beckoning with their painted nails and heavily rouged smiles.

A memory of Papa surfaced, his face lost in the bosom of a half-dressed mulatto woman. I had sneaked from school with Guillaume one night to hide behind the empty crates near the brothel door—a silly dare. And there Papa stood, pawing at a woman who was not my mother.

I turned away from the whores. Time to look forward, not back.

I scanned the line of fiacres and hackney coaches in eager anticipation. Here at last!

"A gentleman hired transportation and rooms for us. Would you see to it? The captain said I am to wait here for a courier." I stroked the creased letter. Aunt Désirée and Alexandre expected to hear from me right away.

"I'll get to finding him." Mimi mopped her face with a handkerchief.

I nodded and turned back to the frigate, my home and prison these past months. The familiar faces of its passengers had dispersed in a hundred directions. A lump of apprehension lodged in my throat. I would make friends straightaway, without doubt. But Alexandre. I sighed. I hoped he would be a man I could love.

The courier arrived, toting his sack of letters. I delivered my own and paid him as I felt a hand at my elbow.

"Our coach is waiting round the bend." Mimi pointed to a road that snaked around the corner of a gray boathouse.

We traveled to an inn on the outskirts of Brest. Knobby pastures dotted with grazing sheep and fattened dairy cows stretched as far as the horizon. Gone were the throngs of travelers and the slate blue sea, though the vacant arc of pallid sky followed us from the shore. The grayness soaked into my skin and filled the hollow in my chest.

Papa couldn't have loved a place as lackluster as this. Certainly Paris would be more appealing. I imagined the King's court of handsome men in pressed coats, swirling courtiers across a perfectly polished floor, their jewels glinting in the light. I smiled. I would visit the court one day soon with Alexandre.

I paced the dilapidated inn for three days awaiting news from Désirée. How long would it take her to respond? Mimi and I strolled through the wilted garden to pass the time. One afternoon as we made our way up the front walk, an elegant carriage pulled into the drive. My palms grew clammy inside my only gloves.

"It must be them." I laughed a shrill sound and clutched Mimi's arm. "I didn't expect to be so nervy."

"Don't worry your pretty head, girl. He'll be taken with you." She kissed my cheek to comfort me.

When the coach stopped, an elegant blond woman alighted. Aunt Désirée glided toward me. Her pale blue dress hung in perfect folds, its embroidery of silver flowers shimmering in the watery sunlight. Her vast skirts swelled around her hips as if pillows were hidden beneath the fabric, accentuating her tiny waist. A ribbed corset wound around her middle to boost her lace-trimmed bosom. Teardrop baubles swung from her earlobes and a ribbon-embellished hat perched fashionably atop her head.

I smoothed my own water-stained shift and flushed with embarrassment.

"Hello, Rose." Désirée embraced me lightly. A feigned gesture—was she displeased with me?

"Hello, Aunt Désirée," I said, kissing her cheeks.

"You were a child the last time I saw you." She had left Martinique a decade ago and she still looked as beautiful as I remembered.

Désirée stepped back to assess my appearance. We stood in awkward silence.

At last she said, "*Chérie*, your lips are blue!" She took my hands in hers. "I have some warm things for you. I haven't forgotten my first weeks in France. It's difficult to bear the cool weather in the beginning."

"Thank you. I have shivered ever since we arrived."

She patted my shoulder. "You will adjust."

I turned. "This is my maid, Mimi."

Désirée nodded. "Your voyage—how did you fare?"

"I've never been so sick. My stomach still rocks." I glanced at the carriage. "Where is Alexandre? Has he come?"

"Of course, dear. He has fallen asleep in the coach." She cupped her mouth with a gloved hand and called, "Alexandre? Alexandre!"

"I'll wake him, madame," the coachman said.

Désirée glanced at the shabby inn. The sign near the door hung crookedly from a single rusty hinge. My aunt's lips pinched as if she tasted something sour.

"Goodness, child. You stayed here? We'll find a more suitable place." She looked at Mimi. "Why don't you see to Rose's things?"

"Madame." Mimi curtsied and rushed off in the direction of the inn.

"Aunt Désirée, I—"

She waved her hand dismissively. "I will pay, of course."

I fidgeted for several long moments.

A door screeched, in need of oil. My breath caught as my future husband staggered from the coach. He stretched, and looked around with a bored expression.

Our eyes met.

Alexandre raised one dark eyebrow in a perfect arc.

I caught my breath. He possessed such fine features—a straight nose and high cheekbones, full lips and light eyes. He held himself like a prince in his white officer's uniform, embellished with silver buttons, ornate lapels, and blue *culottes*. His powdered hair appeared coiffed to perfection. Even his boots gleamed.

I sneaked a glance at my own scuffed shoes and musty dress. My reflection in the glass this morning had shown sun spots and bleached hair from my time on deck. I looked like a commoner, as the wiser women on board had warned me I would.

I straightened my shoulders. I was attractive and I possessed rare charm. Maman always said so.

Alexandre stared, but made no move in my direction. I smiled in greeting. A fleeting emotion shone in his eyes, though I could not identify it from a distance. Surely not disdain?

I flinched and turned to Désirée. She looked away.

He must dislike the lodging, I told myself, to repudiate my doubts. I shifted from one foot to the other. Alexandre lingered for an eternity, eyes roving over the scenery and weighing its worth. I winced. This was not an auspicious place to meet your future wife.

He moved toward me. I stiffened until he stopped before me and bent in a slight bow.

"Mademoiselle Marie-Josèphe-Rose de Tascher de La Pagerie, I'm pleased to make your acquaintance."

"Finally," I breathed. How long I had anticipated this moment.

Surprise filled his eyes. Confused, I glanced at Désirée.

"If you will excuse me," she said, "I will see about another inn."

"Allow me," Alexandre offered.

"Thank you, dear, but I can manage. I'll leave you to become acquainted." She gave me a tight smile before leaving.

I played with the sad bow hanging from my sleeve. Alexandre cleared his throat and looked around.

Silence.

Finally, I asked, "How is the Marquis?"

"Father is in bed most days," he answered in a disinterested tone.

"He is ill? I'm sorry . . . I didn't realize—"

"It's been a slow degradation. He's still sharp of mind. It is only his body that fails him. Even so, I suspect he has many years left."

"Well that's a relief."

Disbelief crossed his features once more.

I frowned. What had I said?

He crossed his arms over his chest.

"And your brother, François?" I tried again.

"Well, thank you. I trust your voyage wasn't too grueling?" He looked over my head at a pair of women leaving the inn.

"It was dreadful. Storms nearly drowned us. And I couldn't eat or drink—the rocking made me so ill. I—" Alexandre's incredulous expression stopped me.

"Do you always speak so plainly?" he asked.

Heat crept up my neck to my cheeks. "Monsieur? You asked about my trip."

"Never mind. We have other, more pressing changes to make than your speech . . . your accent, and . . ." He looked down his nose at my dress.

"Excuse me?" Pricks of anger barbed under my skin. How dare he be so rude!

Mimi emerged from the inn, hauling the trunks.

Désirée reappeared behind her, a list in hand. "I have found another inn not far from here."

Alexandre nodded, a grim expression reflected on his features. My cheeks flamed with embarrassment. His first impression of me had not been a favorable one.

Désirée clapped her hands and pretended not to notice. "*Merveilleux!*"

We began our journey to Paris the following day, traversing pastures and hills that rose in waves of green carpet, forked by streams and covered in brush. Most days clouds blanketed the sky and drizzle filtered through golden and peach-colored leaves. The smell of cool air and wet ground pervaded—so unlike my island's smoky sweetness of burning sugarcane and wildflower perfume. Despite Désirée's wool cloak, the raw weather soaked into my bones.

We rode much of the way in silence. I amused myself by studying the landscape of trees and the few autumn flowers.

"How vivid Martinique must be," Alexandre said. "I hardly remember it from childhood." He had left the island with Désirée to seek a more refined life in Paris.

"I had never given it a second thought until now," I said. "There is a realness. . . . Trois-Îlets has a heartbeat. It is so alive. But it is lovely here, too," I added in haste, not wishing to insult.

Alexandre chuckled, blue eyes twinkling. "Paris may be more alive than you can manage, farm girl." He took my hand and caressed it as if stroking a kitten. "I'm sure you will adore it."

His fingertips left a trail of flames on my skin. I blushed, timid at my reaction to his affection. He did like me. We just needed to get to know one other.

"I'm certain I will." I smiled.

We stopped at an inn after the long day of travel.

"I have a present for you." Alexandre had joined Désirée and me in the common room for an aperitif.

I perked up at once.

"*De l'Esprit des Lois.*" He handed me a worn book and settled into a chair with a brandy glass. "Montesquieu. A great philosophe. His works were not always praised in France, but it is a new era. You'll enjoy his inspired theories of human injustice." Passion lit his eyes.

"Wonderful." I smiled in spite of my doubt. Lessons on music, art, or gardens, perhaps, I would enjoy far more. No matter. His enthusiasm delighted me. "I'll begin reading tonight."

In the morning, I settled into my carriage seat, happy to be spending more time in close proximity with him.

Alexandre smiled. "And how did you find the book? The Americans have taken to his ideals of separation of powers."

I shifted in my seat. I had hardly read the first ten pages before drifting to sleep. "Your views are surely more informed than mine. Would you care to share them?"

"I find his thoughts on personal freedoms . . ."

My attention drifted as he explained theory after theory. His lips, the excitement in his eyes, the way his brow furrowed on his perfect face proved an interesting study. When he paused from time to time, I could not hide how much he impressed me. Nor could I resist attempting to charm him.

"Fascinating, Alexandre." I placed my hand on his arm. "You are so knowledgeable."

He beamed at my obvious admiration. I smiled back at him. Perhaps this marriage would turn out better than I had hoped.

The final morning of our journey we embarked early, eager to reach our destination by nightfall. The ride passed in a blur of sunshine and trees, and by dusk, Paris emerged. As we entered the city gates, the setting sun glowed in a dreamy swirl of pink and orange, resembling the inside of a papaya. Along the horizon arose the largest number of buildings I had ever seen.

I gaped. "It's . . . it's . . ."

Alexandre flashed a brilliant smile and laughed. "Paris is the most remarkable city in the world."

"Incredible!" I clapped in delight.

The sheer number of people rendered me speechless. Hordes shuffled along the roadside carrying packages, toting their children, or walking arm in arm with friends. Odors assailed my senses; rich coffee wafted from cafés, sweaty horses and fetid piles of animal waste assaulted, flowery perfumes and warm bread tempted. Street vendors, juggling performers, and the incessant clopping of hooves whirled together in an orchestra of sounds.

"*Mon Dieu,* look at all the coaches!"

Gilded carriages and speeding fiacres dodged pedestrians and splattered mud in every direction. I gaped at the opulent homes of stone and imposing state buildings guarded by the King's army. The city hummed like a swarm of bees on a cluster of begonias.

Alexandre enjoyed my awe, pointing out the Palais-Royal and Luxembourg, explaining their histories. I tried to listen, but the throngs captured my attention.

After a long ride through the city, Alexandre enveloped my hand in his. "Here we are. Noisy-le-Grand, your new neighborhood."

A pungent stink burned my nostrils. "Alexandre, what is that smell?" I wrinkled my nose in disgust.

"Excrement and mud. You won't notice it for long. I don't smell it at all."

I looked at him in surprise. Of course I would notice it. I covered my nose with my handkerchief to block the horrid odor.

Our coach stopped in front of a two-story house composed mostly of stone.

"Welcome home," Alexandre said.

Désirée kissed my cheek. "Welcome."

"Thank you." I suppressed another delighted squeal—I shouldn't appear too childish.

I stepped down from the coach and surveyed the neighboring houses. Rickety dwellings cramped the spaces between the grander homes, a curious scene. The wealthy separated into their own quartiers in Fort-Royal, but not in Paris, it seemed. Still, the neighborhood pos-

sessed a sense of faded glory, though I had envisioned more elegance
from a *vicomte*.

A servant opened the front door and ushered us into a vestibule
with towering ceilings.

"Bonjour, mademoiselle," another servant said, curtseying. Her
voice echoed in the hall. "May I bring you anything?"

"*Non, merci*." I walked toward the staircase dominating the hall and
ran my hand along the worn banister.

"Rose, the Marquis awaits our arrival," Désirée said.

"Of course." I followed her, studying the rooms and their furnishings as we went.

Despite the golden glow from oil lamps and candles, the house was
cold and dark, like the stone of which it was made. Its depressive ambience lacked the luxury I had expected—so unlike the airy, wooden
mansions of the Grands Blancs in Fort-Royal, decked with palms and
wildflowers. Heavy drapes replaced the gauzy curtains that billowed
on sea breezes I remembered from home. Cool air leaked under doorways and crept over icy marble floors, mingling with the stale air inside.

Unimpressive furniture filled the rooms, save for one stunning table
veneered with layers of priceless wood. Its gilded-bronze finish glinted
in the firelight. I ran my fingers over the smooth veneer, warm from
the heat of the fire. A perfect spot to play cards or read my tarot deck.

"Have a seat, my dear. They'll join us in a moment."

I settled into a blue silk chair facing Désirée. Where had Alexandre
gone? He would greet his father, I assumed. I tried not to fidget.

A servant assisted the Marquis into the room. Another gentleman
followed, likely Alexandre's brother, François. All three men resembled
one another; proud chins and wide blue eyes distinguished them as
family. I stood quickly.

"You must be Rose." The Marquis approached and took my hand
in his. "Welcome. We're happy you have arrived." His smile was kind
and his eyes crinkled at the corners.

"Thank you, monsieur. I am thrilled to be here." I returned his
smile.

"And this"—he motioned to François—"is my other son, François,
your soon-to-be brother."

François bowed, creasing his stiff suit coat sewn with gold thread. "*Enchanté*, mademoiselle. Please forgive me, but I'm afraid I must go. I am late for an engagement." He inclined his head toward me. "If you'll excuse me."

"Of course." I nodded and he hurried from the room.

"Please make yourself at home, Rose," the Marquis said. "We are family, after all."

"You're very kind." Relief washed over me. Désirée and the Marquis were lovely.

When shown to my room to dress for supper, I cheered inwardly. Rest at last. I snatched the blanket at the foot of my bed and snuggled in by the fire. I relished the heat like an iguana scorching in a treetop under the tropical sun. The vision of midday warmed my blood.

It seemed odd Alexandre should allow Désirée to play hostess. I supposed he admired her a great deal, despite her being only a sort of stepmother.

After an hour of rest, I returned to the hall. A dining table had been set with an ivory cloth and fine dishes. I slid into an empty chair.

"Shall we dine?" Désirée lowered her graceful form into a chair across from the Marquis. She had changed from her riding dress to a blue silk gown and twisted her hair into a perfect chignon decorated with pearls. She rang a porcelain bell, bringing a flurry of servants. One filled our wineglasses as others brought parsnip soup. Braised venison and beet salad would follow.

Alexandre joined us at the last moment. "Pardon my tardiness."

Désirée gave him a reproachful look.

He helped himself to a piece of bread and soaked the crust in his soup. After a large bite, he blotted his mouth with his napkin and turned to me. "I do hope you feel at home."

"I don't feel at home quite yet." When his expression turned grim, I amended my comment. "But I'm sure I will very soon." Best not to be too direct, it seemed.

His face relaxed. "Very good, then."

I stared as he shoveled food into his mouth. Not rude, exactly, but hurried.

"Alexandre, the venison will not wander from your plate," Désirée said.

I smiled behind my goblet.

He laid down his fork and knife. "I'm afraid I'm in a rush. I am meeting a friend this evening."

"Oh? May I accompany you?" A pulse of excitement tingled in my stomach. My first night in Paris with Alexandre!

He finished chewing, then replied, "I'm afraid not. I have important business to attend to. I won't have time to introduce you to everyone." He waved his hand in my direction. "You have nothing suitable to wear, at any rate."

"Very well." I tried to control the disappointment in my voice. "Not tonight. But another?"

"Of course." He stood abruptly. "Excuse me, Father, Désirée. I will see you tomorrow morning for breakfast, Rose."

"We will expect you," Désirée said, as if implying a threat.

We finished our meal in relative silence. After a digestif by the fire, we retired to our rooms. I tossed in bed for hours. A few new gowns, music lessons, perhaps some history, and Alexandre would be proud to call me his. I could not wait to see him in the morning, to tell him I wanted to meet with a tutor immediately.

But Alexandre did not join me for breakfast. I did not see him again for two days.

My third day in Paris, I sat impatiently at the breakfast table while Désirée finished eating. I could hardly wait to explore the city.

"Your tutor will arrive at ten sharp. At two, you will have music or dance on alternating days." She paused to chew a bite of her bread. "We take tea in the salon at five and supper at nine. Please be prompt. You have had several days to adjust to your surroundings."

"Yes, Désirée." I shifted in my chair for the tenth time. When would she finish?

"I'm so glad you're looking forward to our excursion, dear."

"I can't wait to purchase a new gown!" Anything to feel more a Parisian.

She drained the last of the coffee from her cup. "To the rue Saint-Honoré."

We rode through alleyways and along grand boulevards. The river

Seine gushed pewter water in torrents as boats pushed upstream. Lively markets flourished in the squares of most quartiers. Cooks inspected lumpy vegetables, silvery fish on trays of ice, and bins of spices in russet, green, and plum. The scent of ripe cheeses permeated the air. Désirée stared unseeing out the window.

For every fashionable boulevard, a pocket of hovels sprawled. I looked past the women and children moaning for bread. Guilt flooded, intense and unsettling. If only I could help them. But nothing could be done, so I pretended not to see them.

The rue Saint-Honoré did not disappoint. Paris's finest boutiques displayed a staggering selection of jewelry, shoes, and fabrics. I fingered silk gloves and delicate lace, and held brooches to the light to examine their dazzling facets.

"The hats, Désirée! A thousand would not be too many." Straw hats *à la bergère* with ribbons; bonnets; broad-brimmed felt hats with feathers, jewels, or lace netting in every color—I would have happily died to own one.

I gaped at ladies browsing in voluptuous gowns that rustled as they moved, their poufs piled high on their heads and powdered pale blue. I could not remove my faded gown fast enough.

"First your corset and petticoats." The dressmaker's assistant jammed me into my undergarments.

"It's crushing my ribs," I cried, as she tugged on the last of the stays. I pulled at the fabric.

"Don't touch it!" she barked. "It should be tight to boost your décolletage and shrink your waist."

"How on earth am I going to wear this awful thing?"

The woman made a tsk-tsk with her tongue and helped me step into a pannier. My eyes bulged at its inconceivable girth. One would suffocate in Martinique in such a gown.

"We need your measurements." She moved quickly, scribbling numbers on her paper. "There. Now we're ready for the gowns." Madame ushered two women forward who paraded an array of fabrics before me—brocades and velvets, silks and lace, cottons and wool in a dozen colors. I tried the few model dresses available. The finer boutiques would never allow such a thing; we had not bothered to enter them.

I twirled for the second time in a yellow brocade. Who was the elegant stranger in the looking glass? Her cheeks were flushed, her form graceful. I smiled with glee.

"Do you like this one, Désirée?" I asked.

"It's lovely. We'll have one made for you. As you can see it doesn't fit precisely as it should. And what about the green one?"

"It's quite expensive. I have already asked madame."

"I am aware of the price. Why don't you try it on? It looks to be about your size," Désirée said.

Madame helped me into the rich silk gown and I moved to the mirror.

"Oh." My hand flew to my lips. "*C'est magnifique.*" I turned slowly, swishing the glossy skirts. I stroked the black lace cuffs that extended the length of my forearms. If only Maman could see me look a lady.

"I believe that gown was made for you."

"I've never worn anything so beautiful."

"Nor owned one, I suppose? Well, you do now, dear." Désirée turned to madame. "We'd like this one as well."

"Oh, Désirée! Do you mean it?" I rushed to embrace her, bumping a small table in my hurry. A set of porcelain figurines rattled as if coming to life. I steadied them, stifling a laugh.

"*Attention.*" Désirée gave me a disapproving look. "You must be aware of your person at all times."

I bowed my head in embarrassment.

"Of course I mean it," she said, her tone softened. "Now. You'll need another for tomorrow. We can't have you wearing your soiled dresses another day. Shall we?"

I squealed and kissed her cheek. "Thank you, thank you!"

By day's end, I had a start to a proper Parisian wardrobe. I chose a gold-threaded brocade glittering with iridescent beads, three day dresses, and one made of navy wool. Hats, shoes and silk stockings, an evening handbag, and gloves. Never had I owned so many beautiful things.

I wondered at the Beauharnaises' fortune. Neither the house nor the furniture reflected wealth, and I had witnessed Désirée scowling at the bills. I dismissed the thought. Not my concern. Alexandre's knees would buckle when he saw me.

⚜

The following morning, I arose early for my toilette. I spent an hour on my hair alone to arrange my curls into a perfect chignon like Désirée's. I applied my new powders with a careful hand and painted my cheeks with rouge. After a dab of perfume, I called to Mimi to assist me with dressing.

"Stockings first, Yeyette." She used my childhood nickname.

I pulled the silky film along my calves and over my knees, and secured them in place with frilly garters.

Mimi laced up my corset, thankfully with less force than the dressmaker. "Can you breathe?"

"Barely." I laughed.

She helped me into my petticoats and pannier, and at last I pulled on a milky white dress dotted with embroidered cherries. It had been the only frock ready for wearing after minor adjustments. The gown happened to be one of my favorites.

I smiled into my hand mirror. A Parisian lady, head to toe—a temptation for any man.

As I swept down the stairs to the hall, Alexandre leaned over the table to select a hunk of bread from the basket.

"How was your evening?" I touched a lose curl on my forehead lightly.

"Quite fine. I've only just arrived." He slathered his bread with apricots and ate it in a few bites, all without sitting.

"I hope I may accompany you one evening soon." I swished my skirts to and fro as I approached him. "I've been to see the dressmaker. Do you like it?"

He eyed me silently for a moment. "It's nice."

Nice? I looked down to hide my disappointment.

He closed the short distance between us. "I'd like a closer view."

My stomach flip-flopped at his silky tone.

He pressed his body closer and tucked his face into my neck. His hot breath reeked of cigars and wine.

"Alexandre," I said breathlessly.

He kissed the sensitive skin under my ear. "You smell divine. Lavender?"

I nodded as he drew his fingers softly over the roundness of my breast. Warmth spread through my limbs.

"I can't . . . we can't . . ." I leaned against the wall for support.

"Shh." He pulled me hard against him and forced my lips open with his tongue. In a swift instant, his hand slid down my frame and lifted the hem of my skirts.

I yielded to his mouth as it became more insistent. He moved expertly, pushing aside my petticoats, groping for bare skin.

"Alexandre." I tried to pull away. "Alexandre!" I pushed at his chest. Fabric ripped.

"Don't you want me?" His hand ran the length of my bare thigh. "I've seen the way you look at me."

I inhaled a sharp breath. "I . . . not now—"

"I know you've had lovers in Martinique. Creoles are known for their sensuality." He drew circles on my thigh with his fingertips. Fire blazed over my skin and I flushed. "You're beautiful in this gown. I can't resist you." He planted a trail of kisses along my collarbone and his hand inched higher.

My head dizzied and I wilted in his arms. The sudden plunge of his warm fingers into my sex made me cry out.

Footsteps echoed from the next room.

"Rose? Is that you?" Alexandre's father called.

The Marquis's cane clunked across the study floor. His slow pace allowed just enough time to adjust my clothing. Alexandre wiped his mouth with a handkerchief. When his father opened the door, all appeared normal, or so I thought.

"Are you well, Rose?" The Marquis's eyes widened when he saw me.

I swallowed hard and squared my shoulders. "I am quite well, monsieur. *Merci.*"

He regarded Alexandre with a weary glance and limped back to his study. Alexandre bounded up the stairs without a word.

I looked into the circular mirror on the opposite wall. My cheeks appeared stained, my eyes feverish, and the torn sash floated from my waist. A single tear slid down my cheek.

One chilly morning the next week, I gazed at the geraniums nestled in their window boxes, their leaves painted with frosty patterns that glittered in the sun. I remembered Alexandre's sudden passion. His kiss. His *hands*. He had treated me like a whore, then never mentioned it again. I didn't know what to make of his behavior—his kindness and charming nature had returned. I laid my head against the pane. It must have been his drunken state that morning. I hoped that was all.

I sighed. How I missed Maman and Manette, even Papa. And my friends—I longed to make new ones.

"Mademoiselle, you'll not learn your history by staring out the window," my tutor scolded.

I could not resist calling him Monsieur Ennui, at least in my head. His lessons bored me to death.

"And your posture is atrocious. Like this." He wrenched my shoulders back and tilted my chin up.

"*Oui*, monsieur." I stared into his cold face. His pale lips were the only spot of color on his over-powdered face. Why couldn't Désirée have found someone more likable? At least my lessons were nearly done for the day.

An unknown voice echoed from the foyer. Company? I forgot my manners in my eagerness and bounded into the front hall.

Désirée gave me an exasperated look. "Like a lady, Rose."

Though she meant well, I tired of the constant admonitions. "Yes, Désirée." I slowed my pace and then stopped suddenly to stare at the colorful woman by her side.

"May I present to you, Madame . . ." a servant began his stiff introductions.

Using her full hips and enormous skirts, the woman pushed him aside. He gave her a pinched look, and I giggled.

"I am Fanny de Beauharnais, wife of François, Alexandre's brother. But you have probably met my husband by now. Please, call me Fanny." She beamed and kissed me on both cheeks. "Welcome to Paris. I've been dying to meet you."

Fanny's style of dress resembled those in fashion, though a bit disheveled and overly vivid in purples and reds. The popular pastels were unsuited for her; her character would not be contained in a pale corset. Heavy curls hung in thickly powdered ringlets adorned with silk feathers, and rouge colored her lips and cheeks to the point of overdone. She resembled a rare bird flitting through the treetops of my jungle home.

A smile spread across my face. "I am very pleased to meet you, Madame—"

"Fanny, love. No one calls me Madame de Beauharnais. I insist." She regarded my face and dress. "You're adorable. And how is Alexandre? Has he shown you around town?"

"No, I'm afraid I haven't seen much of him—"

Désirée interrupted me. "He meets with his garrison and stays with the La Rochefoucould family when he can. You know how dedicated he is to his duties and his friends, Fanny."

"Among other things," Fanny answered with a pointed look at Désirée.

My heart skipped in my chest. What did that mean?

Before I could ask, Fanny changed the subject. "You must attend my salon one evening. With Alexandre, of course. My soirees are quite famous, you know." She rattled off many names, none of which I had ever heard, but I was assured of their importance. Her rapid speech left her breathless and I laughed when she paused for air.

"It all sounds so wonderful! I've been restless in this cold season," I said. "Would you care for a drink of chocolate?"

"Chocolat chaud would be divine. Come. Tell me all about yourself." She took my hand in hers.

"If you will excuse me, Fanny, I must speak with the doctor," Désirée said. "He is upstairs with the Marquis."

I hid a smile with my hand. The doctor had not yet arrived; Désirée wanted to escape. She must not enjoy Fanny's company.

"Of course, Désirée. Give him my love."

"And will you dismiss my tutor?"

"For today." Désirée glided through the door.

I found myself at ease in Fanny's presence. I adored her jovial laugh and frank nature.

"Tell me about your home," she said. "Your friends and family. And I hear there are strange jungle creatures?"

She fired question after question, and I withheld nothing. But her greatest interest lay in plantation life with the Africans.

"And the slaves? What is their life like on your plantation?"

Fanny didn't notice the clink of silverware behind her. I glanced back to see Mimi collecting a dropped knife she had been polishing. I met her eyes. She looked down, concentrating on her task as if her life depended on it.

"They live in huts unless they are part of the household. The dearest, most hardworking dine and sleep in the main house."

Mimi did not look in our direction, but her silence throbbed in the air. She knew she was my dearest—my friend, even.

"Do they work from sunrise to sunset? What do they eat? What's the punishment for a slave that misbehaves? I've heard horrible tales," Fanny pressed.

I found it curious she should be so consumed with their routine. Slaves were not our equals, after all. What could be so interesting?

"All men and women should have rights, regardless of their position, gender, or upbringing, *doucette*," Fanny insisted. "Or the color of their skin."

Mimi's eyes widened.

I cleared my throat and said, "Mimi, could you fetch us some cakes if there are any left?" She placed her polishing rag on the bureau and scurried to the kitchen.

What a grandiose idea. I had never given a slave's freedom any thought, let alone the "rights" of women. I accepted our roles—those of the slaves in their fields and the Grands Blancs running their plantations. Our sugarcane would rot, our plantations crumble without the Africans. Where would we be then? Yet Fanny had given me much to ponder.

Alexandre and I married in a small church in Noisy-le-Grand. The sanctuary sat shrouded in filtered light. Broken patterns of color streamed from stained glass windows and illuminated patches of cold stone floor. Alexandre's cousins and friends filled the pews. Fanny, the only familiar face, reassured me with a wink the moment I emerged from the priest's chamber. I smiled at her, despite the doubt that snaked through my limbs. Did I love Alexandre?

Papa's words resurfaced. "Marriage is about property. Love in marriage is nothing but a silly girl's fantasy."

A blast of organs signaled the commencement of the ceremony. Those in attendance fixed their gaze on me. I gulped and began the procession.

Maman, why couldn't you be here? I imagined her blue eyes shining with tears, pride swelling at my beauty. She would have curled my hair and Manette would have helped me into my dress. A dull ache pulsed in my chest.

I moved down the aisle toward my future.

Alexandre posed near the altar, handsome as ever in his uniform, his face set in a firm mask, making him impossible to read. Had he regrets?

We celebrated at home later that evening with an elegant dinner, complete with hired musicians. A smattering of friends and family arrived. When Fanny appeared, a sigh of relief escaped my lips.

"Congratulations." She wrapped me in her embrace.

"Am I happy to see you!" The first smile of the evening crossed my face.

"After supper we'll chat."

"I look forward to it."

I wound through circles of men and women who stared at me but said little. An outsider in my own home. I held my head high despite my unease. At dinner I sipped my soup in silence, sampled the tarte aux champignons, and indulged in champagne. The bubbles played on my tongue, relaxing me despite my discomfort.

Alexandre sat to my right, enthralling our guests with his discourse. How could I add to their discussions? I knew nothing of theater gossip or the royals' abuse of privileges. The feel of black earth between my toes, the scent of rain on hibiscus blossoms, and the magic of tarot— this was my well of knowledge. I blithely smiled or nodded when appropriate, certain my eyes were glazed over.

I glanced at my empty flute. When the servant arrived with the tray of champagne, I took two glasses. Before long, giddiness coursed through my limbs and I forgot my isolation.

When the music began, Alexandre took my arm. "Darling wife." He kissed my forehead. "Shall we dance?"

Wife. I am a wife. I smiled at the warmth in his eyes. "Yes!" How I missed dancing.

Everyone formed two parallel lines for a quadrille, thankfully a dance

I knew well. Alexandre stood across from me and nodded. We met in the middle, palm to palm, and twirled to the rhythm of the music.

I held my breath as our eyes locked, our hands touched. The heat of his skin made me blush.

"You're blushing, Madame de Beauharnais. And it suits you. You're lovely."

A thought of our wedding bed flashed behind my eyes. My stomach quivered in excitement and nerves; my neck burned. Perhaps I'd had too much champagne.

I slid to my spot in line and hiccupped. A giggle erupted in my throat and I missed the next step of the dance. I laughed at my idiocy.

Alexandre shot me a grim expression. "Rose," he whispered in an angry voice as our shoulders met in the middle, "behave like a lady, please. No more champagne."

"Isn't that what a wedding is for? Merriment?" I hiccupped again. "I am the bride, after all."

"You are the fool with your sputtering and stumbling. You'll sit out the next dance."

"I don't need a break," I slurred.

He stiffened. When the song ended, he led me to an uncomfortable chair.

"I'm not finished . . . d-dancing." My tongue was too thick to form proper syllables.

He straightened his jacket and stood erect. "Stop this embarrassment. You're drunk."

"Oh, silly man." I waved a hand at him in dismissal. "Don't be offended. I'm the guest of honor. I'll do as I please. No one even knows I'm here." The absurdity of my words did not sink in.

He paced away.

Was he serious? I stared after him in disbelief as he joined a crowd of gentlemen.

A cloud of melancholy enveloped me as the hours ticked by. Alexandre ignored me. He glided across the floor, an exquisite dancer with lithe movements. Every man looked on in envy. Women admired him, adoration and lust on their countenances. My temples pounded and jealousy sickened me. But I was Madame de Beauharnais. No other could claim him.

Still Alexandre did not invite me to dance.

Stupid girl, I berated myself.

When I could no longer bear his disregard, I said my good nights and went to my room. A white nightdress lay on the edge of my bed. I stroked the smooth fabric. I would apologize and he would forgive me, and I would forgive him.

"Mimi?" I called through the door. "I need your help."

She rushed into the room and helped me undress. I stepped into a circle of fabric. Folds of satin cascaded from a bustier adorned with ribbons and lace. My bosom bulged into fleshy mounds.

"Sweet Lord, Yeyette. You're going to drive him mad." She tied the last of the ribbons.

I scooped her hands to my chest. "I am afraid."

"It's natural," she said. "But you'll be just fine. You may even like it, if he's gentle."

I kissed her cheek. Excitement tingled in my belly. I would no longer be a maid. If my darling Guillaume in Fort-Royal had had his way, I would have been spoiled on a balmy evening long ago. In this moment, I was glad I had resisted.

I sat on the edge of the bed to wait. I chewed my nails. Such a horrible habit, Maman said. I sat on my hands, but my feet twitched.

I jumped up and paced. What could be taking him so long?

An hour passed and the champagne enveloped me in a tired haze. I climbed between the burgundy sheets and closed my heavy lids. I would rest while I waited.

He would take me in his arms. All would be well.

Alexandre did not come that night. Nor the next, or the next.

Marriage
Noisy-le-Grand, 1780–1782

I didn't see Alexandre until a week later, just before dawn. He climbed into bed, clumsy, his cheeks rosy from the fine brandy he adored.

"Where have you been?" I rubbed the sleep from my eyes.

"Busy with my garrison, darling. We've had many drills of late. But I'm here now."

I wanted to shout my frustration. How dare he leave me alone on my wedding night! I had dressed in my nightgown each evening since, but he never came. I pressed my lips together and rolled away, giving him my back.

His hand cupped my shoulder, slid down my arm, and rested on the curve of my waist. A delicious sensation tingled under the trail of his fingertips in spite of my anger.

"I've missed your sweet face," he purred in my ear. His slurring had evaporated.

"You have a strange way of showing it."

"Shh." He put a finger to my lips. "I'm bringing you to one of the best known salons in all of Paris next week." His silky voice could charm a serpent.

My resolve melted. "Really?" I turned to face him.

He quieted me with an urgent kiss. His hands slipped over the fluid fabric of my nightdress until he found an opening. I gasped at his touch, a fire smoldering below.

Alexandre sensed my change of heart and threw back the covers. "I want to see you." He tugged the shift over my head.

I blushed at my nakedness and lay perfectly still.

Alexandre caressed my shoulders softly, my breasts and stomach, and finally the triangle of dark hair.

A moan escaped my lips. I blushed again at my body's response to him.

"The scent of your skin." He inhaled and took my nipple in his mouth.

I surrendered to his heat, and wrapped myself around him.

Sometime later, I dozed to sleep, warm and nestled in his arms.

Alexandre slipped into bed in the hours before dawn, slept much of the day, and stole away into the night without a word. If he came home at all. During his brief visits, he whispered proclamations of love and soothed my resentment at his absence with gifts. I treasured the baubles and showed enthusiasm for the books he shared. I tried to forgive him for the days he did not return home.

One afternoon, I sat at the cherry desk in the study. A long week of lessons without company had left me dejected. I sighed and thumbed through the pages of a dull novel. A vision of Catherine shimmered in my memory, my sister hunched over the desk in our shared bedchamber, reading about centuries past as her candle burned to the quick.

One such evening, Papa had knocked at our door.

"Come in," I called, shifting my position on the bed. Manette squirmed while I plaited her hair.

"Young ladies, it's time to put out your candles."

"But Papa, I am at the best part," Catherine complained.

He kissed her on the head. "My little bookworm. You make a father proud. Have you done your day's reading, Rose?"

I tied Manette's braid with a strip of cloth. "Well . . ."

He gave me a stern look. "Catherine is younger and yet surpasses you in your studies. A gentleman will never want you at this rate."

I ducked my head. He scolded me so often, one would think I'd have grown accustomed to it. I had not. I wanted to toss my sister's book into the fireplace.

Guilt swam in the pit of my stomach. I hated myself for my envy, for the hateful thoughts that crept in when I thought of those days. I looked down again and the pages blurred. Catherine had been the better choice for Alexandre's wife. I pushed the thought away.

She couldn't be anyone's wife.

I closed the book and ran my finger along its spine. *La Nouvelle Héloïse.* I had wrestled with its dense intrigue all week. I tossed the abominable book on the shelf with a thud. Rousseau could not be that important.

"You throw down Rousseau! Have you finished it?" Alexandre's voice startled me. I whipped around in my chair.

"Yes," I lied. "I don't see what is so great about him." Spite dripped from my tongue. It would anger him if I challenged his favorite philosopher and writer. I relished the opportunity. I had tired of his constant lessons and haughty opinions, never mind his continued absence.

"You're insupportable! How can you not see his genius? His theories of—"

"Please, Alexandre. I've just read his work for two hours. Can we speak of something else?" I was in no mood for another monologue.

"Fine." The muscle in his jaw twitched. "What would you prefer to talk about?"

"The court." I sat on the divan and moved to make room for him. "Queen Marie Antoinette, her ladies, the elaborate balls. How lavish they must be! We are nobility, are we not?" I took his hand in mine as he sat beside me. "I've dreamed of the court since I was a girl. Would you . . . could we solicit an invitation? I have a proper gown. I've been learning etiquette with my tutor. I'm a splendid dancer, as are you. We would make a lovely addition to the court, don't you think?"

"You wish for me to escort you to Versailles?" His eyes bulged like those of a frog trapped in a little boy's hand. "As if anyone would allow you at court!" He dissolved into laughter.

My irritation returned. "What do you mean?"

"It isn't as easy as that"—he snapped his fingers—"to obtain invitations. And you would be hideous in the presence of royalty."

I dropped his hand as if I'd touched a leper. "You needn't be mean."

"You haven't the slightest idea how much breeding courtiers have endured to become so refined."

I lowered my eyes. Perhaps not, but I could learn their manners. How difficult could it be?

His expression softened. "Why don't you choose something to wear tonight? We're going to the salon I promised. We'll leave at eight o'clock." He kissed my cheek and strutted from the room.

I studied the silk rug. I would go to court, I vowed. I would mingle with nobility, with or without Alexandre. But first I must make friends. I would begin tonight.

I took extra pains to be beautiful for our evening together. Pale pink and yellow flowers scrolled in dainty webs across the bodice of my gown. I arranged my hair in a cascade of curls adorned with flowers. I glanced at my clock: five minutes before eight. Perfect. I swished from the room in a cloud of flowery perfume to look for Alexandre.

I knocked at his bedroom door. "Alexandre?" No answer.

I scooted down the staircase as quickly as my skirts would allow. "Alexandre? I'm ready."

Silence.

Where was everyone? I popped into the sitting room, into the empty study, and into the front hall. I climbed the stairs to find Désirée and inquire as to his whereabouts.

"She has gone to dinner with friends," her maid said.

"Have you seen Alexandre?"

"He left while you were bathing, Madame de Beauharnais. He did mention flowers."

I smiled. He must regret our squabble.

For an hour I watched carriages file down our narrow street, wheels thundering over cobblestone. I grew angry, then worried, and angry again.

Another hour passed.

My hope cracked in a hundred places. At last, I raced upstairs and slammed the bedroom door. I kicked my shoes across the room. I had dressed for nothing! The flowers had not been for me at all.

Alexandre punished me with his absence, with his sequestering me to a life without social engagements or friends. I busied myself with letters to

Maman, promenades through the city's gardens, and shopping. Rainy days found me indoors reading to Monsieur Ennui, plucking my harp, or playing cards with Mimi, though Désirée scolded me for the latter.

"Servants do not consort with their masters," she insisted.

"Really, Désirée, Mimi is more than a servant," I said in defiance. She was my confidante, a beacon of home.

Désirée threw me a weary glance. "And do not touch your hair. You will have to curl it over again. Ladies do not fidget."

I sighed in exasperation as she skirted from the room. Mimi smothered a laugh.

"You're much more than a slave, my friend." I kissed her strong brown hand.

Her eyes filled with love. "I know. Since we was girls."

"Thank God for you." Life would be unbearable without her.

One frigid winter evening I huddled in bed remembering Papa's tales of Paris. What I wouldn't give to be admired, influential at the court he had described, to have a life, a *real* life in the city. How different Paris was . . . my husband. . . .

My tears soaked the satin pillows. I had prayed feverishly to leave Martinique, for adventure and love, but here I lay, lamenting a life I could not abide. What man would not wish to sleep in the warmth of his love's embrace? He had told me he loved me many times.

A rapping at the door startled me. I sat up.

"Rose?" Another knock. "May I come in?"

Before I answered, Fanny barged through the door. She glowed, a cheerful orb of gold taffeta, her rouge as thick as ever.

"Fanny." I wiped my eyes with the back of my hand and sniffed. "What are you doing here?"

"You're going out with me, *chérie*. A friend of mine, Madame de Condorcet, is hosting a salon. Let's get you dressed."

"But—"

"No time to waste. Up, up!"

Mimi had heard the commotion from the hall and entered the bedroom. She threw open my armoire and sorted through my gowns. "Time to get on with things, Yeyette."

Yes, time to get on with things. Alexandre be damned.

I leapt from the bed and threw my arms around Fanny's neck. "Thank you for coming!"

"No more tears." She patted me on the back. "That wretched husband of yours isn't taking very good care of you, is he, love? Arrogant ninny! One never needs a husband. I left mine long ago."

My mouth fell open in shock. "I didn't realize you and François—"

"I have no use for my husband's views."

I threw her an admiring glance. How brave Fanny was.

"I'll just wait for you outside." She closed the door behind her.

Mimi helped me into the lustrous green gown I had yet to wear. A quick pinning of my hair with Maman's pearl combs and I stepped into the night.

When we arrived, a servant escorted us through a row of beribboned evergreen topiaries to the entrance. The house in which Madame de Condorcet lived did not impress in size, but it possessed a charm, as did Sophie herself. I admired her intelligence and accomplishments. I did not share her desire to write for publication or give fine speeches on the King's taxation, though if I could be as accomplished a lady as she, I would be happy.

Fanny guided me through circles of people. I participated as best I could, repeating opinions I had heard about the popular Encylopédie or the Queen's latest hat. Mostly, I observed. Parisian women presented an incredible study, their gestures theatrical and conversations dramatic. A slight tilt of the head, a gleam in the eye led gentlemen their way. I made a mental note to practice their expressions.

After an aperitif, Sophie de Condorcet signaled the start of a play. I selected a seat next to several women with powdered poufs. I pitied the souls who sat behind them—they wouldn't see a thing behind the towering wigs.

As everyone filed to their seats, a cloud of mingled odors permeated the space. Perfumes and pomades of lilac, rosewater, and orange blossom tickled my nose and I sneezed. The woman to my right didn't speak, but revulsion twisted her features. I brought my handkerchief to my face and averted my eyes. Really, as if she never sneezed.

A shuffle of bodies near the front of the makeshift theater caught my attention. Newcomers bustled in and moved to open seats, laughing as they went. I noted a pair of squared shoulders and a perfectly coiffed wig.

My breath stopped. Alexandre.

He scanned the curtain-draped room cluttered with *palme*-patterned settees before he selected a place in the row directly in front of me, two seats down from mine.

My heart raced. He had not seen me.

I couldn't focus on the farce about the King and his downtrodden subjects. I fixated on the back of Alexandre's head.

Should I approach him? He was my husband, after all. Or maybe I should pretend not to see him and engage myself elsewhere—show him I could manage alone.

I jumped from my chair when the play ended, and I joined a group deep in conversation. Two ladies eyed me with suspicion and gave me no welcome. A gentleman told a story that made everyone laugh.

I laughed along with the others as a hand tightened on my shoulder. "Rose?"

I turned. "Alexandre, what are you doing here?" My voice was an octave too high. We kissed one another's cheeks.

Astonishment registered on his features. "I could ask you the same." He glanced at my gown. "You're stunning."

My heart skipped a beat. "I wanted to look my best for my friends."

"Your friends? Well, I'm pleased you have made some."

No thanks to you. I smiled sweetly.

"Shall we ride home together later?"

"That would be splendid. If I can get away, that is."

"Until then." He grinned and disappeared into the crowd.

He had seemed happy to see me. Suddenly cheerful, I said a silent prayer of thanks.

My elation dissolved as Alexandre skirted the room, kissing the hands of every pretty lady, sweeping across the dance floor like a prince. Women did not seem to mind that his wife stood in the same room.

My stomach roiled. I placed my glass on a footman's tray and went in search of a washroom. Nausea surged as I left Alexandre whispering in the ear of a beautiful brunette. I closed the washroom door.

Sweat beaded on my forehead. My pale expression stared back at me from a gilded mirror. The fish must have been rotten. I patted my face with cool water from the pitcher and leaned into the mirror. Powder ran in milky streams down my cheeks.

Once my stomach settled, I powdered my face and rejoined the fete, pushing through the sea of faces to find Fanny. I couldn't face another moment of humiliation. Fanny would understand. She stood near the refreshment table. I walked in her direction, until the acidic odor of alcohol hit me with force. I stopped abruptly.

Oh, God. I covered my mouth with my hand.

"Are you well?" Fanny raced toward me.

"I think I ate something spoiled."

She wrapped an arm around me. "Let's get you home."

"Our cloaks are in the study. This way." We weaved through the hall and toward the back of the house, away from the din of voices and laughter.

"Here it is." Fanny opened the door to reveal three couples huddled in the dimly lit room, lost in one another's embrace.

We sorted through piles of overcoats, finding ours at last. I slipped into my own as a couple untangled themselves and sauntered to the door. The gentleman made eye contact with me and stopped.

Alexandre.

"You?" I whispered, mouth agape. What . . . who was she?

"Leaving so soon? Well, good night, then." He pushed past me, escorting his beautiful dark-haired companion.

"Alexandre!"

He didn't turn but closed the door behind him.

"Get me out of here," I choked, clutching Fanny's arm. "*Tout de suite.*"

He had taken me in his arms, told me he loved me. Pain ripped through me, then fury. Why had he bothered endearing himself to me at all? A greasy wave of nausea swept up my throat. "I'm going to be sick." I held my stomach.

Fanny pushed me through the front door and into the garden. I leaned against a stone column for support and gasped in deep breaths.

"I'm so sorry, my dear." She dabbed my forehead with her handkerchief.

"He said his garrison kept him away." I groaned. "I should have known. Papa . . ."

"Alexandre is . . . well, he's always been this way. He has always had many lovers. I assumed you knew."

Another wave of regret crushed me. I was a blind, ignorant girl, just as Alexandre said.

"Do not center your life or your happiness around your husband." Fanny's eyes met mine. "You must create your own."

My head felt as if it would explode. Anger and sorrow warred within. My marriage was everything I had known and nothing I had longed for.

When my stomach had settled, I gave her a rueful smile and stood tall. "I will. I'll do my wifely duties, but from now on, my life and happiness are my own."

Alexandre never gave me the chance to confront him. A month passed without my laying eyes on him. At last, I questioned Désirée in the garden.

"I haven't seen him in weeks," I said to her. I bent to examine the crocuses pushing their way through sodden earth. Désirée did not need to see me upset. "I know about his liaisons."

She inspected the buds on a nearby branch. "Spring is here." She released the branch. It bounced up and down as if thrilled by her proclamation. "I don't know how to tell you this, Rose. I'm appalled he did not tell you himself."

I stood rapidly. A barrage of white dots flushed my vision. I put my hand to my head to steady myself. "What's happened?"

"Alexandre has gone to Italy on holiday. For several months, at least."

Alexandre wrote to me often from Italy, but I did not respond to his letters. I had little desire to please him. I yearned for Maman, in her cotton skirts, for her strong arms holding me. She did not trust men; Papa's trysts had hurt her too many times. She would have plenty to say about Alexandre. What I wouldn't give to be with her.

I considered making the voyage home again, but Désirée pushed the idea from my mind.

"Your place is with your husband. Alexandre will come around and you'll make your own life here."

"He isn't here. Why should I be?"

"Give him time."

I grew ill and fatigued, spending hours in bed. Désirée worried at my lack of appetite and sent for a doctor. He arrived within the hour, toting his brown leather bag.

"She has no fever or chills. Her fluids are normal."

"She rarely eats and when she does, she vomits," Désirée said, her voice concerned.

"And I'm so fatigued," I added.

"Well, Madame de Beauharnais, I have good news." The doctor smiled. "You are with child."

My eyes widened in disbelief. I counted back the days. . . . Weeks had gone since my courses. "*Mon Dieu!* I'm pregnant?" My menses had been the furthest thing from my mind. In my sickened state and ill temperament I had forgotten it entirely.

"Rose is pregnant?" Désirée smiled, her excitement plain.

"Congratulations, madame. You are going to be a mother."

I collapsed backward onto my pillows. A mother! But I still felt like a child. And now I would be fastened to Alexandre's side, dependent on him, the child's father, always. I threw my arm across my eyes and groaned.

A second thought brought a twinge of hope. I detested myself for caring, but I could not hide from my wish. Perhaps the news would bring Alexandre home.

My nausea eased after several weeks, as did my astonishment at being with child. When Alexandre discovered the news, his letters came more frequently.

April 12, 1781

Ma très chère,

    I received word you are pregnant. Why should I learn this happy news from Désirée and not my darling wife? I wait for the post each day, but your letters do not come. I want to hear about the baby's room and the gifts bestowed on him.

I say "him," for I know him to be a son and I am overjoyed!

You must keep up with your studies. I receive weekly reports from your tutor to track your achievements. He says you make slow progress.

Remember your standing amidst my friends and family. It will not do for you to display your ignorance.

I will be home, mon amour, for the birth in the fall. Please take care of yourself.

You know there is nothing more important to me than you, my perfect and sweet wife.

Je t'embrasse,

Alexandre

Nothing more important, indeed. The beautiful phrases he wrote meant little. My tutor insisted I use the same flowery, false shows of affection.

"Demonstrate your prowess at conversation, Rose. Say the phrase again. This time, use your wit. If you have none, be sweet," Monsieur Ennui scolded.

I read the letter once more. At least he would be home for the birth. *Merci à Dieu.* I would not—could not—raise our baby alone, and a child should know his father.

Désirée and the Marquis thrilled at the prospect of Alexandre's firstborn. Désirée had two stepsons but no children of her own. She took tremendous pleasure in purchasing rattles and linens.

I marveled at my changing form, not recognizing the bulges beneath my clothes. I patted my rounded abdomen. The baby kicked at my hand.

"I felt that, my little darling. Who will you be? Your *maman* already adores you."

Maman—I could not get used to my new title. Another layer of my womanhood.

Fatigue plagued me and I slept as if in rapture. I dreamt of home often—my sisters and Maman in the garden, my fingers sticky with guava juice, the smell of salty air. I awoke many mornings in a daze.

My pregnancy came to an end on a grueling September day. My room became a battleground of sweat-drenched sheets, bloodied water, and stained serviettes. I writhed in hot agony for a full day, the pain so intense I surrendered my humanity.

A scream tore from my lips. "Get it out!" I clutched the midwife's hand. "*Please*. I can't do this."

"Mimi, open the window," the midwife said with a calm I could not fathom.

Mimi ripped the curtains aside and unfastened the latch. A breeze lifted the matted hair from my forehead.

Another searing pain ripped through me.

"Maman!" I cried. Desperate tears tumbled down my cheeks. "I want my mother."

Désirée patted my forehead, face, and neck with a cool cloth. "I'm here for you, Rose."

"Just a bit more, love," the midwife said. "The head is crowning. You can do this."

I panted as the spasm seized my abdomen.

"Breathe!" the midwife ordered.

"Uuaaahhhh!" I pushed with all of my might, then dissolved in a coughing fit.

"That's it! One more," the midwife coaxed, pushing my shoulders forward.

I heaved from my core, pulling on the bedpost with what little strength remained.

"That's it, Rose. Yes!"

I choked again and felt the warm rush of a tiny body leaving mine. I fell onto my pillows as the blessed sound of a baby's cry pierced the air.

"It's a boy!"

"A boy," I whispered. My head rolled on my shoulders in exhaustion.

The midwife wrapped his slick body in a cloth and rushed him to a basin of clean water.

"Oh, Rose, he's beautiful," Désirée said.

A small cry sounded from across the room. My limp hand reached for my baby. My son. "Let me hold him."

"You need my attention. You've suffered some tearing," the midwife said.

"I'll get you a clean chemise." Désirée left my baby with Mimi.

The midwife and her nurse assistant tended my wounds and flushed my feverish skin with cool water. When my angelic son finally rested in my arms, I guided his tiny mouth to my breast.

Désirée protested at once. "I've hired a wet nurse, Rose. It isn't proper to feed him yourself. You forget your title."

"I will feed my child, Désirée. I do not care for convention in this matter. I've met others who have done the same."

She pursed her lips as I nestled into the bedcovers with my darling. I had made him. This perfect creature. I closed my weighted eyelids.

I named my son Eugène. I gazed on his perfect face and petite fingers and toes for hours. Adoration filled my heart.

Alexandre returned soon after Eugène's birth.

"Let me hold my son." He caressed his face and coaxed a smile from the infant.

He hardly let the boy out of his sight at first. I forgave him for everything as he showered our son with affection. We started again as if no woman had come between us, nor harsh words.

Fatherhood suited my wayward husband. Alexandre waited on us, mother and child. He loved me; he loved our boy. During our days, we were a family. At night, he folded me in his arms.

But our blissful months together ebbed as Alexandre's ennui increased. He launched into political orations and ramblings about honor. I became bored with his military diatribes.

"I am an honorable soldier in search of meaning! In search of justice! I must defend France from her enemies! Why have I not been stationed at war in the West Indies with my comrades? I, who champion the cause of the French?" he shouted, before collapsing onto the sofa in a fit of drunken snoring.

He refused to escort me into town.

"I'd like to join you this evening. I'd love to meet more lady friends," I said, laying a flower guide on the table.

"Not tonight. I am meeting someone."

Jealousy pricked beneath my skin. "Have you taken another lover?"

"You must not make a fuss, Rose." He tossed the cookie he had been nibbling into the fire. It burned white hot and turned to a blackened lump. "Mistresses are expected. If you weren't so ignorant and ill-raised, you would understand that."

"How dare you!" I stood and crossed my arms. I understood perfectly, but I had believed in the possibility of love. Not with this man.

"Rose," he sighed, "I have loved you as well as any man could."

My mouth fell open as he jumped from his chair and stalked through the door.

I avoided Alexandre for several days, spending much of my time with Eugène out of doors. One afternoon following a long morning walk, I readied Eugène for a nap.

"Sleep well, my little cherub." I kissed his chubby cheek and lowered him into a bassinet. As I tiptoed into the corridor, voices drifted from Désirée's chamber. I paused to eavesdrop.

"She's so lonely. She craves his attention," Désirée said.

"*La pauvre*," the Marquis replied. "She'll have to find her own way."

"I feel guilty, somehow, for arranging the marriage. She's such an agreeable girl."

Désirée's voice dropped. I moved closer and strained to make out her next words. "Alexandre has too many lovers. He behaves like a rogue. I've spoken with him at length about his reputation."

I stiffened. Her words stung, though I knew them to be true.

"And what of Laure de Longpré?" the Marquis asked. "Alexandre seems smitten with her. He supports their bastard child without question. That woman uses him for his youth and money. But he will not listen to me."

"And now he plans to take her to Martinique," Désirée said. "They left for port today."

The air left my lungs. I slumped to the floor.

Abandoned

Paris, 1782–1784

"Rose! Are you all right?" Désirée rushed to assist me. She placed her arm behind my head. I had not fainted, but collapsed in shock. "I heard a thump in the corridor—"

"A child with another woman?" I gasped. "She travels with him! That philandering *con!*"

Sympathy filled Désirée's eyes. She rubbed my shoulder. "Try not to upset yourself."

"Upset myself?" I glared. "I am not upsetting myself!" My voice rose to a scream. "Alexandre has a child with another woman! A woman he deserted me for! Now he takes her to my home?"

A swell of heat crushed my chest. He had insulted me a thousand times! And worse, I would be left behind, unable to visit my family.

Désirée pulled back in surprise. "How dare you raise your voice to me! He has not deserted you. He is stationed in Martinique."

Eugène's muffled cries drifted through the corridor.

"*Merveilleux!*" I shouted. Laure de Longpré had stolen his heart, had borne his child, and would parade *my* husband in front of *my* family and friends. I ground my teeth in rage. How dare she!

Footsteps echoed in the hallway. "What happened?" Mimi asked.

"Can you watch Eugène? I need some air."

Mimi read my expression. "Now, don't lose your head, Yeyette."

"It's too late for that!" I stormed from the corridor.

My head boiled. My throat burned. I would love to torch his fancy uniforms, throw flames in his wig and watch it burn! I ripped the front door open and flew into the street, narrowly missing the sludge splashed by a racing coach.

Merde! I stopped and peered down the narrow street. I could not go out on my own, at least not on foot. I retreated indoors, frustration choking me.

"Ready the coach! I'm going for a drive. At once!" I shouted at no one in particular.

"You cannot go out unescorted!" Désirée rushed down the staircase.

"I can and I will!"

Her mouth clapped shut as the servants scattered. Within moments, my carriage was speeding through the quartier.

The solitary flame I had held—the hope that Alexandre would forget the others as our love grew with our child—fizzled as if quelled by icy water.

I rode, unseeing, for an hour until the Seine came into view. The river soothed in its swirling currents, coursing around each bend, never still. I hated myself for every hot tear I wept for him. Alexandre loved no one but himself.

The tunnel of winter loomed dark and bleak, intensifying my malaise. Yearning throbbed under my skin. What I wouldn't give to be home, to raise Eugène with my parents, my friends, and cousins. My son grew into his chubby arms and legs and toddled through the house. Soon he would no longer be a baby, and my family had missed it all.

"The bunny is going to catch you." I made the animal hippity-hop near Eugène's face. He giggled in his delicious baby way. "Here he comes." I crouched on the chilly floor, chasing him with the caramel-colored animal until my knees protested.

When I left the house, I drowned my loneliness in new hats, shoes with shiny buckles, toys for Eugène, and sugary treats for Désirée. The merchants knew me by name.

"Bonjour, Madame de Beauharnais. Can I interest you in this gown? It mimics the latest style by Rose Bertin. The Queen owns a dozen," Monsieur Caulin would say.

We could not afford gowns from Mademoiselle Bertin herself. A copy would have to do. "Perhaps in blue," I said.

The sanctity of a boutique helped me forget the hollow in my chest, if only for measured moments. I spent every penny Alexandre gave and accrued a stack of bills charged to his name. Guilt gnawed but I could not stop spending.

Exhaustion seeped into my bones. The earthy scent of coffee and the odor of charred meat turned my stomach, and by the second week of nausea I knew—I was with child again.

"We'll need to do the birth ritual again," Mimi said, tucking the sheets on my bed. She had slathered my arms with a soil paste and sacrificed eggs in the fire pit to ensure Eugène's health.

"Tonight?" I pulled back the drapes, bathing the room in gold. Once-invisible dust whirled in the shaft of sunlight over Mimi's head.

"*Oui.* Have you told your husband?"

"No." I slipped an earring in the shape of a daisy through the tiny hole in my ear. "What does he care? He's not even here."

"He loves Eugène."

"I told Maman in my last letter. He can hear the news from her." To withhold my sentiments, to share nothing with him, was my only card left to play.

Alexandre's condescension in his letters strengthened my resolve not to write him.

"Excuse me, Vicomtesse de Beauharnais. The post has arrived."

I nodded to the butler and scooped the missive from his hands. "It's from your papa," I said to Eugène, patting his head. He gurgled as I turned the crinkled paper over and sighed. "I suppose we should see what he has to say."

February 25, 1783

Ma chère Rose,

My commanding officer does not allow me to join our fleets that ward off the attacking British. I am frustrated by my lack of active service, and spend my days in your parents' home. I had forgotten the sweltering heat and discomforts of Martinique. I don't know how you tolerated the insects or the indolence! Progress never happens here. Now I understand why you arrived in such a pitiful state when we first met.

I am discouraged to have had no letters from you. Do you care so little for your husband? I wallow in malaise on this God-forsaken island and long for news from my dear wife, for her comforting words. Can you find no kindness for me in your shriveled heart?

Yours,

Alexandre

I shredded his letter and tossed the pieces into the air. Eugène swatted at the paper as it fluttered like snowflakes to the floor. Maman would be appalled to know he abused the reputation of her home. Thankless, cruel man! I found revenge in my letters to Maman. I knew she would read them aloud.

Her reply did not surprise me. Maman believed a woman's duty was to her husband, regardless of his faults.

March 10, 1783

Ma chère Rose,

I am delighted you are expecting your second child! I didn't realize you had not told Alexandre. He flew into a tantrum when I read your letter aloud. He is vexed by your lack of contact. Darling, he is your husband. You owe him courtesy, despite his shortcomings.

Alexandre does not enjoy his time here and has moved in with your uncle Tascher. In truth, Papa and I grew tired of his complaints and we're glad he is gone. Désirée told me what has happened between you two. I hope your tender heart has not suffered too much.

The slaves ask after you, as does your sister. Manette misses you a great deal, especially since her fever. She is scarred, poor thing, and remains very weak. She will never again be beautiful. I fear she may never marry. Time will tell.

How is our beloved Eugène? I trust he is well. I am told he has his father's eyes and your good nature.

I regret we are able to send you only a little money. We are struggling to pay our debts—your Papa even labors in the fields some days. I hope Alexandre's sums keep you comfortable.

We miss you and send our love.

Maman

Alexandre's financial support? Ha! He had sent little, abandoning me and his children in every way—as a lover, as a father, and as a provider. I tied the letter with twine and stashed it in a drawer. Désirée had paid my bills for months and could not afford them much longer. I laid my face on the smooth surface of the desk. What was I to do?

One spring afternoon, Eugène and I strolled through a park near our house. I watched my son as he wobbled in his unstable way, tripping on tufts of grass. The heavy load around my middle prevented me from playing *cache-cache* behind the bushes the way he wanted. When he sat in the grass to watch a family of beetles, I slipped my hand into the pocket of my woolen riding coat. My fingers brushed the crumpled edges of a letter. Alexandre persisted in correspondence despite my continued silence. I sighed and tore it open.

September 10, 1783

Rose,

How could you keep your happy news from me lest you had conceived another man's child? You behave like a whore in my absence, while I am away at war, protecting your family and your beloved home. Have you no conscience? How can you call yourself a dutiful wife? You are without remorse and incapable of repentance.

Your comportment is abhorrent. You are a cold and vile creature, caring for only yourself!

You must quit your affairs at once. Your duty is to Eugène and to my father, to Désirée and above all to me, your husband! I shall return this summer and I expect there to be no signs of another man's presence in my home.

                                        Yours,

                                        Alexandre

His dramatic sniveling was absurd. The very idea of another man in my bed! I knew few and rarely attended any salons. I shoved the offensive letter back into my pocket.

"Papa loves you, Eugène," I said. And despises me, I thought as I tugged the corners of my son's little hat.

I gave birth to a baby girl in April, a week earlier than expected. Her violet eyes matched those I had seen in my dreams. Two children in less than two years and it felt a lifetime.

My little Hortense did not possess an easy temperament, and her thin frame worried both Désirée and me.

"You must hire a wet nurse," the doctor recommended, "until the baby gains strength and a little more weight."

Her form improved, though she was never an easy child like her brother. Her belly seemed perpetually upset and her cries often kept me from sleeping.

Spring evolved into summer. One radiant afternoon the children and I had settled in for repose when the post arrived. I sprang from bed and rushed down the staircase. A letter from Maman.

                                        June 1, 1784

My Darling Rose,

    I hope beautiful little Hortense is well, and my dear Eugène. I would love to meet them both before they have grown too much. Promise to visit soon.

As for your industrious husband, I have difficult news to share. Alexandre has officially taken up with Laure de Longpré, despite his many lovers. He is shameless! Everyone speaks of it here.

I am sorry to say my news worsens from there. Your uncle Tascher overheard Laure denouncing the legitimacy of baby Hortense. She calls your daughter a bastard. Your uncle was outraged and asked Laure and Alexandre to leave his home.

Still, Laure continues to sully your name. She seeks proof of your indecency with men when you lived at home to validate your "unsavory history" before you were married. I imagine she hopes Alexandre may separate from you without having to support you financially. I am furious, but relieved to hear that those who know you validate your innocence.

Against my wishes, Alexandre visited us again, though only briefly. Your father discovered him attempting to bribe the slaves to slander your name. The fool did not realize the slaves loved you and would protect your honor. Your Papa banished Alexandre from our home for good.

This is the first I have been glad you are far away, taking care of yourself.

Alexandre will leave for France in two months' time, or so he said. I pray he treats you respectfully upon his return. Remember you always have a home with your family, who love and cherish you, should you decide to leave him.

Please give my grandchildren my love.

> Love Always,
>
> Maman

Outrageous! My face grew hot with humiliation. How could he diminish me without cause, belittle our family's name? A bitter laugh escaped my lips. He couldn't doubt the father of our child. I knew no other men!

Later that evening, I reread the dreadful letter by firelight as rain pattered on the eaves of the house. A knot of cold resolve formed in my chest. Let him have Laure. In fact, they deserved each other. But what next for me? I reached for my tarot cards and emptied them from their pouch. It had been too long since I had consulted them.

I shuffled the cards and divided the deck into three. The pile in the middle beckoned. I scooped them up and laid them in a familiar pattern on the floor, then turned them over, one by one.

The Fool—a spiritual card. The search for meaning, without reservation. Two of Rods—a journey, a new beginning. And the third card—the Chariot, for courage.

Embers smoldered in the fire pit. Soon, I would be plunged into darkness.

I would not be Alexandre's pawn a moment longer.

Renaissance

Penthémont, Paris, 1784–1785

"I must go, Désirée." I sorted through an array of gowns in a boutique near Les Halles. "I've done nothing to warrant Alexandre's hatred. I've grown tired of his abuse."

"Oh, Rose!" She forgot her finely pressed lace collar and crushed me against her breast. The scent of orange blossom surrounded me in a cloud. "You must weather Alexandre's faults. It will be too difficult on your own. And we will miss you and the children."

"I'm humiliated! He slanders my name." I pulled away. "I live in isolation and grief." I saw no need to tell her that my dreams had been shattered. It would only upset her more.

"The law does not protect women accused of adultery, whether it is true or false," she said. "He can apply to the magistrate to withhold your financial support. You must proceed with caution, my dear."

"I'm not sure where I will go." I tried to control my rising panic. The money from my parents would not be enough to support us. I plunked down on a footstool by the dressing partition.

"You don't have to leave. Stay with us." She squeezed my hands in hers.

"I cannot. We will visit, though I don't know where—" My voice cracked.

"Many ladies in your predicament move to a convent. Until their situations improve. The nuns offer apartments at discounted rates."

I considered living among other women, all starting over in their lives. Their friendships, the solace of a convent.

I stood. "Then that's where I'll go."

Strange I should be so relieved to pack my things. To become the master of my own life elevated my mood. I would never give myself fully again—I could not risk such abuse of my heart, of my loyalty for a man.

Fanny came to my aid when she heard the news.

"Take this." She placed an envelope in my hand and wrapped her fingers around mine. "It'll help you get on your feet."

"What is it?" I opened the envelope. Several hundred livres were tucked inside. "Fanny! You don't have to do this."

"You'll need it and I have it to give. You forget I make my own money with my letters." She embraced me. "You're welcome in my home at any time."

"Thank you." I kissed my only friend. "One day"—I hugged her package to my chest—"I will repay you in multitudes."

It was a tearful parting from Désirée and the Marquis; living with their grandchildren had livened their home. I promised to visit often. Within two weeks, the children, Mimi, and I were looking from the third-story window of our new apartment at Penthémont, a convent on the rue de Grenelle.

A square courtyard housed a frozen garden scattered with stone benches for prayer or conversation. In the corner opposite our wing, a statue of the Blessed Virgin stretched out her hands as if to disperse seed to the pigeons pecking near her pedestal.

Mimi squeezed my hand in reassurance. "We'll get on."

I nodded. I would see to it.

The convent teemed with women of every age and state—religious, noble, and bourgeois. I had not anticipated so many seeking solace from failed marriages, estranged families, or lost homes. By the end of my first week, I had grown more at ease and mingled with others. One evening, I left the children in Mimi's care to join the ladies for supper.

I selected a place at the table near a cluster of women who spoke in animated tones.

"It's obvious he adores you. Won't you consider spending an evening with him?" a brunette with rounded features asked. Her gray dress and mobcap did little to enhance her beauty, but her demeanor exuded vitality. I liked her instantly.

A striking woman enrobed in russet silk fluttered her lambskin fan. Its delicate surface exhibited a scene of dancers on a verdant landscape beneath a red *montgolfière*, a hot air balloon. "He has no fortune," she said. "He couldn't support my shoe habit."

Everyone laughed.

A servant rang a bell to announce the first course. More servants filled our bowls with a clear broth that smelled of onion. I watched Marie-Josèphe as she handled her serviette and sipped daintily from her spoon with perfect grace. Other ladies replicated her movements. I adjusted the cutlery in my hands to mimic their style. Must be a proper lady—words echoed from my absent husband. A proper lady I shall be.

Anne turned to me. "You are new here. Welcome." She gave me an amicable smile. "I am Anne and this is Marie-Josèphe, Duchesse de Beaune."

The following three evenings, Anne invited me to join them. I had made my own friends at last, though they could not be more different from one another.

One bitter winter day, I drank tea while Anne baked. The scent of sugar and cinnamon hung in the air.

"Plum or currants? I could eat one whole."

"Plum in some, pear in others." She fished in the oven with a long-handled wooden peel and pulled out several tarts. "*Parfait.*"

"Do you have any living relatives, Anne?" I added a dollop of honey to my tea.

"Just the one cousin." She slid the fragrant pies onto the woodblock countertop to cool.

Anne's father had died of consumption the year before, leaving his prized bakery to the only male relative. Her devastation seeped into her voice when she mentioned it.

"So there is no way you can obtain your own shop?"

"Do you know any women who own a bakery?" She removed her apron. "Well I shall be the first!" Anne sewed, washed clothes, and sold her fine pastries. She saved every sou and kept careful contact with would-be customers. She had even designed her own seal. Her determination amazed me. "Would you like to come today? I'm distributing bread to the poor."

I hesitated. Seeing poverty left me in profound despair. The unwashed faces and sickly children.

"I'm not sure I am prepared for it, Anne. They detest us in our finery. I—"

"They're grateful, not angered with those who help them," she said cheerfully. "You'll see."

An hour later, I found myself stuffed in a fiacre with Anne and sacks of leftover food. The sky turned silver-violet as the sun dipped closer to the horizon. A scruffy man dressed in black walked from lantern to lantern, opening their small panes of glass to pour oil inside. A flick of his wrist and the orange flame of a match glowed in the fading light. The coach slowed as we approached the Pont Neuf.

"This is our stop," Anne said.

"Under the bridge?"

We lugged sacks of stale bread to the walkway along the Seine. A horde of beggars dashed in our direction.

"God bless you, Anne," a woman cried, wiping her hands on her dirt-smudged overcoat before wrapping her arms around her benefactor.

I stepped back as the woman's rotten odor wafted in my direction. She reeked of old garbage. Other beggars followed and soon they surrounded us. They snatched the goods from our hands in haste, as if we might change our minds.

The number of them! If only we had more to give—shoes and blankets, soap and firewood. An overwhelming helplessness engulfed me.

"That is all we have for now," Anne shouted. "I will be back at the same time next week."

"God bless you. You're an angel!" a woman shouted back.

"Shall we go?" When Anne saw my expression she laughed and put her arm around me. "We're helping as much as we can. That's all that matters."

"There are so many! I had no idea." Guilt flooded my heart. I had so much to be thankful for; my woes seemed inconsequential. I blushed at my own frivolity. I would join Anne each week to do my part, uncomfortable or not.

"Can you imagine if we didn't have Penthémont to go home to?" Anne said. "We would be among them."

I shuddered at the thought. Désirée could only help with my expenses for so long. I would need to find other means to support us soon.

During the ride back to the convent, my head reeled. I must make my own money. I had only one skill worth something in my social circle. I smiled.

My scheme unfolded at Fanny's Thursday salon.

"Tarot cards?" Fanny asked. "You little Creole witch. I love it."

"I can't believe I didn't think of it sooner," I said.

I sat in the almost quiet corner behind a gold silk curtain, waiting for the lovesick, the ailing, and those in search of money.

"Will I ever find love again?" a young woman asked, wistful.

I hid my surprise. She could not be serious. Her sensuous beauty blossomed from every angle. Her emerald eyes sparkled with mischief, while her silvery blond hair formed an angelic halo. I would be shocked if every man in Paris did not love her.

"A woman of your beauty must be loved already." I smiled. "But we'll consult the cards."

I drew the Devil, followed by the Lovers and the Hierophant.

"You will celebrate love in abundance. But you must take caution, for your lust may result in your ruin."

"I knew it!" Claire squealed. "Jean loves me."

I laughed. She'd heard only the pieces she wished to hear. "I'm certain he does."

She placed the fee on the table. "*Merci beaucoup.* I'll be back next week!"

Later, as I prepared to leave for the evening, our paths crossed again.

"Rose, are you a Creole? Your accent gives you away."

"I am from Martinique." A servant helped me into my cloak.

"And I, Guadeloupe."

"Your fair skin—I wouldn't have guessed," I said.

"We moved to Paris when I was nine for my schooling and to be near court."

"Court? I long to attend!"

"I'm afraid I don't have enough influence to secure an invitation for you. But I'll be attending a soiree hosted by a duchess friend of mine next week. Would you care to join me?"

"I would be honored!"

I smiled. It was time I ventured among the nobility.

Claire and I became fast friends, and many nights I accompanied her to popular salons. On more than one occasion I found her in a closed parlor, locked in a passionate embrace with her lover's hand in her décolletage. I teased her for her caprice in love, though I admired her passion. How I wished I could release my own bitterness. But I was in no hurry to be made a fool again.

Through Claire and Marie-Josèphe, my circle of friends expanded. My evening schedule filled and my confidence grew. Men began to dote on me as I treated them with the playful disregard I had learned from Claire.

"Can I get you a drink, madame?" a gentleman asked at a ball.

"*Merci*, but Monsieur Tautou is bringing me one now. Perhaps later." I smiled and sauntered away.

"I'm going to the opera tomorrow evening," another monsieur said. "I'd be honored if you would accompany me."

"Thank you. I will send word if I am able," I said coyly, leaving him to guess my response until the last possible moment. I would hold the reins.

One evening I attended a play with Marie-Josèphe. She had obtained our seats through her current lover, Monsieur Cotillion, a patron of the theater.

"I wish my gown did not accentuate my shoulders. I look like a square," Marie-Josèphe said.

"Don't be silly." I removed my cloak. "You're stunning."

We wore the newly fashionable English muslin dresses that resembled those I had worn in Martinique—the very style for which Alexandre had mocked me my first years in Paris. Their flowing, unencumbered skirts, cap sleeves, and heightened waists flattered my breasts and willowy arms. Ladies no longer suffered the hoops and restrictive corsets of formal brocades. A painting of Queen Marie Antoinette in an informal, flowing gown and straw hat had changed the fashions completely.

A wave of guilt washed over me. I'd had to borrow from Désirée to purchase my latest gown. My fortune-telling had not generated as much as I had hoped. My spending habits did not help.

Marie-Josèphe never questioned my spending. "The company we keep is the key to leaving Penthémont," she said, "to secure your status, to find a lover's support outside these walls. We must be beautiful and well dressed. It is a woman's greatest weapon."

A woman's greatest weapon was expensive. Remorse set in as bill notes filled the top drawer of my desk.

We settled into our seats, our view of the stage unobstructed.

"Would you like to use a lorgnette?" Marie-Josèphe extended a set of eyeglasses on a long, thin handle made of silver and inlaid with mother-of-pearl.

"Don't you want to use them?" I turned the glasses over in my hands. "These are beautiful."

"I have another pair." She pulled an equally beautiful set from her beaded bag. "I refuse to attend the theater without them. You can see the expressions on the players' faces."

I peered through them and gasped. "I can make out the flower stems on the ceiling mural. Oh! And the ladies' jewelry in the first rows. Look at the ruby pins in her hair! Divine."

She laughed. "Now you won't watch a show without them either."

I studied the crowd as we waited for the play to begin. Lovers leaned together. Friends gossiped, raven and blond heads bobbing as they gestured. Thankfully, wheat hair powder was no longer à la mode.

"Very few men are wearing wigs these days. Have you noticed?" I asked.

"I prefer the wigs, myself."

"Not I. I like to see their natural coloring. And I'm perfectly happy to be rid of hair powder."

"The Queen still uses it, I hear." Marie-Josèphe leaned to my ear so our neighbors would not hear her. "She is criticized for her opulence."

"But isn't that the Queen's duty? To entertain the nobility in finery?" I didn't understand the hatred directed at such a poised and elegant woman. She had done nothing but fulfill the expectations associated with her position. "She must be lonely."

"Why would you think such a thing?" Marie-Josèphe looked surprised. "She is surrounded by ladies and maids."

"In a country that is not her own, without family or friends. Without those who know her heart."

She laughed. "You are a romantic, dear Rose."

Not a romantic, but a woman made to start again after leaving all behind. I felt sympathy for Her Majesty. I heard she escaped the palace as often as possible.

To be a queen would not be so grand.

When the *comédie* concluded Marie-Josèphe and I weaved through the gathered crowd in the vestibule. She introduced me to acquaintances, many of whom invited us for supper. That's when I saw him, his arm laced through one of a pretty woman. I gripped Marie-Josèphe's arm.

"What is it?" she asked. "You're arresting the blood in my arm."

"It's my husband! I don't want him to see me."

Alexandre turned as if by command. My heart pounded as he scanned the room, looking for someone.

"Which one?" Marie-Josèphe asked. "The black coat or the blue?"

"The blue." I gulped. What would I say to him?

His eyes locked on my face. Recognition lit his features, followed by embarrassment and finally guilt. Like a naughty schoolboy.

I turned to a male acquaintance on my right and gave him my hand. The gentleman kissed it lightly and smiled, encouraged by the brief contact. Let Alexandre see how I had changed. No longer did I appear unkempt or unsure of myself, thanks to my lady friends. I had observed and adopted their every mannerism.

Alexandre's stare burned into the side of my face.

I turned again.

Melancholy reflected in his eyes. He wasn't happy. Good. He had estranged himself from his family with his wretched behavior. I yearned to yell at him, to scold him for shattering my heart and destroying my trust. How he had belittled me! My fury mounted and I turned a final time.

He had gone.

Seeing Alexandre had rattled my nerves. Against my will, I searched for his face at every outing. He owed me an apology and his children a visit. Still, I detested myself for thinking of him at all.

One cold spring day, I sipped a cup of warmed chocolate while Eugène played with his soldier figurines and Hortense slept. A rapping at the door interrupted our peaceful afternoon.

The door flew open before Mimi reached it.

I spilled my chocolate in surprise. "What in the world?" I set down my cup and jumped to my feet.

My crazed husband rushed toward Eugène. The acrid smell of brandy surrounded him.

"What is the meaning of this?" I demanded, shocked at his intrusion. "You aren't welcome here. Please leave!"

"I'm taking my son home where he belongs." Alexandre scooped Eugène into his arms and bolted for the door.

"You're drunk, Alexandre! Put him down at once!"

"Maman, Maman!" Eugène wailed, extending his arms to me.

Alexandre pounded down the stairs. "He needs his father!"

"You're scaring him! He doesn't know you!" I stumbled after him, across the courtyard and into the street. "Stop this! You can't take a boy from his mother!"

When he reached the hired coach at the edge of the drive, he chucked Eugène inside.

Panic constricted my chest.

"What are you doing?" I yanked his arm with all my strength. "He's only three. Alexandre, please!"

"I am his father. I have every right to take him to a stable home, better than this"—he waved his free hand—"pathetic place. Let go of me!" He pushed me, sending me backward into a slushy puddle.

I landed on my rear, soaking my skirts. "I hate you!" Hot tears stung my eyes.

"Maman!" Eugène's little voice cried.

Alexandre slammed the door. The carriage pulled away into the unwieldy flow of traffic.

I ran after them, thin shoes slipping on patches of ice, until they disappeared from view. "He took my son! I hate you!" I choked through the rushing tears. "He took my son!"

I stood shivering in the street while pedestrians passed. What in the name of God had made him do such a thing? How would I get Eugène back?

A nun had witnessed the horrible scene and rushed to my side. I fell into her arms.

"My dear," Sister Lucille said, "you will catch your death. Let's find some dry clothes." She patted my face with her handkerchief and led me to my apartment.

When I saw Mimi's saddened expression, my rage exploded. "That stupid, selfish b—"

"Clear your head, Yeyette. We have to get our Eugène back."

"That man had better bring him back by nightfall or else—" I launched an Italian vase he had gifted me at the floor. It smashed into pieces. Startled, Hortense began to cry.

Alexandre did not return Eugène. My son's absence tore at my heart. Where had Alexandre taken him? He loved Eugène; my son would be safe, I assured myself. He must be safe.

I visited Désirée at once to seek advice.

She closed the book she held on her lap. "What the devil has gotten into him? You must meet with the provost and get him back."

"Do you think I have a chance?"

She walked to her desk and rummaged through her drawers. "I will write a testimonial on your behalf."

I toyed with the buttons on my gloves. "Désirée?"

"Hmm?" She pulled out a chair and sat down to write.

"You will not like it. It isn't conventional, and I understand my chances of success are slim, but . . ."

She looked up from the letter she had already begun.

"I'll be doing more than requesting Eugène's return. I plan to file for a separation."

"You have a good case now that Alexandre has taken Eugène, but you must be convincing. Ask Fanny and anyone else you know to write on your behalf. The court doesn't rule in a woman's favor often."

"You aren't disappointed?"

She put down her quill pen. "Alexandre is my stepson. I love him, but he has behaved like a spoiled child. You have my complete support."

I moved to take her hands in mine. "Thank you, Désirée. It means so much to me to have your support."

I would beat Alexandre at his own game.

Claire used her connections to secure a speedy appointment with the provost of Paris. Within the week, I found myself waiting in the court of justice with Claire at my side. I shifted in my seat and fingered my stack of documents. Surely the judge would rule in my favor. I had proof of Alexandre's negligence. I prayed it would be enough.

"Madame de Beauharnais?" At last, a clerk called my name.

"Yes." I stood.

"Right this way."

"*Courage.*" Claire blew me a kiss.

The clerk led me through a series of corridors until we reached the judge's office. I inhaled a fortifying breath before entering. I must exude fortitude.

"*Bonjour.* Have a seat," the judge greeted me.

I described every detail of our marriage—my husband's infidelity, his accusations, his fleeting time at home and lack of financial support. Last of all, I explained Eugène's kidnapping. The provost read through my letters, taking notes on his elegant stationary.

"Madame de Beauharnais, it appears you have suffered a great deal, but it's essential I hear both parties." His pale eyes were kind. "I'll request your husband's presence in two weeks' time. It would be in your favor to be present as well." He shuffled his papers into a pile and placed his wrinkled hands on top.

"*Merci*, monsieur. I am aggrieved at Alexandre's conduct."

"It is my pleasure to help an innocent young woman." He smiled beneath his bushy mustache.

I daresay he liked me. As Claire and I swept into our waiting coach, a spark of hope ignited in my bosom. It was time for my luck to change.

The days before the trial crept along. Visions of Eugène's terrified face plagued me. I couldn't wait to bring him home. The appointed day arrived on a frosty March morning.

Alexandre arrived just as our names were called. The moment I saw him, my anger flared.

"I'm so glad you could make it," I said, the hate in my voice controlled but unmistakable.

"Let's finish this business once and for all, shall we? I'll be glad to be rid of you."

I clenched my fists inside my green wool muff. I would not give him the satisfaction of seeing me upset. I had learned to hold my temper, to appear a lady at all times.

"Right this way." The clerk motioned us through an open door.

The provost addressed us without looking up from his papers. "*Bonjour*, Madame de Beauharnais. *Bonjour*, monsieur. Please have a seat." He waved his hand to indicate the chairs in front of his massive oak desk.

Alexandre sat as far from me as possible.

The judge locked Alexandre in his gaze. "I will come to the point. I met with Madame de Beauharnais on a previous occasion. I have reviewed her letters from your family and friends. They all support her innocence despite your claims of her infidelity. I find it difficult to find her guilty with so many contrary witnesses. Do you have proof against her? If so, I will take your documentation at this time."

My articulate husband bowed his head before the provost. "Monsieur le Jouron, I assure you my wife has not been devoted to me, as required by law. I heard many rumors while abroad, serving my garrison and my country. As you can imagine, I was vexed by such atrocious news." Somehow he managed to conjure tears.

I stared at him, incredulous at his false display of emotion.

"She sneaked from the house to meet her lovers like a common whore." He dabbed his eyes with his gloved hand. "It is I who deserve the rights in this separation. She has never been a respectable wife—"

"Monsieur de Beauharnais," the provost said, "this is no place for insults and fabricated rumors—only facts. You have spent less than a year with your wife in a five-year period. I find it absurd you allege affairs having spent so little time at home. Who were your sources?"

"I relied upon the counsel of my aunt Désirée and my father, the Marquis de de Beauharnais. I cannot divulge my other sources. You must understand the sensitivity of my position."

"That is complete nonsense," the judge said. "Your stepmother and father submitted their word in writing in support of Madame de Beauharnais. I suggest you cease your falsehoods, monsieur, or you may find yourself facing contempt. Is this the only case you can make against your wife?"

Alexandre's jaw set in a rigid line, but he said nothing.

He had been silenced. A miraculous feat, indeed. I studied the judge's face as my heart thrummed in anticipation of the verdict.

"If you have no documentation, all charges against Madame de Beauharnais are to be deemed false and unfounded. Madame, your name is cleared and your honor restored. I grant you the separation you desire, including proper financial support due a wife."

I released a breath I did not know I was holding. Relief washed through me. I smiled, thankful for the judge's faith in my honesty.

"*Insupportable!*" Alexandre cried in indignation. "I won't pay her a single sou." He jumped from his chair and stormed across the room.

My mouth fell open as he slammed the door behind him.

En Avant

Fontainebleau, 1785–1788

The judge stood in outrage. "What in God's name is the meaning of this? No man leaves my court without being dismissed!" A pair of guards rushed to the judge's aid. "Stop that man in the officer's uniform!"

Moments later, the guards thrust Alexandre back into the room and barred the door.

"You are not dismissed!" The judge glared. "I will fine you if you attempt that ridiculous display again. Is that clear?"

"*Oui*, monsieur." Alexandre bowed his head, suddenly meek.

"Sit down."

Alexandre sat soundlessly.

"You have no evidence against your wife; therefore her name is clear," the provost said. "You will give her the monthly sum owed to her."

Alexandre ducked his head. "Of course. I apologize. I was taken by such surprise. I—"

The judge raised his hand. "Enough."

I covered my mouth to hide my smile. Alexandre had a flair for the theatrical, but it did not serve him well in the judge's office.

"May I see the testimonials from Désirée and my father?" he asked. The provost handed him the papers.

We sat in uncomfortable silence while Alexandre read.

I longed to discuss Eugène. I tapped my foot and gazed at a painting of a nobleman on the far wall. His crooked nose and steely eyes sent a shiver up my spine. A hideous painting, to be sure.

Alexandre shuffled the stack of letters into a pile. "It appears I am mistaken." He turned to me. "Rose, I owe you my most ardent apology." He was using his slick bedroom tone.

I smothered a laugh. No one knew his false, obsequious nature better than I.

He sensed my reticence and knelt by my chair. "My accusations were wretched and undeserved. I'm chagrined at my own behavior." The man with whom I had fallen in love had resurfaced, if only for an instant. "Please say you'll forgive me."

A vision of Eugène's face made me stiffen with anger. "I can forgive your slander, dear husband, when you return my son."

"I took him for his own good. I—"

"That is our next topic of discussion," the provost interrupted. "You have violated the law in this regard. Your son is to remain in his mother's custody until he is five years old, as is customary. At five, he will be sent to school under your care. Summers will be spent with his mother. You will return the child to her immediately. If you attempt to abduct him again, you will be arrested."

"I understand."

My heart soared. Thank God! My darling boy would come home.

The provost gave Alexandre a hard look. "You are to restore financial support to assist Madame de Beauharnais with her expenses, including monies for your son's servants and education. Your wife will also receive her dowry from her family—it is not to pay for your needs. Is that clear?"

The judge turned to me. "Madame, have you anything further to discuss?"

"No, monsieur."

The provost nodded his dismissal and I followed Alexandre to the door. I had won—a legal separation, monthly stipends, and my son! I could not marry again, but I could move on, and even take a lover if I chose. I nearly skipped from the building. With Alexandre's support, I could afford my own apartment. Good-bye convent. Adieu, Alexandre.

Alexandre stopped me as we exited the building. "I hope we can be amicable for our children. Our dissidence has divided my family."

"Your behavior divided your family," I snapped. "If you'd been the father and husband you promised, this wouldn't have happened."

His ears reddened. "Had you been a desirable wife, we wouldn't be in this predicament."

I took a deep breath. He wouldn't belittle me again. "You wouldn't know a good thing if it struck you in the face. You care only for yourself."

He ignored my insult. "I've been a good father to Eugène. He may not wish to rejoin you."

"I'll be the judge of that! Bring him home tonight."

"Only if I may meet my daughter as well."

I stared at him, speechless.

"Don't look so shocked. I love my children. Both of them."

"I recall you denouncing Hortense as a bastard."

He bowed his head. "Something I truly regret." Sincerity rang in his words.

"I would like for her to know her papa," I said, eyeing him with suspicion. "If you can be civil to me and not steal her away."

His eyes narrowed to slits. "That may be difficult. To be civil to you, that is."

I clenched my fists in outrage and stormed toward a fiacre.

Alexandre arrived at the convent later that evening, just as I had begun to worry he wouldn't deliver Eugène.

"*Bonsoir*," he said curtly, letting go of Eugène's hand.

"Maman!" Eugène raced across the salon. He wrapped his little arms around my neck and relished my assault of kisses.

"Oh, my darling! I missed you so much." I squeezed him to my chest and stroked his hair. I peered over his head at Alexandre, who remained in the doorway, his expression sheepish. He seemed to regret having acted a fool. "What did you do with your papa, *cheri*?"

"We rode horsies and threw bread at the birds, and Papa read me stories. I ate lots of jam!" he added with glee.

"I'm so glad you enjoyed your vacation." I gave Alexandre a steely look.

"Did you expect I would mistreat my son? Give your papa a kiss." Eugène wiggled from my grasp and sprang into his father's arms.

Alexandre *had* treated him well. It was clear he loved his son. He detested only me.

"Hortense is asleep. We can set another time for you to meet her."

"I shall come in two days, at midday." He put Eugène on his feet. "Does that suit you?"

"No, it does not. I have an engagement. You may come Thursday at two."

I would never be rid of him, but his visits would be on my terms.

Alexandre visited regularly and lavished affection on our children. They adored his visits. I began to forgive his kidnapping Eugène.

I made haste to begin my new life and called upon friends to help me find an apartment in Paris. After viewing a dozen dilapidated buildings, I realized I could not afford a place in the city. My income from Alexandre was smaller than I had realized. We would have to relocate elsewhere.

One summer morning, I loaded the children into our hired coach.

"Where are we going, Maman?" Eugène asked as we pulled away from Penthémont.

"Our new home in Fontainebleau. Where Aunt Fanny and Désirée live." Financial hardship had forced them to move months earlier. I touched the tip of my son's round nose. "And don't worry. We'll still see your papa. We won't be far from Paris."

When we pulled into the drive of our new home, I admired the modest vegetable garden and flower boxes stuffed with petunias.

Eugène leapt from his seat. "Can I play?"

"Let's!"

Our new apartment lacked elaborate furnishings, but we awoke to the warble of birds and cheeping tree frogs. Yet despite the lovely wood, invigorating air, and the calm of Fontainebleau, I grew bored. How many promenades could I take through the meadow? I missed the bustle of the city.

One afternoon, I retied Hortense's ribbons after playtime in the yard.

"Your romping has mussed your hair." I tickled her middle. "As it should be, *doucette*. Your *maman* tumbled through the garden when she was little."

She climbed into my lap. "Want to sit with Maman."

I kissed her head. How fast she had grown! I could hardly believe she was three years old. And Eugène had been sent to school. A lump formed in my throat. I couldn't wait to visit him, though I had no idea where the money for the trip would come from. I worried at my pitiful income. Independence had been more difficult than I'd expected. I looked up as Fanny waltzed into the salon.

"How are my favorite girls?" She stooped to kiss Hortense, leaving a ring of rouge on her face. "Oh!" She laughed. "Let me clean your cheek." She dabbed at the imprint with her handkerchief.

"We're well," I said.

"The royals are in town!" She beamed. "Do you know what that means? With the royals come their sycophants and lackeys, their supporters and enemies. The hunt will begin again and so will my salon, darling!"

I whooped in glee.

Fanny's salons impressed as they had in Paris; the most brilliant minds, the most creative, and the most fashionable outside of the royal court attended. Even Claire came for an extended visit.

One autumn evening, Claire twirled in a new gown. "How do I look?" Iridescent sequins sparkled in the candlelight.

I admired the blush satin on her creamy skin. "Fresh as a peach in summer."

"Ripe for the picking." We laughed.

I pulled on a pair of ivory gloves. "Thank you for the gown. It's lovely."

Claire had tired of a muslin sheath in mint green after wearing it twice. I didn't have a sou to purchase my own. I had no idea how I would accrue rent for the apartment or for Hortense's tutor. Alexandre sent money only sporadically.

At Fanny's, we parted ways to mingle. As I circled the room, I overheard conversations that shocked me. Everyone spoke ill of the Queen.

"*L'Autri-chienne!*" a portly man guffawed.

"A female dog, indeed. The Queen scampers around her harem like a bitch in heat!" a thin man with gold-rimmed glasses added. Their laughter bellowed.

"The dauphin is sickly. Poor bastard. He pays the price for his mother's bawdiness."

What bravado they possessed—to call the Queen such a name in public! The idiots! Someone could report such a statement and they would find themselves imprisoned, or worse.

I scooted across the room to Claire, who flirted with a man I had never seen.

"Rose, darling." Her hand made a sweeping gesture. "Monsieur Jacques, may I present Rose de Beauharnais."

"I was just leaving to search out a cigar," he replied. "Mademoiselle Pellier, it was a pleasure."

Claire showed a perfect smile, the gleam in her eye full of unspoken taunting.

Lord, she had a way with men.

"*À plus tard,*" she cooed.

"You have met a man already?" I teased.

"Of course." Dimples popped from their hiding places in her cheeks. "Speaking of men, the gentleman in navy is staring at you."

I opened my fan and pretended to look past the dark-haired gentleman. He caught my eye and started in my direction.

Claire elbowed me hard in the ribs. "Maybe this time you should do more than flirt. It's time, *mon amie.*"

I regarded his chiseled chin and aquiline nose. "He's not handsome, exactly, but there is something attractive about him. He seems . . . self-assured."

"Well, yes. He's rich and has loads of women vying for his attention."

"Who is he?"

"The Duc de Bordeaux. He's not married."

"Maybe he isn't interested in women at all."

"Ha! I doubt that."

"*Bonsoir,* ladies." The duke bowed. "I couldn't help but notice the most beautiful women in the room."

"You flatter us, monsieur," I said, fluttering my fan.

"I wanted to invite you *à la chasse* and an evening of dining next week. At the château I've rented in town."

"Perhaps we'll see you there." I gave him a coy look.

"Splendid." He grinned. "Now, if you will excuse me, I have business to attend to. Enjoy your evening."

"I haven't hunted in ages!"

"I don't know what I was thinking." I reached for a flute of champagne. "I can't kill an animal!"

"I assure you we'll not see the prey at all. We'll ride behind the others." Claire took her own glass of wine. "It's great fun. And then there's the duke." Amusement danced in her eyes.

"Don't get your hopes up. I don't plan to bed the duke."

I attended my first hunt in a cornflower blue riding habit with narrow skirts and epaulettes. But my hat! Gorgeous and petite, it had blue satin that shone and a perky cerulean feather waving like a flag in the breeze.

"It is fantastic, isn't it?" Claire relished my excitement. "With kid gloves and half boots, you look a natural. *Regarde.*" She pointed at a man carrying a giant curled horn. "It is time to begin."

We mounted our sidesaddles with the help of a stable hand. A cheerful smattering of voices and the whinnies of horses floated on the crisp autumn breeze. Energy pulsed in the circles of waiting hunters. All listened for the horn, the signal to begin. Nothing in Martinique resembled such an event, with its display of horses and their regal riders. My pulse raced at the thrill.

I scanned the crowd. Still no sign of the duke.

The crowd hushed.

I held my breath. My horse, Sable, pranced beneath me in anticipation.

The horn's melody sounded and cheering erupted. A blur of thundering horses and bawling hounds raced for the forest. Sable bolted. Leaning forward in the saddle, I focused on the path ahead. We sailed through thickets of oaks, maples, and walnut trees, their leaves a parade of burnt orange, lemon, and red currant. Wind billowed in my skirts.

"*Va Sable, Va!*" I shouted. Chunks of soil flew from under her speeding hooves. The scent of polished leather, the rhythm of muscles and sinew intoxicated me.

Just ahead, a stream came into view, gushing from the past few rain-soaked days. Anxiety washed over me. Should I pull back? Sable's hooves pounded forward without hesitation. At the bank of the stream, I closed my eyes.

My stomach dropped. Weightlessness overtook me. In one smooth leap, Sable bounded over the stream.

A peal of laughter ripped from my lips. "*Magnifique!*" I nudged Sable faster, to leave all behind. "Onward!"

That evening, I wore rose-colored velvet with gold embroidery and cream satin ribbons. The dress had cost a fortune, but Claire insisted on helping me pay for it. We descended the stairs to wait for Fanny's coach. She would escort Claire and me tonight. When the coach stopped in front of the house, its door flew open.

"Get in! We're almost late," Fanny called.

I bumped my head on the doorframe as we jerked forward. "Ouch!" I blotted my forehead, trying not to touch my hair. It had taken me more than an hour to get it right. Curls sprang from a pink flower pin, the perfect complement to such an elegant gown.

"You're perfect, darling. Not to worry," Claire said. She was ravishing, herself, in yellow silk and diamonds.

"Why are we in a hurry?" I asked.

"I'm meeting friends to discuss reform." Fanny folded her hands in her lap.

"Reform? What sort?" Claire asked, her head swaying side to side to the rhythm of the moving carriage.

"The royal treasury is bankrupt. We'll see another increase in taxes soon."

"I've heard the King will no longer host court in Fontainebleau when this season concludes. How dull everything will become," Claire complained.

"An increase in taxes?" I asked anxiously. "As it is, I have borrowed to survive these last months."

"Times are unstable. We don't want to be associated with the wrong side. Be prudent with your opinions," Fanny warned. "Many fear revolt."

We nodded in silent agreement. The thought of a revolt turned my stomach.

Fanny had no need to be discreet. Everyone debated reform.

"The King should fire the Minister of Finance. His support dwindles," a gentleman said.

"King Louis is an arrogant fool. Too busy hunting and letting the Queen spend the national treasury on frippery," another said.

Remaining neutral was my natural inclination; both sides had their points and dividing my friends concerned me. I thought it ludicrous to lose a friendship over opinions about the King. He would be King for posterity.

I searched for the duke throughout dinner, but did not see him in the sea of faces. As the wine flowed, the guests' discussions became more animated and the ambience darkened. I excused myself to seek fresh air; a headache brewed.

On my final turn through the rambling halls, I spotted a door leading to the main gardens. The chilly air bit at my nose and ears. Stars sparkled against a black velvet sky. Torches lit the mansion's rows of hardy flowers, which thrived in spite of the autumn frost. I descended a staircase leading to a terrace of topiaries and fountains.

"Madame, are you cold?" A voice startled me. "You are shivering."

I squinted at a form in the darkness. "Who's there?"

"Please, take my coat. I am quite warm." The figure stepped into a halo of light from a nearby torch, revealing a familiar chiseled face. The duke.

I smiled. "Thank you, monsieur. That's very kind of you." He slid his coat off and wrapped it around my shoulders.

"You are very beautiful tonight, madame." He leaned forward, taking my gloved hand in his and grazing it with his lips. A tingling spread up my arm. "It's a lovely night, but a bit brisk. I'm surprised to find a woman out of doors."

"The heavy talk was depressing my mood." I smiled. "It appears I made the right choice."

"May I?" He offered me his arm.

"Please." I held his muscled forearm as he led me on a promenade through the garden.

"Times are changing," he said. "We all feel the strain. But we need not dwell on serious talk on such a perfect night."

"*Merci.* I've had enough for one evening."

"And did the riding agree with you this afternoon?"

"Very much. Such a rush of freedom and danger. It feels like flying," I breathed.

He eyed my heaving chest.

"I enjoy it as well. But I enjoy the company of a beautiful woman more." His eyes smoldered with longing.

Heat swelled in hidden depths.

"Perhaps you would consider riding with me tomorrow afternoon . . . if we have good weather?"

I could hear Marie-Josèphe's words of warning: "Don't appear too eager. Rapid surrender will not win his affections."

"I have another engagement tomorrow," I said.

"And the following day? We could ride to one of my favorite spots."

I paused before answering. I enjoyed riding, and I liked him. I glanced back at the impressive château. A wealthy lover would be divine, even if only for a little while.

"Sounds lovely."

"I'll send a coach for you. Now, shall we join the festivities? A concert will begin in a few moments."

I grinned in the dark.

Within a fortnight, I fell into bed with the duke—the first man, beyond harmless flirtations, since Alexandre. To be admired again made me feel alive. Charles possessed an adorable perfection, but with so many willing ladies yet unplucked, his attention faded quickly. I followed his lead and applied myself to the next interesting gentleman, and the next. To feel wanted, even for a short time, invigorated me, as did their expensive gifts.

My financial woes deepened as the prices of flour, sugar, and oil swelled, and I moved in with Désirée and the Marquis to cut expenses.

They adored having us live with them again. Both had missed our visits and those from Alexandre.

One summer afternoon, Alexandre came to see the children, bearing gifts.

"The gifts are lovely, but do you have my monthly stipend?" I asked.

Eugène sat on the floor surrounded by soldier figurines. Hortense held her new doll against her chest and gazed up at her father's face.

"I will deliver it to you next week via post," Alexandre said.

"We won't eat, should you choose not to."

"There is no need to be dramatic. I will send the funds."

"As you always do?" My tone brimmed with sarcasm.

He glared at me and carried Hortense to the garden.

Alexandre did not send the money he had promised. I considered visiting the judge—perhaps he could force my delinquent husband to pay.

Hortense pulled on my hand as she skipped up the drive.

"I wish Eugène were here," she said. "Why does he have to go to school?"

"To learn and become a man."

"Will I go to school?"

"Yes. A school for little girls." Though I couldn't imagine how I would afford it. "Look! There's a bunny in the bushes." I dropped my voice to a whisper. "Shall we sneak up on him?"

"I'll be a bunny, too." Hortense hopped after the animal, startling it.

We turned at the crunch of hooves on gravel.

"Ask Mimi to put on some tea, dear."

Hortense hopped inside as a portly man in elegant clothing descended from the coach.

"Madame de Beauharnais, I presume?"

"Yes. And you are?"

"Monsieur Boucher." The man wheezed as he spoke. "I'm here to collect a sum on account of your husband's debts. Is he at home?" His foulard acted as a tourniquet around his thick neck.

"My husband?" I asked, confused. "But he doesn't live here. We have been separated for some time." The man coughed into his hand-kerchief, a horrible gurgling sound.

Perhaps I should offer him a chair.

He wobbled closer. "This address is listed as his residence."

My eyes widened. "I assure you, monsieur," I began, controlling my growing anger, "he does not reside here. You may find him in Paris, though I do not know the address of his residence there."

The man coughed again. Mucus rattled in his throat. "The next time you see him, please tell him I stopped by. Here is my contact information." He waved a small card at me.

"Of course. Good day."

The man nodded, then hefted his bulk up the short step and into the coach.

I could strangle Alexandre. How dare he send creditors to our door! I stalked inside to begin a scathing letter.

Alexandre's creditors began arriving in droves. He had gambled away most of his inheritance. After some investigating, I discovered it was actually his folly that had been the reason for Désirée's and his father's forced move to Fontainebleau. I fumed at his selfishness. Désirée's budget grew strained supporting all of our needs. I sold my jewelry and harp to assist with the bills, but knew I had to make a change. A letter arrived one spring afternoon that prompted my decision.

March 13, 1788

Chère Rose,

I have troubling news. Manette and your father are very ill and have shown little improvement in these last days. I fear their end may be nearing.

I hope you may consider making the trip. I cannot send you money, but perhaps a friend will understand the urgency of your visit and take pity.

I hope my grandchildren are well.

Je t'aime.

Maman

I had to go to Martinique, no matter the price. I checked the date on the letter. Six weeks had passed. *Dieu*, I hoped I was not too late. I asked the one person who would help me without question, without expectation: Fanny.

Three short weeks later, Hortense, Mimi, and I set sail. I would return home at last.

Return to the Island

Martinique, 1788–1790

It had been nine years since I had set foot on my native soil. I'd left a child and returned a mother. Joy bubbled in my veins.

"Hortense, we're here!" I slid my arm around her and kissed her. Hortense looked confused. "But it's a big forest, Maman."

"Yes." I laughed. "It is." I glanced at Mimi. Tears glistened in her eyes. "We're home," I said, voice soft.

She grabbed my hand and kissed it. "Don't know if I'm happy or sad."

Mimi would rejoin her friends and family, but to see the rugged plantation again might shock her. She had grown accustomed to the easier life in France, I knew. I understood her ambivalence.

Trois-Îlets looked the same, frozen in time like my memories, though I felt a stranger, a woman from another world. Wilderness crowded the island, chewing at signs of civilization. The forest dripped with shades of jade, olive, and lime—and the smell! Earth baked in tropical sunshine, the mingling of wildflower blossoms and lush foliage. I gulped in breaths of fragrant air. Not a single French *parfum* could match it.

Nostalgia swelled as dormant memories pushed to the front of my mind: Catherine seeking shelter from an afternoon shower under drooping leaves; me, stealing hunks of sugarcane and chomping them until the sweet juice ran in my mouth; the two of us hiding in secret coves. Lord, I had missed it all.

The enchantment of my recollections faded with the first sight of my

childhood home. How uncivil the sugar mill appeared. Moss covered
the stone facade, and underbrush from the forest invaded the garden.

I had not yet reached the front door when Maman barged through it.

"Rose!" She embraced me fiercely. The scent of sugar and wet
leaves filled my nostrils. She had not changed.

"Oh, Maman!" I buried my face in her shoulder. A flood of emotion poured from my chest. The hardship of our years apart crushed
me. Heartache, loneliness, struggling to belong. The birth of my
children—every moment I spent far from the shield of her arms. A
torrent of tears gushed down my cheeks.

"Shh. I know. I know." She stroked my hair as I sobbed. "You're
home now."

"I'm s-sorry," I sobbed. "I'm ruining your dress."

"Nonsense, *doucette*." She eyed the cotton sleeve of her sensible dress.

Hortense tugged at my skirts, fear marring her delicate features.
"Maman, what's the matter?"

I sniffled and bent to kiss her head. "I've missed Grand-mère.
That's all."

Maman crouched down to Hortense's eye level, holding a doll.
"Hello, Hortense. I'm so happy to meet you, darling. Your mother has
told me all about you."

Hortense smiled shyly. "Hello, Grand-mère."

"I have a present for you."

Hortense perked up. "A present?"

Maman flicked the rag doll to and fro as if to make her dance.
"Here you are."

Hortense snatched it from her hands. "Thank you, Grand-mère!"

"You're welcome." She beamed, eyes ablaze with happiness. "You
are five now, no? Big girl! And where is your brother?"

"He's at school," Hortense replied. "Papa wouldn't let him leave."

"Alexandre thought it best not to disrupt his education. I disagreed,
but had no say in the matter." To leave my son behind, with an ocean
between us, had been difficult. Eugène's angelic face had crumpled in
grief at our parting. I inhaled a ragged breath to keep from crying
again. I missed him already.

Maman nodded. "Of course. His father decides what is best for
him." Disappointment colored her voice.

"Someday I hope you visit us in Paris." My invitations by letter had been ignored. I thought the idea of seeing her grandchildren would have brought her to my door. I swallowed my resentment.

"And leave all of this glamour?" She laughed.

"*Bonjour*, Madame Tascher," Mimi curtsied.

"Mimi." Maman nodded. "We're glad to have you home again. Janette could use a hand. Especially since we're back in the plantation house. We've finally rebuilt it!" She motioned through the trees to the clearing up the hill. "Now, how about a bath and some coffee? I want to hear everything! From the beginning."

She led us to our home.

As I had assumed, Papa and Manette were bedridden. I read to Manette and filled her head with stories of Paris. When she felt well enough I bathed her.

My reunion with Papa at his sickbed, however, was not what I had expected.

"*Bonjour*, Papa." I set a tea tray on a table and moved to his bedside. How thin he had become. I smoothed the damp hair on his forehead. "I'm so happy to see you."

He stirred and peered at me. "Catherine? My darling girl." His voice came out as a forced whisper.

A pang hit me in the gut. I squeezed his hand and leaned closer. "Papa, it's me, Rose. I'm visiting from France."

Confusion lit his blue eyes. "France? We're not in France. Where's Catherine? What have you done to her?"

My eyes filled with tears. He had always preferred her, and now it appeared I had been erased from his mind. As if I had never been. I kissed his cheek as tears streaked my own. "I'll tell Maman you are ready for a bath."

"No." He tried to push himself into a sitting position. His ashen face twisted into a grimace of pain.

"Do not get up, Papa."

As I slipped my hand under his bony elbow, he jerked his arm away. "Don't send your mother. Janette will assist me."

Janette, his black mistress. He placed his own family below the slaves in importance.

"If you insist, Papa." I walked to the door as Janette entered the room.

"*Bonjour*, madame." Her vivid white teeth gleamed against her coffee-colored skin.

I forced a tight smile and hurried from the room into the garden. I sat on my favorite bench near the edge of the jungle. Papa had had a mistress as long as I could remember. Maman had despised them all, and I had hated to see her in pain.

This time was different. I put my face in my hands. This time I felt it, too, and relived my own.

I didn't adjust to life at the plantation as fast as I had expected. I had forgotten the oppressive summer. Insects the size of saucers buzzed in and out of windows in search of spilled sugar, and the call of birds long before sunrise exasperated me for the first few weeks. What a woman of the city I had become.

Hortense loved exploring. Moisture rose from the ground and hovered to crawl on our skin and saturate our clothing as we walked the plantation. Thunderheads puffed their ominous warning in the distance. I flicked a black insect with vivid blue legs from my arm. Its rotund shell thumped against my fingernail.

Hortense followed me through the garden and happened upon a frog as it hopped down the hillside toward the valley.

"Can I touch him?" she asked.

"If you can catch him." I fanned myself lazily.

She squealed and began the chase, her blond curls dancing down her back. I sauntered behind, but finally plopped down on a fallen log. She flew down the hill just in time to touch the fleeing creature before he would leap away again. I sighed. Eugène would love it here.

When Hortense had been out of sight awhile, I stretched and went to usher her away from the crops nestled in the valley. She needn't go near the slave quarters. It would irritate the overseer to have her underfoot.

As I drew closer to the fields, rich African voices mixed with the thick air. Their beautiful hymns had intrigued me as a child, and still their sorrow vibrated in my chest. The slaves' scorched ebony backs came into view.

Where was Hortense? I continued down the hill. Still no sight of her.

I picked up my pace. As I reached the edge of the slave quarters, the hymns stopped.

A cry sliced the air.

My chest constricted. Hortense! I hustled to the open courtyard in the center of the huts. It wasn't her voice, I told myself. No need to get upset.

I walked faster; my perspiring feet slipped in my shoes. I ducked between huts.

Still no sign of my daughter.

Dieu, Hortense, where are you?

The overseer emerged from between the huts dragging a slave behind him. He jerked the man's arms together and bound them with rope.

"This will teach you to run your mouth," he sneered. He shoved *le noir* into the dirt. I knew what came next, but I could not tear my eyes away.

"We're human. Not beasts!" The slave's face twisted in rage. "We have rights like the Americans! Rise up! Rise up, men! They can't keep us down! Come together and rise up!" He shouted at his fellow slaves as they gathered on the fringes of the scene.

"Shut up!" With a swift kick, the master pummeled the man in the face with the sole of his leather boot. He pounded on the slave's ribs and stomach. Blood spurted in a morbid stream from his nose and lips.

A queasy sensation roiled in my stomach and my breath came in short spasms. Where was Hortense? No one would hurt her, I reassured myself. There were too many whites nearby.

My heart pounded as I weaved through another row of the shabby huts. A layer of scum covered the rickety siding, many dwellings had no doors, and others had holes in their thatched roofs.

Another cry sounded from somewhere in the fields.

Fear spread like poison, evoking horrible thoughts. I broke into a run.

"We'll never have salvation unless you *rise up!*" The slave did not stop his ranting, even with blood streaming down his face. "They can kill me! But they can't stop us all!"

"Didn't you get enough?" The overseer heaved the man to his feet and dragged him to the whipping post. He tied the slave's arms above his head. Others were corralled to the space surrounding the whipping post.

"Make an example out of someone," Papa always said, "if you want to keep slaves in line." An example would be made today.

Within seconds of tying the man, the overseer cracked the whip, snapping bands of flesh from the slave's bare back. Blood oozed. The wounded slave screamed in agony.

My hand covered my mouth as I suppressed the urge to vomit.

"Hortense!" I screamed. "Hortense!"

Several slaves turned to locate the source of the screeching, curiosity and hate on their faces.

"Hortense!" I shouted again.

And there, peeking from behind a shanty, she sat, transfixed by the scene. Relief and then alarm flooded my limbs. My little girl was watching a slave being beaten, her sweet innocence shattered.

An inhuman scream sliced the air as the whip came down again and again upon the slave's back.

"Hortense!" I ran to her as fast as I could in my ruined shoes.

Her head whipped around when she heard her name. At the sight of my face, she began to cry. "Maman!" She leapt into my arms.

I kissed her face a hundred times. "You scared me!" I crushed her in my arms. "Don't ever run so far from me again!"

"I'm s-sorry, Maman. I was trying to get the frog," she sobbed, "and then I heard singing. I wanted to see. . . . Why is he hurting that man?" She pointed at the bloodied African hanging unconscious from the post.

"Let's go." I tightened my grip on her damp hand. We threaded through rows of huts toward the hill leading home.

"He was bleeding, Maman. Why are all the people brown?"

"They're slaves. They work our fields so we have crops. We wouldn't have a home without them."

"Why? What's a slave?" Her childish mind worked overtime.

I avoided the question and pulled her forward.

As we reached the bottom of the hill, a voice called, "You there! Stop!"

"What's a white devil doing here?" another voice said.

I had no time to feel outrage at such a statement. Four slave men and one woman formed a wall in front of us.

"My daughter was lost." Hortense hid her face in my skirts. "We're just leaving." My voice was calm despite my trembling. I glanced at the top of the hill. Safety was on the other side.

"What you think?" one of the men asked another. "Should we let them go?"

The man spat on the ground.

"It's their fault Leon is being tortured. Maybe we should teach them a lesson."

"Daughter of a Grand Blanc! We'd be heroes!"

My blood went cold.

"What about the girl?"

"I'll take care of her," the third man answered.

Hortense wrapped her arms around my leg, her tears coming faster now. Blood pounded in my ears. No fear. I could not show them fear. I scrutinized their faces. The woman looked vaguely—yes, her name was . . .

"A Grand Blanc's daughter? Miss Rose! Is that you?" the familiar woman asked. "You back?"

"Yes, it's me. . . . Millie?" My lips quivered.

"Is this your little one?"

The largest man crossed his arms in annoyance.

"Yes, this is Hortense. Hortense, say hi to Millie."

Hortense waved, her face stained with tears.

"Well aren't you pretty! Boys, Miss Rose was a sweet thing. Well, at least Mimi loved her."

"Thank you, Millie." I changed the subject. "It looks like your shift is unraveling. I'll send another one down for you right away." I forced a smile.

"Thank you kindly, miss." She returned a smile packed with gray, rotting teeth.

Hortense whimpered.

"Well, we had better move along. They'll be looking for us at the house. I should have tended to my sister an hour ago," I lied.

The larger man did not move, but the others parted just enough to let us pass.

My legs shook so violently, I stumbled as we climbed the hill. Hortense's sobs grew louder.

"Shh, *chérie*." I regained my balance. "Just a bit farther." I dragged her alongside me.

The men below argued with Millie. "I don't care who she is!"

"We could teach 'em a lesson. . . ."

"Hurry," I whispered to Hortense.

We broke into a run at the top of the hill. Never had I felt fear among the slaves. I had loved them and they had loved me. Something had changed. Something sinister. The ease I had remembered from home did not exist.

A fog of malevolence hung in the air despite the summer heat. Whites peered over their shoulders and blockaded their doors at sunset. Slaves ravaged crops and burned homes, watching orange flames lick the sky like devil tongues. Plantation homes collapsed amid a chorus of screams. On occasion, the Africans trapped a Grand Blanc and made him pay for his sins. Death did not come swiftly for them.

The plantation owners convened to fight back. Whippings and hangings increased. Maman refused to speak of the slaves' rebellion; to say the words aloud would evoke Ekwensu, the god of war. Despite her Catholic upbringing, she believed in the supernatural, the spirits of the land and sky, over and underneath it all.

Hortense did not sleep well for weeks. Every night she awoke screaming. I held her, stroking her sweat-soaked hair, and sang her back to sleep. But the pain of seeing her live in fear tore at me. When I received an invitation from Uncle Tascher to visit Fort-Royal, I accepted in an instant. A change of scenery would dispel the demons, and I hoped the mood wouldn't be as threatening there.

Being in town helped, as did the charmed amulet I had hung over Hortense's bed. Soon after our arrival in Fort-Royal, her nightmares ebbed and our days became placid again. We played for hours in the jewel-toned water, chasing birds or gathering crabs to prod with a stick.

One brilliant afternoon, I accompanied Aunt Tascher to market.

I squeezed several fresh mangoes. "These look good." I chose a few soft-skinned fruits and paid the *vendeur*. "I'd like to find a toy for Eugène." His name caught in my throat. How I missed him. His letters detailed his time with Alexandre, learning to shoot, and his favorite friends at school. I tilted my head back and gazed overhead to clear the tears from my eyes. Feathery clouds floated like seeds of the *dent-de-lion* drifting through the meadows at Fontainebleau. The very thing Eugène loved to chase on a summer day with his sister.

"Here we are." My head snapped down at Aunt Tascher's voice. "I'll make a new dress for Hortense's doll." She held up a piece of frilly pink cloth.

"Oh, you'll spoil her!" I teased. "You've given her many already."

"I can't help myself. She's such a sweet child."

We strolled arm in arm to the opposite side of the marketplace. As we entered the hat shop doorway, a pretty brown-haired lady exited. I moved to let her pass, but she blocked our entry.

"Good afternoon, Madame Tascher," she greeted my aunt. "Rose! Is that you?"

My closest friend from school stood before me in a pale green brocade gown.

"Juliette Despins!"

"It *is* you!" she squealed as we embraced. "I heard you were home from France, but I didn't know you had returned to town. How is France? You have two children? Are they here with you?"

"One question at a time." I laughed. "I'm so happy to see you!"

"Why don't you join us for coffee? I had the cook prepare a pineapple cake this morning," Aunt Tascher said.

"I would love to."

The three of us returned to the large white house in the center of town. I had loved Juliette like a sister. We created mischief together at convent school, sneaking late at night to meet boys from the school across town, putting salt in bad-tempered Sister Paulette's hot chocolate, and wheedling extra fruit tarts from the nuns.

We gossiped all afternoon, until Juliette excused herself to go.

"I'd love it if you would come to dinner next week. I've invited half the town."

"I'll see you then." I kissed her cheeks.

Juliette had married well. Her house stood impeccably elegant amid rows of mimosa and frangipani trees. In the front hall, a white marble staircase gleamed. Vases dripped with flowers and servants appeared poised in their suits and gloves. The aroma of spiced crab soup and yams poured from the kitchen, and my stomach rumbled. I had not eaten much that day; it would not do to bulge in my gown.

I wandered among the guests, making new acquaintances and re-connecting with others. Yet, strangely, I felt at odds. My blue silk gown did not mimic the formal styles now worn in Fort-Royal. Parisians had shed the style three years prior; I had stepped back in time. The women eyed me with open hostility. I was no longer one of them. I had become an *étrangère* in my own home.

The rude stares worsened as the dancing began. My card filled rapidly, and I spent only short intervals waiting, unlike many of my former friends. After several consecutive dances, I sailed to a chair to rest. I fanned myself and turned to find several pairs of eyes boring through me.

"Rose, where did you find such a gown? Is it the fashion in France? It seems so . . . daring. Don't you wear undergarments?" Annette asked with a malicious smile. "That neckline is positively risqué."

"Yes, quite . . . and your hair . . . it's au naturel," Diane continued, clutching Annette's arm in solidarity.

I regarded their blue powdered hair and heavily padded dresses. "As of late, style has become simpler in Paris. More like the former styles here. Perhaps they are backward." I smiled. "In truth, I'm re-lieved. I'm not as becoming as you ladies in ornate dress. But I've sent for the few formals I kept in France. I do hope they arrive soon. One hates to look out of place."

"The men seem to admire your loose gown," Annette said with disapproval.

I flicked my fan faster. Envious wretch.

I leaned toward them and whispered in a conspiratorial tone, "We know men aren't the authority on taste. That is the ladies' arena. I discredit a man's opinion in such a matter. I'm so thankful I have you two to help."

An absurd assertion. I knew very well when I caught a man's eye, and I loved it. What woman did not?

Diane and Annette said nothing, but looked at each other in a knowing way.

"And how is your husband?" Diane asked. "Alexandre made quite an impression on our little town. How elegant he was."

"An exquisite dancer," Annette sighed.

"I asked for a legal separation. It was granted. He goes his way, I go mine."

"*Vraiment?* Who has heard of such a thing! Paris must be quite progressive," Diane said.

"Or a moral abhorrence!" Annette added, her face lined in outrage.

I had no chance to speak before Diane delivered another blow. "Speaking of morality, Alexandre took Georgette, the woman in navy; Pauline, the blonde; and Elodie in violet as lovers." Diane inclined her head in their direction. "He paraded them around like prostitutes. They didn't seem to mind that he was both married and had an official mistress."

My cheeks grew hot. I needed no reminder of my husband's faults. Or my humiliation.

"And the horrible things he said about you, Rose. He—"

"As I mentioned, we are separated. I see no need to revisit the past." How dare they be so malicious! I rose from my chair. "Now if you'll excuse me—"

A musician shouted to the crowd, "Mesdames, messieurs, this will be the last dance of the evening."

Jean-Luc, a gentleman I had known as a schoolgirl, stepped from the dance floor. "Rose, may I have this dance?"

"I'd love to." I looked over my shoulder at the women who had not been asked. "Enjoy the last dance." The rudest thing I could muster without being dreadful. The audacity of those women! Our years of childhood laughter meant nothing to them. Why was I even here? I missed my son, the plantation was dangerous, and my friends were jealous and mean.

I no longer belonged.

Finding money for three passengers to France proved impossible. I wrote to Claire, hoping she might lend me the sum. I despaired at the months' wait before her response. Being separated from Eugène any longer seemed impossible.

Thankfully, Aunt Tascher held a weekly soiree that helped pass the time. The governor graced the Tascher home often, bringing the King's militia, who had arrived from France. One balmy evening, we welcomed them for dinner.

"Good evening, gentlemen." Uncle Tascher ushered them inside.

The few ladies in attendance ogled the handsome crew while they removed their hats. Nothing was more romantic than a soldier.

"Care for a drink?" Mimi circulated with a tray and the gentlemen selected their glasses.

Uncle Tascher placed his hand on my back. "May I present my niece, Rose de Beauharnais."

"How are things in Paris?" I asked. "Is there any news?"

A fleshy man with a mustache answered. "Yes, but all unpleasant, I fear."

The others nodded.

"Please, go on," I said. "You can't leave us in suspense."

"Rose was always one for gossip," Uncle Tascher teased.

"It's more than gossip this time, monsieur." The man took a swig of wine. "We suffered a terrible winter that killed most of the wheat, so flour has been scarce. Riots broke out at the bakeries. And the Seine froze! Imagine that rushing river solid! Goods couldn't be transported into the city. Hundreds starved to death and their bodies littered the streets. Even the wealthy have been hungry."

I said a silent prayer of thanks Eugène was well fed at school.

"Good God, man!" Uncle Tascher exclaimed. "And what does the King have to say?"

"He says nothing," one soldier said.

"He raises taxes to pay for his wars," another replied. "There's talk of a new government."

"With a constitution and an assembly. Like the Americans and the English."

The room grew silent.

At last, the governor posed the question we all wished to ask. "And what of the King?"

"He would remain on the throne, but with limited powers," the stout man answered. "That is one theory. Some wish to abolish the monarchy altogether."

Another long silence.

"Change is impossible to avoid," a soldier said. "The country is dividing. You are either a Royalist or a Republican."

I did not care for politics, but even I could not avoid it. A change this great would affect the entire order of things.

The tinkle of a bell interrupted our conversation. "Dinner is served," a servant announced.

I sat between my uncle and the most attractive of the militiamen, Captain Scipion du Roure. I could not help but be drawn to his caramel-colored eyes and golden hair.

"This is delicious." The captain took a bite of wine-basted fish.

"Divine." I smiled as I imagined kissing the padded apples of his cheeks.

"Captain du Roure," Uncle Tascher said, "what is your opinion of this constitutional monarchy?"

"I am a servant of God, the King, and my country. In that order." His expression became fierce. "If King Louis chooses a constitution, I also choose one. But I predict we will soon be in civil war."

"We are already in civil war," the stout man said.

"The beginnings of one, at least," the captain agreed.

I stopped chewing. Civil war? I could not envision Paris torn apart.

"Has there been fighting on French soil?" Uncle Tascher asked.

"There are some unpleasant details. It isn't appropriate in front of the ladies, sir," Captain du Roure answered.

"We are not faint of heart, monsieur," I said.

"Please, go on," Aunt Tascher encouraged him.

"Very well. The King's prison was burned to the ground. The Swiss guards were decapitated, and the frenzied crowd massacred innocents in the street."

Shocked silence permeated the room.

"Just before we left"—he motioned to the others with the knife in his hand—"a mob of women marched on Versailles demanding the King address their demands. His Majesty and the Queen are being forced to live in the Tuileries."

A collective gasp stopped the captain.

Riots? Massacred innocents? Eugène! Was he safe? Surely Alexandre would have informed me if our son were in danger. I clutched the captain's arm. "Is there still violence in the streets? My son—he is at school in Paris."

"The violence is sporadic. Try not to worry, madame. The city is heavily guarded. The mobs are after weapons and food. The children are the last thing of interest to them. He's perfectly safe." He placed his hand on mine. "Really, you have nothing to fear."

His insistence calmed me some, though I could no longer eat.

The heated discussion continued until the men retired to the study for cigars. I took a glass of champagne and dashed into the garden to clear my head. I could not protect Eugène from so far away. I had to get to him. But how? I had asked everyone I knew for money.

A door behind me opened.

"I guess we both needed a break." Captain du Roure leaned against a webbed wall of ivy.

"Indeed." My eyes locked on a ribbon of puffed skin snaking its way from the collar of his jacket along the tender skin of his neck, ending under the ridge of his jaw.

"Gruesome, isn't it?"

"I don't want to know how that happened," I said.

"I wish I didn't know either." He laughed. "I'd prefer to talk about the stunning dress you're wearing."

"A gift from my uncle." I looked down at my white satin gown. "Captain . . ." I attempted to suppress my emotion. "I'm worried about my son. I can think of nothing else."

He joined me on a bench under filmy insect netting. "The King dispatched hundreds of dragoons in the city, Swiss and French. As I mentioned, the schools don't hold any value for the rebels. Your husband and his family would have sent word immediately."

I would send letters in the morning. Just in case.

"Thank you for your reassurance. A mother always worries."

"It would be quite unnatural if you didn't," he said. "How long have you been visiting?"

We spoke in the garden for some time before we joined the others to play cards and a game of trictrac.

When the guests said their good-byes, the captain turned to me. "Would you care for a walk on the beach?"

"That sounds divine."

We strolled to a secret cove, hidden by mangroves and palms. Inside the shielding embrace of the trees, the captain took me in his arms. "It has been so long since I've felt a woman's touch." He planted kisses along the curve of my jaw.

"And I, a man's." I guided his hand to my breast.

We kissed until a haze of passion overtook us and we made love on the sand.

I met the captain many times between my abbreviated trips to the plantation. I enjoyed my time with him, but I held no illusions of love. Companionship was enough for now. It would not be prudent to fall for another solider.

My time on the island grew more uncomfortable as news of the Revolution spread. Rumors of emancipation sparked uprisings among the slaves. The Grands Blancs lashed out to keep them at bay. Severed heads and hanged bodies rotted on display in the public square. I feared leaving the house without an armed escort. My hopes for a stable Paris and my longing for Eugène made me desperate to depart. At my insistence, Uncle Tascher arranged a meeting with the Governor in Fort-Royal. He might lend me the sum I needed for passage.

On the chosen day, Hortense, Mimi, and I set out for a walk to the Governor's office. I surveyed the road ahead. No bodies; no danger seemed to lurk—not today. My armed escort had accompanied Aunt Tascher to the market, leaving me on edge, but I refused to miss the opportunity with the Governor. He was my last hope.

We had almost arrived at our destination when the unmistakable prattle of gunshots echoed from a distance.

I froze.

"What is it, Maman?" Hortense tugged on my skirts.

Mimi met my eye. "Gunfire."

"We must hurry," I said.

More gunshots, and voices drew nearer. Angry voices.

"They're coming this way!" I squeezed Hortense's hand. "Back to the house." We retreated in the direction from which we had come.

A blast from a cannon exploded. The ground shook as it landed.

"Run, Hortense!" I screamed over the rising din of voices. They grew louder as we raced toward Uncle Tascher's house.

When we rounded the corner, a throng of slaves and white men crashed into town. They waved makeshift weapons and torches over their heads.

In an instant, the town hall blazed.

A slave dragged a white woman down an alley by her hair, her pleas barely audible in the deafening roar of voices.

Mimi gasped and Hortense began to cry.

"Run, darling!" I dragged Hortense along. Past the market and through the square and we'd be safe at the house.

As we neared the coiffeur, I stopped, yanking Hortense to my side.

Monsieur Bernard, the town barber, was kicked into the street, head sheared with a cane knife. A slave emerged behind him with the curved knife, dripping with blood and chunks of flesh.

My knees went weak. Hortense screamed.

"Don't look." I covered her eyes, though my own were glued to the gruesome scene.

The slave did not notice us, but fixed upon a group of men running across the street. He tore after them.

I slung Hortense into my arms and wrapped her legs around my torso. Mimi raced at my side.

"Hurry, Maman, hurry," she sobbed as I ran. "They're coming."

My arms burned under her weight; my lungs screamed for air. Mimi ducked in front of me to shield Hortense from all sides. Terror propelled us forward.

Townspeople scattered, searching for shelter.

I pushed through a crowd in the square, holding fast to Hortense, and there, on the other side of the square, was the green door of Uncle Tascher's house. I ran with every ounce of strength I possessed. But as we neared the house, a handful of slaves broke through the front door with clubs and knives.

"Oh God! No!" I screamed, halting in my tracks. "My family!" I looked around frantically. *Dieu*, where could we go? Sweat poured down my temples. I swallowed air in large gulps.

Mimi scanned the crowd, eyes wild. "We could hide in the boats at the harbor."

"They're coming!" Hortense screeched.

I turned. A mob of men battled behind us, drawing closer. I looked back at the house. Flames burst from the windows, sending shards of glass in every direction.

I turned, frantic, and plowed full-force into a man, slamming Hortense and me to the ground.

"Maman!" she screeched in terror as we were separated.

I sat up in a daze and turned to pull Hortense fast to my chest. But she had rolled a few paces away.

She lay at the feet of a slave, with a pitchfork pointed at her little body.

Revolution
Fort-Royal and Paris, 1790–1792

The slave towered above my daughter, muscles rippling, face contorted with murderous rage. Time stopped. The world vanished. Only Hortense's stricken face remained.

"Don't move!" A masculine voice tore into my consciousness. A soldier stepped in front of me and aimed his gun at the slave. Captain du Roure.

The slave let loose a battle cry, raising the pitchfork above his head.

"Hortense! Move!" I screamed. Hot tears strangled my throat.

The slave swung downward.

He wasn't fast enough.

A bullet exploded in his chest, ripping skin, blasting through tissue and blood. The pitchfork clattered to the ground. The slave's body fell, a crimson mound of tattered flesh, on top of my little girl.

"Maman!" she screamed.

The captain rolled the body off Hortense and yanked her to her feet.

I wrapped myself around her, too stunned to speak. I wiped her blood-splattered face. I'd almost lost her. I'd almost lost my little girl. Hortense's cries became hysterical. I crushed her against my chest.

Mimi stood still, as if made of stone, and stared at what was left of the dead slave.

"Rose, we've got to go! I'm on my way to the frigate docked in the harbor," the captain shouted, pointing at its sails. "You're welcome to come aboard, if you choose. There is room, but I'm leaving for France and I'm leaving now!"

Our fortune seemed too good to be true. Thank you, God.

"I don't have any money . . . I—" The screeching in the streets drowned out my words.

"Come on!" He wrenched Hortense from my arms, despite her protests, and ran as fast as he could. We weaved in and out of the terrorized mob, around piles of wood and goods thrown into the street.

I dashed behind him, holding Mimi's hand, trying not to trip. The ash-laden air choked me, the smell of burning wood, of death. I threw a look over my shoulder.

Mon Dieu. The town and surrounding fields blazed. Houses collapsed into piles of charred scraps. My family. My throat began to close.

In a few more strides, we reached the dock and dashed up the gangway. Captain du Roure helped a handful of others aboard. We set sail within minutes. A bit farther and we would be out of the harbor.

I stood at the helm, watching my home descend into ash. I scooped Hortense into my arms and stroked her back to calm her. Uncle and Aunt Tascher. They were safe. They had to be safe. I stared out at the chaos. Everything had changed. My childhood home, my haven, no longer existed.

"What are they doing?" Hortense pointed at a pack of slaves wheeling a cannon along the shore.

They pointed it directly at the ship.

"Oh my God!"

Just then, the captain ordered, "Get belowdecks!"

We raced to the cabins and down the ladder. Other passengers crammed in behind us, screaming and shoving, their faces panicked. Mimi, Hortense, and I squeezed into a small cubby to avoid the mass of bodies.

Just in time.

A deafening burst shook the boat. A chorus of screams followed. But no destruction, no bodies or splintered wood catapulted into the air.

"They missed!" someone shouted.

Cheers erupted. A woman wailed into her husband's shoulder.

Five minutes passed. Then ten, twenty.

My head spun as I rocked Hortense in my arms. The cabin was eerily silent despite the two dozen bodies crammed inside. What was there to say?

A clattering of boots on the ladder cut through the tension.

Captain du Roure bounded into the room. "We've cleared the harbor. You can move to your cabins." More cheering erupted as people pushed by him and up the ladder. "Rose, are you all right?" He wrapped his arms around us.

Words failed me. The man who had saved my daughter's life—my life—held me. The enormity of what he had done sank in. Sobs shattered my calm and Hortense, too, began to cry.

"Shh . . . all will be well." He patted Hortense on the head. "You're safe now." When I calmed, he kissed me on the cheek. "I'll catch up with you later." He disappeared above decks.

Mimi sat silent, stunned by the events, her cocoa cheeks streaked with tears. I could only guess at her thoughts.

"What will happen to Grand-mère and Grand-père?" Hortense searched my face.

"Try not to worry, *doucette*," I said in a tremulous voice. "They will be safe. Our plantation is in good order."

I leaned against Mimi's shoulder, closed my eyes, and prayed.

Our water journey proved hazardous, fraught with British warships and ocean squalls, but we survived, arriving seven weeks later at the southern port of Toulon. I sent a letter to Maman at once to assure her of our safety and to verify theirs. After two days' rest in Toulon, the captain escorted Hortense and me to Fontainebleau.

During the weeklong ride the captain kept a watchful eye on the roads, gun loaded.

"Is that necessary?" I motioned to Hortense. "You're frightening her."

"I would prefer to be safe." He placed a hand on his pistol. "Vagabonds have been raiding châteaus in the country and ransacking towns." He pointed to a once-regal statue of the King. The monarch lay toppled and beheaded. "Signs of the Revolution."

Tricolor flags dangled in every doorway. Storefronts were draped in tattered banners that read, THE CITIZEN LIVES FOR THE NATION, or LIBERTY, EQUALITY, FRATERNITY.

"You must take care with your opinions, Rose," he warned. "A great shift is at hand."

"I will mind what I say." I gave him a silencing look. Hortense had seen and heard far too much already.

The wreckage became more frequent, the changes more drastic, as we neared Paris.

Let the bloodshed be over, I prayed. Leaving one war zone for another was more than I could bear. I hid my unease, though I could not escape Hortense's ceaseless questions. I answered them like a protective mother—with a sugar-glazed version of the truth.

The day we arrived in Fontainebleau, the captain continued on to Paris to report to his garrison.

"I will write." He kissed me on the forehead and leapt back into the coach.

Our time together had not inspired love. I wondered at his lack of affection. Neither had Alexandre loved me, nor Charles or the others. Regret washed over me as his coach disappeared down the tree-lined drive.

Désirée greeted us at the door.

"Rose! Little Hortense!" she called out in joy. Her aged features startled me. It appeared the crumbling monarchy had taken its toll. Her gaunt face was a shadow of its former beauty, her once-honey hair streaked with gray. "We're so delighted you're home." She kissed me. "Your clothes are hanging on you, darling. Haven't you eaten?"

"I haven't had much of an appetite." I frowned. "Désirée, are you unwell?"

"Recovering. Hortense, let me look at you." Hortense smiled shyly and let Désirée kiss her. "I want to speak with your mother. We can play a game later, if you like?"

"*Oui*," Hortense raced to her bedroom.

I followed Désirée through a side door and into the garden. "Shall we sit?" She eased into a chair.

"We made very good time." A servant poured tea into Sevres porcelain cups with gold handles. I stared out at the pruned hedges, the flitting robins, and the multicolored leaves, lustrous in the fall sunshine.

The scent of damp earth and leaves was so different here. I sighed. What a relief to be back.

"How is your family?" she asked.

I answered Désirée's questions, assured her of the family's health, and then described the violent slave uprisings.

"*Dieu!* I can't imagine how Hortense must have reacted. Poor dear."

I spread jam on my bread. "I can hardly wait to see Eugène." A surge of longing pulsed in my chest. My little boy. I changed the subject before the tears came. "What have I missed in Paris?"

"You have heard about Alexandre's position?" Désirée selected a chunk of bread from the basket.

"We communicated little while I was away. How is he?"

"Quite well, I imagine. He's the elected president of the National Assembly."

I put down my knife. How in the world had he contrived that? "President? What does that mean, exactly?" I asked.

"From what I gather, the assembly elects a new president each month, at least for now. They're changing the laws so quickly. It is difficult to keep up." She slathered rhubarb jam on her bread. "Alexandre is foolhardy. He shames his father. Even François speaks out against him."

"François disputes his own brother, the president of the assembly, in public?" I asked in disbelief. He seemed the more foolhardy of the two.

"They were so different as children. François will always support the King. As will the Marquis and I."

"And Alexandre is a Constitutionalist?"

"He is a traitor. They call themselves Patriots, Republicans, Girondists, Brothers of Liberty. When the dust settles, they will all pay for their crimes against the King."

A bite of bread stuck in my throat. So much at stake for his views. Alexandre had better be careful. I sipped from my teacup.

"Is the royal family still at the Tuileries?" I asked at last.

"For now."

"Is Paris safe?" A vision of Eugène sent another wave of yearning through me. And fear.

"The violence has ceased, but, Rose, be careful. You either support the laws of God under King Louis, or you do not. The King sends for support from his allies—the Austrians and the Prussians, perhaps the English. There's talk of civil war."

My mind whirred with the news. "Better to be prudent with our opinions," I mused aloud.

Yes, better to be prudent.

I rented a small stone house at 43 rue Saint-Dominique in Paris to be near my son and friends, to send Hortense to school, and to begin again. Patches of purple and white petunias flourished on either side of the blue-painted door, and narrow balconies jutted from the second- and third-floor windows. Marie-Françoise Hosten, a Creole from Saint Lucia, and her daughter lived with us to share the rent. Living as a family made the girls giddy.

"Désirée!" Hortense called to her new friend. "Let's have a tea party."

"Only if I get to wear the blue hat and gloves this time." Désirée smashed the hat on her head.

The last addition to our home was Fortuné, a black-faced pug with sandy fur. He licked our palms and nipped at our heels. I loved him on sight.

I packed my schedule from my first night. To be in Paris again! How I had missed Claire and Fanny and my other friends, and the city's liveliness. But sentiments had changed. Energy pulsed on every street corner, in each tavern and coffeehouse. Everyone debated. Who would run the country? What to do with the King? Should divorce be legal for all? Should slavery be illegal? So much to decide and no one knew the answer.

I had been in Paris a full month before I laid eyes on Eugène. His headmaster made no allowance for a visit before a school break, even for a mother who had been away. I wrote to Alexandre to join us. He missed Hortense and looked forward to seeing me, or so his letter said. I assumed him eager to gloat about his new position.

On the morning we arrived, I gripped Eugène in a ferocious hug.

"Darling, I've missed you more than words." How much he had grown in two years! His once-chubby cheeks had thinned and he looked taller, leaner.

"I missed you, too," he said, voice muffled in the crook of my neck.

"You're growing up, *mon amour.*" He wore a cap, gray coat, and *culottes*, and stood at attention like a soldier.

"Yes, Maman." He grinned.

His smile was still boyish, angelic. "How can you be nine years old already?" I took his hands and kissed them.

Eugène looked behind me, then quickly pulled his hands from mine. I followed his gaze. A pack of his classmates walked along the opposite end of the courtyard.

I embarrassed him—my boy did not want to show affection for his mother in front of his friends. A pang of regret hit me. It had to happen sooner or later. I forced a smile.

Hortense took advantage of my pause and leapt at Eugène.

"Hortense!" Eugène hugged his sister. "You grew."

"Almost as big as you!" she said.

"You are not! I'm almost a man. I'm going to be a soldier and fight the traitors of the Revolution like Papa."

Even Eugène had been affected. By his father, no doubt.

We turned toward the clacking of boots on stone. Alexandre strode across the courtyard, chest out, head high, more handsome than I remembered. His smile sparkled. His stance exuded regality.

"Hello, my boy." He tousled Eugène's hair. "Hortense, give your father a hug." He spread his arms in welcome.

Hortense advanced slowly toward the father she had not seen in two years. "Hello, Papa."

"You are a beauty like your mother." Alexandre kissed her forehead. "I have a surprise for you." He produced a charm bracelet and a doll.

"Thank you, Papa!" She hugged him, cheeks flushed with excitement.

"Rose, how are you?" He brushed my cheeks with his lips, then bent to help Hortense with her bracelet.

"Well, thank you. I'm relieved you are unaffected by the revolts."

"Unaffected?" He roared with laughter. "I'm quite affected! You mean I am unharmed. Unharmed, but on fire with ideals of freedom, constitutions, representation! Times have changed for the better, Rose. Have you heard? I am the president of the National Assembly. You are married to a celebrity, a mastermind of the times."

I smirked at his conceit. No one wore arrogance as well as my husband. "I have heard." Still, I was truly happy for him. I squeezed his hand. "Congratulations. I'm pleased you are so happy." A group of boys passed through the courtyard, their laughter echoing from the walled-in space. "I'm sure you're aware that your father and Aunt Désirée do not share your views."

"Father doesn't possess the courage to embrace the new ways. Foolish old man. France is changed! We are in the midst of a great enlightenment. Rousseau rolls in his grave." He slung his arm around my shoulders. "You should attend a session of the assembly. Seats are difficult to obtain, but as the wife of a distinguished member, you can come when you please. It would broaden your understanding of the shift in ideals. We are making history."

I hesitated, remembering Désirée's warning. I did not wish to choose sides; it was only important that the children were safe. Besides, to be the wife of the president! My stomach fluttered in excitement. I smiled. "It sounds grand. When may I attend?"

"The tyranny of the Third Estate—"

"Maman, do you want to see my horse?" Eugène interrupted.

Bless him for it. Hortense had been chasing the crows, already bored with our conversation. A political oration would be too much today—I came to visit my son.

"Of course, *cheri*," I answered.

"Show us the way to the stable, son." Alexandre nodded.

Tickets for the National Assembly sold for fifty livres per day and were more difficult to obtain than those for the national opera. I wore the latest fashions to the assembly, though the limited red, white, and blue palette and the endless flag ribbons bored me. The American bonnets *à la Constitution* resembled a nightcap, but still I fastened them on. Women wore polished stone and iron jewelry pieces—symbols of the Bastille, symbols of freedom. In all, hideous, but I would not be *démodée*.

I attended one cold January afternoon with Fanny, who had used her influence to secure a seat.

She huddled next to me in our coach for warmth. "Who knew the Beauharnais name would be such an advantage? I daresay our pompous little Alexandre has made it famous. God love him. All of that blathering is good for something after all." She cackled.

I could not help but laugh. "Droll, Fanny, but how right you are."

Our carriage stopped in front of the royal riding house of the Tuileries Palace, the home of the National Assembly. Though it had been remodeled with green felt-covered benches, large sculptures of Roman figures, and the new revolutionary flag, the converted stable retained the smell of sweaty horses and straw. The odor did not bother the attendees; passionate speeches from the pulpit and the parade of gowns in the audience garnered all the attention. The infamous pock-faced Marat, Philippe Égalité, and Madame de Staël sat in the front rows with Robespierre and Tallien. Everyone knew their names, their ideals.

I studied the platform as the speeches began. All men sat according to their political sympathies.

"The Jacobins are the most radical," Fanny whispered. "They're seated to the left of the podium in the section rising from the floor—the Mountain." Alexandre placed himself among them.

"And the Royalists?" I leaned to her ear.

"It's not that simple. Many want a constitutional monarch like England, regardless of other affiliations. Others are touting the new American system. Some fear we will end up a military regime."

Thunderous applause greeted Alexandre as he took the floor. His well-spoken delivery and good looks had developed a following. How elegant and powerful he appeared at the podium, an important man, an influential orator. Our disputes mattered little in the moments when he spoke—or when I received an invitation as his wife from honored guests. Unexpected pride surged through my veins.

"He is marvelous, isn't he?" I whispered.

"Quite." Fanny nodded.

When the assembly concluded, I was not surprised at the women who rushed to meet Alexandre. But the attention I received caught me off guard.

"Madame de Beauharnais, where did you find such a dress? I must have one!" a woman said.

"*Merci.*" I smoothed my blue-striped skirt.

"You are Madame Liberté in your cockade and gown," another woman said.

I laughed. "You're very kind. Thank you."

Three others stopped me, inquiring about my jewelry, my dress, or my coat. It appeared I was on a stage as well as Alexandre. I would take more care with my toilette.

Fanny bustled with excitement. "Madame de Staël has invited us to her salon." Her Bastille stone earrings swayed as she gestured. "Everyone will be there. Robespierre and his sister, the Prince and Princesse de Salm, Talleyrand, and a load of others."

I squeezed Fanny's hand. "Us among the famous! I must have a new dress."

Alexandre had done something right for a change.

I balanced my loyalties as my circles expanded, taking care to learn each group's desires for the new government, their hopes for the future. West Indian plantation owners, financiers, foreign aristocracy, extremists, or Royalists—the mélange of views enriched my company.

Perhaps it would prove useful.

One evening I prepared to host my own salon. Mimi polished the silver candlesticks and set the table with the few nice plates I owned. Marie-Françoise directed our valet with details for place cards and positioning the musicians.

I emerged from the kitchen when a rap sounded at the door. I rushed to answer it.

"Madame de Beauharnais? For you." The courier placed a package in my arms. Maman's scrolled handwriting covered the wrapping.

News from home! I opened it at once. A sack of livres, trinkets for the children, and letters from the family. Now I could pay the governess and one of my creditors. Good timing, Maman.

A pile of twined letters lay in the bottom of the box. I settled in a chair and read through each of them. The last bore a message I had not expected.

March 23, 1791

My Dearest Rose,

I am sad to report the passing of your father. Your Papa's final days were spent in a great deal of pain.

Words do not express my grief. Life is but a brief moment, a dream. Cherish it.

As for the plantation, we are getting along fine. The turmoil in which you left has abated. I miss you and Hortense so very much. Give my love to Eugène.

Je t'embrasse,

Maman

I dropped my head into my hands. Grief flooded my heart.

Mimi appeared from the kitchen with a soup tureen. "What's happened?"

"Papa has passed." I stared at her in stunned silence.

She rubbed her hands over my back. "You need rest. I'll take care of everything." She led me to my room and tucked the bedcovers around me.

I wept into my pillow until my eyes swelled. Oh, Papa. I wish I had made you proud.

When the time came to dress for the evening, I forced myself from bed and chose a gown and linen fichu. I caked my cheeks with powder to hide my distress and slipped down the stairs. Butter-yellow roses filled the vases throughout the house. Their fragrance mingled with the scent of roasting beef and vegetables. I had spared no expense for the meal—wine from Bordeaux, strawberries and *île flottante* with its English cream and meringue, cheeses from Bretagne, and bread that had cost a pretty sum with the scarcity of grain—but my company would expect no less. I would have to give every livre from Maman to my lenders to pay back the borrowed sum.

Once the guests arrived I pasted a smile on my face.

Claire cheered me, as always.

"What about him? He's handsome," she said. The violinist finished his piece and everyone milled about to search out a glass of spirits until the next set.

"He's haughty and never wipes the spittle from the corners of his mouth. The thought of kissing him repulses me," I said.

We giggled.

"And him?" Claire adjusted a pin in her thick blond locks.

I shrugged. "I'm looking for something . . . for someone." I regarded the packed space, a melancholy settling in my bones. A group of gentlemen gestured with enthusiasm, cheeks pink from exertion and the heat of warm bodies.

"I know. The sweet torture of love. We all wish for it."

"You have it every month," I teased, though my mirth had shriveled. Despite the joyful ambience, the swirl of laughter felt hollow and the cheerful clink of glasses resonated like a coin in an empty drum.

"You'll meet the right man and you won't have to marry him!" Claire laughed wickedly.

Angry male voices sounded above the others.

I craned my neck to find the source of the commotion. Two men from the ministries. I set my wineglass on the table with too much force. The ruby liquid sloshed and dribbled onto the linen tablecloth.

"It appears I need to break up an argument." I hurried toward them.

"What is his authority? He has no right to his position. His brother and father are loyal to the King. They're traitors against the Republic," said the tall gentleman, Julien Lacroix.

"Don't be absurd," said André Mercier, a striking older gentleman. "Alexandre is a Patriot to the core. He champions our cause."

My steps faltered. Alexandre's commitment was in question? A man could not be more devoted to the Republican cause.

I slid my arm through Monsieur Mercier's. "Gentlemen, I see my cook has warmed your blood. I am in want of entertainment. Anyone up for a game of piquet?"

"Only if I may sit next to you," Monsieur Lacroix said.

I lowered my lashes. Always a man first, a politician second. "I would have it no other way." I smiled.

"I'll sit this round out." Monsieur Mercier ordered another brandy and stalked to the opposite side of the room, fists clenched.

I would see to him later.

After several rounds of cards, I sought out Fanny. Still, I could not shake my unease.

She read my troubled expression. "What's wrong?" Her breath smelled of wine.

"Two men from the ministries are disputing Alexandre's loyalties. Is there reason to worry?"

"Alexandre is an intelligent man, but you're right to be cautious. The men leading the government are fickle. Don't trust anyone. Not even your women friends."

"My friends would turn against me?" I asked, taken aback.

"Under the right circumstances, yes. Women have led many of the riots and they talk to their husbands. Don't underestimate their influence."

"Women have a lot of power," I noted aloud. I liked the idea. I relished my own influence, what little of it I possessed.

"At times." Fanny eyed me curiously. "Just be cautious. This is a war of philosophies. Everyone has a chance to gain."

"Or lose."

"Or lose."

"But surely we have too many connections to worry about such things?" I asked.

"One never—"

A shrill voice drifted through the open windows from the street.

"Did you hear that?"

"A newsboy," Fanny said.

We moved to the window and strained to listen.

"Should we step outside?" I motioned to the door.

The warm summer night enveloped us and the moon winked from behind a plump cloud. We made our way to the end of the drive. The shadowed figure of a boy not more than twelve sprinted down the street.

"You there! Boy! Come here. What is your news?" Fanny called.

"*Bonsoir*, mesdames." Sweat trickled down the boy's dirt-smudged face and he panted from running. "King Louis and Queen Marie Antoinette have been arrested. They were caught in Varennes in servants' clothing trying to leave France. They're being held by the Committee of Public Safety."

We gasped.

"The King abandoned his people," I said, taken aback.

Fanny placed a sou in the boy's filthy palm. "Be on your way."

He raced across the street and into the night.

The news of the King's desertion exploded like a shot across Paris. Darkness descended upon the city.

"He must go on trial like every other traitor!" Alexandre commanded the assembly. His voice boomed in the cavernous space. "He deserted his people like a coward! He threatens our Revolution!"

"Down with the traitor!" men cheered in the assembly, in the streets, and at the theaters.

Furious mobs destroyed symbols of the *royaume*, attacked nobility in the streets, and massacred guards at the Tuileries Palace. The tocsin heralded a warning of war. Clanging echoed in our chests, day after day. High alert. Prussian and Austrian armies attacked our frontiers to rescue the captured King and Queen.

Terrified of what might follow, I brought Eugène and Hortense home from school. They would not be separated from me, unprotected in the chaos. *Grace à Dieu*, Eugène was too young to fight.

Months passed. My beloved Paris remained in the same chaotic state.

One hazy September afternoon the children lounged indoors and I walked Fortuné in the garden. He stopped to dig furiously at a small patch of grass.

A low rumbling echoed from afar.

I turned my face to the blue skies overhead. Not thunder.

The distant rumbling grew louder. The tocsin rang.

I dropped the leash. A call to arms. I must take cover inside. I bent to retrieve Fortuné, but he slipped from my hands and bounded down the drive.

"Fortuné! Come!" He ran into the street and howled at the noise.

The clamor grew louder. Were those . . . voices?

My blood ran cold. A memory of shredded flesh, of the streets of a burning Fort-Royal, flashed before me.

"Fortuné!" I screeched, running after him. "Fortuné!"

Angry voices drew nearer, drowning out his barking. I stepped on the end of the leash just as he lunged.

A heathen shriek ripped through the air. In the next instant, a pack of citizens rounded the corner onto my street, farm tools in hand.

The air left my lungs.

I dragged Fortuné toward the house. He tugged on the leash, anxious to attack the strangers.

"Fortuné, stop it!" A shrill voice I did not recognize tumbled from my lips. I seized his squirming body and bolted for the door. My heart thundered in my ears.

Two more steps.

A bloodcurdling scream and a cheering sounded behind me.

Mon Dieu! I dared a quick look back as I reached for the door handle.

A man ran straight for me.

"*Le tiers état!*" he shouted. His jacket was smeared with blood; his eyes looked crazed. In his hands, he held a pike.

Atop it perched a woman's severed head.

La Terreur

Paris, 1792–1794

I slammed and locked the door behind me.

"Bar the windows!" I screeched. "Move the bureau in front of the door."

Everyone in the house sprinted to the front hall. One look at my face and they set to work. Mimi, Marie-Françoise, and I barred the entry and began on the windows.

"What's happening?" Hortense asked, her face panic-stricken.

A crash outside. A banging at the door.

"*Vive la République!*" voices chanted from the yard.

"Get in the cellar now!" I screamed.

"Go!" Marie-Françoise pushed her daughter after Hortense.

A stone hurtled through the front window, spraying shards of glass in the air. Marie-Fançoise screamed.

"Go!" I pushed her.

Mimi ran ahead of us, Fortuné yapping at her heels as if it were a game.

We dashed through the house and clambered down the stairs into the inky coolness of the cellar. I barred the door with the thick wooden arm while Mimi and Marie-Françoise lit torches. The children and staff stood frozen. My breath wheezed as I struggled to regain my composure.

Another crash sounded, this time closer, perhaps from inside the house.

"Who's chasing us?" Eugène asked quietly.

I raised a trembling finger to my lips to silence him. Thank the Lord I had taken the children out of school.

We perched uncertainly in the darkness for several hours. At last we grew hungry and irritable. No one had attempted to open the cellar door. The house seemed quiet. I dared a run to the kitchen. Screaming could still be heard, but it sounded distant. I tiptoed through the halls to the pantry and filled my arms with grapes and dried sausages.

I sneaked to the front hall.

The mob had not broken down the door, nor even entered the house. Only two windows had shattered. *Merci à Dieu.* I peeped through a hole in the front window. My potted plants lay smashed on the walk and newspapers littered the lawn.

I gasped at the carnage in the street, on the lawns of my neighbors.

Blood streamed from desecrated bodies twisted in ways only death permitted. I pulled back in horror. God in heaven. What had happened?

A scream pierced the air.

I searched for the source of the terrible sound. Blood splattered the windows of the neighboring convent. And more shrieking.

Mother of God. They murdered the holy.

A wave of nausea rolled through me. I had heard rumors of a conspiracy; some feared the clergy would side with the nobles against us. Absurd nonsense. I had never met a nun who cared enough about affairs of state to risk her life.

A black figure streaked past near the end the boulevard.

I leaned closer to the hole in the window. A nun! She dashed down the street like a spooked horse, her robe a mane billowing behind her. She pounded at the door of a neighboring house. No answer. She moved to another.

A man rounded the corner, hammer in hand.

My heart thumped in my ears. "Go, go!" I whispered.

She raced to a third house and threw her body at the door. It didn't budge.

The man drew nearer.

What could I use to fend him off? I scanned the room. A chair? I lunged for the broom and ran to the door.

My hand hovered over the handle.

The farmer was bigger than the nun and me together. It would risk the children's safety and Marie-Françoise's. The broom slid from my hands. I couldn't put my babies at risk. I wouldn't. Defeated, I turned back to the window.

The corpulent farmer caught the nun's habit and threw her into a crimson puddle in the street.

"No!" I gripped the windowsill. A sob escaped my throat. She screamed and thrashed as the man twisted her garment over her head and ripped at her underclothes.

"Kick him! Hit him!" I said, my voice hoarse.

He pushed himself on top of her and bludgeoned her with his hammer when she resisted. Blood oozed from her skull.

My stomach lurched. I bent to vomit.

Marie-Françoise dashed across the room to my side. "Rose! Are you all right?" She dabbed at my face with a napkin and used it to cover the pile on the floor. "I came to see what was taking so long."

I pointed at the window. "The nun . . ."

She glanced through the window, then winced and pulled back, aghast. "A nun!" I nodded, too stunned to speak. She swept me into her arms.

Another terrorized scream split the silence. Our eyes locked.

"It's at Les Carmes. The mob is murdering them," I said in a strangled voice. "We're probably safe, but I'm not sure we should risk a light in our windows tonight. A few more hours in the cellar. We can come upstairs in the dark for food. No lanterns. For now, we wait."

The next two days, we ventured from the cellar only out of necessity. By the third day, the streets had stilled. I prepared a letter for Alexandre, but he appeared on the doorstep before I finished it.

"Alexandre!" I leapt from my desk as he entered.

He kissed my cheeks and embraced me tightly. "I'm glad you are safe! How are my children? I came as soon as I could."

"We are well, but frightened. We couldn't leave the house. The nuns . . . I saw a mob. . . ." The words tumbled from my lips.

"I'm glad you had the sense to stay put." He gave me a newspaper, damp with sweat.

According to its date, the *Moniteur* had printed the leaflet the day before the violence began. The headlines blasted in bold print: PRISONERS PLOT AGAINST PATRIOTS, COLLAPSE OF REPUBLICAN GOVERNMENT, CLERGY UNITES WITH FOREIGN ARMIES.

"Rumors sparked that madness? Innocent people died!" I threw down the newspaper in disgust. "The King is arrested. Criminals rule the streets." I waved my hand at his trousers. "We dress like commoners and hide our views."

Beads of sweat pearled on Alexandre's upper lip and temples from the swampy heat. "Titles have been abolished. *Citoyen* or *citoyenne* is how we will all be addressed."

"Citizens?" I asked, incredulous. "There is no distinction among us? My friends of noble blood will not agree. More strife will follow."

"Titles divide us. They create boundaries to our freedom. And whether you like the new laws or not, you will follow them or be deemed a traitor." He ran a hand nervously through his damp hair.

"And what of the madness? I saw a nun murdered." I covered my eyes to block the hideous image.

"It's over now." Alexandre embraced me again. "The religious lorded their power over us. It's just as well they were reminded of their new place in our government."

I stared at him, flabbergasted. He would have them die to champion his cause? I pushed his hands away. I no longer cared for his beloved Revolution.

"They didn't need to die!"

His eyes flashed. "There are always casualties in war." He noted my grimace. "Do you think I haven't suffered? My father and brother mock me! My friends speak out against me, yet I continue in the name of what is right. I don't wish to see French blood spilled, but some must die. Without death to mark its value, our Revolution has no meaning. Examples must be made."

"Would you say the same if your children's lives were at stake? Or your own?"

He paused. "Yes, if it were my own."

An exasperated sound escaped my lips. "You would leave your children fatherless!"

"Don't be so dramatic, Rose."

"I am dramatic? You're a fine one to talk."

We stared at each other in silence.

At last he said, "I have important news. I've been promoted to lieutenant general of the Army of the Rhine. It's an honor I've wished for my entire life. I will have the chance to lead against our enemies."

"Congratulations. I hope you can discern who your enemies are."

His eyes narrowed.

Eugène and Hortense walked quietly into the room. I knew they had been listening, by the expression on Hortense's face.

"Papa, you will lead an army?" Eugène's voice belied his excitement.

"Children! I have missed you. Give your father a hug."

"Is it safe to leave the house, Papa?" Hortense asked, stepping from the circle of Alexandre's arms.

"We've felt like animals in a cage," I said.

Alexandre pressed his lips together. "Wait another two days before you leave. The turmoil seems to be settling, but there's carnage in the street. They're loading the dead into carts to be buried. There's no reason to witness it, *doucette*." He stroked Hortense's hair. "Now, shall we have coffee and play a game?"

"Only a little wine and cheese are left," I said.

"Wine it is." Alexandre slung one arm around each of our children and escorted them to the table.

The fall and winter passed in a whirlwind of upheaval. I avoided traveling near the river, where citizens ransacked barges carrying grain and coal and insurrections raged. The poor froze or starved to death under city bridges. Endless lines spiraled from bakery doorways as citizens awaited their rations.

"It's the laundresses." Mimi returned from a long day of gathering items. Her eyes watered from the cold. "Can't afford soap anymore." She set her shopping bags on the floor and rubbed her gloved hands together. "Going to have to make do with vinegar."

I folded the newspaper in my hands. "We can't go without soap. I'll ask a few friends for favors. How much wood did they give you?"

Mimi pulled two small logs from her bag. "Not enough for one night in this cold."

I pulled my wool cloak closer to my body. The most frigid winter in one hundred years, the farmers had said, and it felt like it. Cold seized moving water, snapped branches, and blasted against our windows and doors.

"Tonight we'll burn one of the chairs in the attic."

I bartered and borrowed to fill the pantry. Thank God for my many friends who shared their bread. We detested the national loaf, made with gritty chestnut flour. Eugène and Hortense fed their shares to Fortuné, who sniffed it with disdain and buried it in the yard.

Soldiers detained the horses. Foreign guards patrolled the boulevards. No one could leave. A sinister hush enveloped the city without the clopping of horses' hooves and the whizzing of carriage wheels. Street lamps ran dry from lack of oil, plunging the streets into darkness. Thieves multiplied. I left the house as little as possible, though I despaired at our seclusion.

In late winter, the National Assembly executed our King.

I did not attend his slaying in the Place de la Révolution.

"Such a waste," Claire said, peering into a tiny mirror in her gilded patch box. She prepared to return home before curfew. "Those buffoons in the assembly don't know what they're doing."

"Alexandre is among them."

"Like I said, buffoons." Claire detested Alexandre, her loyalty to me fierce as ever.

"How despicable to watch anyone march to their death," I said, "in front of a jeering crowd, no less. Such a frightful end. And a king! The Queen and her children must be terrified."

Claire snapped her patch box closed. "Truly horrid. People shouted obscenities and threw garbage. One man dropped his trousers! My dear *grand-père* is stirring in his grave." She whirled her cloak around her shoulders. "But the same traitors that booed him slithered under feet to dip their handkerchiefs in the King's blood."

I shuddered. "Whatever for?"

"A king's blood is sacred." She fastened the buttons of her cloak. "His execution endangers anyone with noble blood a great deal." She looked down at her hands. "You should know," she continued, a grim expression crossing her pretty features, "I am preparing my travel papers. I'll leave for Guadeloupe the moment I receive them."

"You're leaving?" I threw my arms around her neck. "You can't go!"

"I know, dear friend." She embraced me. "But it isn't safe. You should consider leaving as well. If not for yourself, for the children."

Thousands fled to Italy, England, the Swiss cantons, or the low country in the north—anywhere seemed safer than France. Even my bold sister-in-law made plans.

"It's not safe in this godforsaken Republic, Rose," Fanny warned. "You must be careful." Her face glowed orange in the firelight. "You have become known for your letters to the assembly. Take heed. You shouldn't draw too much attention to yourself."

Brothers, cousins, and daughters, former nobility and merchants had been imprisoned based on a whiff of doubt regarding their loyalty to the Republic. Complete nonsense.

"Alexandre is well connected, as am I. And those I help provide us with food. I fear we wouldn't get on without their return favors." I re-filled my wineglass. "Besides, I cannot abandon a friend, Fanny. I would do the same for you, regardless of the risks."

"Of course," she said softly. We watched the fire dance over black-ening logs. "I'm leaving next week for Italy. You are welcome to come with the children. Italy is warmer, you know, and we have plenty of room to spare."

The fearless Fanny was leaving? One by one, my friends and family were escaping to safety. I pulled a blanket around my shoulders into a cocoon of warmth. I hid the fear uncurling like ribbons in my belly. There would be no one left.

"Eugène is in school and I can't leave him. Besides, I have connec-tions."

"Are you certain you should stay? Eugène can continue his school-ing later."

"How will I get along in Italy not knowing anyone? I can't rely on you to pay my expenses. But thank you." I kissed her cheek. "I will miss you!"

"If you change your mind, send a letter that says, 'I am in search of a painting for my salon.' That will be our code that means you're com-ing."

I laughed. "As if we were spies."

"Everyone watches you, Rose. Be careful, *mon amie*."

Robespierre gained influence as Alexandre's power waned. I reread a letter from my husband one afternoon.

"He says he'll return to Paris soon." I stood and closed the door. Hortense and Désirée need not hear. "He said he was ill and had to leave his army."

"I heard he has been recalled to Paris." Marie-Françoise fiddled with a thread dangling from her needle. "Rumors say he deserted his army."

"If I know Alexandre, they aren't rumors."

She smirked. "Too busy with his women to obey the assembly's orders?"

"He may find himself in trouble if he isn't careful." I sat on the sofa across from her and opened my fan.

Marie-Françoise held up the pillow cover. "Do you like the mauve or should I use blue?"

"The blue."

She unraveled a measure of thread. "You have adapted well to the times, dear friend."

"What do you mean?"

"You've adopted the sansculotte speech and befriended everyone, regardless of their sympathies. You shed your title without issue. It amazes me. I'll never be more than Creole nobility pretending in a horrible linen dress."

"It matters little if I am called Vicomtesse or Citoyenne. I'm still Rose underneath it all. For now, I'm a Patriot. I prefer not to bring the Committee of Safety to our doorstep." I fanned my face to dispel the odor of rotting flesh. City guards were dumping bodies in open graves and in the sewers. Our lives meant nothing to the great men of our Revolution.

A howl sounded in the distance. Wolves cried outside the city gates, hungry for the dead. Fortuné jumped from his place on the sofa, ears perked. A series of howls bawled in the silence. He crooned along with them.

"Fortuné! Stop that." He looked at me with a mournful expression, then recommenced his howling. "If things worsen we must flee."

I made my decision. Flight from Paris would keep the children safe and free us from the oppression there. Our opportunity arrived when the former Prince de Salm and his sister, Princess Amélie, invited us to their country home. From there, we would escape to England. I gathered the necessary documents in secrecy and packed our things.

If we were discovered trying to escape . . . I shook my head. We must not be caught. I placed Hortense's combs and hairpins in her valise.

"Marie-Françoise?" I called. "We are going."

She whisked into the room. "Please reconsider, friend. You could face arrest, and arrest . . ." She cast her eyes to the floor. "Well, we both know it is death. Are you certain no one suspects you?"

"If something happens to me, you must lie. You don't know anything. There's no sense in putting you at risk." I embraced her and thrust my head into Hortense's bedroom. She didn't know we were leaving indefinitely. I found it difficult to tell my ten-year-old such a thing. "It's time to go, *chérie*. We need to pick up your brother."

"I'm ready." She gathered her favorite dolls in her arms.

We hustled to the front door. I paused and looked back at Mimi. She nodded, eyes watering. I would send for her. And when we returned, things would be different.

"A fine day to travel," the Prince said once Hortense and I were seated. Princess Amélie had left a week before and awaited our arrival in the country.

"I don't know how to thank you." A lump formed in my throat. He was rescuing us from danger—more than I could say about their own father. This man endangered his life on our behalf.

"You would do the same for me," he said.

"I would." I squeezed his hand.

As the carriage moved through the city, euphoria tingled in my veins. To be free of fear of saying or doing the wrong thing, to laugh again, seemed like a dream.

We passed shops with boarded windows and fortresses made of rubble and broken furniture. I did not recognize the Hôtel de Ville with its littered lawn. When we returned, everything would be normal again.

I sighed in relief at the sight of Eugène's handsome face.

"I'm looking forward to our trip!" He smiled as he bounded into the coach.

"We all are, darling," I said. "It'll be nice to get away."

We made good time until we approached the city gates. Our coach stopped behind the others that formed a long line. A pack of soldiers checked documents and luggage racks, their tricorn hats filling with fallen snow. It was a cold day and an odd time to go on vacation. I hoped they wouldn't notice. I watched the flurries coat the filthy boulevard in dazzling white. A measure of beauty in the bleakness.

Time moved as if through mud.

Some carriages made their way to freedom; others were denied. Our carriage advanced, little by little. When at last we reached the exit, a guard beat on our window. Hortense yelped at the sudden noise.

I laughed. "A bit on edge, aren't we?"

"I'd say so," the Prince said as the door opened.

"Travel papers!" a soldier barked in a thick accent.

A German guard to monitor our papers? I gritted my teeth as he snatched them from our hands.

"What would you like to do first in the country?" I forced a smile. "There are horses and walking paths. It's a bit cold, but we may still find ducks on the pond."

"Horseback ride, absolutely!" Eugène chirped.

"I'd be happy to show you the trails, son," the Prince answered.

The guard studied our faces and then slammed the carriage door. He stalked toward the other soldiers.

"What is he doing with our papers?" Eugène whispered as if the guard could hear him.

"I don't know," I said.

Hortense slipped her hand into mine. I had to be strong for them, though my insides quivered.

"He's showing them to another guard." The Prince sneaked a glance through the window. "Here they come."

The door flew open again.

"Citizeness de Beauharnais?"

"Yes?"

"Your husband, Citizen Alexandre de Beauharnais, requests that you and the children return home at once. He has left a standing order and forbids your release, holiday or no."

"Excuse me?" My tone grew clipped. "My husband has no authority over my actions. We've been separated for years. And I have the proper travel documents."

"Your husband *does* have authority, *citoyenne*. He has a seat in the National Assembly. He may dictate who comes and goes, at least in his own family. I'm sorry, but your exit is denied."

"And the Prince? Can he not go?"

"I will escort you home, Rose, and go another day soon."

Our eyes locked. It was not that simple to obtain papers.

"That won't be necessary. I—"

"I will escort you home," he said in a firm tone. "Thank you. We'll go now."

The soldier closed the door and rapped the top of the carriage. We lurched forward.

"Why did you do that?" I asked.

"They kept my certificate of citizenship." A frown creased his brow. "I saw the other guard pocket it. It's impossible to travel without it. I would have been denied entry anywhere, including . . . our destination." He didn't want to alert the children to our planned escape to England.

"Why didn't you ask him for it?" Eugène asked.

"They would have followed me out of the city. I'll apply for a new one."

When the coach turned and made its way back down the boulevard, I burst into tears. "Alexandre!" I fumed. "How can he do this to his own children?"

Hortense put her arms around me. "Papa wouldn't keep us from going on vacation if he didn't have a good reason. Right?"

"Your father always has a reason." Bitterness rang in my voice.

Alexandre! I wanted to hurl my fist into his face. He had ruined our only hope for escape.

Alexandre appeared the day after the children and I returned.

"What were you thinking?" he shouted. "I could be questioned and put on trial. We would be called turncoats! 'The family of an assembly member deserts the Republic!' Do you want me to die a traitorous death?" His face flushed with anger.

"I don't care about your cause!" I screamed back. "I care about my children's safety! How can you put them in danger?"

"They won't be at risk as long as I do my duty."

"Your duty is to your family. Your flesh and blood!" I threw down the serviette and paced, heels clicking on the wood floor. Alexandre crossed his arms and stood like a sentinel. An idea sparked in my mind. "Why don't you go on vacation with us? You could use a break."

His blue eyes widened in disbelief. "I know you plan to emigrate. You're as transparent as glass. And you expect me to go with you? I'll never abandon France! I'd rather perish *à la guillotine!*"

We faced each other with hardened expressions. Alexandre broke the silence.

"Don't you see?" His tone softened. "You could never set foot on French soil again. Hortense and Eugène would lose their inheritance and their honor. How could you do that to them? I'll see to it that they're safe. Please, you must understand."

How had he changed his demeanor so easily? I still wanted to strangle him.

"Things will get better," he said. "We just have to wait it out."

His reasoning melted my defenses. "Alexandre . . ."

"You won't regret it." He placed his hands on my shoulders. "I promise."

I sighed. "For now I'll stay. But you *will* let us go if things get worse."

"That, I'll agree to."

He cleared his throat. "You should know something." He kicked at an invisible stone on the floor. "I am under suspicion as well. Since I withdrew from my military post."

My mouth fell open in shock.

"I've trodden carefully these last weeks. And it is best you cease your appeals. You're drawing attention to yourself. To us."

I chewed the fingernail of my thumb before answering. Fanny had warned me as well.

"They're innocent, good people. I could never live with myself if I didn't do everything I could. Many have been released because of my petitions."

He sighed heavily. "Please be careful." He bent at the waist and kissed me on the lips.

I stepped backward in surprise. "What was that for?"

"A kiss of friendship. Thank you for understanding. Give my love to the children. I'll visit soon."

Queen Marie Antoinette met her end the same way as the others—by the blade. An innocent woman had dedicated her life to her husband, to his country, and had fallen for his follies. I could not sleep for weeks. The vision of her severed head haunted me. The Queen had not been safe, regardless of her position. It was not enough to have powerful friends, to be beautiful and charming.

One must be clever to survive. And brave.

Many mourned our dead Queen, enraging Robespierre. He sought retribution through the imprisonment of hundreds.

One afternoon, I received a distressing letter from Fanny.

10 Nivose II

Chère Citoyenne Rose,

I have returned to Paris in haste, for Marie has been accused of treason against the Republic. She is in prison! What could they possibly have to say about my patriotic daughter? Her record is impeccable, her heart bleeds the colors of our tricolor flag.

If only her father were not a Royalist buffoon.

You are so well-connected. I beg you, please petition to the Committee of Public Safety on her behalf. I am desperate.

Citoyenne Fanny

My head spun. Marie was a Beauharnais—Alexandre's niece— and her name gave her no advantage. I swallowed hard. I had to clear her or we might all . . .

The following day, I entered Minister Azay's office clutching a package of letters from Fanny and Marie. The minister had the reputation for being the most lenient man in the assembly. I prayed the rumors were true.

"What can I do for you?" He motioned me to a seat.

"I'm afraid there's been a terrible mistake, *citoyen*. My niece is an ardent Republican, yet she has been imprisoned without a shred of proof."

"And I assume you possess documents that prove her innocence?" He removed his glasses.

"Here is a packet of her letters. One can plainly see that she is an abiding citizen."

His owlish eyes flitted from my hands to my face and back again. "I'll consider them, but I can't guarantee her release."

"I'm sure you'll do your best to ensure justice. One would hate to see an innocent adolescent girl murdered without cause." I let the weight of my words hang in the air before continuing. "You're so kind for agreeing to see me at all. In such times, you must be terribly busy. I've brought you wine for your trouble. I hope you enjoy it." I placed the bottle on his desk.

He smiled hesitantly. "Thank you for the gift. It could not have been easy to come by."

"Indeed not, but it hardly exceeds the value of a young girl's life."

He shifted uncomfortably in his seat. "Citoyenne de Beauharnais, I must warn you. You share her name. Take care that it is not someone else visiting my office on *your* behalf."

I pasted a smile on my face. "I would worry if my actions were questionable, but they are not."

Sadness filled his eyes. "Take care, my Citoyenne. Take care."

My appeals for Marie de Beauharnais's release went unanswered. I despaired at Fanny's misery, at Marie's suffering in prison. I lay staring at my ceiling in bed one evening when a thundering at the front door startled me. I reached for the candle on my bedside table. My fingers quivered as I set match to wick.

Mimi beat me to the door. "Yes?" She wrapped her night coat around her.

A young man with disheveled hair stood in the doorway. The white foulard around his neck had not been washed in weeks, and his trousers hung in tatters at the cuffs.

"Citoyenne de Beauharnais, I'm sorry to wake you at this hour, but it can't wait."

My pulse raced. "What is it, citizen?"

"Your husband has been arrested."

Captive

Les Carmes, 1794

They would come for me. Lord, they would come for me. A trickle of dread wound its way through my limbs. Alexandre in prison! How could they suspect him? Everyone knew his devotion to the Republic. Was it his Royalist father, his philandering? Those did not seem sufficient reasons to accuse such an ardent Patriot.

I tossed in bed. The father of my children under a death sentence and I, the wife of an accused traitor. Arrest and imprisonment meant death à Madame Guillotine. I could not wrap my mind around the absurdity. I pulled the covers over my head. How would I tell the children?

The next morning, when Hortense and Eugène had finished their breakfasts, I delivered the news.

"I have something to tell you." I pushed aside my plate of untouched food. Eugène looked up from the book he was reading.

"What is it, Maman?" Hortense asked. "Are you all right? You look tired . . . upset."

I traced the flower pattern on the linen tablecloth with my fingertip. "I don't know how to begin." Their sweet faces looked at me expectantly. "I want you to know how much your papa loves you."

Eugène snapped his book closed. "What's wrong?"

I took a deep breath to prevent tears. I must be strong for them.

"Maman?" Hortense prodded.

I covered each of their hands with mine. "Your father"—I inhaled a deep breath—"has been arrested. He's in prison, awaiting trial."

"No!" Eugène leapt to his feet, anger and despair warring on his face. "My father is no traitor! What proof do they have against him? He's in the National Assembly! He's a Patriot!" His bottom lip quivered. "I don't understand."

"I know, my love. I'll do everything in my power to help him. There must be a way to get him released."

Hortense burst into tears. I sprang from the table and pulled her into my arms.

My brave son dropped his head onto my shoulder and wept. "What if they send him to the guillotine?" He sobbed. "What if they kill him?"

"They can't kill my papa," Hortense wailed.

I smoothed her blond hair. "They won't, *chérie*. I will find a way to get him out."

If only I believed my own words.

I fought to have Alexandre freed, exhausting my dwindling contacts in hopes of a miracle. Yet the Committee of Public Safety refused to see me. Nightmares haunted me. The floating heads of the condemned and our murderous statesmen visited me in slumber. I wandered across cobblestones in the Place de la Révolution, the scaffold dripping in blood, and through the gardens of the Tuileries. A secret pathway appeared as if by magic, night after night, weaving through a lush grotto of trumpet vines and bougainvillea bursting with orange, fuchsia, quince—such vivid color I could not be in France anymore, but Martinique. Home, where the cane burned in the late summer sun and the jungle swallowed me whole.

Under the secret canopy a crumpled old woman perched on a stump, casting chicken bones and singing in a strange tongue. Bodiless, I floated through a veil of mist toward her.

She looked up. Black holes remained where her eyes should have been, their depths absorbing all pinpoints of light. I tried to scream, but my lungs filled with seawater.

"Child," the priestess said in a singsong voice. "Don't you remember?" She stroked a fistful of feathers crusted with blood. "It's a violent end."

"No!" I tried to shout, but bubbles emerged from my lips.

I awoke with a start from the dream—always the same—hair stuck to my head in sweaty patches, the back of my nightdress drenched.

A violent end.

It vibrated in my chest like the warning of a tocsin. Was that my fate, or was it Alexandre's?

I sprang from bed and padded across the cool floor to the box in my vanity drawer. Nestled in the velvet lining was my white silk pouch. I snatched the tarot deck from its hiding place and lit a candle. I shuffled the cards in the twilight of my bedchamber and laid a spread.

The Tower—destruction, a violent change. The Wheel of Fortune—a change in luck. The Hierophant—a powerful and loving woman, generous and mothering.

Feverishly I laid a second spread for Alexandre. Destruction, violent changes. I laid another spread and another. All the same.

A violent end.

"No!" I shoved the cards to the floor in cluttered disarray. I dropped my head into my hands and wept.

Nature did not stop for our Revolution, but marched inevitably forward. Spring bloomed. Yet the warm weather did not expel the chill in my soul. After tossing in bed one evening I joined Marie-Françoise in the study. She played cards by firelight, our ration of candle wax already depleted for the month.

"I just received money from Maman." I settled into the sofa across from her. "I'll ask Citizeness de Krény if she can get us more candles."

A rapping at the door made us jump.

Marie-Françoise dropped her cards, eyes wide. Dread uncoiled like a snake in my chest. The last time I had a late visitor . . .

"I'm sure it's nothing," I whispered, words almost inaudible. I stood, forcing myself to remain calm.

"Rose"—Marie-Françoise took my hand in hers—"no matter who is on the other side of that door, we stand together."

The pounding came more loudly this time and a voice shouted, "Citizeness de Beauharnais! Open the door at once!"

My heart lodged in my throat. Dear God.

Mimi stumbled from her chamber, dark hair mussed. "What the

devil do they want at this hour?" She grumbled and turned the key in the lock. Its click echoed through the hall. As the door swung open, a large hand shoved it against the interior wall. It boomed in the silence.

"What did you do that for?" Mimi asked tartly.

"We need to speak with Citoyennes de Beauharnais and Hosten. We are here by orders of the Committee of Public Safety." Three Patriot soldiers stood on the doorstep in shabby uniforms and worn boots. All of them looked underfed. Their eyes rested in hollow pockets above their protruding cheekbones.

I motioned the three men inside. "Come in, citizens. Would you care for a cup of tea? I can put on a fresh pot."

"You are both suspected of treason against the Republic," the leader of the trio answered. The ribbon of his cockade flapped in the rush of air from his breath.

"You have no evidence against me! I am innocent!" Marie-Françoise burst into tears. Mimi moved to console her.

"I assure you there is not a single item of dishonor in this house," I said. "I am a Patriot and an *Ameriquaine*. Citizeness Hosten proudly wears the tricolor of our government as well. You may search all you like." I would not let them see how they rattled my nerves.

Fortuné scampered from the kitchen and tried to bite the largest of the men.

"Better get ahold of it." The soldier pointed the heel of his boot at my dog.

"Fortuné, stop!" I picked him up by his furry middle and locked him in the kitchen. He growled from behind the door.

The soldiers opened drawers, searched cabinets and under cushions, and pushed through the frocks in my armoire. Thankfully, they did not wake the children. Marie-Françoise wept into Mimi's shoulder, her sobs growing more hysterical by the minute. Mimi patted her back and met my gaze. What do we do now, her eyes asked.

I perched on the edge of the sofa. Fear stilled the blood in my veins.

The brass clock on the mantel chimed. I fixed my eyes upon its whirring cogs. What would Hortense and Eugène think in the morning when they found me gone?

"How can you be so calm?" Marie-Françoise asked, wiping her nose.

Because I had known all along. I knew they would come for me. I stared back at her blankly, unable to say the words.

The soldiers returned to the salon with contrite expressions.

"Ladies," the leader said, "you are under arrest."

My insides turned to stone.

Marie-Françoise's cries turned to wails. "Please! I am a mother! What am I to do with my child? You can't take me from her! Please!" She fell to her knees, dress puddling around her.

"What evidence do you have against us?" I asked. "May I see it?"

One of the men waved a pack of letters in the air. How had he unlocked my letter box? I kept the key well hidden. I felt exposed, violated.

"Letters from Alexandre de Beauharnais, a traitor to the Republic. Citizeness Hosten is guilty for harboring a traitor's wife. Unless evidence can be found in support of her innocence, she'll remain in prison as well."

"His letters demonstrate his devotion to the nation," I said. "How—"

"I'm sorry," one of the men said, his voice becoming soft. "The Committee demands your arrest."

"With or without evidence?" No proof and it did not matter. The committee had already decided our fate.

The soldier nodded. Regret filled his eyes.

Marie-Françoise threw herself into my arms. "What are we to do with the children?"

"You may pack a few things," the leader of the men cut in. "We'll wait."

We dragged ourselves upstairs. I tossed Maman's hair combs, a letter from Hortense and Eugène, and my precious tarot cards in the bottom of a bag. Something to remind me of them.

I paused on the landing and drew a deep breath. Eugène and Hortense—I could not bear to see their sleeping faces. I would fall apart. I pushed away the panic, and glided down the stairs.

"Mimi," I whispered, voice hoarse with emotion. "The children . . ."

She embraced me, pressing me to her pillow-like bosom. How did she manage to smell of sunshine and coconut so far from home? I relished the familiar scent one last time.

"Don't worry, Yeyette," she said. "I love them like my own. We'll find a way to get word to you. And to get you out. I'll ask their tutor to petition."

I kissed her damp cheeks. We had prepared for this moment.

"Have her write to Maman for money. Please, don't let the children forget us or forget . . ." Despair threatened to pull me under. I gripped her arms. "Don't let them forget that I love them! More than anything! And darling, Mimi, I love you."

She squeezed me again. "You won't be gone long. Remember the priestess?" She kissed my forehead.

Indeed I did. Destruction, a violent end.

Marie-Françoise stumbled down the stairs and into the front hall, shoulders heaving.

"*Citoyennes*, we must go," the leader barked.

We laced arms and followed the guards to the waiting carriage. The streets were eerily calm in the dead of night. Wispy clouds drifted like phantoms across the sky and the moon hid its pale face. Lilacs seeped their sweet scent into the air as tender leaves rustled in the breeze.

My last breath of spring air.

I clambered into the carriage as if in a dream. Marie-Françoise clung to me during the short ride to the prison. To my horror, we rode only one street away, to Les Carmes, on the rue de Vaugirard, the convent where the holy had been hacked to pieces.

The most heinous prison in Paris.

And yet, the gardens and stone facade showed no sign of misery, save the barred windows.

When the coach came to a stop, a guard ripped open the door.

"Come with me." The jailer yanked my friend out of the coach.

"I'll get us out of here. I promise!" I called after her.

"Farewell, my friend. I love you!" she shouted through her tears. "Don't forget me."

My bravado vanished as the jailer led her inside. This could not be real. I was no criminal. What would happen to me? To my children? My legs collapsed and I spilled onto the ground.

"On your feet!" Another guard pulled me up like a rag doll. "This way." He ushered me through the door.

As we wound past the office and into the belly of the prison, a nefarious odor struck me. A haze of excrement and rot surrounded me in a humid cloud. I coughed in disgust. My eyes stung. Tears streamed down my cheeks to wash away the near-tangible grime. Grubby stains caked the floors and walls. A memory rushed back, from the days just after the massacre. The streets had smelled of vinegar for weeks. Yet it had not cleansed these stones, or maybe there had been too much blood? My stomach turned in revulsion.

I bunched my skirts in my hands, lifting them off the slime-covered floors as we marched through clusters of crowded cells. Many had more than ten people jammed inside, attempting sleep on straw mattresses. Dear God. They lay in their own filth like animals.

Neither bars nor locking doors trapped the prisoners inside their dens. Some moved about freely while others slept. The doors adjoining each corridor were the only locks. I supposed the guards had nothing to fear from a horde of unarmed innocents.

I had not yet reached my cell when I heard a voice calling my name.

"Rose! Is that you? *Mon Dieu.* There is no end to their lunacy!"

My heart leapt. Who could that be?

"Wife of a president. There's no hope for us now," another voice said.

I peered into the gloom, but could not place the voice with any of the faces. The jailer pushed me along too quickly, locking the door to the enclave of cells behind us. After three more corridors we stopped.

"Here is your suite," he snarled.

Thirteen other women regarded me with pitying expressions. I greeted them with a limp wave. My new *camarades*, linked in this nightmare.

The jailer stalked away, slamming the door behind him. I stood dumbfounded, staring at my surroundings. Thin bedcovers, a few mattresses, and heaps of straw posed as beds; a tattered pile of clothing occupied the corner on the far wall; and a bucket of human waste sat outside the door.

My bag slid from my loose grip to the floor with a soft thump. And I wept.

⚜

I ignored the filth as best I could, though it worsened day by day. What did it matter? My heart ached for my children. The thought of their distress surpassed any amount of muck. Did Hortense cry herself to sleep at night? I pictured Eugène pacing the halls, wondering if he would ever see his *maman* or papa again. My head swam with visions of their stricken faces.

At most meals, I pushed away my saucer of chewy gruel and soured wine. My dresses hung from my feeble frame, my hair thinned, and my bones protruded until I resembled the others, a skeleton of my former self.

My sanity hinged on the few hours each day when the guards unlocked the corridors and we roamed from hall to hall, meeting people from other cells. I talked, wept, and prayed with former acquaintances, some with whom I had spent merry nights dancing or gossiping, some I had petitioned for, and strangers of all trades and titles.

One day I bent over an older woman, feverish and lying in filth. She reeked of urine and infection. She would perish, without doubt. "Let me help you." I slung my arm about her middle and lifted her with care, then leaned her against the cleanest spot on the wall.

She smiled weakly. "Thank you for your kindness."

"It's the least I can do."

A guard entered the cell carrying a canteen of fresh water. "Do you have the comb?"

"Yes." I pulled a pearled comb from my hair and caressed it. Maman's comb.

"You're getting nothin' until you pay up!" he growled. "And I want the canteen back." I deposited the treasure in his outstretched hand and snatched the water from him. "You have one hour," he grunted and stalked off.

I poured some of the liquid onto a corner of my dress and wiped the woman's face. She sighed and opened her cracked lips for a drink. I assisted her, then wiped the spout and drank some myself.

If only I could buy my release.

Dukes, carpenters, maids, nobles, and clergy—all were worthless in the eyes of our government. I befriended them, prayed with them, and read their fortunes. In turn, they dried my constant tears.

"Why am I the only one who weeps?" I asked a woman in the brownish light. The sun's rays could not penetrate the haze.

"You're Creole," she said. "You have lively blood. Your anguish is more acute than ours."

"That's absurd. As if you don't have a heart." We walked sluggishly through the corridors. I tried to ignore two faded handprints in dried blood on the wall.

She laughed. "Ah, we do, but Parisians do not access them as easily."

It seemed true. I wept most days. The others remained silent, morose, with occasional flares of anger. Such dispassionate emotion I could not grasp. I swept the hem of my dress into my arms to avoid a spilled bucket of feces. What is this foul hell, I wanted to shout. But my rage dissipated in a fresh torrent of tears.

My second week at Les Carmes, I saw Alexandre. Delphine, a once-beautiful woman who shared my cell, urged me to meet with him.

"He wishes to see you. He has asked me several times to persuade you." A fearful look filled her eyes, followed by jealousy. The poor girl had fallen in love with him. She feared we still loved one another. If she only knew. I wondered if Alexandre felt the same for her. It did not seem possible.

Yet something about her innocence made me want to assuage her fears.

"I assure you there is nothing between us, Delphine. We are married in name and share children. That is all. We've hardly been civil with one another." In truth, I wanted to strike him. He had brought so much heartache and misery to my life, and now this.

Delphine led me through several corridors until Alexandre's familiar form came into view.

One look at his hollow face and I could not withhold my emotion.

"Alexandre!" The past melted away. My anger dissipated. So absurd, our situation—how could I blame him? We were both innocent, and I had put myself at risk with my letters. Everyone had said so.

"Rose!" He took me in his arms, eyes glistening. "It's my fault! Oh, Rose. It's all my fault!" He searched my face. "And the children are alone!" He clutched me to his chest. "God, what have I done?"

"My darlings." A salty gush ran down my cheeks. "What will become of them?"

Delphine waited quietly during our reunion, desperate longing on her countenance.

Alexandre tilted my chin and met my eyes. "We will survive this, and when we do, you'll take the children to Italy and stay with Fanny. Until this madness blows over. For now, we need a strategy to secure our release."

I marveled at his calm. He sounded so resolute, so certain we would be freed. I wiped my nose with the rough sleeve of my dress.

"There's something I need to say. It's important." He paused to scratch at the grungy beard covering his face.

I regarded him warily. Alexandre seldom delivered good news.

"I owe you so many apologies. In these last weeks of my imprisonment, I've had time to think. It's all I've been able to do . . . dear Rose . . ." He gathered my hands to his chest. "I regret that I didn't treat you as you deserved. You're a lovely, graceful woman. The prisoners speak of you affectionately, of your sweetness. I am proud to know you. That you are the mother of my children." He wiped his eyes. "I never deserved you."

Had we been outside the prison walls, I might have scoffed at his sudden change of heart. But not here—not in the clutches of death. My anger drained away despite my despair. He had truly changed, at last.

I stretched on the tips of my toes and kissed him lightly on the mouth. "Thank you. It means more to me than you know. You have been a good father and an example to your countrymen."

Alexandre placed my hand on the crook of his arm and glanced at Delphine. "I understand you share a cell with the woman who stole my heart."

Once, those words would have cut me to the core. That life was long gone—and none of it mattered in the face of death.

Delphine appeared relieved. I smiled to reassure her. Alexandre deserved love as much as anyone.

"I'm happy Alexandre has fallen for such a lovely person."

Dimples carved adorable divots in her cheeks. "Thank you, Rose."

The sound of a bell halted our pleasant exchange.

Fear gnawed in the pit of my stomach. It was ten o'clock. The hour of death. A grave hush fell over the crowd of prisoners. I held my breath as the warden unrolled a scroll.

"On this day, the Committee of Safety calls forth these names for trial at the Conciergerie." He paused for effect, then listed six names.

No one spoke. One by one, the victims climbed into the death carts in quiet surrender.

How did they contain their terror? Scream out! I wailed inwardly. Beg for mercy! I looked at Alexandre's grim expression.

"Rejoice, Rose," Delphine said. "It's not your name or ours they have called."

"I cannot rejoice when the innocent march to their deaths."

The weeks wore on. Spring evolved into summer. Heat pressed on our lungs. Moisture writhed in the air and clawed over soiled bodies and stone. Mold grew on every surface. Even Martinique had not been so humid. Prisoners choked on filth, perishing on their vermin-infested beds before they had the chance to meet Madame Guillotine.

One insufferable afternoon, whistling and laughter echoed from another corridor. I peered through the perpetual twilight. A familiar fur ball skipped merrily toward me, barking loudly.

Fortuné? A surge of joy raced through my limbs.

"Fortuné! My silly, sweet puppy. Come here, boy." I laughed and cried at once. He bounded into my lap and licked my hands and face in a flurry of excitement. I scrubbed his little body with my fingertips. "How did you get here?" He licked my face. "Sweet boy," I cooed while massaging his back.

And then I saw it—a tiny strip of paper tucked under the clasp of his collar. My heart pounded as I unfolded it.

The governess takes care of everything but our hearts.

Eugène's handwriting! He had not said much in case a jailer found the note, but I knew what it meant. My clever boy. They were well, they missed us, and they had petitioned for Alexandre and me. I tucked the note inside my dress as prisoners came to pet the renegade dog. Fortuné yapped happily.

"How did the little rascal get past the guards?" a toothless man asked as he rubbed Fortuné's silky ears.

"I don't know, but how happy I am to see him!" I smiled for the first time in weeks.

My joy was short-lived.

Two jailers ran to my cell and plucked Fortuné from my arms. "How did this bugger get in here?"

"The children brought him," one of the guards replied. "The ones who keep visiting. They must be hers." He flicked his head in my direction. The jailers carried Fortuné away growling and snapping.

Hortense and Eugène came to Les Carmes? A knot of pain throbbed in my chest and radiated through my body. I couldn't see them or hold them. My children were alone. They needed me. I collapsed on the floor. I needed them.

A month passed as if in slow motion. One afternoon I lay drowsy on a heap of straw when a commotion stirred elsewhere in the prison. People shouted and wailed. In protest? I could not make out their words. What in the world was going on?

The rowdiness drew closer. The lock to our hallway opened. I joined the crowd gathered near the door. As it swung open, a guard shoved another prisoner into the room—the striking General Lazare Hoche.

He held his head high, a sarcastic smile playing on his lips.

"Good general!" a man bellowed and extended his hand.

"Sir, how can it be? A war hero has been arrested!" a shocked young woman cried.

The exclamations continued as the guard led General Hoche through our corridor to another. The General had been the very face of the Revolution, revered, loved by all. I had heard endless tales of his bravery and kindness. If General Hoche was jailed, the assembly had lost reason.

The second day after the general's arrival, he approached Alexandre and me as we huddled, plotting our next move.

"Citizen de Beauharnais, citizeness." He bowed.

"Hello, General," we replied in unison.

"Please, call me Lazare."

General Hoche and Alexandre recounted details of their shared army experiences, the swift political changes, and conspiracy. As they spoke, I absorbed the full details of the general's appearance. Dark hair curled around a proud forehead, a slightly crooked nose protruded, and his heart-shaped lips pouted seductively. Tassels and embellishments decorated his navy uniform. He exuded energy and addictive optimism. A breath of fresh air—a handsome, good-humored breath of air.

I did not see the general again for several days. When at last I caught sight of him, a clump of admirers surrounded him.

"What ingrates our leaders are!" a gentleman said. "They imprison one of their greatest generals! Fools."

"Thank you, kind citizen," the general said. "I love my country, despite the current state of affairs. Mistakes are made when fear lurks in the hearts of men, and it is fear that leads us now. That will change. Someone will do the right thing."

"How can you be so sure?"

"Tyranny does not last forever," Hoche said.

"Neither do we!" another man exclaimed.

General Hoche's warm laugh melted like honey on warm brioche. My knees weakened at the delicious sound. I approached him and touched his arm.

"*Bonjour*, general."

"Citoyenne de Beauharnais. If you'll excuse me." He nodded at the crowd and offered me his arm. "Would you care to walk?"

"That would be a welcome distraction."

"Your accent is, forgive me for saying so, seductive. Are you Creole?"

I peeked at him through lowered lashes. "I am from Martinique."

"Of course. Your dark hair, the way you move, the way you speak." He sighed with satisfaction.

Lord, I could be content in the darkest depths of hell with this man. I smiled, the faintest trace of happiness budding in my chest.

"Alexandre tells me you have been separated for some time?" he asked.

He did not waste time. Giddiness spread through me like intoxication. "Almost ten years. He is in love with one of my cellmates, Delphine. I am glad for them. Are you married, general?"

"Yes, just. Adelaide and I married last month. She's beautiful, but naive in the ways of the world." He looked at me expectantly.

Unfortunate circumstance. If only he had been sent a month prior, he would not be married. I shocked myself with such a horrible thought.

"Do you love her?" I asked.

"Yes. But will I see her again?"

"That appears to be everyone's predicament," I said. "When does responsibility end and celebrating life begin? I'd say the moment the gate is locked behind you."

"Madame." A soldier bowed his head slightly as we passed.

General Hoche saluted him. "I've heard you are well loved," he said to me.

I blushed. "I enjoy making friends."

"You've endangered your life to help at least a dozen others here." The general's expression became intense. "That's honorable. No different from being a soldier."

I laughed. "I assure you I am nothing like a soldier. I am far from brave. I can't even hold my tears when they call the names of the condemned."

"You do not know yourself, *citoyenne*. Or the lives you touch."

"You are too kind."

The prison bells rang. Prisoners shuffled to their assigned corridors.

"Will I see you tomorrow?" he inquired.

"I thought you would never ask." I smiled and made my way through the dank hallways.

My relationship with the general blossomed at a rapid pace. Our desperate yearning for connection, for a sense of meaning, fueled our desires. Lazare loved his wife. He made it plain that being wrenched from her bosom to face certain death was the only reason he strayed. Yet we shared a special sentiment.

He put his hand on my dirt-streaked face. "Why did I meet you in Dante's inferno?" He caressed the apple of my cheek with his thumb.

"Lazare." Speaking his name sent a rush of warmth through my limbs. "It's hard to believe, but here we are." I brushed his hand with my lips.

"I miss Adelaide. I long for her, but your friendship, your *douceur*. You are so sweet." He leaned closer. "I love your confidence. Your heart."

My skin tingled with longing.

He led me through the corridor to his cell—he had his own with a bed and received fresh bread daily. Famed generals did not go without like the rest of us.

"But it is almost a real bedroom!" A writing table sat in the corner, stacked with books. Sunshine poured through a sizable window. "You have clean bedcovers?" I ran my hand over the sheets.

"I am very fortunate."

"If one can call this fortunate."

He pulled me to him in a swift motion, placing his warm mouth on mine. We pulled at clothing, hungry for the touch of skin.

Oh, Lazare. Save me from darkness. Let me feel alive again.

"Rose," he breathed.

I stroked him until he moaned. He cupped my rear end and pulled me on top of him. Our need mounted until our cries exploded in relief and anguish.

I lay in his arms as the passion drained away and my living nightmare returned. My children. I was going to die. I wept on his muscled chest.

"Sweet Rose. Shhhh. No terrible thoughts. Things will change. I promise."

How could he be so optimistic? No one had left this prison through the front door.

Chiming bells shattered our intimate moment.

Lazare managed a smile. Somehow he always managed a smile.

Our love affair did not last. A month later the National Assembly ordered Lazare to be transferred to another, less heinous prison. He promised to lobby for my release and to see me beyond the prison walls. Despair suffocated me and I grew ill in his absence.

"You have the prison cough," Delphine said, concern wrinkling her flawless features. The grime did not mask her beauty.

"The death cough," I rasped, leaning against a wall, fingers slipping in the green film that covered the plaster.

Delphine clasped my fingers. "Don't say such things."

My throat gurgled and my shoulders shook. "We . . ." I coughed. "We both know it is true."

The days slipped by, uniform in their misery. One sweltering day, I lay on my mattress listening to the ranting of a priest.

"The one who condemns us to death is called Saint-Just!" he shouted. "What wretched joke has God played on us? He is the angel of death! *La justice* will visit Saint-Just one day. God's wrath will descend upon him for his evildoing. I will look down from heaven and send a curse of vengeance." His voice grew louder; his passion flared as if he preached from his altar. "God's chosen have been fed to the wolves of rebellion! I will see that he burns, that they all burn, that God—"

"My ears are burning!" an apathetic prisoner shouted. "Shut up, old man! No one cares. We'll all be dead in a few days anyway."

While the priest ranted, the sounds of unfettered lovemaking drifted through the halls. Anything to feel alive, to validate our pitiful existence.

I read my tarot cards before the hour of death. Delphine paced while I shuffled.

"I feel a terrible dread." She clenched her fists as she moved back and forth across the small space. Several of her friends had been executed and three of our cellmates. "I don't know. I feel . . ."

"It won't be you, dear."

The bells rang. I stuffed my cards into their pouch, their message not yet read.

We walked to meet Alexandre. He kissed me in greeting.

"Another day, ladies. We've lived another day." Delphine threw her arms around him and kissed him with ardor.

The usual hush enveloped the prison when the warden appeared before us. He stood on his wooden platform and unrolled the list.

Six names. But still he read more.

Anxiety pulsed in my limbs. The list grew longer each day.

The warden paused for effect before delivering the next name. "The Prince de Salm."

I turned to Alexandre in shock. "The Prince? It cannot be! I didn't know he was jailed! I haven't seen him." I burst into tears. "No! It's my fault! He could have escaped to safety!"

Alexandre embraced me. "It's not your fault. The ministers find enemies where there are none."

The warden went on. More names. Finally he came to the end.

He cleared his throat.

"And the last for today," the warden said, "Alexandre de Beauharnais."

My legs turned to mush.

Delphine blanched white and swayed on her feet. We tumbled together to the ground.

"No!" Spasms racked my body. "Alexandre . . . dear friend."

Delphine threw herself into his arms. He stroked her face and hair, her lips.

"My dear ladies, do not cry for me." He remained calm, resigned. "I would die a thousand deaths for my country. Delphine, my love, take my ring as a token. Remember me." He slipped his gold pinkie ring on her finger while she wailed. "Rose, tell the children I love them." He kissed my head softly.

"Where is justice?" I screeched. "Murderers!" I shouted through strangled sobs. The other prisoners looked on our wretched scene.

Alexandre crushed me against him. "God be with you."

I gazed into his sad eyes. "And you." I smoothed the damp locks away from his forehead.

He slipped a letter into my hand. "Give this to Eugène and Hortense. I wrote it just in case. I'm glad I did."

"Into the carts!" a guard yelled.

"Good-bye, my dearest wife and friend. Good-bye, my love." He kissed Delphine again and stood. He held his head high and joined the others. Death would not make him a coward.

I slumped to the ground, rocking a hysterical Delphine in my arms, my own grief pouring from me. Who would tell the children? Who would dry their tears?

"I can't bear it!" I clutched my sides in agony. My breath came in shallow gasps.

A violent end, the old witch had cackled. And now a violent end was upon me.

After Alexandre's death, neither Delphine nor I left the cell. All shreds of hope had vanished. My health worsened; a fever raged. I would die one way or another. Very soon.

A vision of Maman came to me time and again. Her determined eyes, her dark hair hovering around her face in wavy tendrils. Why hadn't she visited? Did I mean so little to her? Did her grandchildren?

I had failed her, failed my father. Tears leaked from my weary eyes. I had nothing to show for myself but a broken marriage and countless debts. I had failed at love, at life.

My skin stretched thin over feeble bones. I faded to nothing, almost no one at all.

A swirl of images flowed through my head. The drum roll thumping in my chest, uneven cobblestones underfoot, the metallic stench of blood. My blood. The blood of Papa and my dead sister.

A familiar pair of dark eyes sprang into my head. "You will become more than queen"—words spoken so long ago echoed from the past for the thousandth time. I snorted in disgust. I was not even human, rotting to death in the dirt. Revolution for our freedom. I laughed bitterly, startling my comatose cellmates. I ignored their questioning eyes. How much longer could I endure?

I awoke at an unknown hour to the ringing tocsin and the sounds of a mob.

I peered at two men in an adjoining cell. One hoisted the other upon his shoulders to peek through the high window. A fattened rat scurried over the stones near my head. I struggled to stand to avoid feeling its matted fur and clawing feet. Vile creatures. I would never grow used to them.

I coughed deeply, uncontrollably, as if I might vomit my organs. I sucked in a ragged breath and leaned against the wall. I ran my hand over the naked skin on my neck. A few days before, Delphine had chopped my locks into jagged disarray with a knife, borrowed from a jailer. My enemies would not shave my head in front of a mocking crowd.

I had kicked at the gnarled heap at my feet. "I never knew I had so much hair."

"Better for it to go now," Delphine had said. "At least we'll go to the scaffold with dignity." She handed me the knife. "My turn."

Dignity? It would not be dignified at all. I took the rusted blade from her hands and sawed through her once-lustrous locks.

Delphine wept as she watched clumps fall to the floor. "We're going to die, aren't we?"

We would certainly die.

I focused my attention on the gentleman looking out at the street. Others had gathered.

"What is it, Gérard? Can you see?" a man asked.

"People are dancing. They're cheering!" Gérard stuck his hand through one of the bars, motioning to someone. "What's happened?" he shouted at citizens we could not see. "A woman is motioning something. I can't . . . quite . . . *robe?* . . . stone?"

"Robespierre!" a prisoner cried.

"Robespierre! Robespierre!" Gérard bellowed. He drew his finger across his neck, then looked down at everyone below him. "*Il est mort!* The tyrant is dead! The tyrant is dead!"

Cheers exploded in the room and spread through the corridors.

Robespierre was dead?

"Does this mean we'll be freed?" a woman asked.

"It's hard to say," someone answered. "We're still considered traitors."

I stared in vacant disbelief. Fever warmed my face. My eyelids grew heavy as exhaustion claimed my body. I lay without moving.

Please, God. Please. Set me free or let me die.

Several days later, the heavy door at the end of the corridor swung open and the warden entered.

"Rose de Beauharnais! Are you here, Rose de Beauharnais?" his voice called in the gloom.

Me? He wanted me? Too weak, too defeated, I could not find my voice. I whimpered. It was my turn. The scaffold awaited. Death at last. I rested my head against the floor.

"She's here!" one of my cellmates called.

Heavy boots resounded like a drumroll. Closer, until their polished black points stopped in front of my face.

"Rose de Beauharnais? On your feet!"

I didn't move. I barely breathed and black dots filled my vision. Or was it the rats eating holes in the floor, the walls, the boots near my head?

The Phoenix

La Chaumière, 1794

I awoke to find two men carrying me between them, jostling my
limbs as they moved. Prisoners gathered on either side to watch as I
bounced by. Their dirt-streaked faces told me nothing. I struggled
against the jailers' grip but couldn't break free.

"Where are you taking her?" a familiar voice shouted. "*Citoyenne de
Beauharnais!*"

"Let me go!" My hysteria surfaced. "You can't kill me!" I shrieked,
thrashing wildly. "My babies need me! Let me go!" I kicked with all of
my strength. My foot connected with something hard.

"Oww! Stupid—"

The warden gave the jailer a dirty look. "Calm yourself, *citoyenne*."

My screams pierced the air. The men set me on the ground and
one pinned me against the wall. "Stop screaming and listen, woman!"

My chest heaved as I gasped for air. Sweat poured down my back
in rivulets. My dress could not absorb the moisture in its saturated
state.

"You are being released!" the warden said.

I stared at him in shock, mouth open. I was free to go?

"You are to be released!" My captor shook my shoulders. "Gather
your things."

I looked at a group of prisoners. One woman flicked her hands as
if to shoo me away. Go, her face said, go quickly.

"Is this real?" My voice shook.

"Move it or you'll rot in here!" one of the jailers snarled.

I shuffled in a daze, leaning heavily on other prisoners' arms as I moved through the corridors. My cellmates, the priest, men and women at the end of the hall cheered as I passed. They stomped their feet and clapped in happiness at my fortune.

Stunned, I did not return their sentiments.

Finally, we stopped at the central office. I hacked for a full minute before the men helped me into a chair. I flinched as the hard wood met my bony hind end. Once seated, I eyed the men with wary suspicion.

The warden pushed a pile of papers in my direction and presented me with a quill pen. I took it with an unsteady hand. The words swam and my head ached. I was so sick, I would die anyway, even released.

I smiled a vicious smile. God mocked me.

"What day is it?" I scribbled my name.

The warden gave me a hard look. "Nonidi of Thermidor, year two."

Still the annoying revolutionary calendar. I ticked off the months on my fingers. August. It had been less than four months! Only four months, but a lifetime of suffering.

"You are free to go." The warden stamped a few papers and said, "Joseph, show her out."

I carried the only thing of value tucked under my arm—my tarot cards in their now-gray pouch.

The jailer tugged me forward. "We sent word to your family. They're sending a coach to collect you. Wait outside."

He ushered me into the street and slammed the door behind him.

I squinted in the blazing light. I hadn't seen the sun for months. Passersby bubbled with enthusiasm and laughter. Children skipped. I ogled them in shock. The happy crowd in the street stared back as they passed.

A man and woman walking arm in arm waved to me. "Just from prison? Have you heard? The tyrant is dead! We are free!"

I touched my wet cheek. My family, my children. I had wept so much. How could there be more tears? Elation surged through me, lifted my soul, my heart, to join the sparrows soaring overhead. A foreign sound escaped my lips. A laugh? Then a horrible cough.

I reached my arms toward the cerulean sky, the most beautiful I'd ever seen. I twirled, breath whistling in my lungs, head thrown back in exultation. Giddy in the brilliant sunbath in the middle of the glorious street.

I was free.

When the carriage fetched me home, I hobbled up the front walk. The children burst through the front door. My heart exploded in happiness.

"Maman!" Eugène ran to assist me. Hortense followed.

"Oh, Maman! What have they done to you?" Horror registered on Hortense's pretty face. "Your hair." She fingered a greasy tuft. "Your clothes." Her voice trailed off and her eyes filled with tears.

She and Eugène supported me, one on either side.

"Shh. I'm here now, darlings. I've missed you so." I hacked and wheezed in uncontrolled spasms.

"You're sick." Hortense wiped my face with her handkerchief.

"I will be fine, *mon amour*. We'll send for a——" A cough strangled my words. "A physician."

"Don't try to speak," Eugène said. "Let's get you inside."

Mimi appeared at the door. "Yeyette." Tears sprang to her eyes. She folded me in a gentle embrace. She rubbed my back as if I might break. Had I grown so fragile? "Let's get you a bath and clean clothes, and I'll put on some tea."

I sighed and melted in Mimi's embrace. A delicious warm bath, a cup of tea.

Home.

I thanked God for the chance to begin again. But the purity of my freedom would be forever marred by the cost I endured—that we all endured. I couldn't make sense of the masses of rotting bodies, the price France paid in souls and flesh. Their images assaulted me when I closed my eyes and haunted me in sleep.

I detested those who tore our country apart. Battles in Lyon and Toulon, on our frontiers, between families, brothers. I detested those who belittled our lives. They did not fight for freedom—they fought for pride, for nothing at all.

My hair fell out, my courses failed, and headaches crushed my skull, but the doctor assured me I would recover. Fortuné did not leave my side for weeks.

I clutched Hortense in my arms as if she might slip away.

"I'm here." My daughter smoothed my hair. "And take your laudanum. It should ease your headache."

"Precious girl." My voice grew thick with emotion. "I almost lost—"

"Do not speak of it." Hortense stood and closed the drapes in my bedroom. "We're together now, by the grace of God."

The grace of God, or a twist of fate? I wasn't sure I believed in either.

Fanny visited the moment she heard of my release. She sat on the edge of my bed, dressed in indigo from head to toe, her cheeks as red as ever. The times had changed if one could wear such vivid colors again.

"I managed to find a little sugar." She added a cube to each of our cups.

"Dear Fanny." I caught her hand in mine and she kissed it.

"I wrote to the assembly on your behalf . . . for both of you. Citizen Tallien secured your release, but it was too late for Alexandre." She looked down at her steaming cup.

Pain squeezed my heart. "If you had seen how brave he was, how kind." My vision blurred with tears. "We became good friends." Fanny squeezed my knee but said nothing. I blew on the hot liquid in my cup, sending tendrils of vapor into the air. "How is your daughter?"

"Home and recovering." Her eyes glistened.

"Did you send my petitions for Marie-Françoise and Delphine's releases?"

"Yes. Delphine is already home as well, and Marie-Françoise is to be released in two days' time. I received word this morning."

"Oh, Fanny! *Merci au bon Dieu.* As soon as I'm well, I'll write to Citizen Tallien to thank him." A pitiful thanks for saving my life, the lives of my friends.

"He's one of the men responsible for Robespierre's death. They say his lover prompted it. Theresia Cabarrus. She was imprisoned at Les Carmes, too, you know. Of course it takes a woman to get things moving."

I smiled. "I'm grateful for my freedom, regardless of the impetus."

"I'm grateful you are alive."

By the end of my third week home, my cough had subsided and a glow had returned to my cheeks. Friends visited, though I was too weak to entertain for long. One afternoon, I had just settled in for a *sieste* when a caller arrived.

"Yeyette, you awake?" Mimi rapped at the door. "General Hoche is here."

My heart swelled. Darling Lazare.

"Send him in!" I pinched my cheeks. Thank goodness I had dressed today.

The door creaked. A slender Lazare entered, handsome in a fresh uniform and gold sash. Though he smiled, death haunted his eyes. He had aged a lifetime in only a few short months.

"Lazare!" I threw off my blanket and leaped from my chair.

"Don't get up. You're ill." Concern filled his dark eyes.

"I'm nearly well." I threw myself into his arms.

He set his hat on my bureau and showered my cheeks with tender kisses.

"I've been so anxious to hear of your release," I said.

He carried me to the bed and sat next to me. Strong, warm Lazare. Why must he be married? Passionate love, the kind that lasted and consumed, the kind for which I ached, would be easy with him. He caressed my cheek and smoothed my shaggy hair. I burrowed into his chest, ignoring the cool buttons and scratchy medals.

"How is Adelaide?" I asked. "Have you been to see her?"

He loved her and would return to her, I knew. A wave of sadness gripped me. What did it matter? There was no room for love—not for me, not ever.

Lazare watched a sparrow dipping in a wind current near the window. "I needed to see you first." He kissed the tips of my fingers. "I want to be with you, Rose. I love her. I can't leave her, but it doesn't change how I feel about you. What we have been through . . ."

"I know you must go back, *mon amour*." I smoothed the crinkled line between his eyes. "But I'm happy you're here now."

We lay together, listening to the bustle in the street and Fortuné yapping at the birds. Lazare caressed my arms, my neck and face. His touch soothed my nerves.

He broke the silence. "I should let you rest."

"No! You just arrived. Please stay." I caressed his thigh with my thumb and forefinger, moving my hand up his leg.

Hunger lit his eyes, sparking a sensual stirring in my belly. He tilted my chin toward him and met my eager lips.

I quivered with desire. All of the horror seeped into each kiss, each touch, releasing the poison trapped in my soul. I longed to feel alive and whole again. Enraptured, we moved as one, loving one another. Afterward, we lay for an hour, not speaking of our terrifying time in prison, or of our future.

I spent five weeks with Lazare before he left for his post in Caen.

"Must you go so soon?" I asked as he escorted me through a garden near his apartment. "You have another week before you have to report to your garrison."

"Before my garrison reports to me." He smiled. Lazare was general-in-chief of the Army of the West, a prestigious title for a man of only twenty-six.

I swatted his arm. "You know what I mean."

"Yes, *mon amour*, I must leave tomorrow. My battle dress is at home."

"With Adelaide." Sorrow pooled in my stomach. Damn his marriage. "Eugène will be devastated. He admires you so much. I don't know how to tell him you're leaving."

We sauntered through hedges of boxwoods and along a path lined with purple asters. A breeze laced with the chill of fall lifted the hair on my neck.

"He misses his father," he said softly.

I kicked at a pebble underfoot. I couldn't shake my unsettled feelings about Eugène. He picked arguments with Hortense and launched into diatribes about the country's unrest. He was full of his own ideals. For him to remain at home, open to the strife in the streets and tempted by the lure of rebellion, worried me.

"I don't know what to do with him." I sighed. "I can't afford tuition for military school. I'm afraid he'll join the ruffians in the streets. If only he had his father. Or a male role model to look out for him." I gave Lazare a beseeching look.

"I could appoint him as my aide-de-camp. He would learn a great deal about becoming a soldier."

"He would love to go with you!" I threw my arms around his neck. "I don't know how to thank you."

"Consider it a token of my affection." He kissed my nose.

Lazare and Eugène promised to write as they left the following week. Lazare placed a heavy envelope in my hand. It was filled with assignats, the new revolutionary currency.

"For rent and to pay for Hortense's schooling," he said.

"Thank you, my darling." A lump formed in my throat. "Take good care of him."

He kissed me and climbed into the coach. Eugène waved as they pulled away.

I wept all afternoon, though I knew their leaving was best.

Despite Lazare's sum, I could not afford the inflated rent in Paris. I moved back to Croissy with Hortense and Mimi. Citizeness Campan, a former lady-in-waiting to the Queen, invited us to stay with her and to place Hortense in her school. I accepted her offer, flattered she would take us in, though I knew she also sought to rebuild her life.

I dedicated my time to clearing Alexandre's name and to restoring our family property. I had no other source of possible income—the British blockade prevented funds from Martinique and Alexandre's properties had been seized after his death—so I borrowed from friends to stay afloat. But I knew I would soon need to find another way, another man to do my bidding. I wouldn't want for anything again.

I pushed away my ache for Lazare, bitter I should lose another. But I could not banish the emptiness, or escape my need for comfort. I slept away the pain, losing track of hours, of days. Winter came early, spraying shimmering crystals on the trees and gusting air that seared exposed skin. Yet I walked daily in the garden surrounding the château, as the doctor had prescribed.

"To lighten the heaviness in your chest," he had said.

I grew stronger as I pushed against the elements, breathing in life around me and sharing my sorrow with the sleeping trees. My nightmares ebbed—Alexandre's bloodied body was laid to rest. I no longer startled awake from fear of rats or the call of the warden's voice. Still, I could not grasp a sense of meaning, of understanding of my loss. So little seemed important.

My first formal invitation in months arrived as winter neared its end. Citizen Tallien invited me to a ball at his Paris country house, La Chaumière—a fete in honor of his pardoned lover, Theresia, our Lady of Thermidor. I longed to meet the heroine of the Republic and thank Tallien for my release, my life. I accepted at once.

A week later I rode to La Chaumière, watching Paris fly past. The dreary weather did not affect the vivacity of the people. Parisians crammed into brasseries and newly opened restaurants with windows aglow in cheerful lamplight, or crowded into the dozens of new dance halls alive with music.

I squealed in delight as we passed my favorite theater. It had opened once again. Warmth radiated from the center of my chest and spread through my limbs.

"Thank you, God," I whispered. "I am alive."

The coach traveled along the Champs-Élysées and to the outskirts of Paris. Finally, it stopped in front of a large red cottage. The thatched roof resembled that of a charming farmhouse, nestled in a tree-lined nook near the Seine. My heart skipped with excitement. I had not attended a fete in so long.

A butler dressed in black livery took my overcoat, while another escorted me to the salon. Warmth I had not felt since the summer months embraced me—wonderful, blissful heat. Columns wrapped in ivy, frescoed walls, and sculpted busts of the ancients decorated each room. A Roman-inspired Republican household. I would do the same when I could afford it.

I had arrived early. Only three gentlemen and a woman I did not recognize mingled in the salon. Most of the furniture had been removed, displaying polished wood floors. There would be dancing. A giddiness came over me. Lord, how I missed dancing.

I sauntered across the room to tables loaded with mangoes, pome-granates, and pineapples. My eyes bulged at the feast. Such a variety I had not seen in years. I couldn't imagine how Tallien had had the fruit delivered; the Seine had frozen again. I supposed with enough money one could buy anything.

A servant walked by with a tray of champagne. He bowed as I accepted a flute of the lively liquid. I caught sight of my reflection in the goblet. My locks fell in waves to my chin; my eyes glittered in the candle-light. It had been almost awkward to take care with my appearance—a frivolous endeavor in the wake of imprisonment, of all that death. Nothing more than a tool to secure one's station, like the ruse of love.

Boisterous laughter caught my attention. A former acquaintance waved me over. I had not seen him since before my time in Les Carmes.

"Citizeness de Beauharnais! What a surprise to see you here." Gerôme LaCourte left a lingering kiss on my cheek. "You're as beautiful as ever."

He had expressed his interest on several occasions, poor man, but his bulldog appearance did not appeal to me.

"Citizen LaCourte," I said. "How lovely to see you again. *Bonsoir*, Citizeness Degrange." I had met the woman at his side one evening. I never forgot a name or face.

She pursed her lips as she regarded my dress of powder blue mus-lin, draped and fastened by a slender rope belt. "How the times have changed, Citoyenne de Beauharnais."

Rude and prudish—what a combination.

"One does not want to be caught in the past," I said, looking over her shoulder.

She glanced down at her velvet gown and lace fichu. Pretty, but no one wore a fichu these days. "Yes, one wouldn't want to be deemed traitorous."

My eyes narrowed. How dare she imply my guilt! She knew noth-ing of my sympathies, of all I had given, of all I had lost. I sipped from my glass to calm my nerves. "Well, it's a relief neither of us fit that description."

Her mouth fell open, but the woman said nothing.

Citizen LaCourte looked embarrassed and changed the subject. "How do you know Citizen Tallien?"

"A mutual friend introduced us," I said. "I owe him my life."

"We all do. Theresia Cabarrus and Paul Barras as well. Without them, La Terreur might still be happening."

"Paul Barras? An assembly member?"

"Yes, and a member of the Committee of Public Safety. A very powerful man."

"A scoundrel, to be sure," Citizeness Degrange added in disdain. "He parades a collection of mistresses like a pack of whores."

"Hardly, *citoyenne*. They are respectable women," LaCourte said.

"I suppose it depends on your definition of respect."

Her disdain piqued my curiosity. I would have to meet this scoundrel. I glanced around the room as guests filed in.

"If you'll excuse me," I said, "I'd like to say hello to some friends. Enjoy your evening."

The woman looked relieved.

"I will find you later for a dance, if I may?" LaCourte asked.

"Of course." I smiled.

When the dancing began, I twirled to the rhythm of the violins and stamped my feet in time with the pianoforte. My cheeks flushed and heart thundered, and tendrils of hair stuck to my glistening neck. Exhilarated, I gave myself over to the music, releasing the anguish tormenting my sleep, the grief over the loss of my husband and so many friends, and dear Lazare. Months of distress and illness melted away in the glow of La Chaumière.

After spinning for hours, I sought repose in a chair at the edge of the dance floor. I gulped down a glass of water and unfastened the fan hanging from my belt. I waved it to cool my face.

Citizen Tallien spotted me from across the room and closed the gap between us. "It's good to see you. Thank you for coming." He kissed my cheeks.

"How does one say thank you for their life?" I gripped his hand in mine.

"It was my duty and my honor. You look well. I trust you have recovered?"

"I've been in hiding, but yes, I am finally well."

Musical laughter drifted over the merriment. A woman with black hair and creamy skin glided through the room with the ethereal grace of a goddess. Her red gown barely contained her décolletage. Eyes widened as she crossed the room.

"Have you met Theresia?" Tallien asked.

I had heard of her legendary beauty, but I was not prepared for an enchantress. She radiated perfection. Not a single gesture went unnoticed as she weaved through the crowd. I instantly wanted to befriend her.

"I would be honored to."

"Theresia?" he called. She placed her hand on the young man's arm with whom she spoke as if to apologize for the interruption, and floated toward us.

Tallien slid his arm around her waist. "*Chérie*, I have someone I would like you to meet. You share a past at Les Carmes." He nodded in my direction. "*Je te présente la Veuve de Beauharnais.*"

"*Bonsoir.*" A dazzling smile lit her features. "I've heard so much about the widow Beauharnais." She kissed me on each cheek.

Taken aback, I laughed. "And I you, our Lady of Thermidor."

"Please, call me Theresia."

"And I am Rose."

"If you will excuse me, ladies, I have business to attend to." Tallien motioned to a gentleman from the National Assembly. "I hope you will join us again, citizeness."

"You may count on it," I replied.

Citizen Tallien lifted Theresia's hand to his lips possessively. "Darling, I'll see you later."

Theresia leaned in and kissed him passionately on the mouth. Someone whistled through the din of music and voices. The hero and heroine of the Republic laughed before Tallien disappeared into the crowd.

Theresia and I shared details of our time at Les Carmes, past husbands, and our shared love of fashion, dancing, and meeting new people. In a short time, I felt as if I had known her since birth. We linked arms and swept around the beautiful array of candied fruits and pastries. I hadn't seen so much sugar in years. I sampled a dozen pieces, taking care not to spend much time chewing them. My sensitive teeth began to ache, nonetheless, so I chucked my final plum, half-eaten, onto a servant's tray.

"Pure bliss." I sighed.

Theresia laughed at my enthusiasm. "You're definitely Creole. Living without sugar must have been the most unnatural thing in the world."

"I had no idea how much I missed it."

We plunked down onto an empty sofa in the adjoining study.

"It has been such a lovely evening with you, Theresia. I feel as if I've known you for years."

"As do I." She patted my hand.

I swigged from my wineglass. "Forgive me for mentioning a solemn subject on such a fine night, but it weighs heavily on my mind. From one woman to another, I'm certain you'll understand."

Curiosity crossed her angelic countenance.

"I'm plagued with the disgrace surrounding my husband's death," I continued. "After his execution, the government sealed his properties and accounts. The Beauharnais name carries a black mark and my children and I must bear his shame. I've petitioned, but I am ignored. I'm not sure where else to turn except to your Tallien. But he is so busy. I don't want to be bothersome."

She fingered a shiny black curl. "Say no more. I'll make sure he pleads Alexandre's case. Too many innocent Republicans have suffered. Your husband's execution was a crime."

A little inebriated, I threw my arms around her neck and kissed her. "I cannot thank you enough."

She laughed and patted my back. "You may thank me by coming for dinner tomorrow night."

Excitement fluttered in my stomach. "I would love to, but I have traveled from Croissy. I did not make plans to stay in Paris."

She understood my meaning. Theresia knew I possessed little and would need to arrange to stay with a friend. "You shall stay here. And do not try to argue. I insist."

A broad grin crossed my face. My luck had proved capricious, but this was a start in the right direction.

Theresia and I became inseparable. We waltzed evenings away at the dance halls or attended art exhibitions. When spring arrived, we played games in the country and rode horses with friends, relishing the *fraîcheur*, the smell of grass and sunshine. Nature had never appeared so divine—a gift—as it had in those months after our incarceration. I marveled at its eternal renewal, and threw myself into the celebration of life I had taken for granted.

Most evenings we languished at La Chaumière. My circle of influential friends expanded and I borrowed from powerful bankers who liked pretty women. Theresia's admirers abounded and soon, so did mine, though I remained in her shadow. I worked to preserve my youth with creams I concocted, facial masks, and expensive rouge, though it felt all for show. But a show is what I must give them.

Ten years my junior, Theresia was a blooming beauty, but my thirty-one years threatened my position among our beautiful friends.

Theresia laughed at my concern.

"You're graceful and lovely. Men flock to you. Haven't you noticed?" she teased one afternoon as we lay under an oak in the garden. Tallien fed her grapes.

So easy for her to dismiss my concern when her own youth stretched before her. I fingered the silver ribbon on my new hat. It complemented my purple dress perfectly. Both had cost far more than I could afford, but I had to reinvent myself once more, else I might find myself destitute. I shifted in the grass. The thought made me ill at ease.

"My dear friend"—I stole a grape from the dish—"they flock to you and merely tolerate me."

Tallien laughed. "Really, Rose. That's absurd." He popped a grape into his mouth.

"I have a favor to ask of you," I said. "I've dreaded this moment because you have already been so kind, but my conscience won't let it rest."

"Ask away."

"I have a few friends still at Les Carmes." I looked down at my hands. Guilt pooled in the pit of my stomach. Here I sat with friends, enjoying fine food—freedom—while they wasted away unjustly in prison. I had to do what I could for them.

Tallien noticed my change in humor. "I will see to their release. Give me their information and I'll look into it first thing in the morning."

I sighed in relief. "They're good people. It sickens me that they are incarcerated without cause. How will I ever repay you?"

He sat for a moment, lost in thought. "Perhaps you could amuse Citizen Belfour. He arrives tonight from Bern and will be in want of company."

I grasped his meaning. It would not be the first time I had entertained men in exchange for someone's life. It was a small price to pay and sometimes it was amusing.

I nodded. "Of course."

I relished letters of Eugène's progress and visited Hortense when possible. How I missed them.

Citizeness Campan assured me Hortense was an industrious student.

"She's well liked and a prodigious pianist." Citizeness Campan looked through a ledger scribbled with notes. "Hortense's scores are quite high." She ran her finger down the page. "She's attentive during classes. I wish I had more students like her." She closed her book.

I could not have chosen a better teacher. Citoyenne Campan knew more about etiquette than anyone. Republican or not, my daughter would possess the manners of a well-bred lady. I would not wish for my daughter to suffer as I had at a young age.

Hortense grew more like a woman each time I visited. Her figure blossomed, her round face thinned, and her smile grew confident. We laughed and talked as women, though she was only twelve.

"Darling, you're beautiful," I said as I kissed her.

We settled on a red *canapé* in the sitting room. Hortense blushed. The pink stain on her cheeks accented her violet eyes and blond hair all the more.

"You have to say such things, Maman." She fingered one of her elaborate braids.

I laughed. "That may be, but it's the truth. Soon, you'll catch a young man's eye, if you haven't already."

More blushing. "Please, you're embarrassing me."

"Then my work here is done. I'll speak no more of it." I winked. "I have good news, darling." I covered her hand with mine. "Your papa has been exonerated!"

"Oh, that's wonderful!" She jumped up to embrace me.

"Our name is clear again." I patted her back. "But there is another matter I have to contend with. His properties have been restored, but I will have to sell them to pay his debts. And ours."

Her face fell. "We'll have no inheritance."

"I'm afraid not." I gathered her hands in mine. "But we have our honor. And we have each other. What could be more important?"

Hortense kissed my cheek. "How right you are."

I motioned to the pianoforte. "Will you play for me?"

On Sunday afternoon, I looked at my latest bill note. Three thousand livres. I chewed a fingernail to the quick. The jeweled hair clip could be returned and my dress would still be stunning. What would I do about the other bills?

Mimi set a tray on the desk. "Chocolate and bread."

I rubbed my face in frustration.

"What is it?"

"I'm hopeless with money." I sighed and folded the papers on my desk.

"It's all them dresses, Yeyette. Your *maman* would scold you if she saw you acting so frivolous."

I studied her face: round nose and pillowy lips, high cheekbones— all so familiar, so dear. "You're right. I have plenty of dresses for the season. And Theresia will let me borrow hers."

Wealthy friends ensured my financial support, but keeping pace with them drove me further into debt—a vicious cycle I could not escape. I needed a husband, but I would not marry just anyone. I sighed. And what of love? I tired of the constant search, the constant failure. Love and marriage certainly didn't go hand in hand. Alexandre had taught me that.

One cool evening in the month of Floréal, Theresia and I rode in her violet carriage to a soiree at the Palais-Égalité. Paul Barras, current president of the National Assembly, had invited us. I could not wait to meet him. His reputation for scandalous parties intrigued me. I hoped tonight would be no exception. The theme—*bal des victimes*—demanded guests wear red velvet ribbons around their throats. Prison survivors assumed positions of honor at the tables and a dance mimicking a beheading would commence the ball.

Theresia and I wore matching blood-red silk gowns and had pinned our shoulder-length locks in tight curls. We had not covered our arms in gloves or our heaving breasts with fichus. Shocking the crowd was too much fun.

"I thought these beautiful." Theresia pulled two gold tiaras from her bag. "One for each of us."

I clapped in delight. "They're beautiful."

Theresia pinned hers in her hair. "What do you think?" The dim lighting glinted off the glittery band.

"Perfect."

"No man will resist us tonight, *mon amie*." She blew me a kiss.

"Is Tallien coming later?"

Her expression grew guarded. "I don't know. I left him."

I gasped. "When?"

"Three days ago. I am filing for divorce. That man has battered me for the last time."

"Oh, darling!" I braved the rockiness of the carriage and slid into the seat beside her. "I didn't realize he was violent." I squeezed her hand. "You're so brave for leaving."

"It's not brave. Everyone is divorcing."

"Not many women."

She sniffed. "I'm not just any woman."

I put my arm around her shoulders. "No, you aren't! Do you have a place to stay?"

She dabbed at her eyes with a handkerchief. "With Tallien for now. He said he would support our daughter and me until the affair is settled with the provost."

"That was generous."

"He felt guilty." She straightened in her seat.

"You're doing the right thing."

She folded her handkerchief and stuffed it in her handbag. "Let's forget I mentioned it. I want to have fun tonight. Meet a handsome stranger or two." A watery smile illuminated her face.

"I have my eye set on Paul Barras."

"*Dieu*, then you are the one who is brave." She laughed.

During my last visit to the Palais-Égalité, the château had been called the Palais-Royal and housed the now executed Duc d'Orleans. Since, Barras had snapped up the empty palace and gutted the whole estate.

"Goodness, look." I pointed to a cluster of tables covered in white lace. In the center of each, red flowers surrounded miniature replicas of *la guillotine*. The hair on my arms stood on end. My abhorrence of it would never fade.

"Paul loves a good show, they say." Theresia smiled a devilish grin.

I rubbed my bare arms. "What is that look for?"

"His reputation in the bedroom is legendary." We walked arm in arm to the main ballroom.

"I look forward to meeting the wicked Barras. I've only seen him from afar."

Servants dressed as executioners circulated with gilded trays of delicacies. Musicians played harps in one room and the pianoforte in another. The salon had been converted to a stage; hired players practiced their lines for the performance scheduled later in the evening.

Theresia and I accepted glasses of wine.

"*Merveilleux*," I said as we entered the main ballroom.

Rich scarlet and purple fabrics flowed from the ceiling like a shroud encasing the dance floor. Guests wore their finest white muslin, silver brocades, or black lace decorated with red shawls and ribbons, red hats and gloves. Theresia and I wore the only two crimson gowns, making us the most conspicuous women in the room—exactly as we had planned.

The evening began with a sumptuous eight-course feast. Servants whisked gold-plated trays of cold vegetable salads, potage, and roasted meats to the tables, one after the other. But the food displays between courses inspired the most delight among the guests.

"*Regarde!*" Theresia pointed.

A fish jumped through hoops of fried onion from a sea of blue icing. A carved potato gentleman waltzed with a woman in her endive gown.

I clapped. "*Magnifique.*"

Guests applauded each exhibition—until the final dish.

Severed heads made of sponge cake.

A collective gasp echoed in the great hall.

I covered my mouth and stared at the horrific creations. So realistic the fondant eyes appeared, frightened and glazed, and the ribbons of red sugar that dangled from each chin. Revulsion swept through me. The servants promptly removed the frightening cakes. I gulped from my water glass to clear my palate and wash away the terrible image.

The final course met cheering—platters of glistening sugar-coated fruits, iced creams, sweetmeats, and jellies. I sampled a few and mingled with the crowd.

Later when the dancing began, I moved to the ballroom. With each new song, the crowd grew wild, thumping and spinning until dizzy. My head buzzed with wine and sugared fruit. I lost myself in the crush of bodies until the back of my gown grew damp with perspiration. I sought an open window in a quiet room. An abandoned pianoforte faced rows of empty chairs, and dozens of lit candles sputtered in the breeze. The cool night air whisked the sweat from my temples. I sat on a chair to rest my aching feet.

Quelle fête. I would need to seek out Paul before I danced the night away. Maybe he would help me forget Lazare. A dull ache pulsed in my chest. I couldn't help but compare each gentleman I met to him.

A sudden movement near the door caught my eye. An imposing man dwarfed the grand doorway. Or perhaps he would find me.

Paul Barras stepped into the room.

His scarlet coat stretched over his muscled frame and a cascade of black hair waved to his chin. A sarcastic smile played on his lips. Devilish, some called him. Now I understood why.

I hid my face with my fan and met his eyes. An invitation. He did not hesitate, but crossed the room like a rushing bull, brandy in hand. I stood to greet him.

"Citoyenne de Beauharnais, we meet again." He bowed before brushing my hand with his lips.

"I do not recall our last meeting." I fluttered my lashes. I remembered him perfectly well, though we had not spoken. The occasion had been a tropical themed party at La Chaumière. I had worn snake bangles with a black-and-white-striped tunic modeled after a zebra. Theresia had asked me to do tarot readings, at which Barras had laughed, or so she'd told me.

"I have admired your beauty from afar. Tonight, you leave me breathless." His black eyes danced. He did not release my hand. "If I didn't know better, I would swear you were a witch."

"I've been known to cast a spell or two on an unsuspecting soul." I waved my fan back and forth.

His laugh was brusque, dangerous. Delicious. "Did you bring your devil cards tonight?"

"No, but I'd be happy to beat you at a game of brelan."

He snorted with laughter. "You think you can beat me? I am a master card player. Besides, it isn't proper to humiliate a woman at games."

I loved a good challenge. I arched my back slightly, pushing my breasts forward. "Paul Barras is proper with women? That is news to me."

His smile grew wider. "Shall I find a deck?"

"Your arrogance begs to be taught a lesson."

His laughter boomed. "What a droll little minx. Would you care to wager?"

It was almost too easy to capture his interest.

"A wager makes everything more interesting," I said.

He placed my hand on his arm and led me to a room resembling an office. A fire roared in a pit taller than Barras. Several gentlemen sipped cognac and smoked cigars near a set of doors that opened to a grove of chestnut trees.

Barras found a deck of cards in a drawer and handed them to me. "You are my guest. And you'll be paying me soon. Why don't you shuffle?"

"We shall see." We took glasses of absinthe from a servant, a new delicacy from the Swiss cantons.

He held his up for a toast and tapped the side of my glass with his. "To a beautiful woman."

"To winning." I took a sip.

We played two games of whist, and one of brelan. I beat him at two of three hands.

"Impossible! How can you beat me again?" he asked, tossing his cards on the table.

"It is amazing, considering you cheat," I teased. I placed the cards in a stack and leaned forward to give him a glimpse down the front of my dress. "I believe you owe me."

He paid me triple the small sum we had wagered. "Shall we dance?" He held out his hand.

I smiled and took it. "With pleasure."

We made our way to the ballroom. Many of the guests had departed, but a few still whirled across the floor. Theresia sat in a far corner, shaded by a swath of fabric—I would know her silhouette anywhere. She and a gentleman leaned into one another as if alone in the room.

Barras held out his hand. "A waltz."

The dance was popular for its sensuous moves, allowing a man to take a woman in his arms. He pulled me against his chest and guided me through the room.

We danced a set, and when the music concluded, he leaned close to my ear and whispered, "I would love to show you the new furniture in my apartments upstairs. As a woman of taste, I am certain you will find it fashionable."

I looked into his wolfish eyes. They glittered like onyx.

"I do possess a sense of style." I ran a finger down the side of his face and along his jaw.

He took my hand and escorted me upstairs.

It would be several trips to his mansion before I noticed the baroque armoire and vanity, the footstool and mahogany writing table. That night, I admired his black satin sheets until golden rays of sunlight spilled through the windowpane.

Creole Beauty
Palais-Égalité, 1795

Barras was as rich as a prince, living in a multitude of homes from the infamous Palais-Égalité to Grosbois, his country palace. He owned more finery, possessed more influence, and enjoyed a soiree more than any man I had ever met.

"King Barras," the papers called him, "treacherous, dishonest, and hedonistic."

He exhibited glimmers of all those traits, but I found him cunning and generous. I assured naysayers of his commitment to the Republic, which he loved more than anyone I had ever known, save my murdered husband.

I relished Paul's stories of his travels, especially of India.

"An exotic land like yours," he said, "filled with stunning women. And the spices!"

Paul delighted in my poise, soft Creole accent, and dealings with the occult, or so he said. But it was my social connections and lovemaking skills that kept his interest.

"You had the bedroom redecorated?" Paul stroked the carved mahogany head of an elephant by the fireplace.

"An Indian harem," I said.

Sheer fabrics in gold and aquamarine dipped from the bedposts. Pillows patched with glittering fabrics lay heaped on the bed. Jasmine incense perfumed the air.

"Stunning." He smiled, unbuttoning the brass buttons of his coat.

"This," I said, letting the overcoat I wore drop to the floor, "is stunning."

I revealed a jeweled top exposing my stomach. My skirts flowed from a gold-encrusted belt and swept about my ankles. Slits in the fabric bared my naked thighs. I moved my hips in a circular motion and shook my shoulders back and forth. A delicate thread of golden bells jingled on each ankle.

Paul sat on the edge of the bed, awestruck.

I performed a sensuous dance around the room. I smiled at his rapacious expression. My sexual prowess captivated him.

Barras showered me with jewelry, opera tickets, flowery *indiennes*, and the most expensive undergarments money could buy. He made no secret of his lust for lacy things and I did not disappoint. But despite my status as official mistress, Barras did not curb his roguish ways.

"Be careful, darling," Theresia warned me one afternoon as we walked in her garden. "You know Paul has other mistresses. He was not alone while you were gone." I had just returned from a fortnight in Croissy to pay Hortense a visit.

"I have no delusions of his character. He is incapable of giving himself to one woman." He loved me for now, but I knew he would tire of me, and I would be on my own again, scrambling for security. A memory of Lazare's laughing eyes came to mind. My steps faltered as the pain coursed through me. I hoped my longing for him would pass.

"You should hear what is being said of you—the evil Barras and his doting mistress!"

I snorted. "Do tell!"

A flock of pigeons pecked at invisible feed on the path ahead. They did not frighten, but parted as we passed.

"Apparently we're all involved in sexual orgies. Men with men and women with women. But you and I, they say, prefer our sexual encounters in public."

I howled with laughter. Paul and I did not always behave appropriately, but I possessed a sense of decency.

"They enjoy slandering those who are the center of attention. We can't help it if we captivate men," she said. "Nor do we want to help it."

I frowned as a disturbing thought crossed my mind. "I hope the children haven't heard the rumors."

"No one would tell a child such things. Besides, I'm sure they're proud their mother consorts with the most powerful people in Paris."

I hoped they hadn't heard. I would hate to disappoint or, worse, embarrass my darlings.

⚜

Paul was generous to a fault, despite his insatiable appetite for women. He rented a fashionable property on the rue Chantereine—a dream location near the theaters—to surprise me. The afternoon he obtained the keys, we toured my new home.

"You'll need to hire a gardener, a cook, and a servant or two if you plan to host a soiree with proper company." Paul's baritone voice echoed in the empty underground kitchen. We mounted the stairs to the first floor. I peered through the salon window at the carriage house. "And a footman for the coach."

My own coach. *Quel luxe!*

"I'm not sure how I'll afford them all."

"I can help, but it would be best if you found another source of income."

"Of course. I'm so grateful for everything, darling." I stood on the tips of my toes and kissed him. "I can't thank you enough for Fanny's appointment with your painter. And Marie-Françoise is quite comfortable with the money you gave her."

"I can't say no to you." He smiled, his eyes shining. "Have you considered dealing in business? With your contacts and the way you manage people—"

I pulled away from him, eyes wide with feigned innocence. "The way I manage people? I am empathetic. That is all."

"Come, Rose. Do you think I'm a fool? You say just the right thing to get your way. And I am a victim of your charm." He kissed me harder, and on the mouth.

I had caught him in my web, but I knew he could escape whenever he chose. Unease niggled in the pit of my stomach.

I changed the subject. "What type of business?"

We continued through the house and out the front door. The late afternoon sun threw long shadows onto the drive.

"Military supplies." He had made his fortune, in part, selling supplies to the revolutionary armies. "I know a few gentlemen looking for a middleman. You would be perfect."

"I do enjoy negotiating." An income was precisely what I needed to keep up with my bills, to support a larger staff in my new house.

The footman held the coach door open. I nodded my thanks and chose a seat inside.

"I'll secure a meeting. You can go from there," he said.

"When do I begin?"

I met with Citizen Ouvrard and several other bankers the following evening. They connected me with others and by the end of the week, I had secured my first contract. As one of the few women, I had everyone's attention, earning more money on my first sale than most. I spent the sum in a hurry; a new home required furnishings.

I lavished the salon in sky blue silk and sheer muslin, a veneered mahogany table, and the harp I had longed to play since quitting Désirée's home. My attention to detail created the illusion of wealth. One must always look the part.

As the last of the architects packed their supplies to depart for the day, the post arrived. Lazare's blocky handwriting stood out on the envelope, erect and formal, like his posture.

My stomach flipped. The scent of Lazare's skin, the softness of his touch, had not faded from memory, despite my liaison with Paul. I prayed with each of his letters he would tell me he had divorced.

I opened the missive with care.

15 Messidor III

Chère Rose,

How are you, amour? Eugène is well. He excels at horsemanship and has garnered the respect of every soldier he meets. What a gallant, intelligent young man he has become. You should be proud of how well you have raised him.

I have missed you these last months. I think of you every time I look at Eugène.

I look forward to our reunion this winter when I return.

I have heard you've made new friends in Paris. I hope you do not succumb to their greed and questionable morals. Paul Barras is lacking in character.

I worry your sweet nature may be compromised. Not all have your best interests at heart.

In truth, I write to you with news, dearest Rose. I wanted you to be the first to know—I am going to be a father! Adelaide is expecting our first child. I can share your joy as a parent, at last.

I hope you are well. I look forward to taking you in my arms.

Je t'embrasse.

Lazare

His words squeezed my heart like a vise. Adelaide pregnant? Of course he would have a child with his wife. He loved her. And he would never leave her for me.

I laid my head against the windowpane and wept. Sudden fatigue seeped into my bones. I was so tired of the pretenses. It seemed I would never find safety, financial freedom, love to fill the gaping hole within.

I sent for Eugène. I couldn't accept Lazare's aid any longer, or hold on to a dream that would never be. Within a week, I enrolled my son at McDermott Academy, a prestigious military school. I pushed Lazare from my mind and threw myself into the merriment around me, eager to forget.

One afternoon in the month of Fructidor, before the leaves began to change, Theresia and I attended a painting exhibition chez Barras for Citizen Isabey. I hoped Paul's guests might purchase a piece to support my artist friend.

I weaved through the beautiful tableaux in my lemon yellow gown, chatting with acquaintances. I had yet to speak to Paul. He had been flirting with a pretty brunette from the moment I arrived.

Malaise roiled in my stomach. His invitations had ebbed in the past two weeks. I did not love him as more than a dear friend, but still, his easy dismissal of our relationship stung. Dread crept along my spine. I would be alone very soon, made to start again.

I watched a cluster of gentlemen near a refreshment table. I had met each of them at some point. I sighed. One was a braggart, the other always drunk. A third, I thought, would like me to be his mother. I shuddered. No thank you.

I moved to find Theresia. She stood in a bath of sunlight streaming through a window, angelic in her beauty, her pale blue gown a piece of fallen sky. The soldier with whom she spoke appeared awestruck. He scratched his neck nervously every few seconds.

I wrinkled my nose. Who was that?

The gentleman was disheveled with greasy hair, and his soiled uniform fit him poorly.

Theresia laughed at something he said. She dismissed him with a wave of her hand and he trudged to the doors in a huff.

She took a glass of champagne from a silver tray and linked her arm through mine. "There you are," she said, as though she had been searching for me all afternoon.

"Who was that man?"

"The general?" She laughed again and tossed her head. "He asked me to accompany him to a dance later. Imagine dancing with that cretin! I couldn't help but laugh. I told him I had far more interesting things to do. He didn't seem happy, did he?"

"Shame on you." I led her across the room to a painting I had admired twice before. "You could have feigned interest to spare his feelings."

She rolled her eyes. "He looked as if he hasn't bathed in weeks."

I giggled. "Still, you could have been kinder."

"At least he won't ask me again."

"Certainly not." We stopped before a self-portrait of Isabey with his daughter, one of my favorites. "I haven't spoken to Paul all evening. I fear he is taken with the brunette."

"Darling, he's always chasing someone. Perhaps you should move on."

I studied the little girl's dress in the painting. "Marvelous, the way he paints fabric. See how the folds in her frock catch the light? They look soft."

"Stunning."

"Perhaps I should find a husband."

"You don't mean that." She leaned closer to examine the strokes. "You adore your freedom."

"I'm not sure what I adore any longer."

Crisp autumn air blew in as the month turned to Vendémiaire, but the falling temperatures did not cool the rumors. The country was bankrupt and Royalists would invade to restore the crown. Riots broke out in the streets. Many friends whispered of hopes for the monarch's return.

I hoped Barras would quell the disorder.

I sat writing letters to the children when the sound of an approaching carriage floated through the open window. Someone had come? I sprang from my seat and peered out. The setting sun poured amber light over the lawn.

Paul's coach pulled into the drive. He had not visited me for weeks. Relief and uncertainty swept through me. I hoped nothing was wrong.

"Mimi," I called, "put on tea and prepare some refreshments. Barras is here."

Mimi put down her feather duster. "Should I set a place for supper?"

"I will let you know."

Paul's footsteps thundered through the front hall. I rushed to greet him.

"It is good to see you, *mon ami*." We kissed on either cheek. "Would you care for a cup of tea?"

"I could use a jolt." He set his pistol and sword on a table with a clunk. "I haven't slept for days."

We sat in the salon as Mimi placed a tray stacked with galettes and quiche before us.

"What's happened?" I selected a *sablé*. The buttery cookie crumbled in my hand and onto my lap. I brushed at the crumbs.

Paul dug into a slice of quiche. "Royalists plan to overthrow the government in two days. They've surrounded the Tuileries. I've commissioned a general to take matters into his hands."

"So the rumors are true? There will be more riots?"

"I believe so. I came to warn you. Leave Paris. Go to Croissy or Fontainebleau. I'll send you word when it's safe to return." He popped an entire *sablé* into his mouth.

"I'll pick up Eugène tonight and leave first thing in the morning." I had witnessed enough bloodshed to last a lifetime.

Eugène and I stayed with Désirée and the Marquis in Fontainebleau. Six days later a letter arrived from Barras.

> 12 Vendémiaire III
>
> Chère Rose,
>
> All is well. The Assembly survives, the Republic lives! Several hundred men were lost, but the message was sent—the Republic will triumph. You may return when you choose, but I would be honored for you to accompany me to a celebration at the Palais du Luxembourg septidi next, honoring my new protégé and nominated head of the Army of the Interior.
>
> General Vendémiaire we call him.
>
> I hope you will join me.
>
> Je t'embrasse,
>
> Paul

A shift was at hand. For Barras to appoint a new general-in-chief and throw him a celebration meant the man was important, indeed. I would attend in all my finery—to connect with Barras's new right-hand man, to secure my influence from all sides.

The new general might prove useful.

The Curious General

Rue Chantereine, 1795–1796

"I have someone I would like you to meet," Barras said on the night of his celebration.

"Who would that be?" I asked innocently, nibbling a petit four—delicious, sugar-coated perfection.

"My star general. He's a bit unsightly and aggressive, but purposeful. Someone you should know. Perhaps you could teach him some manners."

"Manners? Goodness, that doesn't sound good. Is this the general that has everyone worked into a frenzy?" I asked, looking down at my frock. If my dress did not win the general over, he wasn't male. I'd had it designed after a painting of Venus, the Roman goddess of love. Folds of pale blue muslin fell from my décolletage and an opening in the bodice revealed the dewy skin of my right thigh, visible through sheer stockings. Silver-strapped sandals wrapped my ankles and calves, and a delicate wreath of flowers decorated the curls piled high on my head. Theresia mirrored my style in pale green. A handful of guests had clapped when we arrived. We laughed and swished across the dance floor like nymphs.

Barras led me through the room. "Yes, and he's my new appointed head of the Army of Italy and the Army of the Interior. I find him . . . amusing."

"How so?"

"You will see."

As we approached the general, my hand flew to my mouth. This man? It was the same bedraggled soldier whom Theresia had spurned and mocked. He could not be the hero of the Republic!

His uniform engulfed his meager frame. His scuffed boots had lost their shine. Unkempt brown hair hung over his collar and looked as if it had not been washed in weeks. As Theresia had said, it appeared the general did not practice hygiene.

I looked at Barras for assurance. He nodded. I recoiled inwardly. What an ungainly man—hero or no.

"*Bonsoir*, Bonaparte," Barras said, shaking his hand.

The general stood a little straighter. "Good evening." He spoke with an Italian accent.

"May I present to you, the widow Rose de Beauharnais."

"*Citoyenne.*" Bonaparte bowed his head, gripping his brandy glass a little tighter. His fingers turned red, then white.

I waved my white silk fan. "General Bonaparte, how very nice to meet you."

The general said nothing. His blue-gray eyes appeared cold and flat like cobblestones. No warmth emanated from his person, yet his intensity was distinctly noticeable.

I smiled to ease the tension. "You've accomplished an amazing feat. Extinguishing the violence and commanding a group of rebels. Paris rests easy tonight knowing our safety is in your hands."

"It *was* amazing. Tactical, really," he answered through tight lips.

My smile froze on my face. Unkempt and arrogant. What a man! Such a combination would not endear him to the exalted company he sought, not for long.

He stared straight ahead and said nothing more.

Barras laughed and clapped him on the back. "I like your self-confidence, man."

General Bonaparte didn't smile or answer.

Paul swigged from his glass and said, "If you two will excuse me, I need to speak with Monsieur Ouvrard." He left in a rush.

I would scold him for leaving me with this man. I cleared my throat. "You must have some intriguing stories, as a soldier and hero."

"Of course." His eyes roved over my frame.

A loud clanging—the dinner announcement—interrupted our pitiful attempt at conversation.

I touched his arm gently. "I am meeting a few of my lady friends. Perhaps we can chat later?"

"All right," he said, staring at my gloved hand.

"Wonderful to meet you, general. Good evening."

Bonaparte bowed and made his way toward Barras.

I rushed in the opposite direction. What a relief to be rid of him, the odd little man.

Escaping the general was not easy. His unnerving eyes followed me the remainder of the evening. After much dancing, I glistened with perspiration and sought the courtyard for fresh air. Couples sat along the outer rings of the garden, locked in embraces or engrossed in conversation.

I ran my fingers along the cool surface of the fountain. Amazing detail, the way the artist had made the marble appear fluid, lustrous. I peered into its pool at my reflection. My gown shimmered like an apparition in the moonlight.

I turned at the sound of footsteps.

General Bonaparte. His eyes sparkled, hard as diamonds in their hollowed sockets, and his long nose protruded from his bony face. He studied me from head to toe as if memorizing every detail.

"You've enjoyed dancing this evening, Citoyenne de Beauharnais."

He had manners after all.

"I love to dance. Don't you, general?"

He stiffened. "I don't partake in activities that make me look a fool. I'm a soldier. My dance is on the battlefield."

"That's a shame. Women love to dance." I gave him a flirtatious smile. A cool breeze made the hair on my arms stand on end.

"Indeed." He stared through the thin material of my dress.

"A lovely evening." I looked up at the moonlit sky.

Bonaparte took my hand in his.

"General?" I startled at his touch.

"May I read your palm?" He began to stroke it. "I'm well versed in reading fortunes."

"You?" I laughed. "I would have never guessed. You're so . . . guarded."

"I'm from Corsica. We take palm reading very seriously."

"As do I." I grinned, amused by his brazen behavior. "What does my future hold?"

He pulled my hand closer. His hot breath tickled my skin while he traced the lines with his finger. After a short study, he froze, then dropped my hand as if it were a poisonous snake.

I laughed. "Goodness, what do you see?"

His face paled. "*Mi perdoni* . . . I must go." He turned on his heel and fled. Without a backward glance or a word to anyone, he escaped into the night.

The general's behavior fascinated me. I couldn't imagine what had upset him. It was my palm, after all. When I told Barras, he said I would grow used to the general's unusual mannerisms, maybe even grow to like him.

I doubted that.

The next time I saw Bonaparte, I visited him of my own volition. He had ordered the surrender of all unauthorized arms in the city to prevent further tumult after the recent coup—without exceptions.

Eugène became enraged.

"I won't surrender Papa's sword! It's my inheritance. I have nothing else left of him!" He balled his hands into fists and paced our small salon. The wood floor groaned beneath him.

"I know it's upsetting, darling, but you can't disobey." I envisioned my adolescent son standing before the Committee of Public Safety. I shivered. "You *must.*"

Pain filled his eyes, a dagger to my heart. How I grieved to see him distraught for the love of his father.

"But Maman," he pleaded, "you know many ministers on the committee. Isn't there someone who owes you a favor?"

My son knew his mother well. I made sure others owed me as I owed them. I moved to the front window. Passersby hustled along the street in the dismal weather, their hats brimming with rainwater.

"I've already asked Barras," I said. "It was out of his hands. The general-in-chief—" I stopped midsentence. "The general-in-chief is Bonaparte!"

"Who's Bonaparte?" Eugène asked. He ran his hand along the intricate scabbard. One could not help but be impressed by its brass etchings.

"The general who gave the order. He might be persuaded with the right prompting. Put on your nicest uniform. Polish your boots. We'll go this afternoon."

Bonaparte sat at his desk, head bent. The vast ceilings and immense windows dwarfed his already small frame. Surprise registered on his features as I closed the door behind us. He dropped his quill pen on a map labeled "Italian States." Several books lay open around it and papers cluttered his tabletop.

"How the devil can you read?" I peered at him in the semidarkness. "Have you no oil for your lamps?"

"Citoyenne de Beauharnais." He jumped to his feet, ears turning as red as the collar of his jacket. "What brings you here?"

I eyed his new uniform. What a difference clothes made.

"May I present my son, Eugène de Beauharnais. Eugène, General Bonaparte."

"Pleased to make your acquaintance, general." Eugène saluted, then returned a possessive hand to his sword.

"What brings you here on such a dreary day?" He flitted from lamp to lamp, lighting them in haste. The vaulted ceilings appeared less cavernous as light cheered the ambience.

"We received some very distressing news—"

"Excuse me, Maman," Eugène interrupted me. "General, if I may?"

Bonaparte nodded.

My son squared his shoulders and puffed out his chest. "You've commanded the surrender of all weapons. I do not wish to refute your order, but I came to plead my case. My sword belonged to my father, a Patriot and soldier like you. He was unjustly imprisoned and executed for crimes he did not commit."

Eugène exhaled a ragged breath to control his emotion. "All I have . . ." He swallowed. "All that remains of him, of his honor, is his sword. I will become a soldier soon myself, and it would be a great honor to carry it. Please, general—"

Bonaparte held up a hand to stop him. Eugène bristled, bracing for a rebuff. "Young man, you may keep your father's sword."

Eugène exhaled a breath and bowed his dark head. "Thank you, general. I'll be forever grateful."

Pride swelled in my chest. My son had grown into a man.

Bonaparte's rigid frame relaxed. His eyes softened. "You're welcome."

"*Chéri*," I said to Eugène, "would you step into the hall for a moment? I'd like to speak to the general. Alone."

"Of course, Maman. General." He replaced his hat and saluted Bonaparte, palm forward.

When the door closed, I eliminated the distance between us until only the corner of the desk remained. "You can't imagine what that sword means to him. Or what it means to me that you allowed him to keep it. Thank you."

Bonaparte cleared his throat and shifted his posture. "He's a passionate young man. He'll make a fine soldier."

"He longs for that day. I only hope he may be as inspiring a soldier as you are," I said.

A smirk lifted the corners of his lips. "Perhaps one day."

At least he had attempted a smile. "I presume I'll see you this evening at the theater?"

Sudden excitement lit his features. "I look forward to it."

"Good afternoon, general."

His gaze bore into me as keenly as a knife. "Good afternoon."

The evening's comedy ensured a packed theater, as did the exceptional players Julie Carreau and Joseph Talma. I unfolded my lorgnette and tried to forget the young brunette at my side. Barras had invited the beauty to join us. I had never accompanied him to an event with another woman, other than Theresia. Jealousy pricked under my skin. It was only a matter of time until Barras discarded me entirely, unless I discarded him first.

I leaned forward to escape the fog of lilac perfume surrounding my competition. I didn't envy her beauty, nor even her hold on Barras. I longed for her carefree youth, her ceaseless options. But I had my own options. Many suitors waited for the day I left Barras's side, I reassured myself.

My eyes raked the crowded room before the curtains opened. I knew many in the audience: Citizeness Hamelin and her husband, a few others from the ministries, and, of course, Citizen Ouvrard and Theresia. I smiled. Theresia had admitted her interest in the handsome banker only the night before. She moved quickly.

A player drew the curtains. The crowd hushed. The only light blazed from the lamps illuminating the stage.

General Bonaparte shuffled onto our balcony and plunked down beside Barras just as the play began.

He leaned forward to catch my eye. A slow, magnificent smile spread across his face, transforming his features.

Dieu, how handsome he was when he smiled. I could not help but return one.

He tilted his head in a polite bow and returned his eyes to the stage.

I sneaked glances at Bonaparte throughout the show. He didn't seem the theater type, yet he appeared entranced by the stage. The general appeared entranced by anything he admired.

After the show, our party made its way to the Hôtel de Richelieu for dinner and dancing. A bustling throng greeted us when we arrived.

"General Vendémiaire!" many men shouted.

Bonaparte puffed his chest slightly and Barras clapped him on the back. "Still the hero." Paul's sardonic smile played on his lips. "We have business to tend to. We'll meet with you later."

"I have business myself," I said. "Save me a dance, Paul." I waved coyly and walked in the opposite direction. Always business, even in the midst of our diversions, but I had several military contracts to solidify.

After two hours had gone, curiosity gnawed at me. I wondered at Barras and Bonaparte's activities. They had been inseparable in recent days. I strolled through the room to find them, happening upon one of my favorite people, impossible to miss in a green silk gown and matching wig.

"Fanny!" I shouted over the raucous chatter. "I had no idea you would be here tonight." I kissed her with exuberance.

She held me in a fierce embrace. "You owe me a visit."

"I have missed you."

"You look ravishing." She eyed my high-waisted gown. "Pink suits you."

"I'm not the one who is ravishing tonight." I laughed. "You look like a wood fairy heralding the spring."

She cackled. "I couldn't resist the color. Why don't you come to my salon next week before everyone arrives?"

"Splendid. I have plenty of gossip to share."

"Speaking of gossip," she said, "have you met the general everyone is talking about? Such a meager little man. I don't see what all of the fuss is about."

I moved to avoid a threesome of men; two of them supported a staggering third, intoxicated, without a doubt. "He's strange, but he seems to be warming to me."

"I bet he is!" She laughed wickedly.

"I was just looking for Bonaparte and Barras. Have you seen them?"

"Isn't that him?" She tilted her head.

Bonaparte stood in the center of the adjacent room. A cluster of people surrounded him. I recognized the handsome Captain Junot, a financier, and four women I had met at other events. To my surprise, Bonaparte took one of the gentlemen's hands in his.

Palm reading. I laughed aloud. He was not so unlike me after all.

"What's amusing?" Fanny asked.

"He surprises me," I said, more to myself. I watched the people around him laugh. One of the women pushed to his side and put her hand in his.

"The general?" A mischievous smile crossed Fanny's face. "Maybe he'll read yours."

"I wonder what he would see in my palm?" I gave her my own wicked look. She needn't know he had read it already. "I will see you next week?"

"Yes, darling." We embraced. "Enjoy your evening. *À tout à l'heure.*" Fanny disappeared into the crowd.

I joined the others surrounding Bonaparte. "Are you enjoying your evening, general?"

He looked up from the woman's palm.

That smile again—it melted his hardened demeanor.

He dropped the woman's hand. "Pardon me, citizens. I have been waiting to make the acquaintance of Citoyenne de Beauharnais all evening." He placed my hand on his arm. "Shall we?"

A bold move when not invited.

I smiled. "*Bien sûr.*" We traversed the room. "You enjoy palm reading. But not mine?"

His jaw clenched. "I was at a loss for words that evening."

"You ran from the courtyard!" I laughed. "Did you see something dreadful? You've left me rather anxious over it."

"I was taken aback by its message." Bonaparte pulled out a chair for me to sit. "Our futures are intertwined. I'm not sure how, but our lines appear identical."

He took my hand in his and traced a line on my palm. "Here." He looked up, his eyes probing mine.

I laughed uneasily and motioned to a waiter for a glass of wine. My future could not be linked to this man's, except through Barras.

"You mock me?" He gazed at me in his brazen way.

"Of course not, general. I would be blessed to have our future paths cross." I rested my hand on his arm. "You're very accomplished. Your principles are inspiring."

He moved closer, his lips brushing my ear. "You flatter me. Why? You're the most desirable woman in the room. I can barely breathe next to you." He regarded my expression. "You're amused?"

"You've had too much champagne," I drawled, lids half-closed. He had become smitten with me in such a short time.

He kissed my hand softly, never losing eye contact. As if to possess me. "I know what I want," he said. "I always know what I want."

Suddenly uncomfortable, I pulled my hand from his grasp. "I've barely eaten today. Shall we see about some light fare?"

"If you'll allow me to accompany you, I'd be delighted."

I flirted with General Bonaparte another hour, then joined the dancing and forgot him altogether—until the end of the night, when he caught my eye. Desire burned on his countenance.

I waggled my fingers in a flirtatious wave and left him staring after me.

Barras encouraged my relationship with the general.

"The man is besotted with you." Paul stretched out on a *canapé*, thumbing through a book. Rarely had I seen him settle in to read. "He would court you. If you let him."

"Do I have a choice? He is already pursuing me." I rang for a servant. I needed coffee for such a conversation. Paul was hinting at our going separate ways.

"Can you blame him?" He gave me a wry smile. "He makes a good salary and he is ambitious. His wife will not want for much." He flipped through several pages. "The man has a peculiar understanding of human nature. Uncanny, even. But then, so do you, *mon amie*." He blew me a kiss.

"Do you mean to marry me off, Paul?" A servant set a tray on the nearby table. I chose a *petit* cup and added sugar.

"I only mean for you to be happy. And cared for." He sat up, swinging his legs to the floor. "I adore you, Rose, but we both know our attachment is little more than friendship."

I felt as if punched in the stomach. So that was it, then. I had been replaced. I stared at the floor in silence. I didn't know if I could bear it—another relationship without passion. I leaned back into my chair, weary, and closed my eyes.

Bonaparte's passion unnerved me. Yet I found myself spending more time with the general, fascinated by his distinct brand of magnetism. His gaze fastened upon my movements; he abandoned company in the middle of their speaking to leave a lingering kiss on my cheek or compliment my gown, to press my hands between his in a possessive gesture.

I grew to like him, despite his odd manners and sharp observations, or perhaps because of them. He amused me, though he could not control his tongue.

"Women have too much power in this city. In this country!" Bonaparte raved one evening during dinner at Paul's.

Citizeness Hamelin choked on a swig of wine. Paul's eyes bulged and a series of mouths fell open like gaping fish. Such provincial think-ing from the Corsican. I swigged from my glass to hide my smile.

"A woman wishes for something"—he waved his knife like a sword—"and she has it. She speaks her mind, places a dainty hand on a broad arm, and the man trips over his feet to do her bidding. Women blather on about nonsense and gossip too much about politics, an arena where they have little understanding." He dipped a chunk of crust into the cream sauce on his plate.

Silence fell over the table. Only the scraping of silver on china could be heard. He did not realize he was offending everyone in the room.

"You insinuate that neither I nor any other lady present has any-thing valuable to say." I couldn't help but goad him. "How positively primeval, general."

The tips of his ears flamed red. I smiled sweetly, then slipped a forkful of haricots verts into my mouth. Bonaparte turned the stem of his goblet between his thumb and forefinger, his agitation apparent.

"Your opinions should be shared at home," he said, "privately. With your husband. Women complicate situations and cloud a man's mind."

"Men are not ruled by their minds at all."

Everyone laughed.

The general's sallow complexion took on a rosy hue—from anger or embarrassment, I could not be sure.

"I don't deny a woman's influence or intelligence, but find it ridicu-lous they should have so much power. Madame de Staël, Theresia Cabarrus"—his brow furrowed—"they have no real business but to cause trouble."

I laughed again. "I won't tell them you said so."

It would do no good to mention the men I had swayed and the sums I had collected from my own business dealings; it would only inflame him. No matter. I would do as I pleased—my life was no busi-ness of his.

One winter evening, I threw a small soiree to welcome Hortense and Eugène home from school. I crushed them in my arms when they arrived, Eugène in his smart uniform and Hortense a blooming beauty in blue muslin. A mother suffered when separated from her children.

I spared no expense for the festivities. Our company included my closest friends: Theresia and Ouvrard; Marie-Françoise and her daughter, Désirée; Barras and General Junot; Fanny; and a handful of others. At the last moment, I invited General Bonaparte.

As guests trickled in, the hired pianist began to play. General Bonaparte arrived with an armful of gifts: flowers, ribbons for Hortense, and for Eugène a book of military strategy.

Eugène's countenance lit up as he read the title. "Thank you, general."

"*Merci*," Hortense said, clutching the small box to her chest.

"You're welcome." General Bonaparte leaned toward Hortense and tugged her earlobe.

"Ouch!" Her hand flew to her ear. "I beg your pardon, general. That hurt!"

He laughed, a sharp, uncomfortable sound, and slipped his hand inside his jacket in a nervous gesture.

I gave Hortense a stern look. My daughter had no trouble speaking her mind. I took Bonaparte's arm. "You were so thoughtful to bring us gifts. Would you care for a brandy?"

"Yes," he said, winking at my daughter.

"I hope you enjoy your evening." Hortense attempted to be polite, though disdain shone in her eyes. She turned on her heel and left to find Désirée.

Barras arrived moments later with Jolène, the same brunette from the theater. The sight of the two of them sent a tide of regret through me. I pushed it away and forced a smile.

"Welcome." I kissed their cheeks, then went in search of wine.

My head reeled. I had not been prepared to be so saddened to see them together. I looked over the rim of my glass and met Bonaparte's eyes. He patted Eugène on the back and walked toward me, a smile on his face.

I invited Bonaparte to escort me to Fanny's salon a week later. A band of her friends could not wait to meet Barras's protégé, the new general-in-chief to the Army of the Interior. Fanny insisted I bring him. My gracious friend hosted a simple affair, with Bonaparte at the center of attention. After dinner and music, the crowd dispersed. We hustled into our waiting coach to escape the cold.

The general sat as close to me as possible.

"I didn't see you all night," he said. "Did you enjoy yourself?"

He had, without doubt—his blue eyes sparkled in the dim light; his smile beamed. He was handsome when happy and well dressed.

I did not pull away, despite his proximity. "Fanny's parties are always entertaining. You were the star of the evening."

He swept aside an errant curl on my forehead. "My star could never shine as brightly as yours, sweet Rose."

I covered my mouth to hide my smile. Who knew Bonaparte could be so sentimental?

He tucked my hands in his. "Such tiny hands you have. So feminine and delicate." He stroked them for a moment.

I shifted in my seat, anxious at his display of affection. He held me with his gaze. I grew still as captured prey. Warmth spread beneath my skin.

"I have something important to say. I need you to just . . . think about it . . . to think before you answer." He shifted in his seat.

"Are you well?"

"Quite." He smiled again. "My darling . . . Barras doesn't love you. You're just another woman to him—one he will discard very soon, if he has not already."

Another winning comment from the general. I tried to pull my hands from his grasp, but he tightened his hold.

"Please. Let me finish." His voice became soft. "What I meant to say is, you're ravishing. Intelligent, graceful. I've never met a woman with finer breeding. And you possess . . . a sense of calm and quiet confidence." He kissed my palm. "Rose." He said my name as if a caress. "I am in love with you. Consumed! I can't eat or sleep. I dream of your long, lovely neck." He rubbed the small exposed patch of my neck. "Of your lips . . ." He traced my lips with his forefinger. "Of the swell of your breasts." He looked at my chest as if hoping to see through my winter cloak.

"Bonaparte." I swatted his hand hovering just above my bosom.

"You can't be in love with me." I moved to escape him, the vitality that emanated from him. To escape my drowning.

"You're not young anymore."

"Thank you for that." I glared. Exasperating man. He always managed to say the wrong thing.

He gripped my hand in his as if I might slip away. "You need a husband. Marry me! No man could love you as I do. *Amore mio*, make me the happiest man alive and become my wife."

My jaw dropped. I hadn't expected this. Admiration and longing, perhaps a proposition to be his lover—but a marriage proposal? I stared back at him in silence.

Marriage had not suited me well. I had given everything I had— and for what? I was left with nothing. Alexandre . . . I sucked in a sharp breath at his memory. Peace be with you, dear friend. I tore my eyes from Bonaparte's to hide my sudden emotion.

"You're sad." He ran a finger along my jaw.

I looked down. "Bonaparte—"

"I have enough love for the two of us. My star is rising. I'm respected and well connected. Your children will not want for anything as long as you live." He kissed my hand again. "And *je t'aime*."

I sat, unmoving, studying the intensity etched on his features. This man loved me.

"You don't have to answer now." He sat back in his seat. "But say you will consider the possibility."

A sensation, an instinct, rolled through me and clouded my vision. The hair on my arms stood on end. I shivered.

"Are you cold, my darling?" He wrapped me in his arms.

I could not ignore my intuition.

"A dark stranger without fortune," the priestess had said.

"Yes, Bonaparte. Yes, I will marry you."

Citoyenne Bonaparte

Paris, 1796

In truth, I thought of Bonaparte often—his strength, his sentimental side, and love of beauty. The way he observed everyone and seemed to know their hearts. How unlike my first husband he would be.

Still, I wrestled with doubt one afternoon in my salon. I shuffled a deck of cards absently.

I needn't settle for one man. I possessed my own influence with so many friends in the ministries. Many men pursued me and would support me, for a time. But how long would I be desirable at my advancing age of thirty-two? Bonaparte would bring security, a father figure for Hortense, and a mentor for Eugène. His status improved daily. Yet would I hold his attention? The others had slipped away. A familiar ache throbbed in my chest.

The apartment door slammed.

"Where are you, my lovely bride?" Bonaparte's voice boomed from the front hall.

"In the salon." I sighed and placed my cards on the table.

"Come to me," he bellowed as he entered.

I ignored his hand. "How was your meeting with Barras?"

"Later," he said firmly. He lifted me into his arms. Layers of petticoats fanned over his arm in a frilly display. A beatific smile crossed his face.

"Put me down." I laughed. "You're going to throw out your back."

"My wife will be carried! Worshipped!" He carried me up the winding staircase.

"I am not your wife."

Bonaparte stopped midstep and fixed me with a penetrating gaze. I squirmed under his keen stare until he pressed his lips on mine. My mouth softened against his, and his urgency rose.

Warmth flooded my belly.

After a feverish moment, he pulled back and we gasped for air.

"You *will* be my wife." He leapt up the remaining steps, swept me into the bedroom, and thrust me onto the vanity tabletop.

"Bonaparte!"

He silenced me with his lips. This time, he worked them softly.

He paused, holding me captive with his eyes. "I love you."

His trousers hit the floor with a thunk. I covered his mouth with mine as he lifted my dress and pawed at my undergarments. Moments later the hard length of him pushed against the sensitive skin of my thigh before sinking into my secret folds. I cried out, then wrapped myself around him.

"You're an angel." He held my face while he rocked me, possessing me. "My angel. I'll take care of you, *amore mio*. Always." He clutched me to him, thrusting faster.

I abandoned my fears, my doubts, losing myself in his heat.

Our pleasure exploded, one after the other.

My husband-to-be sagged against me for a moment. I melted into his arms as he carried me to the bed. He cradled me in his arms. How tender he could be.

"What's your full name, *mon amour*?"

"My full name? Why?"

He stroked my cheek. "I'm disgusted at the thought of another man touching you. I want to possess the true you, yet untouched. You will be reborn as Citoyenne Bonaparte."

"Marie-Josèphe-Rose de Tascher de La Pagerie de Beauharnais," I said.

"You're not a simple Rose." He clucked his tongue. "You will be Josephine. Josephine Bonaparte. Wife of a leader."

"Reborn . . ." With so many metamorphoses of my person, of my stations in this life, I did not mind another name, another layer of my womanhood. In fact, I relished the thought. "Yes . . . I like the sound of that. Josephine Bonaparte I will be. *Your* Josephine."

My own Josephine.

We didn't announce our engagement to anyone except Theresia, Barras, and Captain Junot, who worked under Bonaparte. I guessed Bonaparte feared telling his family, though I could not be sure. I had no need to proclaim my status to anyone—being independent suited me—particularly Hortense and Eugène. But they were not as sheltered as I had hoped.

One afternoon, I finished a letter to my dear Claire, still in Guadeloupe, while Hortense composed a song for a school recital.

She stopped playing abruptly and spun around to face me. "You aren't planning to marry him, are you?"

"Who, dear? Why did you stop playing?" I dipped my quill pen into its inkwell. "Your song is lovely."

"You can't avoid me, Maman," she said snidely. "You have been seeing General Bonaparte. Everyone talks about it."

"There is no need to be hateful." I rubbed a spot of ink on my fingers without meeting her eyes. "And who is everyone?"

"Désirée and Eugène. And Madame Campan asked me as well." Her face screwed into a look of disdain.

"And they are everyone?" I laid down my pen and folded the letter.

"I don't like him. I don't care if he gives me gifts. He yanked my ear! He's abrupt and forceful." Her voice shrilled in a whiny tone only an adolescent can master. "Eugène says he'll try to take Papa's place." She crossed her arms over her chest. "He would make a terrible father."

My temper flared. "No one will take your papa's place. It's true the general courts me. He has been nothing but gracious to us. You and your brother will show respect. Do you understand?" I could not bear to tell her the truth. Not yet.

Hortense looked at the floor and mumbled, "*Je comprends, Maman.*"

"Now, let's hear the rest of the piece you're composing. Thus far I adore it." I slipped the letter into its envelope. I would do what I thought best for the family. End of story.

Bonaparte and I spent most of our evenings in the company of Barras and his companions. My husband-to-be was still his protégé, after all. One night they debated the threat of war.

"Don't be a fool!" Bonaparte sloshed rum on his hand as he waved his arms about. "The Austrians have made advances for months. *With success.* They now control all of the eastern frontiers. Do we wait until they invade France? If we aren't prepared, they could destroy the Republican armies. Put a king back on the throne. How much do you value your head, Paul?"

Barras's face grew flustered. "General—"

I linked my arm through Paul's. "What Bonaparte means to say is that it's imperative the borders be fortified. There's no sense in putting the Republic at risk. What harm could there be in sending an army to protect what we have fought for?"

Barras looked from me to Bonaparte. We had become our own army.

"If you're so passionate," Paul said, "go to the Italian border to assess the situation. But you do not advance without my consent. Is that clear?"

Bonaparte nodded, a lock of his hair falling into his eyes. "I'll begin preparing at once."

I smiled sweetly. "If you will excuse me, gentlemen, I need to catch up with Theresia."

On a gusty spring day I prepared for my second wedding—a civil ceremony to take place in the Mayor's office, now located in the home of a former émigré. At seven in the evening, my notary, Citizen Calmelet, escorted me inside. We greeted my witnesses, Theresia, Barras, Tallien, and the Citizen Mayor.

"*Bonsoir, mes amis.*" I leaned my umbrella against the wall near the door. "Dreadful weather, isn't it?" A steady drizzle had commenced earlier in the day and I had been unable to shake my chill.

"Miserable." Theresia kissed me on either cheek in greeting.

"Bonaparte isn't here," Barras said. He turned his black stare on the man who would wed us. "Citizen Mayor, are you in possession of any brandy?"

"Of course." The large man retrieved a brass key from his pocket and unlocked a cabinet behind his desk. In a flash, the Mayor produced a pitcher and poured the rusty liquid into glasses.

We chatted while we waited for my bridegroom, shifting in our uncomfortable chairs.

An hour passed. No Bonaparte.

Light rain trickled down the windowpanes. Candles guttered in their tins. I played with my tricolor sash as the Mayor poured more brandy for Tallien and Barras. This time I accepted a glass.

Inside I fumed. Bonaparte had better have an explanation.

When another hour passed, the Mayor stood and put on his overcoat and hat. "Citizens, I must go. Pardon me"—he tipped his hat in my direction—"but it is late and I have not yet eaten. I'll leave my assistant in my stead."

Heat crept up my neck. "I apologize for his tardiness." I would give Bonaparte a tongue lashing for embarrassing me. To beg and plead with me to marry him and then leave me waiting! It was absurd.

When the grand clock on the mantel chimed ten, my anxiety grew. Surely he had not changed his mind?

Another quarter hour passed and Tallien stood to leave. "I regret, I must go. I'm sorry, Rose. It's time I returned to La Chaumière." Everyone stood, joining him, and began to put on their overcoats.

So that was it, then. Bonaparte had made a fool of me. I burned with barely controlled rage. "I'm sorry you all came for nothing."

Theresia put her arm about my shoulders. "How could you have known he would not show? The ingrate does not deserve you anyway."

Just then footsteps sounded in the hall and the door burst open. Bonaparte tore into the room, out of breath. "I'm here!" He ran a hand through his damp hair and looked about the room.

"Bonaparte! Where on earth have you been?" I crossed my arms over my chest. "We thought you weren't coming. The Mayor has already gone."

He strode across the room and held me against his chest. His rain-drenched coat soaked the front of my dress. "I'm sorry to keep you waiting. You know how busy I have been preparing for departure."

I pushed at his chest. "You're soaking me to the bone." He rubbed my shoulders to dispel my anger. Not likely. I glared at him.

"I would never miss my marriage to you, dear one."

"Good God, man, it's late. We had best get on with it," Barras boomed.

"You could have let us know, general." Theresia said, seething. "Contrary to the exalted opinion you have of yourself, the world does not await your every breath."

He gave Theresia a look that could freeze fire.

Tallien cleared his throat. "Shall we proceed?"

"Theresia's right," I said. "You could have sent a note."

"Please don't be angry with me." He tugged at my arms, unlacing them. "Can we just get on with this?"

The Mayor's assistant, silent through the entire scene, spoke up at last. "General, I'm afraid I have no authority to marry you. The licensed official has left."

Bonaparte grabbed him by the collar. "If he left us in your care that is authority enough. You will marry us at once!"

"As you wish." The man avoided Bonaparte's murderous visage.

Bonaparte shoved him with a violent thrust. The slight man stumbled backward, then straightened his jacket. Expelling a loud breath, he selected the proper manual from the desk and began to read in a pinched tone.

In a few short minutes, I was Rose de Beauharnais no longer.

Bonaparte kissed me tenderly. "I have more work to do, but I can work from home."

"You're going to work more tonight?" I asked, incredulous.

"I must." He kissed me again, on the forehead.

"Congratulations," Barras said stiffly.

"You'll visit this week, I hope," Tallien said to me.

"Of course, and thank you for waiting, gentlemen."

Barras and Tallien shuffled into the hall.

Theresia hugged me one last time before we followed the others.

"I hope you know what you're doing," she whispered in my ear.

Bonaparte sorted through the cloaks in search of mine.

I stood dumbfounded. Had I made a mistake? I looked back at her, panic twisting my stomach into knots.

"*Bonne chance, mon amie.*" She left in a cloud of lavender perfume.

Luck might have been precisely what I needed.

Notre Dame des Victoires

Palais du Luxembourg, 1796

The next morning, Bonaparte appeared more haggard than usual. Purple circles ringed his pale eyes and he shuffled as he walked. His uniform jacket looked a fright.

"You never came to bed." I patted the cushion beside me on the settee.

He dropped onto it with a thud. "I had last-minute details to finish."

"How long will you be gone?" I hoped it would be a few months. I cared for him, but his affection overwhelmed me. I still clung to my independence.

"It's difficult to say. I suspect six months to a year." He rubbed my hair, mussing it, then planted a wet kiss on my cheek.

"I expect you'll keep me informed of your whereabouts?"

"*Bien sûr.* But you will join me soon." His eyebrows formed a tightly knit arch. "Won't you?"

I fumbled with a tassel on the pillow behind his back. "I was hoping you'd return soon enough that I wouldn't have to travel."

He rubbed the sensitive skin on my wrists. "Six months is too long without my wife at my side."

I frowned. "You would have me join you in the fields? At war?"

"You will be safe at my side. I swear it. I would rather die than let anything happen to you." He swept his fingers over my breasts, then squeezed them as if choosing a ripened fruit. An embarrassed servant rushed from the room, duster in hand.

"Bonaparte, please. Not in front of the others."

A mischievous smile stretched across his face. "She has left." He leaned forward, placing his face in the middle of my décolletage.

I pulled away, annoyed. "I couldn't possibly come before the summer. I haven't told the children we are married. I need to find a place to live. And it's still winter in the Alps. You can't expect—"

"I'll send a fleet of men to escort you." He pulled me to him for a kiss and led me to the bedroom.

Bonaparte had been gone only a week when his letters began to arrive, one and sometimes two daily. He gushed admiration that bordered on worship, guarding none of his innermost sentiments. He smothered me with his need to possess me, even from afar. How glad I was to be in Paris, with days of travel between us.

One afternoon my playwright friend, Citizen Arnault, was practicing lines with Theresia and me, when one of Bonaparte's couriers arrived.

The sharp rapping at the door startled us. Arnault looked up from his script.

"We were just getting to the good part," Theresia said, a pout puckering her pretty face.

A soldier darted into the salon, slightly out of breath. Crusty blood covered the breast of his uniform jacket in a frightening display. Mud caked his boots and he smelled of horses. He appeared fresh from the battlefield.

"Pardon me for interrupting, Citoyenne Bonaparte," he said, removing his hat. It left a slight ring in his matted hair. "The general insisted I deliver his letter without delay. He instructed me to record your reaction when you had received it."

I took the letter from him. "Thank you, citizen. You may tell Bonaparte that my heart leapt with joy, that I cherish his loving words." No need to be unkind to my husband, even if this had become a daily ritual.

Theresia snorted.

"Citizen, would you like something to eat? Or a bath, perhaps?" I asked.

Theresia rolled her eyes. She lectured me on being too kind to those beneath me. I argued that no one was, that our stations could change in a flash.

"Merci, *citoyenne*, but I must go. The general awaits my return. Have you letters I might deliver to him?"

"Not today."

The man cringed visibly.

Bonaparte probably berated him when he returned empty-handed. Poor fellow. He was but a messenger.

"Wait a moment." I dashed up the staircase to my bedchamber, found a handkerchief, and sprayed it with lilac perfume. I returned to the salon and wrapped the cloth in a piece of parchment and ribbon.

"Here. Tell him there will be two letters with the next courier."

Relief crossed his features. "*Merci.* Have a good day, Citoyenne Bonaparte." He put on his hat and left as quickly as he had come.

"Well? Let's see what he has to say," Arnault said.

I smiled and opened the letter to read aloud.

Citizeness Bonaparte,

Not a day passes without my loving you, not a night but I hold you in my arms. I cannot drink a cup of tea without cursing the martial ambition that separates me from the soul of my life. Whether I am buried in business, or leading my troops, or inspecting my camps, my adorable Josephine fills my mind, takes up all my thoughts, and reigns alone in my heart. If I am torn from you with the swiftness of the rushing Rhône, it is that I may see you again the sooner. If I rise to work at midnight, it is to put forward by a few days my darling's arrival.

One day you will love me no more; tell me so, then I shall at least know how to deserve the misfortune. . . . Good-bye, my wife, my tormentor, my happiness, the hope and soul of my life, whom I love, whom I fear, the source of feelings which make me as gentle as Nature herself, and of impulses under which I am as catastrophic as a thunderbolt.

Forgive me, soul of my life. My mind is intent upon vast plans. My heart, utterly engrossed with you, has fears that make me miserable. . . . I am waiting for you to write.

Bonaparte

"He is a poet," Arnault said from his position by the fireplace. "A rather intense fellow, isn't he?"

"Perhaps too intense," I said. "He didn't mind that his sentiments weren't returned when we married."

"Well, 'soul of my life,'" Theresia said with a smirk, "shall we continue with our script or do you need time to write a response? Please, let the passion flow from your heart."

I tossed a pillow at her. "How could I possibly respond to such a letter?"

Despite my marriage, I remained a part of Barras's privileged circle of friends and deputies. As the unrest in the streets rose anew, they conspired for a change in leadership, a Directoire of five men, for the next year's elections—for any way to preserve the Republic. I thought it wise to elect a single man to lead the country, to silence those in favor of a returning king. The deputies did not agree.

One evening, I moved the lace curtain aside and watched a throng of picketers outside Barras's *palais*. "There are so many! At the Tuileries, too, darling. A change must come swiftly or they may revolt."

Paul struck a match and lit his cigar. He puffed on its end until it glowed orange like an angry eye in the dim light. "Bloody émigrés. Their return is upsetting the order we've established."

"They're grateful to be on French soil. I don't believe they threaten the Republic. Not now. To welcome them, to integrate them will only strengthen it. Make the divide less gaping." I adjusted my colorful scarf *à la Creole*, which wrapped my hair, and settled into a chair.

He tapped ashes into a dish and studied me in the brooding silence. "We elect our new leaders tomorrow. I've alerted the police. Keep your ears open. Inform me at the first hint of an uprising."

I leaned to kiss him on the cheek. "Not to worry. I am always listening, dear friend."

He winked and took another drag on his cigar. "That husband of yours has had luck in Italy. Parisians are elated by his victories."

"It seems so. Has he lost a battle yet?"

"Not that I am aware of. But he appears to be losing his battle for your attention."

I laughed. "I care for him as a friend, as my protector. Nothing more. He's a bit, well, dramatic. He sends me three letters per day! I wonder if he's been to battle at all."

Barras's laughter boomed.

"No matter how often I reply, he scolds me." I sighed in exasperation. "I assumed he would take a lover like every other soldier."

"Give him time. He'll take someone to his bed. Quell that desperate affection."

"The man who guts the Austrian army writes me poetry. A rather odd juxtaposition, don't you think? Sometimes I question his sanity."

I did not take on a new lover—until I met Lieutenant Hippolyte Charles at La Chaumière.

"Who is that?" I hid behind my fan and watched the soldier in a sky blue uniform mock the dancers. He twirled, then stumbled and fell to the floor. Everyone around him laughed.

"The hussar?" Theresia asked. "That's Lieutenant Charles. Have you not heard of him? He's . . . quite popular, shall we say." She motioned to a group of ladies watching him from the edge of the dance floor. "And comical, for certain."

The lieutenant jumped to his feet, dusted off his rear, and made his way around the room, slapping the backs of friends and winking at ladies. Every pair of eyes followed him. At last he stopped near Theresia and me and filled his glass with punch.

"Good evening, ladies." His dark eyes twinkled with mirth. "You're dazzling tonight. I, on the other hand, am hideous." He shielded his monkeylike face with his hand. "Please, look away. I wouldn't want to offend you."

A giggle bubbled in my throat.

He noted my amusement and smiled, his mustache turning up at the corners. "Would you care to dance?"

"Not unless you toss me to the floor." I tried to hide my smile.

His grin broadened.

"Suddenly I'm dying for fresh air." Theresia gave me a knowing look and left the lieutenant and me alone.

"Shall we dance, then?" The lieutenant offered his arm.

I slid my hand over his strong forearm. Suddenly I wished I weren't married.

In the lieutenant's arms I felt still young—despite the nine-year difference in age—alive and carefree, and the faintest hint of guilt. Bonaparte loved me. Would it crush him to see me in another's arms? I shrugged. I had to maintain my life, my independence, outside of Bonaparte. I knew his feelings wouldn't last. A man's affections always waned, and this time I would not play the fool.

One evening the lieutenant arranged to meet me at the Feydeau Theater, soon after we had become acquainted.

I disrupted the flow of the crowd as I pushed in the opposite direction toward the vestibule. Hippolyte was late. The show would start in a few moments. I stood on the tips of my toes to peer over the sea of feathered hats and male shoulders.

Where could he be? Perhaps he did not care for me after all. He had not shown for our last engagement.

"Gentlemen, ladies, please take your seats," a theater hand bellowed in the corridor. Disappointment dimmed my buoyant mood.

Just then, I spotted the lieutenant's dark head. I waved my fan above my head to gain his attention. A grin lit his face and my heart skittered in my chest.

"I thought you weren't coming." We exchanged kisses on either cheek. "How sad that would make me, lieutenant."

"I'm sure you would cry yourself to sleep if you missed my unsightly face."

I threw my head back and laughed. "No one makes me laugh as you do."

"And no one is as alluring as you, Madame Bonaparte." The title of Citizen had become less and less fashionable—and good riddance. Everyone detested it.

I slipped my arm through his. "Barras and Theresia are already seated."

A blonde in purple silk resplendent with diamonds gave Hippolyte a provocative look. I felt a stab of jealousy. Could she not see he was with me?

Hippolyte ignored her. He had grown used to the women who swarmed him, no doubt. "Shall we?"

We mounted the creaking staircase to our box. Just as I stepped through the doorway, applause erupted.

Hundreds of faces slowly turned toward our seats to stare—at me.

I blushed, then looked at Barras, puzzled. Paul shrugged. I fished my lorgnette from my mauve sequined handbag and looked toward the stage. A soldier with ragged boots presented two bloodstained standards. Flags of Milan and Venice.

"General Bonaparte has vanquished the Austrians!" the soldier shouted. "They have fled from our neighboring republic to the south. France destroys her enemies! Bonaparte liberates!"

Uproarious cheers shook the theater. "Long live Bonaparte! Long live our Lady of Victories!" the soldier chanted.

The cheering deafened.

I smiled and waved at the crowd, trying to appear at ease. My husband was a hero! Unexpected pride surged through me.

Bonaparte had been a proper choice of husband after all.

As spring passed, Bonaparte's letters became more urgent. I fabricated excuses to stay on in Paris, to delay my joining him at the war front, but he grew crazed.

Citizeness Bonaparte,

What art did you learn to captivate all my faculties, to absorb all my character into yourself? It is a devotion, dearest, which will end only with my life. "He lived for Josephine": There is my epitaph. I strive to be near you: I am nearly dead with desire for your presence. It is madness! I cannot realize that I am getting further and further away from you. So many regions and countries part us asunder! How long it will be before you read these characters, these imperfect utterances of a troubled heart of which you are queen! Ah! Wife that I adore. I cannot tell what lot awaits me; only that if it keeps me any longer away from you, it will be insupportable, beyond what bravery can bear. The mere thought that my Josephine may be unwell, or that she might be taken ill—above all, the cruel possibility that she may not love me as she did—wounds my heart, arrests my blood, and makes me so sad and despondent that I am robbed even of the courage of anger and despair. I cannot go on, dearest: My soul is so sad, my mind overburdened, my body tired out. Men bore me.

I could hate them all; for they separate me from my love.

My love to Eugène and Hortense. Good-bye, good-bye. I am going to bed alone. I shall sleep—without you by my side. Night after night I feel you in my arms. It is such a happy dream, but alas, it is not yourself.

Bonaparte

As the summer neared, I planned to confront the children. They must learn of my marriage sooner or later and I preferred they heard it from me. One warm weekend in the month of Floréal, they joined me at Grosbois. Barras had offered the use of his country château, though he remained in the city.

Our first afternoon together, Eugène, Hortense, and I boated on one of the ponds scattered throughout Paul's property. The incandescent glow of early summer settled over the water in a green-gold hue. A family of ducks paddled lazily off the far shore. The harmonious swishing of water lulled us as Eugène tugged on two long paddles, disturbing the fabric of lily pads.

I relaxed in the warm rays of sunlight while Hortense complained about a new girl in her class.

"She's so rude. She shares the cost of her gowns with everyone.

Can you imagine? No one speaks of such things!" She twirled her pink and white parasol in her palm as she spoke.

"Not everyone has been raised with proper etiquette, *mon amour*."

A fish flopped on its belly, creating a ripple in the placid water. Eugène stopped rowing to point. "Did you see the fish?"

"Yes," Hortense and I said in unison.

"Do you think it will eat bread?" Hortense asked.

"Perhaps," I said.

Hortense gave Eugène a crusty slab that we had brought to feed the ducks. They shredded their portions and tossed crumbs into the water. The fish did not surface, but a mama duck heralded her ducklings in our direction.

While they tossed bread overboard, I broached the dreaded topic. "I have something to tell you."

Eugène looked up from the honking ducks. "What is it?"

"You will not like it, but I made the decision for the good of the family."

Hortense stiffened. Eugène's expression became guarded.

"I have decided to . . . I have married General Bonaparte."

"You what?" Hortense demanded. "You *married* him?"

The ducks scattered frantically.

"How could you marry him without telling us?" Eugène started to stand and rocked the boat violently.

I clutched the sides of the boat, knocking a paddle into the water.

"Sit down, Eugène!" Hortense grabbed the corner of his jacket.

He plunked onto his seat and scooped the floating paddle back into the boat. Water dripped from its edges and soaked my shoe.

"I know you don't care for him," I said, "but give him a chance. Bonaparte is generous and thoughtful. He asks after you both in almost every letter he writes."

"Letter? Is he not in Paris?" Hortense asked.

"He's in Italy," Eugène replied, head lowered. "I heard a rumor at school that you were married, but I didn't believe it. I didn't believe you would keep it from your own children!"

"How could you not invite us?" Hortense said, pouting.

Regret washed over me. "It was a civil exchange of vows and paperwork. It all happened so quickly. It was late at night." Excuses tumbled from my lips as tears welled in Hortense's eyes. "I'm so sorry, darling."

I squeezed her hand. "I know you both disapprove, but you need to trust me. I know what is best for this family. You both need a father. Someone to look after your interests. Someone to take care of your mother." I attempted a smile.

"But he isn't even here, is he? He's in Italy," Eugène said. "How can he care for us from there?"

"He's in Italy for now. And I will be joining him."

A week later Barras signed my travel papers. I had to join Bonaparte. My husband's letters had reached a fever pitch and the Directoire feared the general might thwart the Italian campaign and desert his army to be at my side. But I was not yet ready to leave my beloved home. I did not want to go at all. Aunt Désirée and the Marquis were to be married, at last, as was Fanny's daughter, Marie. I would not miss the weddings, even if Bonaparte lost his mind.

One rainy afternoon I left Fanny and Marie with the dressmaker and stopped at the Palais du Luxembourg. Barras's office sat on the third floor overlooking the circular fountain in the courtyard.

"*Bonjour*, Rose. I mean, Josephine." Barras cocked his head to the side with a mocking smile.

"That's Lady of Victories to you," I scolded him with mock superiority.

"Pardon me." He stood from behind his desk and bowed.

I laughed.

"I'm glad you stopped in for a visit. We need to talk about your lieutenant." He walked toward me over his plush oriental rug.

"My lieutenant?" I asked, feigning innocence.

"You know very well of whom I speak." Barras put his hands on my shoulders. "You must be more careful in public with him, *mon amie*. You'll make your husband furious if word gets back to him. He's temperamental as it is."

"It is my business and mine alone."

The gold-plated clock on the wall chimed four metallic strokes.

"Everyone knows your business. You're the Lady of Victories, and your husband is a hero. Everyone is watching you. Joseph Bonaparte examines your every move. I'm certain he is filling his brother's ear with nonsense as it is."

I looked out his office windows. Manicured hedges lined the promenade and stone pots overflowed with geraniums. Despite the ominous sky, the garden was exquisite.

"Joseph dislikes me. He hardly speaks to me."

"He's no fool. He suspects you're betraying his brother. And let's face it. Corsican men aren't exactly . . . enlightened. You would be appalled at the things the Bonapartes say about your sex."

"I know what my husband says about women. But his opinions do not degrade my influence."

"It's important that he's assured of your love. He may risk dismissal, even desert his army to be near you. It could cause a scandal and a national crisis, for Christ's sake. Can't you at least write?"

I threw my hands in the air. "I do write. Every week. I will not spend my days doing nothing but writing letters. That's what he would have me do. I care for him a great deal, but he—"

"He's impetuous. But he has brought France more victories than any general in decades. The people adore him. Don't make him your enemy."

I watched men weave through the garden toward the entrance of the palace, umbrellas in hand. "I should end it."

"Yes, you should. And it's time you headed south. When the weddings have concluded, off to Italy you go."

"How can you send me to war?"

He rolled his eyes. "I've hired your lieutenant and Officer Junot to escort you. And I just received word today that Joseph is going as well."

"You've arranged this without my permission?" I asked, furious.

"You can't avoid Bonaparte any longer. It's time to be his wife."

The evening of departure, I had scarcely laid down my fork when Barras and Theresia led me to my waiting coach.

"We will miss you, _chérie._" Theresia kissed my cheeks. "I will visit as soon as I can."

I wiped my eyes. "I didn't bid my children farewell." I threw my arms around Theresia's tiny waist. "And I'll miss you. I'll miss Paris."

Barras pulled his silk handkerchief from his pocket and dabbed my face. "Write to them." He kissed the top of my head. "You'll be home before you know it." He held the carriage door open.

Fortuné barked from inside and leapt from Lieutenant Charles's lap onto a startled Joseph Bonaparte.

"Get off of me, you mangy rodent." Joseph pushed my dog to the floor and brushed at his trousers with a stormy expression.

"I beg your pardon, Monsieur Bonaparte." I scooped Fortuné into my arms and settled in a seat between Hippolyte and Officer Junot.

A cloud of despair engulfed me. I would be riding for days with this wretched man in the sweltering heat. At the end of the miserable journey, I must start my new life—as Bonaparte's wife. At least I cared for him.

Barras closed the door and waved.

"Farewell," I whispered to the window as I watched Paris slide away.

Italian Sojourn
Italian Principalities, 1796–1797

We did not rush to Milan, but stopped to rest for a day or two in the larger towns. I had little patience for long days of bumping over rocky terrain and pitted roads. Our carriage swayed past hectares of vineyards and olive groves, and over Alps that stabbed the sky with dagger peaks. The temperature grew warmer as we moved south.

Headaches blinded me for much of the trip. Joseph Bonaparte's constant complaints did not make the journey more pleasant. He squirmed and whined in discomfort, though his precise ailment eluded me. His sour temper irked Hippolyte and Officer Junot as well. I hid my annoyance, unlike my friends, for I did not want to give my brother-in-law a reason to dislike me.

"We're nearly there, brother." I patted his knee. "I will order tea and a hot bath for you immediately. Is there something else I can do to ease your discomfort?"

"No." He pulled away from my touch and scowled. "And I'll see to a bath myself. I don't need your assistance."

I prayed the other Bonapartes were more endearing.

When at last the Serbelloni palace gates appeared on the horizon, a collective sigh escaped our lips. Gleaming columns of pink and white marble reflected the fading sunlight in a rosy glow. The air smelled of citrus blossoms and dry earth, parched from the unyielding heat of midday. Militiamen and a bevy of servants stood at attention, poised for our arrival.

Bonaparte had done well. Still, it was no Palais du Luxembourg.

I slipped from the coach with all the grace I could muster after our trying journey. Hippolyte glanced at me with a resigned expression. Our trysts were at an end.

My husband burst from the palace and rushed to me, arms outstretched.

"My beloved!" He smashed me to his chest.

For an instant I could not breathe. "Bonaparte." A muffled laugh escaped my lips.

He pulled back to look at me. "How I have longed for this moment!" He wrapped one arm about my waist, pulling me to his lips for a passionate kiss in front of everyone.

I reddened. "You mustn't show such affection in public, *chéri*." I smiled to soften the reproach and took his offered arm.

He ignored my reprimand. "Why did it take you so long?"

"Many roads were blocked by Austrians. Your brother was ill, as was I, with constant headaches. We were forced to stop often."

He stroked my arms and traced his fingertip over the tops of my breasts.

"Bonaparte!" I glared at him. I looked at the others to see who had noticed.

Hippolyte pretended to admire the palace, while Joseph stared at the ground. Bonaparte laughed and scooped me into his arms, then twirled me around.

At the palace door he turned to the others. "Welcome, everyone. You'll be shown to your rooms for a respite. I expect to see you at the fete tonight to honor my dear Josephine."

Bonaparte did not let me rest. Every moment of the afternoon he cradled me, stroked my hair, or kissed me as if I might slip away. He decorated my body with jewels, impressed me with paintings, ancient Roman vases, and expensive furniture. The luxuries did not make up for the loss of Hortense and Eugène, my friends, or my home. How I wished my darlings had come. Still, I was strangely happy to see him.

For the evening festivities, I dressed in white gown, head scarf *à la Creole*, and bangles. Bonaparte insisted I wear one of several antique rings tucked into a velvet-lined jewelry box.

"Where did you find this?" I wiggled my finger so the gem caught the light. The circular ruby flashed an exuberant red.

"A prince sent it as a gift to the new ruler of Milan." He attached the last tassel to his uniform. "Me." He laughed with glee. His power thrilled him.

I fastened on a pair of matching ruby earrings. "Gorgeous."

"Not as gorgeous as you." He kissed me. "Are you ready?"

I nodded. Ready as I would ever be.

My husband led me through corridors filled with servants rushing to and from the kitchen, their hands laden with platters. Each stopped to bow as their new ruler passed.

Such a fuss for a man who is only a general in Paris. I smirked. He would be enraged to know I thought such a thing.

The rumble of voices grew as we approached the ballroom. The central room was magnificent, with low arced ceilings decorated with mosaics of heaven. Sculptures came alive from their footholds on the wall. I paused to study a naked male statue. The lines of his muscle looked as real as my own, his expression of anguish heartrending, and the curved etchings of his hair exquisite. I reached out to trace the contours of his neck.

"You'll have time to study them later, darling. Come." Bonaparte tugged me across the room.

French soldiers milled about in uniform. Italian noblemen pranced in their *culottes* and stockings, flowing coats, and wigs. The Italian women, though as lovely as Parisian ladies, wore the formal gowns we had abandoned ten years ago. I pitied them—laced, tied, and corseted within an inch of their lives, every patch of skin covered and hair powdered. Passé from head to toe. Theresia would be in hysterics at such a sight.

"I'd like you to meet my officers," Bonaparte said, dividing groups as we crossed the room.

A woman gasped at my style, eyebrows raised. Another waved her fan as if dying from heat.

How uncivil I must seem with bared arms, light fabric, and low neckline. I held my head high and smiled. I was their ruler's wife. I would wear what I wished.

The evening passed at a tortoise's pace, with no one of interest to talk to. I searched for Lieutenant Charles. I scanned the room again and again, but came upon only one face I knew: Bonaparte's. He teemed with pride and adoration, exuberant to have me in Milan. In the rare moments he drifted through the room without me, women swarmed his small frame. He seemed annoyed by their attention, always catching my eye to assure me of his devotion, unnecessary but endearing.

Everyone treated Bonaparte with deference and he accepted their praise as if born to lead. My awkward little general had grown, indeed.

When we were seated for supper there was still no sign of Hippolyte.

"I haven't seen the others." I dipped my spoon into the velvety soup in my bowl.

"My brother did not feel well. He's resting in his room. Officer Junot is here somewhere." Bonaparte craned his neck to look for him. "Are you offended my brother could not make it?"

"Not at all. He was quite miserable on the ride. I pitied him." And wished someone would whack him to shut him up.

"Serves him right. If he hadn't spent time in the company of French whores, his loins would not burn." Bonaparte slurped from his spoon.

I choked on my soup. So that was his source of discomfort.

"Bonaparte!" I smothered a giggle. "How can you say such a thing?"

"It's true. Lord knows what he contracted from them."

I leaned forward. "Shh. Someone may hear you. You don't want to humiliate him." I took a bite of bread. "And what of Lieutenant Charles?"

His spoon stopped in midair and he studied my expression. "He went on to headquarters in Brescia." Suspicion lit his eyes. "Were you hoping to see him this evening?"

My heart plummeted, but I could not show my disappointment. "That's too bad. He was interested in meeting a Milanese woman. He mentioned something about his grandmother being a beauty from Milan. Family tradition or some such nonsense," I lied.

"He'll have his chance with plenty of Italian women." He kissed me on the nose.

Bonaparte remained at the Serbelloni palace only two days before he returned to war. Without him or a single friend, I was consumed by loneliness. I wrote letters, strolled through the palace gardens, and admired the art Bonaparte had collected during his campaigns. The spoils of war. I shuddered to think of how he had attained the treasures he now possessed.

One evening as I dressed for dinner a clatter of grapeshot shattered the tranquil evening air. I rushed to my window to locate its source. Soldiers and courtiers scattered to the far corners of the garden or ducked behind topiaries.

I moved away from the window as another round blasted. Screams pierced the air.

Mon Dieu, were the Austrians here? I snatched my cloak and darted into the hall.

"Madame Bonaparte, we must leave at once." Officer Junot bounded up the marble staircase. "An Austrian brigade has surrounded the town."

War again. The stays of my chemise cut into my flesh. I leaned against the wall for support. Bonaparte wasn't here.

Junot cupped my shoulder. "Madame?"

"More violence." My pulse raced. "I don't know if I can bear it again."

"I will ensure your safety. Let's get you out of here—"

"No." I shook my head with vehemence. "I can't leave until I receive word from Bonaparte."

"Madame." He took me by the arm. "I insist. There are bodies in the street and the Mayor has been taken hostage. I cannot allow you to stay."

I freed my arm from his grasp. "You're as much a stranger to this country as I. You haven't the slightest idea where we should go. I'm not leaving without my husband's orders."

"I don't think that's wise." He ran a hand through his wavy blond hair in exasperation. "If the Austrians invade the palace—"

"Bonaparte will send for me. He would never abandon me."

Officer Junot dispatched a courier with a message to Bonaparte. I prayed the courier would arrive swiftly. If Bonaparte did not receive the message . . . I paced from bed to window and back again.

No—I would not think of it. He would send word.

I dressed in riding clothes and called my maid, Louise, to prepare my trunks. Ready to flee at any moment.

As the night wore on, the courier did not return. I lay awake in bed, fully dressed, cringing each time gunfire split the silence. Fortuné stood by the window, a rumble in his throat.

The clock sounded every hour, its brass clanging like cannon fire in the stillness. I started each time.

Bonaparte, where are you?

In the early morning hours I drifted into a fitful sleep. Almost at once, Louise pounded at my door.

"Madame Bonaparte! Madame!"

My eyes flew open. Fortuné yapped and sprang at the door. I threw back the duvet. "What is it?"

"It's from the general, madame." She held out a note, her hand shaking.

The heavy footsteps of bustling men echoed from the floor below. Officer Junot took the stairs by twos to meet us.

"We're to leave for Castelnuovo to meet Bonaparte immediately." I stuffed the letter in the pocket of my riding coat. "He sent his best cavalrymen to escort us."

"The Austrians are advancing," Officer Junot said. "Are you ready?"

I gathered Fortuné in my arms and stole into the violet dawn.

We rode in heavy silence. No one dared speak his fears aloud. Rotting bodies littered the streets: French dragoons, Austrians, Italians; their allegiance made no difference when they were dead.

I suppressed a wave of nausea and turned my focus to Fortuné. I fingered his leather collar and its silver bells. "I belong to Madame

Bonaparte," the tag read. I buried my face in his fur. Let us be safe, I prayed. Let me get to Bonaparte.

As we passed through the city gates, a spray of bullets ricocheted off the ground and nearby trees. I shrieked. The horses galloped at a frantic pace. The carriage teetered, throwing us against the interior wall. I gasped, clutching the leather riding strap that hung from the ceiling. Louise clasped my arm and began to cry.

"Shh, Louise," I said. "Be calm. Tears will not help us now."

"It's all right, ladies. We'll make it." Excitement shone in Junot's eyes.

Why did men love danger, the threat of violence and destruction? I would never understand. I peeked through the streaked window. We were passing a lake. Its glassy surface reflected the surrounding elms, evergreens, and beech trees, and a stream of smoke snaked from the top of the dense forest. White specks moved from behind the cover of the trees, first one, then a dozen, then more. Fortuné perched his front paws on the edge of the window and growled at the moving blobs. Gunfire crackled as the white specks moved closer.

Soldiers pointed guns directly at our coach.

"Austrians!" Junot pushed Louise and me to the cramped floor. "Stay down!"

A hailstorm of bullets rattled the coach. The frightened horses bolted. The carriage rolled. Louise screamed as she smashed into the wooden seat corner. The sharp edge gouged her cheek, opening a bloody gash.

"Louise!" Junot pressed his handkerchief to her cheek.

I looked at them together. So the rumors of their romance were true. He stroked her hair as he held her wound closed. Junot met my gaze. His eyes pleaded with me to guard their secret. An officer could not consort with a maid. I would confront this matter later.

An animal scream split the air. The coach became airborne. In an instant we collided with the ground.

The three of us lay in a heap, immobile. After a moment of shouting and confusion, the door creaked open.

A dragoon from our escort poked his head inside. "Everyone out! A horse is down. Junot, we need you to help unhitch it. Madame Bonaparte, come with me." He bent at the waist and held out his hands.

I grasped his sweaty palms and allowed him to lift me. Fortuné bounded out after me. Junot assisted Louise and we stood in the open, watching a flurry of soldiers shove the dead horse. The rest of our crew returned fire at the Austrians.

"Bonaparte . . ." I said, looking around wildly. "What—"

"Take this trench along the road," the dragoon shouted over the gunfire. "It travels southwest and leads to Castelnuovo. If we're separated, use the road to guide you."

My eyes widened in shock. "I am to walk alone?"

"You're a target in the carriage. At least until we make it around that bend." He pointed ahead.

"Shouldn't I wait here while you—"

Musket fire blasted from all sides. One of our men clutched his chest and dropped to his knees. He heaved for a horrifying moment and then fell to the ground. Scarlet blood seeped into the dusty earth beneath him.

A soldier shielded me with his body. "You must go!" He helped us into the deep trench alongside the road.

I stumbled forward, legs shaking. Fortuné sped ahead. Bullets whizzed overhead, splintering wood and bouncing off trees.

Louise sobbed so loudly, I became annoyed.

"Be brave!" I would not think of death. "More swiftly. Come." I dragged her by the hand.

"Y-Y-Yes, madame."

I looked back to check our convoy's progress and saw another man shot through. The soldier's body toppled from its horse and splayed grotesquely on the ground.

"Oh!" I stumbled and fell face-first in the ditch.

"Madame!" Louise screamed.

Another round of gunfire ricocheted around us.

I jumped to my feet, kicked off my heels, and ran. Perspiration poured down my back in the blazing Italian sun. A little farther and we would round the bend, out of sight of our attackers.

Bonaparte, I need you. I gulped one ragged breath after another.

The sound of galloping horses beat behind us. I dared not look.

"They're coming. Run, Louise!" I screamed.

She fell farther behind, still wailing.

I raced around the bend. My breath sputtered. Thundering hooves drew closer.

I wouldn't let them take me. Faster, faster, I chanted in my head. My lungs burned.

I screamed in terror as a horse rode up beside me.

"Madame Bonaparte!" a voice shouted. "Madame!" It was Junot's voice.

I halted abruptly, wheezing.

He stopped his horse and dismounted. He pulled me from the ditch, then Louise, who had sidled up behind me. "The Austrians aren't leaving their post by the lake."

"Thank God." I bent over, clutching my sides.

Our convoy rounded the bend. The coach stopped long enough for us to jump inside, and then raced away through the Tuscan countryside.

When we reached Castelnuovo, the sight of Bonaparte sent a flood of emotion into my throat. My husband, the man who loved me. My protector, my provider.

The man I . . . the man I loved.

I threw myself into his embrace. "I was so afraid! I couldn't leave without getting word from you. I . . ."

"Shh." He wiped my face and rocked me like a child. "You're safe. You did the right thing trusting your husband. I'll always protect you."

"Why didn't you come?" My anger flared suddenly.

"I couldn't, *amore mio*. This is our stronghold. If I had left, chaos would have ensued. It would have been impossible to ensure your safety. I sent my best men." He kissed my face a dozen times. "They'll pay for the fear they've caused you."

Junot, who had stood quietly during our reunion, cleared his throat. "General Bonaparte, we lost three men and a horse. I don't believe the Austrians will advance, but you should take note of their proximity."

"Thank you, officer." Bonaparte carried me inside.

In the following months we traveled from one town to the next, through an Italian winter and spring. I saw little of my husband. He would come and go, staying a few days and then joining his men in battle. He left me largely alone—amid the Italian nobles, wealthy merchants, and courtiers, but utterly alone. I distracted myself with military supply contracts. My credit became endless, a great perk for the wife of a famous general.

I developed the gardens of my ever-changing homes and promenaded through the grounds. In each town I purchased gifts for the children and Maman, pottery or paintings for Barras and Fanny, and fabrics for Theresia. So many beautiful things, such lovely vistas, and no one to share them with.

I yearned for Paris.

I invited friends from France, though the one I most longed to see never came; Theresia would not leave her place of power. Nor would she spend time in my husband's house. She had never liked him.

"He's an arrogant imbecile," she said.

She filled her letters with excuses. I tried not to begrudge her choice. In her place, I wasn't certain I would travel to Italy in the midst of war. But others less dear visited and I could not help but question her loyalty.

Bonaparte proved himself a good husband; he protected me, provided tuition for Hortense and Eugène, and indulged me with every luxury. When he was not in the fields, we lay tangled in the sheets. He whispered his ambitions and promised me the world. I valued his friendship more than I had ever expected.

One morning we sat on a balcony eating a breakfast of bread, cured ham, and coffee. The breezy spring day refreshed my mood and helped clear the fog of fatigue. Sleep had evaded me for days. Rumors of another invasion, of Barras's retreating power, and of unrest in Paris weighed on my mind.

"You look fatigued." Bonaparte took a bite of bread. Crispy flakes of crust rained on his cravat.

"You say the sweetest things." I frowned. "I didn't sleep well again. I have a terrible feeling." The blood drained from my face as the sentiment washed over me again. "I think we should leave Milan—today. I had another dream. The Austrians will invade."

He stopped chewing. "Tell me exactly what happened in your dream." He took my premonitions earnestly. "Every detail."

I relayed my nightmare and my recurring malaise.

"Call the maids. I'll see the convoy readied." He kissed my forehead and pushed back from the table.

I sighed with relief. How fortunate I was to have a husband who listened. Within the hour we galloped away from Milan.

Two hours after we settled at Brescia, Bonaparte received a dispatch.

"Milan has been surrounded by Austrian troops," he read. My husband's face paled. "My incomparable Josephine." He kissed me fiercely. "You are my lucky star! My perfect wife."

A vision of Hippolyte came to mind. Guilt sloshed like an oily pool in my stomach.

Perfect, indeed.

The Bonapartes
Mombello, Italy, 1797

O n the second day in the month of Messidor, my husband's family
arrived at sunset. Tangerine and pink, butter yellow and lavender streaked the sky. The palace marble glittered and the gardens burst
with violets and roses. Orange blossoms effused their delicious scent
into the air and olive groves dotted the hillside. Paradise, to be sure.

Surely the Bonapartes would be pleased with such splendor.

When their carriages pulled into the drive, my husband pulled me
from my card game. "They're here!"

I held my breath as the train of carriages stopped. I had tarried
over my new family's apartments, insisting on silk sheets and verbena
flowers. The cooks would prepare the freshest frutti di mare, pour
wines ripe with peaches and sunshine, and serve almond tarts and an-
ise treats. Nothing was too fine, too extravagant for my in-laws. I hoped
they would approve. I folded my hands to hide their shaking.

"Mamma," Bonaparte called to his mother as she descended. He
rushed to her side and kissed her on each cheek.

"Nabulione." She used his Italian name. She kissed him and
straightened her black lace gown. She had the posture of a nun and
looked as if she might strike anyone who disobeyed her. Odd she
should look so severe and still so beautiful.

"It is Napoléon now," he said in a sheepish tone.

"You aren't French and you never will be," she replied curtly. "This
pretense is foolish."

Bonaparte bowed his head.

I looked on in disbelief. His mother had toppled his confidence in an instant, as if he were a child.

Bonaparte straightened and offered her his arm. "Mamma, may I present my lovely wife, Josephine. *Mon amour*," he said to me, "Letizia Bonaparte."

Her piercing eyes roved over my frame. I had taken no chances and looked more conservative than usual in rose-colored silk with shortened sleeves and long gloves. I met her gaze evenly. I had been scrutinized a hundred times at the Luxembourg and elsewhere.

"Madame Bonaparte"—I kissed her cheeks—"I'm very pleased to meet you."

"I should have been invited to the wedding," she answered, her tone clipped and disapproving. She motioned to the house. "Look at this monstrosity. I see you have indulged our *Napoléon*." She stressed his name, voice thick with spite.

Now I knew where Bonaparte had learned his pitiful manners.

I forced a smile. "My husband chose the house himself. He thought it might please you to walk through the orchards in the morning. To be surrounded by the luxury you deserve, madame."

"I could not have said it better, darling." Bonaparte gave me an appreciative smile as the others fanned around us.

"Hello, dear brother." One of his sisters embraced him. "What a gorgeous place!" she gushed, blue eyes sparkling. She was the most beautiful of the Bonapartes—save her handsome mother.

"Josephine, this is Pauline."

She studied me with narrowed eyes. "They say I'm the prettiest. I see that is still true. Nice dress." She smirked.

My smile froze on my face. What had I done to deserve this instant hatred? She need not be so cruel. I would smother them with kindness.

"You are quite lovely, aren't you? Bonaparte did not do your beauty justice." My retort left her speechless.

Bonaparte introduced Caroline, Elise, and his second brother, Louis. Lucien would not be joining us, and Jérôme, the youngest, attended school with Eugène. Both would arrive within the week. A rush of warmth filled my body as I thought of my son. Time could not move swiftly enough.

The other Bonapartes were not as ungracious, though Caroline eyed me with contempt. Through it all, I smiled.

"I am sure you would like to refresh yourselves after the journey," I said. "We'll show you to your rooms. If there is anything I may do to make your visit pleasurable, do not hesitate to ask."

Not a single Bonaparte said a word of thanks.

The Bonapartes' insults only increased.

"Ladies do not show their skin," Letizia said, or "Modesty is becoming in a virtuous woman."

I tried to ignore her; she followed Old World rules, not those of our progressive Revolution.

Despite their ingratitude, I remained a doting daughter-in-law, devoted sister, and amorous wife. My generosity was considered an illustration of my spoiled, superfluous nature, or so I overheard Caroline tell Bonaparte.

One evening after supper, his sisters made certain I understood their sentiments. They stood within hearing distance.

"He spoils her. It's disgusting." Pauline scanned the crowded ballroom as if looking for someone. The room buzzed with activity. An orchestra sat in the farthest corner and Italians mingled among themselves, ignoring the French visitors. "*La vieille* is wearing another diamond necklace. It's ugly on her."

I stiffened. *La vieille*, indeed. Thirty-four was hardly an old maid. Indignation rose in my throat, but I did not move away. Part of me wanted to hear the rest. I studied one of my favorite paintings of the Italian countryside.

Caroline giggled. "*La vieille*. What a perfect name. Or better yet, *la puta*. I've heard she takes new lovers to bed every night."

I flushed in anger. I had taken a single lover since my marriage to their brother, and I had not seen him in months.

"Nabulione always had poor taste in women. It doesn't shock me that he chose the biggest tramp in Paris." Pauline gulped the rest of her wine.

My vision tinted red. As if that little tramp didn't fall for every man she met! Bonaparte had reprimanded Pauline for loose behavior at least four times since their arrival. I set my water glass down and left to find Eugène, who had arrived two nights before. Bonaparte's desperate yearning for love made sense—he came from a family of hateful, poor-mannered leeches.

Let them drown in their poison. I would not invest an inkling of feeling in them.

A fortnight later I hosted an elegant dinner for Eugène, a few friends visiting from Paris, and the others. We dined on the terrace under a string of blue and white lanterns. Children chased winking fireflies on the lawn, trapping them in a jar. The luminous insects did not exist in France, and we all delighted in their flashing bodies.

After a lengthy meal, our party chipped away at lemon ices. A delirious happiness settled over the militiamen. Bonaparte's army had finally vanquished the Austrians, driving them to surrender. A treaty would soon follow. All seemed possible for the Republic. We would return to France as victors, as leaders.

Though thrilled to be returning to Paris, I didn't join the merriment. Fortuné, my happy pug, had been chased and killed by the cook's dog the day before. By morning I had another puppy, but could not erase the image of Fortuné's broken body from my mind.

Caroline's callous comments worsened my mood.

"Really, Josephine. I can't understand why you're so upset. It was just a dog. You already have a new one." She sucked on a mouthful of sugared ice with a disgusting slurping noise.

"Fortuné did not deserve such cruel treatment." Neither did I.

Caroline glared at me. I gave her my back and turned to Eugène.

"Little bugger," he said. A firefly had landed in his ice. He flicked it and laughed at one of Bonaparte's comments.

I reminded myself that these were the people I loved and I was here for them.

At the end of the evening I fell into bed, weeping for my murdered dog, the pain of missing my daughter and friends, and the hate emanating from my in-laws. Minutes later, Bonaparte slammed the bedroom door behind him.

I sat up, startled.

His scowl faded when he noticed my tears. "What is it? What's wrong?" He dashed to my side and took me in his arms. "I hate to see you cry."

I sobbed into the warm skin of his neck. "Your sisters and mother hate me. My dog is d-dead. I miss Hortense." Saying her name brought a fresh wave of pain.

"*Amore mio.*" He cradled me in his embrace. "My family doesn't hate you. They disapprove of me marrying without their knowledge. They take it out on you." He stroked my face. "They can be unkind."

Unkind? I would call them vicious. I pulled from his embrace, suddenly angry. "Why do you not defend me?"

"I can't change their opinions, no matter what I say."

I threw back the covers and jumped to my feet. "You haven't even tried. The least you could do is silence them!" I stalked to the other side of the room, my fury mounting.

His expression grew stormy. "Don't raise your voice to me. I am your husband!"

"I will raise my voice when I please!" I shouted. My blood boiled. I detested his horrible family.

He cornered me and gripped my arms. "Not to me, you won't. If you ever—"

I wrenched free of his grasp. "You say you love me, yet you do nothing to protect my honor."

"I would sail to the stars for you!" he thundered. He took a calming breath and closed the distance between us. "I would reject them all. Give up everything for you." His voice softened. "Please, my love. Don't be angry. I know my family well. Be your adorable self. They will come around in time."

I had heard that before from Désirée. It had not worked out so well.

"*Je t'aime.*" He kissed my eyelids, my cheeks.

My anger dissolved. I would try to ignore them. For him. I allowed him to lead me to the bed.

As I slid under the covers, I remembered his slamming the door. "Why were you angry?"

"Pauline." Irritation clouded his eyes. "I caught her having sexual relations in the corridor with Jean LeClerc." His jaw clenched. "She behaves like a *puta*. I insisted LeClerc marry her at once to salvage what's left of her reputation."

I didn't tell him his sister's reputation was beyond repair. She did not deny the rumors of her many partners. When Caroline had confronted her, she laughed and mocked her sister as a prude.

"You did the right thing," I said. "She would be in far more trouble to find herself with child and no husband."

"That won't happen. They will marry next week. Here in Mombello. Can you assist with the preparations?"

"Of course, *chéri.*"

He leaned over me. "You are an angel. My lucky star. I don't know where I would be without you." He kissed me again.

In the end, I arranged marriages for not one, but two Bonaparte sisters.

I granted their every desire, yet neither said a word of thanks. My patience wore thin. I grew weary of the pretension with the Bonapartes and with the Italians at court. I loathed the plastered smiles and judgmental leering.

At the end of the month, when Letizia, Elise, and Caroline announced their departure, I nearly wept with relief. My leaving would soon follow, once Bonaparte solidified the peace treaty. I would take a tour in Venice—far from the remaining Bonaparte clan—and make my way home to France.

That evening, I lay in bed in the dark. Headaches had plagued me all afternoon.

"Josephine?" Bonaparte entered the room and set his lamp on a bedside table. "You've been in bed all day." He kicked off his shiny boots.

"I have a blinding headache." I turned down the covers next to me.

"It must be your guilty conscience." He thumped down into a chair and crossed his arms.

"What are you talking about?" I propped myself up on my pillow.

"You know very well what I'm talking about. That bastard lieutenant"—he gritted his teeth—"put his hands on you. On *my* wife!" He kicked the footstool.

I swallowed hard. He had heard about Hippolyte.

"What lieutenant?" I feigned innocence. "Bonaparte, really, what are you talking about? No one has had their hands on me but you."

Despair and uncertainty warred on his features. He dashed across the room and sat beside me on the bed. He gathered my hair in his hands with too much force.

"I will execute any man who so much as looks in your direction. Is that clear?"

I tensed against his grip. "Who told you such nonsense, darling?" I rubbed his cheek with my thumb. "You know I love only you."

"Joseph and Pauline."

"I've barely laid eyes on the lieutenant this whole year in Italy. You've seen him with his mistress many times. The beautiful Carlotta? Your siblings create falsehoods to ruin my reputation."

He released my hair behind my shoulders. It swished against my silk nightdress.

"Pauline has been known to lie. But why would Joseph fabricate a story to hurt his own brother?"

"My love"—I pressed his hand against my heart—"you saw how your siblings treated me. Don't you think others would have seen me with the lieutenant?"

His hand closed around my breast. He kissed me in a desperate way, as if searching for the truth.

When we parted, I said, "He means to turn you against me."

"Nothing and no one can turn me against you, my beloved."

Fallen Angel

Rue de la Victoire, Paris, 1797–1799

Bonaparte insisted on signing the peace treaty before we left for Paris, but his temper did not endear him to the Austrian negotiators.

I took to smoothing over his tantrums.

"Please forgive my husband's ill humor," I told the chief Austrian diplomat. "He awaits word from the Directoire and is anxious to proceed with the treaty. He detests wasting your time."

Bonaparte cared nothing about wasting his time. His tantrums were about having his way or none at all.

I motioned to a servant to pour more brandy.

"I only wish to reach a peaceful agreement," the Austrian said.

"I have full confidence in your abilities to negotiate." I laid my hand on his arm. "It will be grand to end the animosity between our countries! To be allies, and friends, monsieur." He blushed and fussed with his cravat.

"How lovely it is to see a proper cravat," I said. "The Italians don't seem to grasp the style of the day."

His blush deepened. "You flatter me, madame, but how right you are. The Italians are a rather archaic society, though the food is divine." He heaped his fork with braised fish. "You've done wonders with the grounds. I hear you are quite the horticulturalist."

He motioned to the vases of verbena and freesia.

"It's satisfying to nurture them and watch them grow into something beautiful." I dabbed my mouth with a napkin. "Quite like a friendship. Wouldn't you agree?"

We spoke for some time. All the while, Bonaparte made a show of his displeasure with the other officials. Had I not enjoyed a dance with the Austrian or shared his interest in flowers, the Republic's hopes of a truce would have collapsed.

Despite my obvious assistance, Bonaparte sulked before bed. "Women have no place in politics. You saw what happened. You reduced that man to a sniveling idiot."

"Don't be daft, my darling." I frowned. "That's precisely why I belonged there. Now you have your treaty." I slid under the covers.

He bounced onto the bed beside me. "You did manage him."

"I have my ways." I kissed him lightly on the brow.

He sat for several moments in silence, lost in thought. As I extinguished the lamp beside the bed, he said, "Perhaps I should bring you to more of my official dinners. You might be an asset."

"Indeed I would be."

He took me in his arms.

The Directoire's approval of the treaty came weeks into the autumn season, though Bonaparte took liberties with their demands. He left for Paris immediately, leaving me behind to conclude official appearances. I sighed with relief once safely on French soil.

But I had not been prepared for the greeting I received.

I stared out the coach window in utter amazement. Hundreds gathered in every village to hail the wife of their hero. Torches lit our passage and cannons boomed to announce our convoy.

I laughed aloud. Bonaparte's popularity had spread. How had this happened?

"*Vive* Bonaparte!" citizens cried. "Our Lady of Victories!"

I returned their waves. "Have you seen anything like it, Junot?"

"Not since Marie Antoinette made her royal progress." The captain gawked at the townspeople in the dark.

An uneasy sensation tingled in my limbs. "I am no queen."

He started at the tense tone of my voice. "Madame Bonaparte, do not fear. You are certainly not a queen."

We reached Paris two weeks later than expected. As we pulled into the drive of my lovely home, emotion surged through me. Home again. I jumped from the coach and skipped up the walk to find sentries guarding the door. Since when did we need guards?

"Yeyette!" Mimi greeted me.

I squeezed her with all my might. "How do you always smell of sunshine, Mimi?"

"Best not waste time. General Bonaparte is mighty anxious to see you. He's at the Palais du Luxembourg."

"It's Bonaparte's fault I am late. I had to stop in every town because of his supporters. The National Guard escorted us all the way to Paris." I removed my cloak. "I've missed you! Italy was lovely, but lonely. I've missed the children!"

Mimi tugged me toward the stairs. "Hortense will be here in the morning. Now, let's go. You're going to enrage that husband of yours."

"His temper doesn't frighten me." I dismissed her concerns with a wave. "I'll just take a quick tour. I've been dying to see the renovations."

She rolled her eyes. "I'm glad I won't be there. He's going to—"

"Never mind, Mimi." I breezed into the salon. Mahogany furniture filled the room, gold curtains draped the windows, and mosaics tiled the floors. The airy classical style had become passé. I climbed the stairs to my bedroom and pushed open the door.

I gasped. "I love it!"

A cascade of blue-and-white-striped fabrics fastened at a point in the ceiling, mimicking a soldier's tent. Several drum-shaped footstools circled the bed and a vanity and armoire sat on opposing walls.

A maid rushed in holding three gowns. "Madame, you must hurry. Which will you choose?"

I bathed, dressed in a white gown and gold hat in record time, and rushed to the soiree.

"Where have you been?" Bonaparte demanded when he first laid eyes on me. "Talleyrand spent a fortune to welcome you home. He has rescheduled it twice!" A vein in his neck began to pulse.

I caressed his chin with my finger and laced my arm through his. "Careful, *mon amour*. Everyone is watching. And we both know this fete is really to honor you." I smiled to make it appear as if we were sharing endearing words. "I arrived as soon as I could. Your admirers made the journey much longer than necessary. The French adore you."

The storm in his eyes cleared. "I'm glad you're home." He sighed and kissed my palms. "Can you believe this?" He nodded toward the grand ballroom crowded with guests.

Talleyrand had ordered evergreen garland, bells, red ribbon, and exquisite ice sculptures chiseled in the likeness of forest animals. In the adjacent room, several long tables were set with lacy cloths and dishes for a formal dinner.

"He did a wonderful job. I will tell him so when I see him." Bonaparte escorted me to a refreshment table. I accepted a crystal goblet of pink punch. "You do realize he is courting you? He plans to see you appointed as a deputy in the Directoire."

"Has Barras told you this?" He examined my expression.

"No, but he wrote to you every week while we were in Italy."

"You pay attention."

"Always." I sipped the sweet punch. "The farmers want a man with simple Republican values. The people grow restless for change."

Bonaparte surveyed the room for eavesdroppers. He leaned closer. "Change is what they will have. This will be our last banquet for a while. It's best to demonstrate that we don't confer with corrupted deputies. That we aren't greedy for power."

"Whatever you say, Bonaparte." I smiled.

My husband was proving to be more ambitious than I had expected.

I received Theresia and Barras at the rue de la Victoire or visited them at their homes, but made sure to stay out of the public eye. I worried about Bonaparte's neurosis, which increased with his popularity.

"The Directoire plans to assassinate me. They fear my power," he said one evening.

"Barras is a dear friend. Sending you to England is hardly a death sentence." I rubbed his shoulders while he hunched over his desk. He would depart in a week's time to assess the English ports for a possible invasion. It was a plan to protect our Republic.

"It removes me from Paris and takes me from my people." He motioned toward the window. A throng gathered each morning to chant his name or call for me, his "lady luck."

In truth, I looked forward to his absence. I might have a bit of peace. He wouldn't be gone long, at any rate—not enough time to miss him.

"Their adoration has not gone unnoticed," he said. "The ministers squirm in their beds at night."

I nodded. The near worship Parisians displayed for my husband threatened our unstable government. I could not help but worry, at least a little, about his welfare.

"Then perhaps it is best you are gone awhile," I said. "Let the Directoire regain their confidence. Meanwhile, secure as many victories as you can. The people will only love you more."

He turned from his stack of papers and whisked me into his lap. "*Je t'aime.*"

Before Bonaparte departed, I insisted we tour properties outside the city. The constant mass of well-wishers crowded me. A country home not far from Paris would be the perfect escape.

"Our haven," I told him. "Away from everyone. We could create our own amusements, bring the children. Invite our friends."

"I'll look with you, but I am in no position to spend a large sum."

We had toured several properties, but I knew the house I wanted on first sight: the lovely Malmaison. Its land extended across hectares of rolling hills and streams, several gardens, and a well-maintained vineyard. Farmers tended the land and lived off the meat, dairy, and grains. The château needed remodeling; the roof was in disrepair, the glass windows clouded, and the interior filthy from pigeons nesting in its rafters.

"It needs a bit of work," I said, "but it's perfect. Oh, Bonaparte, this is the one!"

"It's three hundred thousand francs!" He threw his arms in the air, sending the pigeons into a flurry of squawking feathers.

I ducked to avoid one that dived toward my head.

"I have yet to pay the one hundred thirty thousand for your remodeling," he continued. "Maybe one day, but certainly not now."

I stuck out my bottom lip. "Very well."

On our ride back to Paris, my mind whirred. I could use the sums from my contracts and borrow from Barras. I needed my own land, a real home. Malmaison would be mine.

While Bonaparte traveled, I settled into my routine. I visited Hortense and Eugène, met Fanny and Désirée. My military contracts boomed from my husband's war. His success had given me limitless credit, despite his ignorance of my dealings. I managed to save most of my earnings, with the vision of Malmaison fresh in my mind.

One evening I dined at Barras's country estate. After a meal of roasted duck, Barras and I played cards while Theresia entertained us at the pianoforte.

"Any news on the British?" I asked.

"Not yet." Paul threw down his hand of cards. "Bonaparte insists the best way to attack the British is in Egypt. Head off their route to India. But the Russians are there as well, and we'd risk war if we blockade their passage routes. The best way to get at the bastards is directly on English soil. But it's already been decided."

"What has been decided?" I collected his cards, shuffled the deck, and distributed two piles.

"Egypt." He snagged his cards from the table. "When Bonaparte returns from England, preparations will be made for a spring departure. Eugène will be his aide-de-camp and his brother Lucien will accompany them."

I went cold.

"Eugène? He's seventeen! He can't go to war!" The thought of someone pointing a gun at him made my heart stop. I groaned as another thought occurred to me. "Lucien will turn Bonaparte against me."

He patted my hand. "Maman, it is time to let your son be a man. Bonaparte will look after him. And Lucien is a snake, but he can't sway your husband's feelings. Napoléon loves you beyond reason. Near madness, I'd say."

A husband and son at war. Dread settled into my bones. Something would change. I could feel it.

When Bonaparte returned home from his travels, he pored over maps and history books as before, but traded English coastline for Egyptian desert. I had to tempt him from his study in the late hours each night.

I sat on the edge of his desk in a lacy nightdress.

"When are we leaving for Egypt? I need to make arrangements." I could not remain behind with so much at stake.

"You aren't going." He looked up from a blueprint. "At least not right away. It isn't safe."

I changed my tactic. "But how will I get on without you?"

"Wives don't come to battle, dear one." He stroked my thigh. "I will not put your life in jeopardy."

"But you will put my son in harm's way?" My bottom lip quivered for effect. "And you sent for me in Italy."

"This is different. Egypt will be an arduous journey over sea and land with few comforts, if any. No place for a woman." He pulled me onto his lap. "I will protect Eugène. But he has been well trained."

"He's thrilled to go." I brushed a lock of hair from his eyes. "Don't you need your good luck charm?"

"I'll bring your portrait. It will have to do for now. I'll send for you soon. If it's safe." He smoothed the lines on my forehead. "We'll be fine, *amore mio*. I swear it."

And in the clutches of your horrible brothers. Apprehension rose in my throat.

I could not bear to lose either of my men.

Within the month, we traveled south to Toulon. The morning of departure, I joined Bonaparte and Eugène on the dock. The southern sun glittered on the shifting cobalt waves. A crowd of onlookers massed in the streets to watch the horde of frigates bob in the bay. The warships expanded as far and wide as the horizon.

I stared at the fleet. How many would return with tattered sails, or not at all? I inhaled a gust of briny air to calm my nerves.

A horn blared. Soldiers scurried to their ships.

"It's time." Eugène kissed my cheeks. "You must let me go." He laughed his boyish laugh. I had clutched his arm all morning. "I'll be home soon. Don't worry."

"*Je t'aime.*" I smiled bravely to mask the pain. He skipped up the gangway. A last wave and my son's dark head disappeared amid the other soldiers. "Good-bye, son," I whispered, turning my face into Bonaparte's neck.

"I'll take good care of him." He rubbed my back. I pulled away to study his face. His usually pallid skin glowed and determination stamped his features. I straightened a button on his gray coat.

"My sweet Josephine." He caught my hands. "I long for the day I return to your arms. I love you. A thousand times I love you." He kissed me passionately in front of everyone. The crowd exploded in a chorus of cheers and applause. He smiled and waved at the onlookers.

"I must defend the honor of France," he added, projecting his voice. Another cheer erupted.

Sorrow welled inside me at the thought of him being in danger. "Please be careful! I couldn't bear it if . . . if . . ." I touched his lips with my fingertips.

"Do not be anxious. Write to me." He kissed me again.

My fearless husband slipped from my arms and climbed aboard.

I remained in Toulon for a few days to enjoy the salty air and to delay the detestable journey home. Yet despite the respite, my insides churned and prayers tumbled from my lips. I could not shake my dread.

Yes, keep Bonaparte, but my son—Lord, save my son.

By week's end, I had traveled north toward Plombières-les-Bains, a small town in the Vosges Mountains famous for its healing springs.

"The springs promote fertility," Bonaparte had said.

He didn't hide his desire for children. He caressed my abdomen each time we made love, willing it to bear him a baby. I, too, longed for a child. A baby would ward off the doubts of his rigid mother and secure an heir, should there need to be one.

Doctor Martinet, a famed physician, devised a routine of salts and herbal elixirs, scheduled bathing regimes, and exercises to stimulate my menses. I followed his orders as if they were my religion.

"My courses have been disrupted since prison," I complained to Madame de Krény. "It may be six months before I see it again."

She had joined me from Paris to soothe a pain in her ankles. She dangled her feet in a pool of scalding water. It bubbled and hissed as she splashed.

"I was hoping to be with child already," I said.

"Try not to despair. You are still of childbearing age."

I dispelled the rising steam around my face with my hand. "There's no sense in dwelling on it, I suppose. With my husband away."

Bonaparte wrote to me as promised. He depicted the ancient land as I had imagined it: blazing heat that made the horizon shimmer like copper, ancient structures weathered by time, merciless sand flies, and warring men in mismatched robes and headcloths. Thirst that made him ache. He detailed Eugène's impressive comportment on the battlefield and with his officers. Such a noble young man I had raised.

After several victories, Bonaparte asked me to join him. Relieved, I prepared my travel arrangements with haste. The afternoon before my leaving, I enjoyed refreshments with Madame de Krény and Madame Garer, a friend from the bathhouse.

"Why don't we sit outdoors?" I carried a tray of pretty cakes iced with pink and green sugar. "It's so lovely today."

They followed me onto the balcony overlooking the street. A mountain breeze cooled the stifling summer air. We settled into our chairs as ferocious barking drifted up from the street.

"What in God's name . . . ?" I peered over the iron railing. A red-haired poodle crouched in attack position, prepared to pounce on a spaniel puppy. The dogs' owners jerked their leashes in an attempt to separate them.

"Goodness! That's a lot of racket." Madame de Krény joined me at the railing.

The sudden splintering of wood crackled. We looked at each other in confusion.

"What in the world?" Madame de Krény said.

I turned just as the dishes slid from the table and shattered. When the last fork and spoon clamored to the ground, the floor gave way beneath my feet.

Our shrill screams pierced the air. My stomach dropped with the sensation of falling.

I felt a thud, heard a horrible cracking, then blackness.

A beam of light blinded me.

I moaned and closed my eyes. After a moment, I peeled back one lid, then the second, and tried to focus my gaze. A brown square blurred across the room. An armoire? Where was I?

I turned my spinning head. My tongue stuck to the roof of my mouth like parchment. I swallowed and lifted my head. Someone had stuffed my body under layers of covers.

Memory burst through my hazy mind like a torrent of water. I had fallen two stories and crashed to the street. Our balcony had given way!

I groaned and moved my arms, one at a time. Painful, but nothing broken. I attempted to sit up, but could not push my torso into an upward position. A tingling tickled my toes and I tried to move my legs.

No heavy weight of limbs.

I tried again. Nothing.

"I can't feel my legs!" I screeched in a gurgled voice—as if I had not spoken for days. "I can't feel my legs! Someone help me!"

Doctor Martinet rushed into the room. "Madame! Calm yourself!"

"I can't feel my legs!" I screamed, my panic mounting. "What's wrong with me?"

He adjusted the round spectacles teetering on the tip of his nose. "You had quite a fall. You broke your pelvic bone and it seems you're suffering from temporary paralysis."

An alarm pounded against my temples like a hammer. "Paralysis? Broken bones? No." I shook my head. "I must go. Bonaparte! My husband! He'll think I've abandoned him. His vile brother will tell him lies about me."

I tried to roll to my side. A gasp escaped from my lips. Pain throbbed in my torso. Sweat beaded on my forehead and upper lip. I gave up and burrowed my face into the pillow. This could not be happening.

"Don't try to move. You may make it worse. I've sent word to your husband already." My eyes fluttered open. "With the extensive treatments I've prepared, I believe you'll have a full recovery, but you'll not be able to travel for six weeks. I've sent for your daughter and maid. They're on their way from Paris this very minute."

"Hortense and Mimi?" I asked, dumbfounded.

"Yes."

"My other friends! How—"

"They're a bit battered, but are well. You're the only one who broke a bone."

I recovered slowly. The prescribed laudanum and tonics twisted my reasoning, and nightmares tormented my already fitful sleep. I saw Eugène captured, my husband executed in the grainy dunes of the desert. The Bonapartes banishing me from my home. My screams woke me night after night.

Bonaparte refused my request to join him when I could finally walk again.

"It's too dangerous in your condition," his letter said. "Be well, *mon amour*, for my return."

Summer faded. Fall blew in with lumpy clouds and the constant threat of rain. Gusts of air grappled our hats and skirts with cold fingers, and tore at leaves clutching their branches. I had no desire to spend winter in the mountains. I longed for Paris. At last, the doctor cleared me to ride home.

Unsettling news awaited me in Paris. The entire brood of Bonapartes had relocated to the city to influence assembly members on Napoléon's behalf, or so they claimed. Their obvious greed appalled all who met them.

"What a nasty lot they are! The cretin spoke to me as if I were beneath him." Theresia spoke of Joseph. "A stepping stool he might tread upon. Ugly misogynist."

I leaned forward in my chair. "Shh. He's seated just there."

He sat three places away at our table.

"Did you hear what Pauline Bonaparte said to our dressmaker?" Julie Récamier asked from behind her pyramid-painted fan.

"Oh, do tell." Theresia loved gossip as much as I.

"While being fitted she said she was always the most beautiful at any event, but"—Julie leaned in and lowered her voice—"she said she wanted to 'make Josephine and her friends look like the whores they are.' Imagine saying such a thing aloud! To *our* dressmaker! Little wretch. Of course monsieur told me immediately."

I gasped. Did Pauline not know she was creating powerful enemies? Foolish woman.

"The Bonapartes share a special hatred for me," I said. "I hope my husband appoints them posts in Italy and rids us of them all."

Joseph and Louis Bonaparte formed alliances with those who wished to slander my name. Yet I never spoke an ill word against them, and even invited them to my home. My in-laws ignored my invitations, save Letizia, who believed in keeping up appearances.

Joseph in particular relished cruelty; he lorded his limited power over me.

I met him at his office one afternoon to collect my stipend as designated by my husband. When I entered, Joseph appeared on edge, as if he might spring from behind his desk and strike me.

"Good afternoon, dear brother." I pretended not to notice his hostility—he would not intimidate me.

He grunted and closed his book. "What can I do for you? As you can see, I'm very busy."

"I'm here to discuss my living expenses."

He removed a handkerchief from his breast pocket and trumpeted into it, then said, "I will distribute an allotted sum once per month. Nothing more."

I hid my dissatisfaction. "Bonaparte said I would be well provided for, that I may ask for what I need. I'm sure you'll fulfill his wishes."

"You are frivolous with your money, madame. You will not receive advances for lavish parties and extravagant clothing. There's simply not enough for such trifles."

My face grew hot until the roots of my hair tingled. Joseph knew full well Bonaparte would give me the moon. The wretched man had purchased his own colossal country estate only two weeks before. My entire house could fit in one of his bedchambers.

"Extra sums won't be necessary, Joseph. And if I may say so, I'm happy my husband has a brother in whom he places such trust." A scarlet blush moved up his neck to his ears. "You may tell him I am content with what he has allotted."

"Good. Then we understand each other. You may go." He dismissed me as if I were a servant.

"I hope you're enjoying your new estate. I heard its splendor is awe-inspiring," I said sweetly.

He gripped his pen and gave me a steely gaze. So glad we understand each other, thieving greed-monger. "Good day, Joseph."

The Bonapartes left me longing to escape Paris. The idea of Malmaison shone like a new coin. I didn't need to revisit the property—I knew what I wanted.

I met with Barras to put my plan in motion.

"I've managed to save one hundred and fifty thousand," I said.

A look of shock crossed Paul's face. He laughed a jolly sound. "How did my spendthrift friend manage that?"

I set my empty wineglass on a servant's tray. "I sold jewelry and vases from Italy and saved the many months of trading profits. Monsieur Récamier lent me a sum as well."

"Good work, *ma chère!*" He clapped me on the back. "I'll give you whatever you need."

I became the proud owner of Malmaison, the house and all of its animals, orchards, and vineyards. I retreated from the city the moment I held the keys, eager to begin renovations. The first morning I stood in the gravel drive and stared up at the house's charming facade. Much of the property needed work, but this would be my home. I skipped merrily through the door.

I had the rooms painted, windows replaced, and the slate roof mended. My gardener planted three dozen varieties of flowers in the first week, and I kept my designer busy. By month's end, my bedroom was remodeled and the study was furnished with shelves for Bonaparte's endless books. I could not wait for him to see it. He would be thrilled to find his leather bindings dusted and placed in alphabetical order. In a matter of weeks, I invited friends and deputy members to enjoy the country air, the swans and horses, and wine from my vineyards.

One summer morning, I awoke to the lonely cooing of a mourning dove. I spread my arm out over the empty space in the bed. If only Bonaparte were here. He hadn't responded to my last few letters—neither had Eugène. A familiar fear gripped me. My son. I swallowed hard. And without Bonaparte, I would face an uncertain future, again.

"My darlings, where are you?" I whispered to the empty room.

Even Barras had heard nothing. I inhaled a steadying breath. Perhaps their convoy had been diverted. I could not . . . would not consider the alternative. Not yet. I squeezed my eyes closed against the sudden rush of tears and rolled from bed. I had to keep myself occupied.

After breakfast on the terrace, I wiggled my hands into a new pair of gardening gloves and traipsed through the hedges with pruning shears. I was pounding my muddy heel against a brick when an unexpected guest arrived. A gentleman—a soldier—in an azure coat. He bobbed atop his horse down the gravel drive.

I would recognize his impish grin anywhere.

"Hippolyte!" I darted across the lawn. He dismounted and ran toward me. "My dear Hippolyte. How have you been?" I leapt into his arms, inhaling his spicy scent. A flash of our last encounter rushed my senses, of his smooth hands. And those lips. I shoved away the image, and the unsavory prick of guilt.

"I've missed you!" He held my face in his hands. "I heard you were badly injured. Have you recovered?" His elegant cravat impressed as always and his merry eyes danced. I had missed him.

"Mostly, though my hips ache when it rains. But let's not talk about such a dreary subject. Are you well? What brings you to Malmaison?"

Sunlight filtered through the oak leaves, illuminating an errant lock of brown hair that had escaped from under his hussar cap.

"What brings me? You, of course!" He laughed and took my hand. "May I see your new home?"

"I thought you'd never ask."

Hippolyte visited me often at Malmaison, entertaining me with his wit and gossip from the city, though business stocks dominated our conversations. He had accrued military contacts as a soldier but was looking to expand his contacts. He joined me in working with the Bodin Company, my most profitable contractor. I avoided intimate settings with the lieutenant. Shame overcame me each time I considered betraying Bonaparte—until one balmy summer evening as we walked in the garden.

A full moon spilled pearly incandescence over the hedges and lit the path. The scent of wet grass and roses enveloped us, and the crickets chirped their melodies. My limbs buzzed with the happy warmth of wine and a delicious meal.

I smiled. Quite an intoxicating evening, and an intoxicating man.

Hippolyte pulled me into his arms under a trellis of tea roses. "My darling, I still have feelings for you. I've had other mistresses, but—"

"Shh." I placed my finger over his lips. I stared into his shadowed face as he traced the outline of my nose, my eyebrows. My stomach flipped in excitement and desire.

No one need know of our tryst. Bonaparte might not return and where would I be? Alone, devastated again. The thought made my insides ache. Yet Hippolyte was here—warm, tempting, a skilled lover. My cheeks flushed.

"What are you thinking about?" He ran his fingertips over my exposed neck. I gasped at his touch and he chuckled.

"The future," I said, voice soft.

"Ahh, well. There will always be one." A crooked smile crossed his face.

I laughed, until his mouth fell on mine.

Dreams of Bonaparte haunted me while Hippolyte lay in my bed. I watched his chest rise and fall as he slept. Something felt different. Marriage had never equaled fidelity in my mind, not since I was a girl, and not even then. A memory of Papa slapping a slave girl on the rear flashed in my mind. Yet I had pined for loyalty and fidelity from Alexandre. I had come to understand my dreams were just that—a fantasy—and marriage would never be as I wished it to be.

Yet guilt gnawed at me. And the thought of Bonaparte touching another woman made me ill.

I sat up in bed and watched a robin hop across the floor of my balcony, its rust-colored chest puffed out proudly. An image came to mind of my husband standing on the dock at Toulon, kissing me possessively as the people exulted in their hero's affection for his beloved wife.

My stomach lurched, suddenly queasy. I loved Bonaparte—deeply. How could I have been so blind? The wine, the ease of being with Hippolyte, the time away from my husband . . . I covered my face with my hands. It would crush him. I could lose him forever if he discovered the truth.

Hippolyte rolled toward me. His smile faded when he saw my expression. "What is it?"

"I'm disgusted with myself. I can't . . . I just can't . . . we must end this. I'm so sorry." I clutched my middle. "I feel ill."

He tucked a strand of chestnut hair behind my ear. "I knew this would come. The guilt. I can see it in your eyes. You truly love him, don't you?"

A pang of despair rolled through me. I had not realized how much.

"Yes, I love him. *Dieu,* I love him, more than I ever guessed. What have I done? Had I realized . . . I've been so stupid." Tears rushed down my cheeks.

He embraced me gently. "He doesn't have to know. We'll never speak of this again."

"You mustn't come back to Malmaison." I wiped my face with the back of my hand. "I . . . we can manage business through letters or a courier."

Sadness filled his eyes. "I understand." He catapulted from bed and dressed quickly.

"Good-bye, sweet Josephine." He disappeared through my door for the final time.

My affair ended none too soon. Two weeks later, Theresia visited to deliver a warning. We followed a path behind the house and entered the stables. The earthy scent of animals and damp hay permeated the air.

"You're so thin. Are you well?" she asked.

Food had not appealed to me. I had been too racked with self-loathing to eat or sleep. How I wished I could erase my despicable deed.

I sucked in a deep breath. "Well enough."

"I've missed riding," she said.

The stable hand assisted Theresia and me onto our horses, and we trotted to the field behind the barn.

"I've ridden every day this week," I said.

"I'm jealous." She clucked her tongue at her horse. "Speaking of jealous, have you heard about Madame Delait?"

"No. What's happened?"

"Her husband seeks a divorce!"

"No!" I said, shocked.

"Apparently he discovered Jeanette with her lover. Poor man. It must have been an uncomfortable scene."

"Monsieur Delait was practically her slave. Completely devoted to—" I stopped midsentence.

My stomach dropped to my feet. The man had been devoted to his wife, like Bonaparte was to me. Now he was shattered and sought a divorce.

Theresia didn't notice my sudden pause. "Completely. A man could not be more in love with his wife. He's enraged."

A pang hit me like a blow and I fell forward in my saddle.

"Do you need to dismount?" Theresia asked, tugging on her reins to slow her horse.

"No, no. I am all right." I blinked back tears. I would be faithful to Bonaparte, come what may, I vowed. No matter the cost, no matter my fear—even if he cast me aside. *Dieu*, I loved him.

We rode up the hill in silence.

"Are the rumors true about you and Lieutenant Charles again?" Theresia asked at last.

"Oh, Theresia." I gave her a pained expression. "I can't forgive myself. I feel wretched."

"Whatever for? You don't love Bonaparte and he's been gone for months. I'm sure he has taken a lover of his own."

I did not respond.

She studied my face. "No! You do love him!"

"More than I knew." I looked away, toward the edge of the wood.

"Everyone speaks of the lieutenant's visits to Malmaison. Including Joseph. I heard him mention it to Madame Hamelin yesterday."

Joseph knew? Dread pooled in my stomach. "Hippolyte came for business only, until a fortnight ago." I snapped my mare's reins and she increased her pace. "And Joseph has no proof."

Theresia's skin glowed butter yellow under her wide-brimmed hat. "The Bonapartes don't need proof. You know how they are. They enjoy making your life a misery. I hope you terminated your contracts with the lieutenant." She gave me a worried look. "And I'm afraid I have more bad news. The Bodin Company—one of your suppliers?"

I gripped the reins a bit tighter. "My most profitable."

"I feared so. The Bodin brothers have been arrested for selling inferior, stolen horses to the armies."

"*Merde!* Are you certain?"

"Positive."

The happy sky and lush fields of clover blurred. I would have to dump my contracts with them at once.

Theresia's warning came a day too late. The scandal exploded the following morning before I could extricate myself. Every journal in Paris featured the story, and to my horror, my name appeared in bold black print among the investors. I crumpled my newspaper and pitched it at the wall. Bonaparte would be furious. I could be tried and convicted.

A sheen of cold sweat stole across my skin at the idea of jail—of divorce. My husband would not forgive me for deceiving his beloved armies. But how could I have known the horses were stolen?

I sought the counsel of a lawyer friend, who reassured me about my position. When it appeared I would escape a sentence, or even a fine, I wept with relief. But my relief did not last.

Barras invited me to join him for dinner at the Palais du Luxembourg. He had something pressing to tell me, his letter said.

I left Malmaison on edge.

To my chagrin, our private party included Joseph Bonaparte and his wife, and Caroline and her husband, Joachim Murat. I spent most of the evening avoiding them. I reassured myself Eugène and Bonaparte were well. Barras would have told me the minute he knew of their whereabouts. Yet after wandering through the main ballroom, I cornered Paul just before dinner.

"What is it? I can't stand the suspense."

"Later. After the Bonapartes leave. I can't say anything in front of them without it becoming front-page news. Besides, dinner is being served. Shall we?"

Food was the furthest thing from my mind, but I found my place at the table. I had the misfortune of sitting next to Caroline. I managed two courses without speaking to her, but when the pork was served she turned to me.

"Have you heard?" Her dark curls bounced as she sawed a pork filet with her knife.

I raised an eyebrow to show polite interest, though I did not care what she had heard. God knows how she would twist its meaning.

"English forces seized several Egyptian ports and captured a cargo ship carrying mail to France. They're blockading supplies to Bonaparte. I suppose you didn't notice his letters had ceased. You've been too busy with your lover. . . ." She paused for effect. "And stealing supplies from the army."

I dropped my fork. It clanged against the porcelain, drawing the attention of everyone at the table. I didn't know whether to slap her or cry. I had refused to consider the reason for the missing letters—that my men were in grave danger.

"Excuse me." I apologized for the disturbance. I gave Caroline a frigid look. "I do not have a lover, Caroline. Friends and ministers visit Malmaison. That is all." Not that it was any business of hers. "And of course I noticed Bonaparte's letters have waned, as have my son's. But I have been too terrified to consider"—I looked down to control my emotion—"the alternative."

She laughed, a mocking sound. "They aren't dead or captured. But—"

"That's enough, Caroline," Barras interrupted.

I gripped the edge of my seat. My head pounded dully.

"She has a right to know now. The English—"

"Caroline!" Barras said.

"—have printed Napoléon and Eugène's letters in their papers."
She rushed to finish before being interrupted again. "Bonaparte has
discovered your affair. He's incensed! He has even taken a lover in revenge. I bet he'll demand a divorce."

Pain sliced me like a hot knife. He was punishing me for hurting
him. It was what I deserved. I had jeopardized everything—he *was*
everything. And yet I could not believe it. I sat unmoving, detesting
myself, trying to hold all together.

Everyone continued eating to cover their embarrassment. Such
private information should not have been shared over dinner. Caroline
had the manners of a child.

"Not hungry?" Triumph shone in her eyes.

"If you will excuse me, messieurs, mesdames." I pushed back from
the table. The guests murmured their salutations as I left the room.

Barras followed me out. "I'll speak to him. We'll resolve this issue,
doucette." He kissed my hands. "Go home. Get some rest and try not to
worry. I'll visit you in a couple of days. We'll mend this."

I kissed his cheek with numb lips and climbed into my carriage.

What had I done? I clutched at my sides, suffocated by regret. I
couldn't imagine my life without Bonaparte. I could forgive his affair
in an instant, if he would only forgive mine. I loved him. Lord, how I
loved him.

Trees flew past as I rode home. I had to reach Bonaparte before his
brothers, reassure him of my love, beg for his forgiveness. But I must
reach him first, the moment he landed on French soil.

A month later, the news came. Bonaparte and Eugène had landed and
would be home within the week. I excused myself from a gathering at
La Chaumière and rode home. Hortense met me moments later. We
packed and left in a rush to meet the convoy en route.

We raced south at high speed along the Burgundy Pass toward
Lyon. Each time our coach slowed it rattled my nerves.

"His brothers must have learned of his arrival. Do you think they're
on the road?"

I stared out at an agitated sky; clouds pushed against one another,
wrestling the wind as a storm moved in.

"Don't worry. He loves you." Hortense tried to soothe me. "He won't believe his brothers' lies. I'm sure of it."

I cringed in shame. I couldn't bring myself to tell her of my affair. That I had used love as a means to get my way, and now I didn't know what my way was. All I knew was that suddenly I could not breathe without Bonaparte.

When the houses of Lyon came into view, I exhaled a sigh of relief. Our next stop would be the army post.

But luck was not mine.

Bonaparte had headed north earlier that morning by another route.

I collapsed against the cushion as our coach turned back toward Paris—now well behind my enemies.

"They have met him, I'm sure of it!" I wailed.

"Maman, you'll only give yourself a headache. I'm sure there is no reason to be afraid."

I smiled weakly. "That pushy little man has stolen my heart."

Hortense smiled her approval. "It is about time. He's a good man. To all of us."

Two days later, we pulled into the drive of our Paris home at midnight. Despite the late hour, several windows were lit. I bolted up the walk with Hortense on my heels.

"Good evening, Madame Bonaparte." The sentry stationed outside the main door greeted me. "I'm sorry, but I can't let you in. The general gave his orders."

He didn't want to see me. My stomach plummeted to the cold stone beneath my feet. I forced myself to remain calm. "This is my house. Let me in at once."

Hortense stood beside me, silent and shivering.

"I'm sorry, madame. I cannot."

"I know he is angry, but we'll work this out. Surely you won't leave women in the cold in the dead of night?"

The guard looked from me to Hortense, who blew into her hands to warm them. He bowed his head. "No, madame," he answered slowly. "But I warn you, he is very distressed."

He swung the door open and we rushed inside.

Mimi embraced me in the main hall and pointed to the stairs. "Broke two chairs. He's been throwing books at the wall. He shouted like a madman when you weren't here to greet him."

I started up the stairs on shaky knees.

"Maman!" Eugène sprang from his room, arms outstretched.

"My darling!" I clung to his tall frame. "I'm so glad you're safe." I kissed his cheeks and squeezed him in a fierce embrace. "And Bonaparte . . ."

His blue eyes filled with worry. "He's upset. More than you can imagine. He has spoken of nothing else since he heard about your lover. He means to turn you out of the house. To buy it from your creditors. And—"

"I will mend this." My lips quivered.

"Go to him," he said and reached for Hortense.

I continued up the stairs and hesitated for an instant outside the bedroom door. I leaned in to listen and tapped lightly.

No answer. I tried the handle. Locked.

"Bonaparte? It's me, my love. I'm so happy you're home. We've been apart too long. Unlock the door."

No response.

Perhaps he'd fallen asleep.

I knocked again, louder.

"Bonaparte! Let me in. I've missed you."

A loud thump sounded inside the room, but he didn't answer.

"I've just arrived." My breath came faster. "I traveled the Burgundy Pass to meet you on the road. I couldn't wait to see you. Let me in!"

His silence deafened.

"Your brothers will do anything to separate us. You know that. They're jealous of our love. They're jealous of your power, your strength. I don't have a lover! I made a mistake! It's over!" Tears slipped down my cheeks. "I love you so much. Only you. Please, you have to believe me."

No answer.

I dissolved into a puddle at the base of the door.

More crashing sounded from the study. And then a roar. "How could you do this to me? *Tu as brisé mon cœur!*" Another smash, and glass splintering on the floor. "You broke my heart!" he wailed, his voice full of pain.

"I'm so sorry. I'd do anything to take it back." I lay against the edge of the door. "I was foolish, weak. . . . I didn't know the depth of my feelings, how much you mean to me. . . . *Mon amour*, please open the door."

Bonaparte did not open the door.

I wept for hours. When the clock in the hall chimed four, I climbed to my feet, weary and distraught. I had sabotaged my only chance at happiness. I plodded down the staircase with a heavy heart.

Hortense and Eugène sat at the bottom of the stairs, eyes laden with despair. They had grown to love their stepfather, too; Bonaparte had given them everything.

Another pang rippled through me. My selfishness, my careless disregard, had hurt my children. Had hurt us all. What I wouldn't give to turn back the clock.

"Is it hopeless, then?" With the sound of Eugène's voice came the sudden creak of a door.

Bonaparte stepped into the hall.

Ingenue

Rue de la Victoire, 1799–1800

Hortense and Eugène jumped to their feet. I whipped around to face my husband, heart pounding in my ears. Bonaparte's face was thinner than usual, and his eyes swollen. His gray civilian jacket lay open at his chest.

He bounded down the stairs and pushed past me. "Daughter! Son!" He held out his arms. "I will not desert you. I love you as my own." He embraced first Eugène and then Hortense, who blubbered into his shoulder. "There, there. I can't bear to see my children cry." He smeared the tears on her cheeks with a rough sweep of his hand. "Your mother and I will work through this."

My legs gave way in my relief. I grasped the banister to keep from falling. *Merci au bon Dieu.*

"Now, go to bed," he ordered them. "I need to speak to your mother alone."

They hurried from the room without a word.

He stared at me in silence for a long moment. Without warning, he gathered me in his arms and carried me to the bedroom.

We shouted our frustrations, pleaded and cried, and loved each other before falling into an exhausted sleep. When we awoke at midday, we lay in bed, not yet willing to part.

"I love you." I held his face in my hands. "I would prefer my heart be ripped from my chest than to ever be without you."

His fingers trailed along my bare shoulder. "There will be no more men. Ever. Do you understand? I plan to move up in this pathetic government. We can't have domestic squabbles for the public to scrutinize."

I wrapped my arms around his neck. "No one could fill your shoes, my love."

"And you must stop your military trading. It has almost ruined our name."

"I need some way to pay my debts. I—"

"I will pay them. I have made more than enough in my wars." He stroked my hair for a moment in silence. "And that woman," he continued. He closed his eyes, remembering his own mistake. "I wasted my time on that stupid woman who was not my soul, my heart." He kissed me ardently. "I am sorry, too."

"We'll never speak of it again."

He stroked my face, pain emanating from his eyes. "As for the lieutenant—"

"I'll never forgive myself. There will never be another man for me."

Bonaparte forgave me, but something inside him had shattered. His loving gaze no longer lingered; his adoration had shifted. I did everything in my power to please him, to earn his love. I even placed his needs before my own.

"We're not to attend any salons or events in the coming weeks," he said. "I'll need you to help . . . to handle the men, shall we say."

My ambitious husband aimed to overthrow the government—the five-member Directoire had caved in upon itself and lost the assembly's support. If the coup proved successful, Bonaparte would be one of three consuls leading the country. For now, he would direct the army.

"*Bien sûr.*" Handling men was what I did best.

I hosted intimate dinners for the plotters in our home, redirected their tempers, and convinced them to take my husband's side. Bonaparte grew tenser as the days passed and the government scrambled for order. At last, on the chosen morning in the month of Brumaire, the key players convened in our courtyard.

A filmy layer of frost coated patches of browned flower stems.

Horses clip-clopped and pranced about while their riders debated in excited tones. Golden epaulettes glinted in the pale sunshine.

I could not stand still. To send my husband into the face of a possible riot unnerved me. I retreated indoors with a pack of anxious soldiers for tea and fresh brioche.

As the hours wore on, the men's skittishness increased. Finally, a courier banged on the front door at midday.

Bonaparte read the missive hastily, then tossed it into the fire. "It's time!"

Militiamen roared in the cramped space. In a flurry of swords and hats, the cavalry rushed to their horses.

My heart thudded in my ears as Bonaparte mounted.

I rubbed his Arabian's nose to calm us both. "Be careful, *mon amour*."

He looked down at me, determination etched on his face. "I'll send word as soon as I can. Gentlemen"—he motioned to me—"my lucky star! Our Lady of Victories!" Another cheer erupted and fists waved. He punched the space above his head and led the crowd through our front gates.

My heart constricted as I watched him recede from view. "Luck," I whispered.

He would need it to enact such a complicated plan.

After they left, I rifled through my dresses, rearranged my jewelry, and wrote a dozen letters. All the while, I chewed on my bottom lip, tapped my foot against my chair, and stared at the immobile clock. The hour for supper came and went. Still no news.

By evening, a dull ache throbbed at the base of my neck and skull. Rain pelted against the window. I lay on the sofa, willing the pounding in my temples to subside. I could not stand the suspense much longer.

Horses pounded up the drive.

I dashed into the hall as Letizia, Pauline, and Caroline burst through the front door.

"Josephine!" Letizia shrieked. Her face glistened with tears.

"Come." I wrapped my arm about her waist and escorted her into the salon. "Sit by the fire and calm yourself, madame."

The sisters followed without a word. Pauline's red eyes betrayed her emotion, but Caroline looked bored.

I inhaled a calming breath, refusing to panic. "What's happened?"

"We were at the theater"—she wiped her eyes—"and the production was interrupted. A man ran on stage and announced that Napoléon is dead!" Sobs racked her body.

"No!" I shook my head. "No! I don't believe it," I choked. "I would have heard. . . ."

Letizia's wails grew louder while her daughters sat in stony silence.

I struggled to maintain my composure. "I'm sure it is a rumor. You know how dramatic players can be. I would have received word if he . . . if he . . ."

Dieu, let Bonaparte be alive.

Someone rapped at the door. Monsieur Fouché, the minister of the police, promptly dashed into my salon. His hat and cloak dribbled puddles of rain onto the floor. "Madame Bonaparte. Excuse me for the intrusion, but I have a letter for you from the general."

I pushed the air from my lungs. "He's not . . . ?" My hand covered my heart.

"He's alive and well, madame."

I exhaled. "Thank God!"

Letizia made the sign of the cross.

"We heard a horrible rumor. Your arrival is well timed." I took the letter from his outstretched palm. "Would you care for an aperitif?"

"I may as well. Bonaparte instructed me to wait with you."

"Why don't you warm yourself by the fire?" I motioned to a servant to help him with his coat, then ripped through the seal of the small note. I read its message aloud:

> The Republic is saved! Do not worry, my love. All is
> well. I'll be home tonight.

B

The remainder of the evening passed in a blur. In the early hours of dawn, I awoke with a start to a metallic thump.

"What in the—" I pushed up in bed in a fright.

"It's me." Bonaparte had dropped his loaded pistols on the table near the bed. He slipped into the silk sheets and folded me in his arms.

Bonaparte had succeeded. The Directoire was abolished and my husband became one of three consuls leading the country. Parisians went mad with excitement, overjoyed at his rise to power.

All except Barras.

Paul's protégé had duped him; Bonaparte forced Barras's resignation and sequestered him at his country home, excluding him from his promised position of consul. I was aghast at his betrayal—the one part of his plot about which I knew nothing. Theresia informed me of it all.

I returned from my visit with her in a rage. I stormed through the front door, an icy blast of wind at my heels.

"How could you? You kept this from me! He is our friend!" I shrugged out of my woolen cloak and threw it onto the back of a chair.

"He lied to everyone!" Bonaparte exploded, throwing down his book. He rose from his desk and stalked toward me. "He stole money and sold information to the Royalists! The French wouldn't place their faith in the consulate if he remained in power. You heard the rumors. More riots, more war! Is that what you want? Barras cheated everyone!"

"Except you," I said in a chilled tone. "He gave you everything. He gave me everything." I despaired at the thought of Paul's pain at our betrayal. My dear friend had rescued me from poverty and obscurity. He'd given Bonaparte his beginnings, his trust. I couldn't envision Barras banished like an outlaw, or bear the thought of never seeing him again.

"I did the right thing. His greed would have led to a revolt and another king on the throne."

I gave him my back. Who was this man who cast his friends aside so easily? I raced up the staircase and slammed the bedroom door.

Bonaparte relished his power. He awoke humming every morning, overjoyed and proud of his new position. Commanding others came naturally to him. Even I found myself wanting to obey him—I, who obeyed no one.

The "Son of the Republic" could do no wrong, and within a month, the assembly elected him the sole consul. First Consul and Consulesse Bonaparte, we became. The children were awed by our newfound status.

"Leaders of France!" Eugène exclaimed. "The only position more honorable than a soldier."

"I'll meet the finest musicians, the handsomest men! And help you with your duties, of course," Hortense added hastily.

I found their enthusiasm contagious. After weeks of missing Barras and wrestling with my shame, at last I felt myself looking forward to the coming months. But I had not considered the difficult changes my title would demand.

"Eugène will be my aide-de-camp in battle, but for now, he must learn government matters," Bonaparte said. "Hortense will continue her lessons at home. She must behave as the daughter of a leader. At least until we find someone suitable for her to marry."

He tapped his boiled egg with a spoon until he had made many dents in the shell.

I paled at the thought of my little girl married. Yet she was sixteen, nearly the age I was for my own first wedding so many years ago.

"I've sent Bourrienne to settle the remainder of your debts," he continued.

"I cannot tell you how much that relieves me." I munched on cru-dités.

"The mistress of France must be a model citizen." He looked pointedly at my décolletage. "Without debts or immodest dress. And no more gaudy friends that act like whores and speak out of turn. You know who I mean. Theresia and the other ridiculous women. Your days of mischief are at an end."

"Surely you don't expect me to discard my friends!" I said, incredulous. "I will not abandon them! You know I love Theresia like a sister."

"I know it upsets you. For that I'm sorry." He rubbed his thumb across my cheek. "But she is associated with the Directoire—the greed, the corruption. It's a sacrifice we must make."

I pulled away from his touch. "The sacrifices seem to be all mine!

Do you intend to isolate me? I would not be who I am without my friends. I can't turn my back on them. Bonaparte—"

"Do you wish to end my leadership when it has just begun? You think only of yourself, woman!"

My mouth fell open at his accusation. "How can you say such a thing? I wish for nothing but your happiness, for our success."

"Everyone of our rank must make sacrifices." His tone softened. "I'm sorry for your loss, but you are charming, and already well loved. You'll make new friends quickly. You'll see."

After supper, I wrote Theresia a letter and sent it in secret. When she did not answer the following day, or the day after, I sent another and another, my fears escalating. My closest friend did not return a single note.

Did she despise me already? My head dropped into my hands. Our betrayal of Barras, of our inner circle, had destroyed our friendship. In the name of the government, for the love of my husband, I had sacrificed my dearest friends.

Bonaparte's new position meant relocation to a home more suitable for the leader of France.

"We'll have a celebration the day of our installation." He flopped onto the settee next to me. "A parade. The French crave lavish displays. What do you think?"

"A parade would be lovely, but—"

"Military bands marching in unison, artillery, garrison dressed in full uniform. My most important ministers in our convoy, and family, of course." He kissed my nose. "Purchase a new gown, my love, and arrange a soiree."

A servant knocked at the door. She held a tray loaded with cured meats and a bottle of wine.

"*Merci.*" I accepted the tray. "It sounds lovely, but greet us where? You haven't yet said where we are to live."

"The Tuileries Palace."

I nearly dropped the heavy tray. The wine bottle wobbled until Bonaparte rescued it and placed it on the table.

"The royal family's former residence?" I asked. "I would prefer not to live where Queen Marie Antoinette—"

His incredulous stare silenced me.

"Do not speak of that ridiculous woman! You'll bring a curse upon us." He snatched a slice of ham from the tray. "And you may redecorate as much as you like."

Redecorate? Adorning the massive windows with silk and filling the walls with tableaux would not remove its history, or the ghosts that haunted its rooms. I had not set foot in the ghastly place, and yet I could already feel the oppression of its gloom.

"Really, Bonaparte. There are so many beautiful châteaus. Must we live there?"

"The people want tradition to some degree, and every leader of France has lived there. But take heart, dear one. We'll bring change. New life behind its walls." He poured wine into our goblets. "You have a fortnight to make it habitable."

An architect and Hortense accompanied me on a brief tour of the palace. We saw only the main rooms—I needed to see no more.

I groaned inwardly. What a monumental task it would be to remake its appearance. Thieves had pilfered everything of value, cookware and dishes, paintings, and furniture. Vandals had defaced the palace walls with crude drawings and profanity in colorful paint. Cannon shot scarred the plaster; stones and glass blanketed the floors in a prickly carpet.

"We will need a large team." I fingered the dusty remains of a window covering, now shredded and strewn across the floor. "And a miracle."

We had our miracle.

Moving day arrived on a cold, clear day in Pluviose. I admired my dress in the looking glass. White muslin *à la grecque* suited me perfectly. As I pulled on my gloves, the sound of hooves resounded from the drive.

"Our carriage has arrived," I called down the corridor. I slipped a rabbit fur cloak about my shoulders and rushed down the staircase.

The children bounded after me. Eugène looked a fine young man in his elegant blue coat and Hortense glowed with her blond locks and dewy complexion. I could hardly believe they were eighteen and sixteen years of age.

I smiled and waved them on. "Quickly now. Into the carriage."

Once settled I said, "You both look beautiful. You've accepted your new roles with finesse and gratitude. A mother could not be prouder." I squeezed their hands.

"And we are proud of you." Hortense leaned to kiss my cheek, her eyes glistening.

"No tears. Today is a happy day," Eugène scolded.

Cannons boomed, one after another, and the line of hackney cabs in front of us began to move. Our convoy rolled in a slow procession from the Palais du Luxembourg to the Tuileries along the grand boulevards. Throngs of citizens crammed together behind soldiers lining the streets. The clapping of boots on cobblestone thrummed the air.

My pride swelled until I felt as if I would burst. My husband was first consul, leader of France! How had I gotten here? I waved at the women flourishing multicolored scarves from their balconies despite the icy wind. Scarves like those I had worn as a child in the heat of the jungle. I laughed at the absurdity of my new life. I had come so far.

A shadow of doubt fell across my good humor. Could we fulfill our duties? Withstand the pressure?

Napoléon followed at the end of the procession. I wondered at his sentiments. How proud he must feel. He looked so handsome in his new uniform.

I had awakened in time to see him slide into a red velvet coat laced with gold. He had kissed me and slipped from the house like a thief in the periwinkle light of dawn. It was our last morning in our charming little apartment.

The coach stopped in front of the palace. Bugles sounded, followed by an earsplitting roar from the crowd. I waved at the masses. *Dieu*, they packed the street. How many thousands welcomed us? I waved again and we filed inside.

"This way, Madame Bonaparte." A servant showed me to a window to watch Bonaparte arrive.

When his white Arabian horse came into view, joy surged through me. My darling husband looked so regal. How could this man love me? I didn't deserve such fortune. I controlled the rush of emotion—I would not cry.

Hortense grasped my hand. "What a sight he is, Maman."

I nodded, not trusting my voice.

He sat rigid, head held high as he cantered toward the Tuileries. When he reached the steps, he dismounted. The crowd hushed.

One by one, the leaders of each battalion presented him with their revolutionary flags. Stained, scorched from bullet holes, and tattered, the flags reminded us of all we had lost, all we had fought for.

Bonaparte removed his hat and saluted our beloved colors.

My vision blurred. I dabbed at my eyes and glanced at the statesmen clustered near me. Not a dry eye among them. Such was the people's great hope in my husband. Such was my hope in him, in our love.

Moments later, Bonaparte joined us indoors. He motioned me to his side, beaming.

"Ladies and gentlemen," a minister said to gain the guests' attention, "introducing, the First Consul and Consulesse Bonaparte."

Applause erupted as we crossed the room.

Monsieur Bourrienne, ever the flatterer, bowed his head. "You wear your position like a silken robe, madame. With fluidity, elegance, and beauty. Or better still, like a queen. The French are exuberant with your installation as their first lady."

I stiffened at his compliment. Why must he compare me to a queen? The priestess's eyes flashed in my mind and I nearly stumbled. A queen, indeed.

The evening passed in a blur of congratulatory gestures and fine food. When the last of our guests departed, the cheery luminescence in the main ballroom faded. The candles had burned to nubs and shadows stretched from their corners, plunging much of the room into darkness. My new silk drapes floated like apparitions and floorboards moaned underfoot as if alive.

My heart skittered in my chest. Our first night in the palace and where was Bonaparte? I did not wish to sleep alone, regardless of convention. I walked quickly through the corridors to his apartments.

"Will you sleep in your own bedchamber?" I asked.

He studied my face. "There are dozens of guards. You will be safe."

"I would prefer we slept together." I burrowed into his chest. What frightened me could not be remedied with swords or guns. Mimi had only solidified my fears earlier in the evening.

"Something lurks," she said just after supper.

I shivered at the memory of her black expression.

"Very well, *amore mio*." He rubbed my back with his rough hands.

We walked to my new rooms on the ground floor, in the former apartments of our dead queen. Foreboding seeped into my bones as we undressed and climbed into bed. Within minutes, the lanterns were extinguished and Bonaparte's uneven snoring filled the air. He did not fear the walking dead after so many nights on a battlefield, but I lay paralyzed under the bedcovers, straining to catch the slightest sound.

Was that the swish of fabric over stone? A moan of the murdered?

I sat up and lit a lantern. I threw on a cloak and tucked a deck of cards in the deep pocket of my overcoat. Perhaps one of my attendants would be interested in a game, or Hortense if she were still awake. A guard if I were desperate.

I snatched a lantern and swung open the bedchamber door.

A towering wall of solid muscle filled the doorway. Dark eyes glittered in the dim light.

I gasped, nearly jumping from my skin. "Roustam, you scared me!"

Bonaparte's favorite Egyptian guard never left his master's side. How imposing he appeared in the dark corridor, immense curved knives dangling from his belt. A quick slash of the throat would end an intruder's life in seconds.

"Madame Bonaparte, are you well?"

I closed the door behind me. "I am in want of entertainment. I can't sleep in this haunted place."

"Many have died under this roof." He did not deny the spirits' presence.

My voice dropped to a whisper, as if they could hear me. "And they are unquiet."

A toothy grin crossed his features. "Don't worry, madame. I'm wearing my evil eye pendant and it is I who protect you. As for entertainment, the family has gone to bed."

"Perhaps a walk, then?" The glass sheath of my lantern tinked against its metal frame.

He eyed my trembling hand. "Are you comfortable enough to walk alone? I can't leave General Bonaparte."

"I'm not afraid in the lit corridors." My voice betrayed my uncertainty.

"There are twenty guards on this floor alone. If you need anything, you may call out and they will assist you in an instant."

"Thank you, Roustam." I gathered my nerve. I could not spend another minute tossing in bed. "Just a short walk."

Roustam grinned again. "I will be here when you return."

My footsteps resonated in the empty corridor. I pulled my cloak close. Strange that I felt blasts of cold air when the closest window was across the room. I shivered. I would not consider their source.

I paused to admire Egyptian vases, tableaux, and sculptures from Italy; gilded handiwork and detailed tapestries; points of beauty in the gloom. Guards greeted me with a curt nod as I meandered from room to room. Their presence soothed my anxiety and my unease waned.

In a moment of bravado, I climbed a set of stairs to a room not yet renovated. The odor of dust and mold filled my nostrils and coated my tongue. No one had been there for years. I held up my lantern to assess the damage. Broken furniture littered the floor. The walls were grimy and defiled with handwriting. I moved closer to cast the lantern's glow on the lettering.

My hand flew to my mouth.

"The King is a traitor," it said. "Long live the Republic." "Liberty, Equality, Fraternity."

Someone had sullied the King's name in his own house. Even years after his humiliation and murder, I could not believe it. I shook my head as a cold draft enveloped me. I bristled and turned.

The nearest window remained closed.

Bumps rose on my arms.

"At what cost?" a faint voice whispered in my ear.

I spun around on my heels. "Who's there?" My voice echoed in the hollow space, then silence.

A crescent moon winked through the streaked windowpane.

"Every reign must end." Another whisper.

"Hello?" My heart hammered in uneven beats.

A crow cawed somewhere in the distance.

I bunched my chemise in my hands and darted toward the stairwell. I bounded nearly to the bottom of the staircase before I realized it was not the same way I had come. Or was it? My head reeled. My breath came in shallow spasms. What had I heard?

I placed a steadying hand on the wall and gasped for air. I couldn't faint in this wretched place. So many unmarked stairwells and abandoned rooms yet to be refurbished. It could be hours before they found me.

I sucked in several deep breaths before I noticed the muddy brown stain beneath my fingertips. I jerked my hand back. What . . . ? I leaned closer to the wall and peered at the irregular splotches of brown. They were everywhere. Something had splattered the walls.

"Blood," said the gravelly voice.

A scream tore from my lips. Terror propelled me up the stairs.

Where was the other staircase? I stumbled over the final step and struggled to regain my balance.

"Traitors," the voice said.

I bolted across the ghostly room. Blood pounded in my ears. My foot caught the edge of something hard. I screeched as I crashed to the floor.

My palms scraped splintered wood. My lantern smashed. The room went black.

I scrambled blindly to my feet and staggered to the nearest doorway. "Guards!" I shouted in a strangled voice.

A shadow in the corridor lurched toward me.

I shrieked and ran in the opposite direction.

"Consulesse!" a gruff voice called after me. "What are you doing here? I heard you scream."

I stopped in my tracks and doubled over, grasping my sides. "I . . . I . . ."

"Is there someone here?" The guard searched the room as others filed in behind him. "You gave us a fright."

"I . . ." I caught my breath. "Went for a walk and got lost. This room, it's—"

"Let me assist you. Bonaparte would be furious if he knew you were unescorted."

"Thank you." I collapsed against him.

The soldier shifted in surprise, then steered me through a maze of corridors. I could not believe how far I had wandered. Every room appeared like the next.

When we reached my apartments, I closed the door quickly behind me. I washed the scrapes on my hands and leapt into bed. Bonaparte did not stir as I curled beside his warm body.

I buried my face in my pillow. So many souls lived among us. I pulled the bedcovers over my nose and lay staring into the eerie darkness. How did I get here? I asked myself for the tenth time.

After another hour or more, I slipped into a light sleep, in which the ghosts of citizens hacked to death, of kings and queens past, sought me in the dark.

Madame la Consulesse
The Yellow Salon, 1800–1802

I grew accustomed to the palace; or, rather, I forced myself to accept it. Bonaparte warmed my bed each evening and I fell into his arms, fatigued from the day's rigorous schedule. A never-ending stream of dinners and state duties occupied my time, while Bonaparte attended meeting after meeting. Between appointments, if only for a moment, my husband would dash to my salon and pull me into the privacy of my boudoir.

"I need a few moments of peace with my little Creole." He closed the door behind him. I squeezed his hind end and he groaned in satisfaction.

"How is your day going?" I asked.

"I have news." He pulled me onto his lap. I ran my fingers through his hair. "It's the blasted Austrians. They've broken the treaty. I'll have to invade the Italian provinces again."

"You aren't going, are you?" I looked at him with disbelief.

"It will only be a few weeks, and I'll leave in the middle of the night. Tomorrow. No one must know of my absence until I'm on my way. I've instructed the army to convene in Toulon, but they don't know I'll be joining them. It must be done."

"Why can't you send another general? There must be a trustworthy man among them. The country depends on you. The instant you leave—"

"Every faction will conspire to overthrow me." He set me on the cushion beside him and jumped to his feet. "That is why I need you here. Talleyrand, Bourrienne, and Fouché will be working with you, but they don't know it yet. You can tell them in two days' time." He paced like a stalking tiger.

I grimaced. Confronting his political enemies alone would be difficult; facing his siblings would be hell.

"Let me go with you." I crossed the room and wrapped my arms about his middle.

"A battlefield is no place for a woman. Especially not Madame la Consulesse." He cupped my breast and kissed me tenderly. "I won't be gone long. If things don't go well in Paris, I'll appoint my replacement and return at once."

I remained behind to do his political bidding and in a few short months Bonaparte secured another victory. We celebrated his homecoming with a small but elegant meal in the garden at Malmaison.

"Congratulations on your victory, first consul." Monsieur Bourrienne raised his glass.

"To the Republic!" Bonaparte swallowed a large gulp.

"To the Republic!" Everyone followed his lead.

We feasted on lobster and fresh strawberry tarts. After our celebratory meal, the men retreated indoors to Bonaparte's study. The few ladies in attendance remained on the patio in the twilight, sipping champagne.

"I have a delicate matter to discuss with you, Josephine. Ladies, please excuse us," Madame de Krény said to the others. She escorted me to a bench under a willow tree.

"Are you in some sort of trouble?"

"No." She set her glass on the bench. "I'm afraid the news involves Bonaparte." Pity filled her eyes.

My stomach clenched. "Go on."

"Giuseppina Grassini traveled with your husband's convoy. She's moving to Paris."

I remembered the famed opera singer from my time in Venice. I pushed down my rising panic. There must be a good explanation.

"Bonaparte enjoys the theater and music a great deal. I'm not surprised he invited such a talent to grace our own opera."

"Madame . . . I don't know how to say this. . . ." She looked down. "He has taken her as his mistress."

"Are you . . . are you certain?" I whispered. Suddenly, my gown was too tight and I could not breathe.

"Oh, darling." Madame de Krény threw her arm about my shoulders. "I didn't want you to overhear it by accident. I'm so sorry. I know how much you love him."

How had I failed him? Had his love for me waned? After all we had been through. His poetry, his words of love meant nothing. "I think . . . I think I'll lie down. Please excuse me."

I said good night to the others and staggered to my bedroom.

My pale expression had not escaped Bonaparte's notice. He joined me the moment our guests were settled. "Are you ill?"

I ignored his question and removed the pins from my hair, placing them one by one on the vanity.

"I've missed you," he said. "Come sit on my lap, my darling."

I spun on my stool. "Hire your mistress to sit on your lap. I'm sure we can fetch her from town."

He ducked his head. "That woman means nothing to me."

"You rented her an apartment in Paris! I'd say you care a great deal!" I pushed the array of brushes and cylinders to the floor. They clattered and rolled in every direction.

"Damn it, woman! Am I to be alone when you're absent? She's a physical distraction. Nothing more."

"Maybe I'll take a lover when you're gone!" I shouted, fury choking me.

He gripped my shoulders, his fingers digging into my flesh. "Has another man been in my bed?"

"What do you care?"

His face twisted into a furious scowl. I had gone too far.

"You're the mistress of France! Not a whore! My wife will not make me look a fool!" He shook me. "If you want to be free of me, free of your position, then go!"

I shoved him with all my might. "You would cast me off so easily? Like everyone else in your life?"

He caught my arms and pulled me to him. His mouth fell on mine. My lips pushed angrily against his.

When at last we pulled apart, I dropped into a chair. My anger dissolved into sobs. "I thought we were beyond this. How could you bring her here?"

"I don't love her." His face softened and he knelt beside me. "I swear it. Another woman will never possess my heart." He cradled my face in his hands. "Or my soul. Ever."

Tears streamed down my cheeks. I had set it all into motion with my folly. Now I could not escape it. Our love wasn't enough. All I was, all I gave, would never be enough. A fresh wave of pain rippled through me.

He lifted me to the bed. "Sweet Josephine." He smoothed the hair away from my face. "*Je t'aime, mon amour. Je t'aime.*"

Bonaparte's appetite for me did not change, and to my relief, the vivacious opera singer didn't last. She enjoyed her male admirers, it was said, and by month's end Bonaparte had disposed of her. Despite her leaving, I remained uneasy. Another mistress would follow unless I became pregnant. Of this I was certain. Bonaparte waited each month for happy news, but it did not come. I consulted Paris's finest doctors, took potions from midwives, and prayed each night, willing my womb to conceive.

As Christmas approached, I filled our calendar with holiday fetes, a welcome distraction from the obsession over my barrenness. Bonaparte had dismissed the revolutionary law banning religious holidays and moved toward readopting Catholicism.

"To appease the farmers and fishwives. Let them have their religion. They need it," he said.

On Christmas Eve I poked my head into Bonaparte's study to remind him of the time. In less than an hour we would leave for the opera. I did not wish to be late to Haydn's much-anticipated *The Creation.*

"Excuse me, gentlemen. It's eight o'clock."

To my dismay, my husband, who had been in a happy mood, appeared ruffled. Officer Fouché, the minister of police, stood erect in the center of the room, a stern expression on his countenance. Bonaparte motioned me inside with an impatient wave.

"Good evening, madame." Fouché tipped his hat and placed his hand on the shiny pommel of his sword. "I have troubling news. My men discovered large quantities of gunpowder in a warehouse outside the city. We believe it was meant for an assassination attempt. A plot most likely devised by the Royalists."

"It was those damned Jacobins!" Bonaparte paced along an invisible line in the floor. "I want the bastards arrested! Tonight! Do whatever it takes. I'll hire more policemen if necessary."

The blood drained from my face. "Assassination attempt? Are we safe in the palace?"

"You're perfectly safe *here*, madame. First Consul Bonaparte insists you continue to the opera this evening. I have advised him against it—it would be prudent to remain out of sight until we've arrested a few suspects—but he insists."

"Bonaparte—"

He stormed to the door. "I'll not be made a prisoner by those bastards! Rumors of the arrest are spreading as we speak. Our citizens must see I'm not afraid. That all is well. We're going and that's final." Bonaparte pulled on my hand. "You look lovely. Are the others ready?"

"Nearly."

"Let's go." He nodded to Fouché. "I'll see you after the show."

Fouché nodded, his thin face pinched. "As you wish."

Bonaparte freshened his appearance and chose a cashmere shawl to complement my velvet gown. "The black. It matches your gloves."

Hortense knocked and spoke through the closed door. "Are you ready, Maman?"

"Come in, darling."

"You'll charm every man in the house in that gown." Bonaparte tugged her ear.

"Thank you." She blushed and smoothed her glittering waistband. My angel in white silk.

"I need to speak with someone before the show." Bonaparte adjusted his belt. "I'll meet you there. My coach is waiting."

"We'll be right behind you. Your sister should be ready any moment." I had not been thrilled when Caroline ordered rather than asked for me to purchase her a ticket, but I had suppressed my annoyance and welcomed her as a sister should. "I'll check on her now."

The moment Caroline finished dressing, we rushed to our coach and sped toward the opera house. During the ride I could not shake my malaise. I peered at the crowds, searching for a sinister face in the shadows. How could Bonaparte dismiss an attempt on his life? He endangered us all with this pretense.

"How are you feeling, Caroline?" Hortense interrupted my thoughts.

"Like an elephant." Her pregnant belly stretched the fabric of her sapphire gown. "I'm uncomfortable and swollen. My stomach gurgles and I don't sleep. I can't wait for this child to be born!"

I patted her hand. "It will be over soon and you'll have a newborn to adore."

Caroline jerked her hand away. "So far this child has been nothing but a burden."

Hortense gave me a knowing glance. We had spoken of Caroline often in confidence. I pitied the poor child who would have Bonaparte's sister as its mother.

The next instant, our carriage jerked to a stop.

"What in the—"

The horses reared on their hind legs and I slammed into Caroline. She shoved me off of her. "Pay attention! You're going to—"

A blast erupted in an earsplitting boom.

I was catapulted from the coach and all went black.

The burn of smelling salts filled my nostrils. I opened my eyes and locked on Hortense's worried expression. The footman and several guards stood behind her.

"Maman?" She slid her arm under my head.

I groaned and sat up slowly. Splintered wood and shards of glass littered the street. Our carriage, or what remained of it, lay on its side in a filthy puddle. The surrounding houses had lost their windows in the blast. Some had caught fire.

"What happened?" I rubbed the back of my neck. Hortense sat beside me, mute and trembling. Blood dribbled down her arm and pooled on her white gown. "You're bleeding!"

"I've cut my wrist." Her voice shook. "I need a bandage." A guard produced a handkerchief from his pocket and wrapped her wrist, securing it with a piece of twine.

"How is—my God! Caroline!" I looked around frantically. "The baby! Caroline!"

"She's here, madame," the footman reassured me. "She appears unharmed."

The guard moved to reveal several policemen, a few dazed by-standers, and a stupefied Caroline rubbing her belly.

"The baby is kicking. The little thing didn't enjoy being thrown to the ground."

"Are you well? Is—"

"Fine," she snapped.

"Madame Bonaparte, there was an explosion," a policeman said. "We are preparing another coach for you. We believe the bomb was intended for the first consul."

My heart stopped. "Is he—"

"He had already moved on to the opera house when the explosion occurred."

I leaned into the guard, weak with relief. *Merci à Dieu.*

"Shall I take you back to the palace?"

"Take us to the opera. My husband will be expecting us."

Bonaparte waited in our box, pale and on edge.

"Thank God." He crushed my hand in his. "They told me you were safe, but I wouldn't believe it until I saw you myself. You did the right thing in coming. We must show we're in control. Not the bastards who did this. I'll have their heads."

After the initial relief of seeing Bonaparte, my anger grew. His mule-headed decision could have had us killed. I put a shaky arm around Hortense. She smiled weakly and returned her gaze to the stage.

Something had to be done about the Royalists. There must be a way to neutralize them. If Bonaparte would not address their involvement, I would. I packed my lorgnette into my handbag. I could not use it anyway; my hands trembled too much to see the stage clearly.

The police confirmed the explosion was a Royalist plot. Bonaparte ignored the evidence and ordered the arrest and exile of dozens of Jacobins. Uprisings sprang up throughout the country.

"Let them have their voice." Monsieur Talleyrand smoothed his black coat and perched on the edge of a chair. "One who cannot speak grows first apathetic, then angry. Need I remind you of La Terreur?"

Bonaparte rubbed his chin. "What do you suggest?"

I looked up from the letter I was writing. "I will invite them to my Yellow Salon. I'll hear their requests and write to the ministry on their behalf. If the émigrés may return to their families and homes, they'll be less likely to oppose the new government."

They stared at me in dumbfounded silence.

I dipped my quill pen into its well. Sometimes men did not see the obvious. "To reunite their families would make them very grateful and in your debt."

Bonaparte adopted my strategy, permitting me to request pardons for as many Royalist émigrés as I chose. Day after day I prepared my salon and served refreshments to visitors seeking my aid. I turned away no one, regardless of title or station. I could not deny those who had suffered, their fathers or daughters murdered, their heirlooms destroyed or property confiscated.

The exiled trickled back to France and within a few months, the former nobles appealed to me in droves.

"I am growing bored of the same stories," Hortense complained one morning. She yawned and stretched her limbs. I insisted she attend to learn a sense of responsibility in her position of power—to learn to be generous and show mercy. Besides, one never knew when they might need to rely upon another's kindness.

"Everyone has a tale of woe," I said. "It is true. But imagine if we could not return home. If not for the generosity of others, we could have starved during the Revolution. Or worse."

I peered out at the gardens. Saplings grew in place of the ancient trees that had been defaced or ripped from the earth during the riots. A family of robins hopped about, pecking the sodden ground in search of a meal. How I wished to be at Malmaison, digging in my own gardens. My schedule had become grueling.

Hortense lowered her head in shame. "I am grateful, Maman. And I'm happy to show others kindness."

"When you're in a position to give, you do so. It's the right thing to do, to help another in need." I smiled to myself. Perhaps I had learned a thing or two from those years of studying Alexandre's beloved Rousseau. One man for another, regardless of station.

She joined me at the window. "Why do you risk Bonaparte's anger?" She shuddered at the thought. "He'll be enraged when he learns of the ten thousand francs. You could have granted the orphanage the two thousand they requested."

"Two thousand is a meager sum that will barely keep the fires lit. Those poor children."

"They call you our Lady of Bounty. Have you heard?"

I laughed. "Another nickname for the wife of Napoléon Bonaparte."

"You are far more than his wife."

I stared at Hortense. Perhaps she was wiser than I had thought. I tucked a blond curl behind her ear. "I suppose I am."

My charity extended beyond émigrés, orphanages, and hospitals. Every member of my family applied for financial support or a favor. I solicited Bonaparte to bestow them with titles and pay their debts. Aunt Désirée and Fanny, Alexandre's brother, François, and every other Beauharnais relation wanted for nothing. Uncle Tascher relocated from Martinique with five cousins in tow.

I appealed to Maman to join him. When her latest packet of letters arrived, I sought the refuge of my boudoir, anxious to read her reply. Surely she would come to Paris now.

I sat at my vanity, poring over each letter. Everything seemed well at home. She missed us. And in her last missive, she once again refused my invitation to visit.

I tossed the letter on top of the pile. Why wouldn't she come? I couldn't understand her reluctance. She lived alone. Her grandchildren, her daughter, now Consulesse of France, and a life of luxury wouldn't bring her to France.

I threw myself on my bed and beat my pillows in frustration.

My reputation for generosity spread. Soon, every past acquaintance appeared. One warm summer day, a single visit tested my sense of charity more than all others combined.

"Pardon me, madame." A servant interrupted my letter writing. "A woman is here to see you."

"Who is it?" I asked, laying down my quill.

"Madame Laure de Longpré."

I paused in stunned silence for a full minute.

Laure de Longpré! She had stolen Alexandre's heart, borne him a child, and spoken falsehoods about me to my own family. What bravado she possessed showing her face! Wretched woman! I could turn her away, have her thrown into the street. Bonaparte would follow my request in an instant.

"Madame?" The servant looked at me expectantly. "Shall I send her in?"

I tapped my fingers on the polished mahogany desktop. What could she possibly ask of me? I could at least hear her request, then deny her if I chose. But how would I control my temper? I detested few people as much as I did her. I stared at the door for a moment longer.

The temptation was too great.

I moved to a flower-patterned settee and smoothed my skirts. The white muslin dress with blue ribbons had been a good choice. She would see me looking my best.

"You may show her in."

Laure entered my salon, head held high. I knew at once why Alexandre had fallen for her. She carried herself like nobility and her blushing beauty suited his tastes. I noticed her dated appearance with satisfaction—her gown, a pretty *indienne* of pink flowers, appeared worn and her hat was no longer in fashion.

She curtsied. "*Bonjour*, Madame Consulesse."

"Have a seat." I motioned to a floral chaise across from me. "Would you care for coffee or galettes?" I plucked a silver bell from the table.

A servant appeared instantly. "Madame?"

"Coffee, *s'il vous plaît*." The servant nodded and hurried from the room.

I stared at Laure coldly, relishing her discomfort.

"This is very awkward." She fingered the lace trim of her fan. "I owe you an apology. I was a fool." She lowered her eyes. "My mother would have disowned me had she known I treated another woman in such a way." She began to flutter her fan wildly.

She had a heart after all.

I said nothing for a long moment. Finally, I waved my hand in dismissal. "A million years have passed."

Silence.

I shifted in my seat.

Laure surveyed the room and fixed her gaze upon the oriental carpet, with its curling vines and bulging rosebuds.

"Is there something I can do for you, Madame de Longpré?"

"*Oui*, consulesse." She stopped fanning. "My husband is dead and I've discovered his fortune was a lie. My parents lost their plantation in the slave revolts. I find myself destitute. My son—Alexandre's son—has had no proper schooling. I don't know where to turn."

"You are in need of money?"

The crease between her brows deepened. "I have no one else to turn to. I have heard of your generosity. . . ."

I took pleasure in helping those who deserved it, not those who had wronged me in every possible way. I stared at her in silence. I would enjoy telling her to seek help from a convent, as I had, to find her way.

Her bottom lip trembled. She looked down at her hands. "I know I don't deserve your kindness."

I placed my coffee cup on the table. I could not stand to see a woman in desperate need. The past was as much Alexandre's doing as hers, and I had made my peace with him long ago.

I touched her arm. "I'll call my financier and set up a meeting with you next week. We can discuss an appropriate sum. And perhaps a military post for your son."

She heaved a sigh and her shoulders fell. Tears filled her eyes. "I don't know how to thank you."

"I cannot deny a fellow woman in need. Now, if you will excuse me, my next appointment is here."

She gazed at me gratefully for an instant, then turned and rushed through the double doors.

I smiled. Her guilt would be payment enough.

My days became a routine dictated by Bonaparte.

"You will take appointments until four, then do as you wish and dress for dinner. We'll meet at nine in your boudoir, unless there is a state affair, of course," he said. "You may meet with your ladies or friends after we dine. And I expect you to be at your most dazzling."

"I will 'dazzle' them, as you say, but do not complain when the bills arrive," I said.

"Monsieur LeRoy is robbing me blind," he growled.

"He's a brilliant dressmaker. You remark at every gown he creates for me."

He swatted my rear end. "The gowns would not be as becoming on anyone else."

I followed the schedule exactly as he requested without complaint, though the days grew ever more packed. Our exhaustive work in the city left us longing for the peace of Malmaison. Many Fridays we raced to our haven with the children the moment the final meeting ended. On one such blissful weekend, we awoke Saturday morning to the sound of the barnyard cock. The scent of leaves and hay floated through the open window.

I shivered from the cool air and pulled the duvet up to my chin. "I'm meeting with the botanist today. We're to find a place for a heated orangery and greenhouse. I'm considering an aviary as well." I would re-create Martinique just beyond the noise of Paris, with flowers and exotic birds. My own land, my home. "What do you think?"

"Whatever you like." He lay on his back, staring out at the cheery morning sky. "I have some documents to review, but let's be a family this afternoon."

In the afternoon hours we rode along the forest paths and played trictrac. Bonaparte and Eugène took turns reading poetry and Hortense and I played the harp and piano. I sighed in complete happiness when we had finished a supper of stewed pheasant, parsnips, and meringue, all grown and prepared from Malmaison's farm.

The children excused themselves and Bonaparte and I moved to a sofa in his study. I lay beside him, entangling my limbs with his under a blanket. The wind whistled as it blew against the eaves of the house.

"The weather is changing," I mused aloud. Flurrying snowflakes swirled in violent bursts before perching on grass and windowsills.

"Winter is almost upon us."

I braided the fringe of the wool blanket, dreaming of a baby. I dared not broach the subject, though I knew it weighed as heavily on his mind. Months had passed since my last courses.

He broke the silence at last. "Eugène is a handsome young man."

"Yes. Women admire him."

"As they should. He's an able soldier. Intelligent, well mannered, graceful. The stepson of a ruler."

I tugged on the blanket to cover my arms. "I'm proud of who he has become."

"And Hortense nears her nineteenth birthday," he said. "It is time, *amore mio*."

I sighed. I knew this day would come. "She has many suitors. They can't resist her blond curls and sweet voice."

"She's angelic. A gifted singer and she tempers my bawdy tongue."

I laughed. "She has a way of inspiring virtue."

"Whom would you choose for her?"

"I want her to be happy."

"I'd like to see at least one member of our family properly married. My siblings have chosen poorly." His voice rose an octave as his anger grew. "It's an embarrassment. If they had obeyed my orders—"

"I know, darling." I stroked his cheek to calm him. "We don't wish that for Hortense."

We discussed a dozen names, speculated about their families and their ability to integrate into our own. How would Hortense feel about this one or that one?

"And my brother Louis?" he asked. "What do you think of him?"

I didn't like him at all, though he was the least detestable of the Bonapartes. I couldn't imagine giving my only daughter to him.

"I need an heir," he said quietly.

I blushed. The child I had been unable to give him thus far.

At last, I said, "They will have children." A flicker of hope welled inside me. An heir could be named if I did not become pregnant, if the child was my daughter's instead. It would secure my marriage.

He clutched my hands and his determined eyes met mine. "Exactly."

❧

I wrestled with my emotions. Hortense would despair at a marriage to Louis. I hated to disappoint her, my only daughter. When I expressed my doubt to Bonaparte, he made his decision clear.

"It's the perfect solution. I've made my decision."

I could have argued his point, but I did not.

The following evening I told Hortense of her betrothal as we sewed by the fire.

"How can you suggest such a thing?" She threw down her pillow. "He is melancholy and anxious! You wouldn't choose for me someone who fakes constrictions of the throat!"

I moved to a seat beside her. "He's a bit eccentric, but not unhandsome. He would treat you well. I'm afraid, darling, that Bonaparte has decided. It's the best thing for you and the family."

Anger darkened her purple-blue eyes. "I don't love him!"

"Love will come. I was reluctant to marry Bonaparte and now he's the only man in the world for me."

She dissolved into tears, defeated.

The wedding arrived on a bitter winter day. We held it at our former home on the rue de la Victoire. Mimi laid out the exquisite gown Monsieur LeRoy had created for Hortense. I fingered the lace detailing, the pearls expertly stitched onto the white satin bodice.

All would be well. Hortense would grow to admire Louis.

When the ceremony began, Hortense descended the stairs in a simple white sheath. Not the elaborate gown I had prepared for her—a symbol of her own sacrifice. Her eyes appeared puffy from crying.

A ripple of pain shot through me. "Oh, Hortense." My throat ached against the dam of tears.

She ducked her head. "I am ready."

She gave all for me, to ensure my position, to secure my marriage and our livelihood. She never spoke the words aloud, but I saw them in her eyes.

Later that evening, I wept bitterly into my pillow for her lost innocence, for my own selfishness and Bonaparte's. My only daughter. What had I done?

Bonaparte's support grew as he built schools and museums and, above all, created jobs. The strength of the franc grew under his new laws, and industry boomed. When speculation circulated that he might be named first consul for life, malaise stole over me and nightmares plagued my sleep. Though I enjoyed my position, I looked forward to our retirement to Malmaison, an end to the ceaseless functions and the constant threat of being overthrown, of danger. Worse still, my greatest fear resurfaced: A consul for life mirrored the duties of a king; Bonaparte would need an heir and I would be unable to oblige.

I rubbed my throbbing temples one evening at dinner.

"You haven't touched a morsel." Bonaparte forked a roasted potato into his mouth.

"I am uneasy." He raised an eyebrow in question. "I feel it's a grave mistake to accept such a position. Consul for life is no different than king. I fear your election will enrage Republicans and the Royalists alike. Please reconsider." I took his hand and pressed it to my heart. "I am your lucky star. My intuition has never been wrong."

He kissed my hand and then stabbed another potato. "It is out of my hands. The assembly votes tomorrow. I will give the people what they ask for. Who am I to deny them?"

My husband became first consul for life, as predicted, and I agonized over my barren womb. I didn't eat and I grew thinner by the day. I sought the advice of Europe's finest doctors but each one said the same.

"You suffered too much during the Revolution. Now, at your advanced age of thirty-eight . . ."

Mimi scolded me when I collapsed on the bed one afternoon, fatigued and distraught. "Have you forgotten where you come from, girl? These men in their fancy coats know nothing of a woman's body or spirit."

She plunked down beside me on the velvet bedcover and rubbed my back. "Famian is angry you don't seek her help. The new moon, we'll make an offering."

It had not occurred to me to contact Mimi's spirits. So far had I traveled from home, from the comfort and ritual of African magic.

From Maman. A tide of longing choked me. What I wouldn't give to retreat beneath the blanket of jungle and wildflowers, free of expectations.

"Tell me what I must do."

The evening of the new moon, Mimi and I waited until the palace had quieted. We slipped through a door off the kitchens.

A guard stopped us as we stepped into the night.

"We'll just be in the garden near the edge of the wood," I said. "Please leave us undisturbed."

"You have one hour. Bonaparte would have my head if he knew I let you out of my sight."

I followed Mimi across the lawn, dew seeping into my brocade shoes. My candle flickered in the blackness, casting its paltry light over the landscape. I sneaked a glance back at the palace. How sinister it appeared in the dark; its facade towered over the lawn like a great hulking monster with mirrored eyes. I shivered and walked faster.

Mimi clutched a sack close to her body and ducked behind a chestnut tree. I followed, stumbling over an exposed root.

"Watch it, now." Mimi continued to a dark corner of the garden. She bent to light a haphazard stack of logs. The wood caught fire and a spray of flames shot toward the moonless sky. The fire burned silver, then orange, throwing an eerie glow on Mimi's cinnamon skin.

She chanted in her Ibo tongue.

A warmth spread through my limbs. Despite my unease in the dark, a sense of comfort stole over me. How at home I felt in the open air, beside *ma noire* and her gods.

Mimi pointed to her sack. "You take one, I'll take the other."

I retrieved the collection of twigs and dried herbs inside.

"Light it."

We lit our sacred boughs and danced around the ring of fire. Mimi tossed a sachet of dried herbs into the flames. The sweet smell of dead grass filled the air.

"Take this and do as I showed you." She handed me a burlap pouch filled with vesta powder.

I ran my thumb over the rough material and stared into the fire.

Lord, let this work.

I chanted Mimi's prayer and sprinkled powder over the flames.

When a small amount of powder remained, I pitched the rest into the middle of the pit. It ignited in a small burst. We circled the fire once more, then threw dirt on the flames.

"We'll do this again on the full moon."

I nodded and followed her indoors.

The ritual proved successful. My courses returned for six months. But still I did not become pregnant.

"Then it's not meant to be," Mimi said when I lamented my infertility.

"But it must!" I said.

In my desperation, I sought the advice of Madame Lenormand, a fortune-teller.

Once again, I stole into the night after Bonaparte went to bed. Madame Rémusat, my closest maid next to Mimi, accompanied me.

"When Bonaparte finds out you've left the palace without cavalry, he'll be incensed," she said.

"He won't know, and we have a guard with us. Besides, no one will recognize this old carriage." I tucked my hands into my muff to warm my freezing fingers.

"But don't you fear the gossips?" She read my grim expression. "You know I would never tell a soul."

I gave her a pained smile. "You are the only one, my friend."

When we arrived at the Palais-Égalité, Madame Rémusat remained in the carriage. The market still buzzed with activity, despite the late hour. Prostitutes posed against their doorframes, adjusting their exposed chemises and calling to passersby. Raucous laughter sounded from the taverns and pale light poured from a gambling house, packed with cigar-smoking scoundrels. I pulled my hood over my head and hurried toward the dilapidated shop nestled in the far corner. The smell of hot waffles drifted from next door.

I paused and looked behind me. No one appeared to be watching.

A cloud of incense and smoke assaulted me as I entered. Black and purple silk swathed the front windows and stars and fake birds dangled from the ceiling.

"*Bonsoir.*" An assistant appeared and ushered me to the back room.

Madame Lenormand sat at a small table puffing on a cigar. A halo of smoke rings floated above her head.

"Ah, there you are, madame."

"I apologize for the late hour. It was the only time I could get away."

She shrugged. "I am awake all night. It is when I do most of my business. Now, the fee." She held out her plump hand, covered in tarnished rings. I placed a sack in her palm and sat gingerly on the worn stool.

Madame Lenormand perched her cigar on a tray. "Let's see." She spun her hands above mine. With a swift movement, she grasped them in hers and closed her eyes. I watched her chubby face for movement. At last, her piggish nose twitched and she cleared her throat.

"I see a lost child."

I inhaled a sharp breath. Would I become pregnant only to lose it? I fought the mounting panic in my chest.

She released my hands, though her eyes remained closed. "A heavy crown. And enemies prepared to strike. Beware."

My head began to swim. Enemies? Of France? Or . . . the Bonapartes? They would do anything to rid themselves of me.

Her throat made a horrible gurgling sound. She hacked and spat into a cup filled with murky liquid. "Ahh, yes . . . and there will be a new beginning."

Empire
Palais des Tuileries, 1802–1807

In the fall, my spirits lifted with the birth of Hortense's joyful baby boy, Napoléon Louis Charles Bonaparte. Little Napoléon brightened the Tuileries and dispelled my depressive humor. Hortense, too, seemed happier—her supreme love for her son distracted her from Louis's fastidious demands.

Bonaparte couldn't hold his grandson enough. He tickled the baby's belly and smelled his fresh skin at every opportunity. I struggled to control my emotions when I watched him heap affection on my daughter's child.

How I longed to give Bonaparte one of his own.

One evening after Hortense had tucked little Napoléon into bed, she joined me and my ladies for light confections and a game of cards in my private rooms. Bonaparte had long since gone to bed.

"Such a night owl I have become." I played a seven of spades from my hand.

"It must be difficult for you to sleep alone in such a grand room. I cannot imagine it." Mademoiselle Fornet placed her nine of diamonds on top of my card with a snap. "Nine takes seven." She gathered the cards and placed them in her stack, then plucked a candied orange from the dish.

"The room is rather dreary," I said, "but I don't sleep alone. Bonaparte is always there."

"He is? But I've seen . . . I mean, I have heard . . . never mind. I beg your pardon." Madame Tricque blushed crimson. "I don't know what I am blathering on about, madame."

Hortense noticed my confused expression and shot me a warning look. Ignore their remarks, she seemed to say.

"Well? Go on," I said. "You can't say such things and not continue."

Everyone cast their eyes to the floor but Madame Rémusat. I gave her a questioning look. "Then you truly have not heard?" She sighed and tossed her cards on the table. "I despair that I am the one to impart such news."

I sat rigid, bracing myself. I knew what she would say.

"The first consul has taken many mistresses these last months." Her words came out in a rush.

I sat frozen on my chaise.

Sympathy filled her eyes. "I am sorry, madame. I know how much you love him. He seems to care little for them and treats them poorly, if that is any consolation."

Many mistresses? He betrayed me a thousand times. A knot clogged my throat. How could he belittle me so, in front of the palace, before all of France?

I leaned on the table for support. How had I not seen them? He must have taken great pains to hide his affairs. The room began to spin. How could I be here again—blinded by love, selling my soul to the man I loved?

A hand caught my elbow. "Madame?"

Hortense slipped her arm around me. "Ladies, we will say good night. Please excuse us."

"Of course." A chorus of *bonsoirs* followed them out of the room.

When the door closed behind them, I burst into tears. Hortense did not say a word. She embraced me until the tears dried.

Sometime later I stood and kissed my daughter's cheek. "Thank you for being with me, my darling. I'm going to retire for the evening. We'll not speak another word about it."

Hortense squeezed my hand. "Whatever you wish, Maman. This isn't truly shocking, is it?"

"No," I said tersely. "It isn't. Yet it does not lessen the pain."

When she had gone I walked slowly to my bedchamber. I was surprised to find Bonaparte awake. Fresh from a late-night tryst?

My blood boiled at the sight of him.

He closed his book. "You've been weeping, *amore mio*. Come here."

"You outlaw prostitution, yet you take whores! In our house!" I removed my shoe and launched it at the wall. "Are women nothing more than pawns to prove your manhood? I suppose I'm not enough for you!" A second shoe landed near the first.

He leapt from the red satin sheets. "I am more than five men put together. Let he who is greater challenge me!"

I rolled my eyes at his assertion. "How can anyone challenge you when you surround yourself with a hundred armies? When every word you utter is law?"

He clutched my arms. "Yet you, a mere woman, brave my anger!" He shook me, jarring my head back and forth. "You know those women are nothing to me!"

I wrenched free of his grip. "Everyone knows of your philandering! I'm humiliated!"

"I'm not having this conversation again, Josephine."

I threw my hands in the air. "We wouldn't have this conversation if you kept your trousers buttoned! You aren't a schoolboy any longer."

His face turned an alarming shade of purple.

"If I catch a wench in my house—"

"*You* will not command *me!*" He bent over me, fuming.

I met his gaze evenly.

After an instant, he tied a robe over his chemise. "No one expects a ruler to be faithful. And I *am* faithful—to my heart, to your heart!" He stormed through the bedroom door.

The following afternoon, Madame Rémusat and I rode to Malmaison to escape the stifling confines of the palace walls and the sympathetic stares of my ladies-in-waiting.

We strolled arm in arm through my orangery.

"I can breathe again." I drank in the sight of sun's rays filtering through the thick glass and warming the air. Flowers bloomed in clusters of fragrant white stars, and a constant trickle of moisture watered the trees. I pulled a branch toward my nose and inhaled. I wished I could hide among the trees, be lost amid the roses and trumpet vines like a songbird. I puffed out a long sigh.

Madame Rémusat patted my shoulder. "This will pass, madame. He'll tire of those women. But you must not argue with the first consul. You enrage him with your jealousy and he pushes you away. Do not let someone come between you."

Her words shot through me like a poisoned arrow. How could I keep silent while he ripped me apart? I did his bidding at every turn. I had given my life over to him.

I tread upon the petals littering the walkway, their once-white silkiness browned and their edges curled. He would desert me in time and I would be left with nothing. Empty, floating on a vacant sea. My hands began to tremble.

"What if he falls in love? Or one of his women becomes pregnant? I have failed him."

"You haven't failed him. You're his friend, his lover, and good luck charm. Besides, he has had many women and not a single one is with child."

I pushed away a clawing branch. "All he needs is proof he is fertile and—"

"Be his oasis, the only person who does not vie for his attention or his power. He will be pulled in many directions if he becomes emperor."

He had spoken of becoming emperor for weeks. I hoped the idea would be forgotten.

Suddenly, the perfumed air clogged my throat and the sun's rays bored into my skull. Bonaparte would be forced to travel constantly as emperor. How many beautiful maidens would he meet in Prussia, Italy, Spain?

"Why can't little Napoléon be named his heir? And Hortense is pregnant again." Madame Rémusat said. "Her children carry the bloodline."

"We planned for that very thing, but Louis forbids it. He refuses to be passed in the line of succession, even by his own son." I opened the greenhouse door and a blast of cool air rushed in around us. "I don't understand a man who doesn't wish for his son's honor. Hortense has pleaded with him to reconsider. And now if Bonaparte becomes emperor . . ."

"He would never d—" She stopped short.

I nodded. "Yes, divorce me. You can say it."

"He would never divorce his empress."

My eyes grew wide and the first smile in days tugged at my lips. "No, he would not."

Bonaparte declared the French Empire in May, though he could not decide if I would be granted the title of empress.

"What does a woman do with such a title? It isn't necessary," he said. "It doesn't change your power."

"It would improve your reputation," I said. "Your wife would make history alongside you."

"The people do love you," he mused aloud. "We will see."

Once the empire had been declared, we attended an impossible number of official dinners and traveled from town to town, too far from my little Napoléon, the children, and Malmaison. A depressive humor came over me, made worse by my detestable in-laws.

"Bow to your emperor!" Bonaparte bellowed from his place at the table during a family celebration.

"You aren't emperor yet," Elise retorted, sinking her teeth into a roll. Through a mouthful of food she asked, "When will the coronation take place?"

"Elise! Do not speak while chewing," Letizia said.

Elise glowered at her mother.

"It will take months to prepare. I'm aiming for December." Bonaparte dabbed at a spot of *sauce hollandaise* that had splattered his jacket.

"And what will my new title be?" Elise demanded.

"I don't intend to distribute new titles to everyone," Bonaparte said. "Joseph, Louis, and Eugène will become princes for the sake of the bloodline. Their wives will become princesses. The rest of you will remain as you are."

My heart plummeted. He had decided. And I could be replaced. I focused on the lacy pattern on the tablecloth to hold my rising emotion at bay.

"How can you condemn us to obscurity?" Elise asked, incredulous. "Your own flesh and blood! I should be made a princess!"

"At least *she* won't be named empress," Caroline quipped, eyeing me with contempt. "After all, she's quite unable to fulfill her wifely duties, never mind her duty to the empire."

My mouth dropped open in shock. She spoke as if I weren't in the room. Before I could reply, Bonaparte slammed the table with his fist.

"Enough! You behave like greedy swine! After all I have given you, you demand more!" His face burned scarlet. "And my wife has done nothing to deserve your scorn! She's been gracious and kind. You spurn her sisterly affection without merit."

"Nabulione," his mother began, "you should consider the problem of your heir—"

"She *will* be my empress!"

Relief and gratitude flooded my heart. Then love. I smiled at my beloved husband.

Caroline's ears burned. Louis directed a pointed look at Joseph and then his mother.

Bonaparte noted the exchange. "Madame Mère, I believe you're sitting in my wife's seat. Her Imperial Highness, Empress Josephine should be at the head of the table."

"How dare you speak to our mother that way!" Caroline shouted.

"Son, your head has grown too large for your body," Letizia said in a glacial tone. "I'll move when I like. You're not my husband or my master."

"I am your ruler!" He pitched his fork at his plate and stood.

I flinched at the clang of metal on porcelain.

"You ungrateful ass!" Elise said.

"Who is the ingrate here?" Bonaparte roared. "Leave my table at once!" He swept his goblet to the floor. The crystal smashed to pieces.

"Gladly! It's clear I'm not respected here! You tyrant!" Elise pushed back from the table with such force her own glass wobbled.

"You haven't seen me act the tyrant yet, sister!" The veins in his neck throbbed.

"I'm not afraid of you! You and *your empress* can go to hell!" She stormed from the room.

Caroline jumped to her feet and followed. Once they had gone, Madame Mère, Joseph, and Louis turned their eyes to me. I alone was to blame. Every family issue, every fault of Napoléon's stemmed from his marriage to me, their eyes said.

I met their looks with placid resolve. They would not bully me any-more. I could not be cast aside, forgotten and belittled. I would do my duty to my husband and my country, not to them.

I would be empress.

Summer faded to fall while we prepared for the coronation. Bonaparte pressured the Pope to attend, and he would, it seemed. I worked with a team of valets on clothing, banquet food, and musicians. Everything must be perfect for the historical day. In the evenings after a day of endless preparations, the imperial party studied a model of our procession made with paper dolls. No one could misstep or move out of position, lest they disrupt the entire ceremony.

The night before the coronation, snow dusted the gardens in a fluffy powder. Fitting, I thought, to begin anew in a blanket of white. But by morning, the dazzling carpet had turned to slop under driving rain. When the time came to set out for Notre Dame, the children and I rushed into the carriage to remain dry.

Onlookers gathered along the boulevards, throwing flowers despite the rain that beat their flimsy umbrellas. Crowds had traveled from afar to pay homage to my husband, the emperor.

A lightness settled over me, despite my nerves.

I would be Empress Josephine.

I smiled as much to myself as to the citizens in the street. My posi-tion would be secure—all I had worked to maintain for my family, for myself, would be safeguarded. Bonaparte had fended off his family, at last. They could not separate us.

When we reached Notre Dame, my hairdresser whisked me away to the priests' chambers in the rear of the church. He had already applied chestnut coloring to the patches of gray the evening before. Now he threaded diamonds among the strands and affixed my golden diadem.

"Voilà," Monsieur Justin said, tilting a silver-backed mirror this way and that.

My hair sparkled like a glittering halo. My cheeks blushed petal pink and my eyes sparked with excitement. Fit to be empress.

"It is time for the dress."

My stomach somersaulted. My ladies-in-waiting moved around me in a tornado of hands and fabric, assisting me into a form-fitting gown with a high waist—Monsieur Isabey's design—in white satin stitched with silver and gold thread and diamond studs. A stout lace collar jutted from my shoulders toward my chin, cupping my face.

Bonaparte, adorned in white satin, entered the chamber, followed by a crowd of servants and Monsieur LeRoy, who flitted about in a nervous frenzy.

"The family is ready," Bonaparte said. "They've all gone to their stations." He brushed my cheek with his lips.

I squeezed his hand as the crowd shuffled into the church and filled the pews.

"No time to waste, Your Imperial Highness." Monsieur LeRoy clapped his hands and the servants brought forth the last pieces of our ensembles, scarlet velvet robes lined with ermine and embroidered with golden bees.

I stepped in front of the looking glass. My petite frame dripped in rubies and diamonds and beautiful fabrics.

"*Amore mio*, you are a vision," Bonaparte said, eyes filled with joy. "We make history today."

My heart skipped a beat. Empress of France, of all Europe.

"With the emperor of my heart." I blew him a kiss.

Martial music blared, signaling the beginning of our march. My stomach buzzed as if the golden bees on my robe swarmed within.

We entered the frigid church in the slow procession we had practiced. The Bonaparte sisters took their places behind me, supporting the weight of my lengthy train. Onlookers shivered with awestruck faces. A full orchestra played. Light filtered through the towering stained glass windows, and candles glowed.

I fixed a smile upon my face and counted my steps as we moved. One at a time.

Once everyone took their places, the Pope and his cardinals began a lengthy mass. I studied the throng of familiar faces. Our ministers and supporters, family members and friends sat in silent reverence. Finally, when Pope Pius called Bonaparte forward, all eyes fixed upon my beloved husband.

The Pope raised his hands above Bonaparte's head and anointed it with oil. "May the spirit of our Lord and Savior, Jesus Christ, guide you and keep you. I hereby anoint thee, Napoléon Bonaparte, Emperor of France and of all her territories." The Pope lifted the crown from its velvet pillow.

In one swift motion, Bonaparte stood and snatched the diadem from the Pope's holy hands.

A gasp echoed in the stillness of the room.

"Emperor Bonaparte, I am thus crowned." My husband placed the heavy circlet upon his own head. "Emperor of France, Emperor of Europe." His voice thundered in the vast church.

I glanced at the startled faces in the crowd. Bonaparte did not seek anyone's blessing. The service had been for show. I was not shocked at his behavior, but no one knew him as I did.

My husband inclined his head in my direction.

I began my ascent to the altar. Could they hear my heart pounding?

I moved slowly, steadily. When I took my final step, a great weight yanked me from behind. My sisters-in-law had dropped my mantle. The wretches wanted me to fall.

I struggled to regain my footing.

Bonaparte glared at his siblings with such ferocity they gathered my train at once.

I inhaled an even breath. I would not waste another thought on them on this most important day.

I knelt before God, the congregation, the Pope, and my husband.

Bonaparte lifted my own diadem and said, "I crown thee, Imperial Highness Josephine Bonaparte, Empress of France, Empress of Europe." He lowered it to my head.

My heart leapt in exultation.

I bent over my folded hands and serenity filled me. Empress of the French, Empress of Bonaparte's heart.

My duties did not change, though the expansion of our royal court burdened everyone, even my husband, who had demanded it.

"The finery and lavish displays demonstrate my power," he insisted.

We sat through lengthy introductions and state affairs, Bonaparte fidgeting on his throne all the while. I thought three sets of curtsies and a kissing of his ring a bit extreme, but enforced his wishes among my ladies-in-waiting. He enjoyed their attentions.

"You're exquisite, Mademoiselle Larouche." He held her hand an instant too long and gazed into her eyes.

I pretended not to notice, though I would love to expel her from court. Or give him a swift kick.

My bustling salon and Bonaparte's constant meetings consumed our days. Our evenings alone waned as Bonaparte's time on the road increased.

I lamented of it to Hortense one afternoon while playing whist. "I feel as if he's never here and when he is, his mind is consumed."

"An emperor's responsibilities must be infinite. And wearing on an empress." Hortense sorted through her cards and placed them in her preferred order. "I worry about you, Maman. You will make yourself ill with your schedule. You suffer such strain and for what? The admiration of courtiers who care for nothing but rank? You should take some time away. Come with me to the springs. Your grandchildren will be thrilled to have you along. A visit to the spa will do you some good."

The door flew open.

A round-faced cherub galloped into the room with a young nurse-maid in his wake.

"Napoléon, *mon petit chou*, I thought you were napping." Hortense frowned at her son.

He ignored her and jumped onto the settee beside me. "Grand-mère, can I play?" His chubby hands grabbed at my cards.

I laughed. "Of course, *mon amour*." I kissed his plump cheek and sifted my fingers through his fine blond hair. "I will show you how."

He plopped into my lap without a care and wriggled until comfortable. "I love to play."

"Napoléon, this game is for adults." Hortense turned to the nurse-maid. "He should be napping."

"*Oui*, madame. I beg your pardon, but he would not lie still and jumped from bed. I chased him through the halls." She curtsied. "I apologize for interrupting your game."

"My three-year-old angel is welcome anytime." I planted a kiss on the crown of his head. I could not kiss him enough.

He jumbled my pile of cards, pink tongue wagging.

I laughed. "Such concentration for a little man."

"One game and then back to bed," Hortense said.

Little Napoléon looked at her with sorrowful blue eyes. "Only one game, Maman?"

"One."

"How can you resist such a face?" I squeezed him again. "And a vacation would be heaven."

Hortense and I had been absent for only a month when Monsieur Talleyrand, Bonaparte's foreign minister, heard troubling news from the Austrian front. I returned to Paris at once.

Austria had joined the Russian forces to declare war on the empire. Bonaparte and Eugène prepared to march. I despaired at the thought of sending my son and husband into harm's way once again.

"Surely you won't go yourselves?" I asked.

"It will give the people hope to see their leader defeat the enemy," Bonaparte said. "We'll leave for Prussia in two days. Speed in battle, the element of surprise is more important than supplies or men. I'll form an alliance with the Prussians and divide the Russian forces. This time, my little Creole, you are coming, too."

We departed Paris straightaway. The Prussian King agreed to Bonaparte's scheme and our armies advanced at once. I remained in Bavaria as a correspondent, receiving foreign ministers and accepting honors on my husband's behalf. As often as possible, I left my antiquated lodging and visited the wounded in the hospitals.

I stood over a French captain who lay unmoving on his cot. His face was ashen, lips bruised, and his skull wrapped in dirty bandages. He could have been Eugène. Bile rose in my throat at the horrific thought. I accepted a cloth from a nurse and dipped it in a basin of water, then wiped the exposed skin of the soldier's cheeks and neck.

His single uncovered eye fluttered open. "Empress Josephine? God bless you." His voice came out as a forced whisper. "Have we defeated them?"

"Do not strain yourself, captain. You must heal. But yes, victory is imminent." God willing.

His head rolled to the side. "*Grâce à Dieu.* Long live the emperor."

Bonaparte secured a prompt victory. The evening before the treaty was to be signed, Talleyrand warned him not to act with haste.

"You have a chance to make them allies," he said. "With Russia, Austria, and Prussia backing us, we may defeat the British. Without them, we may be lost."

"With my family as heads throughout the empire, we don't need allies." Bonaparte looked to me for confirmation.

"Our family is no substitution for proper leaders," I said. "I must agree with Monsieur Talleyrand."

Bonaparte ignored his minister of war and formed the Confederation of the Rhine, carving up the territories he had freed from the Austrians. He distributed them among the Bonapartes and my children like cards.

One evening, Bonaparte and I lay in bed, discussing the next moves for the family.

"I would like to adopt Eugène and Hortense," he said, "and make them official successors."

I sat up in bed with a start. "It would mean so much to them! And me!" I cradled his face in my hands and kissed him in twenty places.

He laughed at my enthusiasm. "They have been the best children a man could hope for." He looked away, realizing the implication of his words.

I turned his face toward mine. "What is it?"

"You know that Eugène cannot accept the throne?" he asked.

I nodded.

"But I will appoint him Viceroy of Italy and Louis and Hortense will be King and Queen of Holland."

My happy bubble burst. They would be so far from Paris, and with my grandchildren. I looked down at my hands.

He tilted my chin toward him. "You will still see them."

I stared past him. How often could I travel to Italy or Holland with all my appointments? It seemed impossible.

"I have more news. The Elector of Bavaria has agreed to Eugène's marriage to Princess Augusta."

My mouth fell open. Eugène to be married! "When? Have they met?"

"No, but do not fret, my love; Augusta is beautiful and sweet. Eugène will be mad for her. He will join us tomorrow. They will marry the following day."

The moment I saw Eugène with Princess Augusta, I knew he had fallen for the fair-haired beauty. She appeared to share his feelings. They could not be more perfectly matched.

"I'm in love," Eugène said not three weeks after his marriage. "Augusta is the loveliest woman on earth." A twinkle shone in his eyes, his hair was mussed, and his cheeks were rosy. Yes, my son was in love.

"I'm so happy for you." I embraced him.

An infectious grin crossed his face. "My cheeks ache from smiling. I am beyond reason!" He laughed. "I don't want to live a single day without her."

"You won't have to." I smiled, thrilled to have made a perfect match for at least one of my children.

Bonaparte and I returned to Paris for one season before Russia marched on the borders of his Confederation of the Rhine. Just as Talleyrand had warned. My husband departed at once for Poland. I remained in Paris with the court to ensure morale in the capital remained high, though fear consumed me, for more than one reason.

I had heard Polish women were very beautiful.

The months wore on. My regimented days continued. Bonaparte did not return and his letters became clipped. Exhausted and distressed, I sought refuge at Malmaison among my plants and forests, away from the meddling of the courtiers.

One afternoon, I walked among the purple magnolias as a courier thundered up the drive. He dismounted, breathless, and pulled letters from his saddlebag.

His hurried manner sent a chill over my skin.

"What is it, monsieur?" I asked. "Is it the emperor?"

"I have letters from His Imperial Highness and also from King Louis of Holland."

I snatched the letters and walked to the garden, dropping to a bench in the shade of a cherry tree. Louis, Hortense's husband, had written to me. I shredded the envelope with shaking hands and scanned the curled writing. Little Napoléon, my spirited, adorable grandson, was ill with fever and a rash. Louis could not calm Hortense.

Fear seized me. I would leave immediately. She needed her mother.

I tore open Bonaparte's letter as I rushed toward the house.

He knew of little Napoléon's illness? How long had my little darling been unwell? Bonaparte demanded I stay in Paris despite my grandson's condition.

I bolted inside. Was Bonaparte mad? I would not abandon my daughter in her time of need. My first duty was to my children, not his ridiculous court.

"Ready my carriage!" I shrieked. "I'm leaving within the hour!" A servant dashed off to alert the coachmen.

I stared unseeing through the coach window as the countryside sped by.

Lord, let my grandson recover, I prayed. *Please let him live.*

Rumors
Palais des Tuileries, 1807–1809

I was too late.

Little Napoléon died in the early hours of the morning in Hortense's arms. When I arrived, I found my daughter huddled in a corner of her son's room. She rocked back and forth, cradling one of his toys. Her hair had come loose, forming a crimped halo around her head. Her dress looked as if it had been wadded into a ball.

Sorrow hit me like a blow. "Hortense!"

Her vacant eyes met mine for an instant, then flickered away.

I gathered her in my arms and caressed the pale skin of her face. "Oh, my darling." I rocked her wilted body in my arms. "My darling."

She said nothing. My own sobs filled the silence.

For days Hortense trembled violently or lay limp in her bed, but through it all she did not weep or even make a sound.

I sent for a doctor.

"She's in shock," he said, closing his bag. He lowered his voice so Hortense would not hear him. "It's very difficult to lose a child, Your Highness. She would do well to—"

"Difficult?" Her shrill voice interrupted him. "It's difficult?"

Hortense sprang from her bed. Her lace nightcap fluttered to the floor. Purple smudges ringed her frantic eyes. She looked as though she had been beaten.

"Hortense!" I rushed to her side.

"Napoléon!" she screamed. "My baby boy!" She ran from the

room. "God let him die! He took my baby boy!" She raced into the salon, nightdress billowing behind her.

I felt as if stabbed with a knife. My tears began again as I stumbled behind her.

"It will do you no good to excite yourself," the doctor said.

Hortense turned to snarl at him, but tripped over a corner of the burgundy rug. She hit the floor and gasped for air, then screamed, an inhumane sound. Shrieks tore from her lips over and over again as if she were being tortured.

I pulled her shaking body onto my lap and wrapped myself around her. She did not fight me. After many minutes, her screams dissolved into sobs.

"I want to die! I can't do this. I can't . . . Maman, make it stop. I can't . . . the pain . . . my baby boy."

I crushed her to my chest, rocking her for hours as she wailed.

How could God take him? How would she go on? A mother could not recover from losing a child.

Hortense was inconsolable. She refused to eat. Her skin sagged on her bony frame. Her eyes bulged and I feared for her life. I bartered, pleaded, and begged with God for her recovery.

She could get through this. She *would* get through this. She had to. She had another son who needed her.

To my surprise, Louis remained by her side. He was loving, patient, and kind. He carried her into the garden every morning, read to her, and rocked her in his arms. I wrote to Bonaparte from Holland. He claimed he was devastated by little Napoléon's death, but he did not come. I grew wretched, aching for my lost grandson and my ailing daughter.

I grew furious with my absent husband. Bonaparte had deserted his brother and daughter, his wife in our time of grief. I no longer knew the man I had married. He, who had been given all, had abandoned those who loved him.

"I'm at a loss, Louis. What will we do?" I asked one afternoon while Hortense slept.

"Maybe a trip away will help," he said.

"Yes. Maybe your country home near Brussels? I'll invite Eugène for the summer. She adores him."

Eugène left Italy at once to console his beloved sister. When he arrived, Hortense threw herself into his arms.

"He's gone, Eugène." Tears streamed down her hollow cheeks.

"Hortense." He rubbed her back. "Dear sister, I'm so sorry."

Days passed one by one.

Hortense responded well to her brother's love.

"You must eat, sister," he would say. "Just a bite of bread and jam." She nibbled at first, then consumed the entire slice.

He kissed her hand and smiled. "That's my girl. You must regain your strength."

Day after day, Eugène read to Hortense, strolled with her in the gardens, and sat beside her at the pianoforte. She did not smile or laugh, but the shroud of death lifted from her features. She poured her grief into exquisite melodies that floated through the palace day and night.

One note at a time, she began to heal.

By summer's end, I had returned to Paris with a promise from Hortense to visit before the holidays. Two days after my arrival, a letter was delivered from Martinique.

Maman had passed away in her sleep.

Grief weighed on me like a heavy cloak. I had not been there to lay my mother to rest, to say good-bye. I fell into a pit of despair and introspection. My family was gone. My own mortality stretched before me. My skin would wither, my mind would weaken. What was this life that I led?

Happiness seemed illusory. I drifted through my duties, the political nonsense. I waited, though for what I was not sure. For Bonaparte to return?

For the darkness to lift. For understanding.

Bonaparte scolded me for showing my despair. "Your letters are stained with tears. You indulge your sorrow. Be strong. The empire requires your guidance."

I bristled at his harshness and ceased to write to him.

A visit from Hortense pulled me from my emotional malaise. She planned to stay in Paris for several months; Louis no longer demanded she remain in their palace, isolated from family and friends.

After supper the first evening, we retired to my apartments alone.

Hortense settled into a chair. "I have news." A smile spread across her face—the first I had seen in months. She rubbed her belly. "I am pregnant!"

"Oh, Hortense!" I threw my arms around her. "I'm so happy."

A sparkle had returned to her eyes. "We needed good news, you and I." She kissed my hands. "And how are you, Maman?"

I frowned. "Do not worry about me. I am well enough."

"I've heard the rumors," she said softly. "The Bonapartes send mistresses to His Highness."

"So my friends tell me." I struggled to maintain my composure. "They wish to prove his fertility."

Hortense sat speechless for a moment. She knew my husband's family sought to undermine my position.

"He returns tomorrow."

A loud rapping sounded at the door.

"*Entrez.*"

A servant entered and curtsied. "Empress Josephine, the chief of police wishes to speak with you in private."

"Oh! I forgot. We're to discuss the security details of Bonaparte's return. Hortense, would you mind, dear?"

"Of course." She rose to go as Officer Fouché strode into my salon in his usual crisp black uniform, lapels embossed with gold thread. His face resembled a fox's with his almond eyes, high cheekbones, and pointy nose.

"Your Highness." He bowed, then adjusted his red sash. "I have a delicate matter to discuss." He clasped his hands behind his back in a nervous gesture.

"Are we to follow the usual protocol with the armory?" I asked, plucking a sugared cherry from a dish.

"Yes." He looked at the floor.

"What is it, Fouché?" I stopped chewing.

"This is very awkward, so I'll come straight to the point." He cleared his throat. "The emperor has a bastard child."

I choked into a napkin. I discarded the fruit and stared at him in disbelief.

"Your Highness?" he prompted.

"What is your point, monsieur?" I fixed him with an icy glare.

"The emperor's love for you is well known, but he needs an heir."

"Are you telling me this to be cruel?"

"Empress . . . Your Highness . . . How do I proceed?" He paused. "It's your duty, as a loving wife, as the mother of France, to file for divorce. You are loved, but your country needs an heir. Spare Bonaparte from making a scene. Step down and divorce him yourself. If you love him, you will do what is right, what is expected."

"How dare you!" My throat burned. "This is none of your business. Leave at once!"

My tone alerted the guards. In an instant they burst through my double doors. "Empress Bonaparte?" a soldier demanded, pistol drawn.

"Monsieur Fouché was just leaving." I pointed to the door.

"I hope you may convince the emperor otherwise. There are many Bonapartes as successors." He bowed and turned to go. "Good luck, Your Highness."

A guard closed the door behind him.

I cried for hours, until the walls grew too confining. A child! The barrenness was my fault and they had proven it at last.

Despite the late hour and snowy weather, I called for a coach. I stared into the bleak night as the carriage whizzed through slush. An occasional citizen bustled along, carrying parcels of meat and bread or bundles of wood in the dead of night. Bakery and tavern windows glowed, throwing light into the street. All other storefronts sat dark and silent.

Near the Luxembourg garden I ordered my driver to stop. A walk would clear my head.

"I don't advise it in the snow, Your Highness," my guard warned.

"I did not ask for your opinion. You may follow behind me. At a distance." Sodden clumps of snow dripped from branches of dormant pear and chestnut trees. I tramped through puddles, soaking my boots and dragging my skirts behind me.

Bonaparte would have a child with another woman. Would he marry her? I would not step down. My anger mounted. How dare he ask Fouché to say such a thing! Could he not face me himself?

I squished melting snow beneath my boot as three citizens rushed along a nearby path. I pulled my hood over my head to avoid recognition—a moment too late.

"Empress Josephine!" A man dropped to his knees. The others followed.

"You saved our ailing daughter, Your Highness. I am eternally grateful."

"Long live Empress Bonaparte!" the other man said, bowing his head.

"God bless you, gentlemen." I waved before turning toward my guards.

How could I abandon my people?

Bonaparte returned without a mistress. I nearly fainted with relief, though I began saving sums in secret. Within three short months, Bonaparte prepared to depart once more, to address the riots in Spain. This time, he insisted I go with him.

"To charm the diplomats, as you do," he said. "My brother has made a mess of things and he's threatening our alliance. The Spaniards detest Lucien."

I went with a glad heart; my role was invaluable.

Bonaparte despised the Spanish more than the Austrians, if possible, and handled his meetings like a child fraught with tantrums. I softened his behavior as best I could and helped secure the alliance.

Our last week in Spain, I encouraged him to take a vacation.

"We need to rest. To play and make love. Enjoy the sea before we return to our duties in Paris."

"That sounds like a fine idea, *amore mio*. We'll stay a few days." He ran his hand through my hair as I sat at the vanity rubbing cream on my face. "Why don't you take a walk on the beach? Get some fresh air. I'll join you as soon as I'm done with the meeting."

"Don't be too long." I blew him a kiss.

On the way to the beach, my yearning for the sea intensified. How I had missed the ocean, the smell of waves, warm grit between my toes, my hair rippling in the wind. *Home.* An ache radiated in my chest. How I missed home. *Maman.* My eyes watered at the image of her face. Some aches never healed, no matter how much time had passed.

When the coach stopped, I leapt from it and skipped along the shoreline, parasol in hand. Slate blue waves glistened in the sun. The scent of seaweed permeated the air, and wheat-colored sand stretched until the mountains met the sea. A lone fisherman cast into the waters, bobbing his line to attract his prey.

I envied his simple sense of purpose.

I secured my straw hat under my chin and plunked down onto the sand. Lost in thought, I did not notice Bonaparte, barefoot, barreling toward me. He pounced, sending a spray of sand into the air. We laughed and rolled, a tangled pile of limbs and muslin. My pink parasol rolled from my hand and blew into the waves.

"My parasol!"

"We'll get another." He pushed himself on top of me and trailed his fingers over my forehead, tracing my eyebrows and then the swells of my cheeks. He searched my face as if for an answer.

I focused on the love in his eyes. There would be no distress, no fears or jealousy on this perfect day.

He burrowed his face into the soft skin of my neck. "Darling, I've missed you. I need you near me. Always."

I brought his lips to mine and kissed him as if the world would end.

We spent six blissful months together. Bonaparte was attentive and tender. He slept in my arms every night, the way he used to. We were happy—until he departed for another campaign. I called upon Madame Rémusat to report every rumor, though they became more vicious.

"They say he plans a divorce and a marriage simultaneously," she said. "He has chosen a bride with the help of Tzar Alexander and his brothers."

The pattern of doubt, despair, and loathing became familiar and exhausting. Who I had become, where I longed to be, eluded me. I could not find myself among the hundreds of strangers at court, amid the constant competition, or even in my rooms alone at night. Adrift, I floated through bleak days. The price of being Empress Josephine, of being Bonaparte's wife, weighed on my soul. I knew something had to change.

When Bonaparte returned from his stint abroad, he arrived with the worst disposition I had ever witnessed. It seemed as if a devil had possessed him.

He barged into my salon in a fury. "What are you doing? I told you to meet me at two o'clock. It's a quarter past." He stalked across the room. "You, madame, will leave at once." He pulled the headmistress of the Society of Charitable Mothers to her feet.

She paled and straightened her hat. "Forgive me, Your Highness. I had no idea—"

"Go!" he roared. She bolted to the door.

"Bonaparte," I began, "what in God's name—"

"When I tell you to do something, you do it! I am your master! You obey me!" He stamped around the room, smashing my glass figurines. He swore and kicked the furniture. I stood behind the settee, waiting for the storm to pass. After several moments, he stopped and looked around the room, then at me. His enraged face crumpled and he flung himself into a chair.

"What am I doing?" He put his face in his hands. "I'm sorry. So sorry."

I moved behind him and placed my hands on his shoulders. "Whatever it is, *mon amour*, we will work through it. We will face it and carry on. You're fatigued and under a lot of strain. Why don't you rest? I'll send up a tray of tea and brandy."

He pulled me into his lap and kissed me hard. "I will always love you." Guilt shone is his eyes.

His desperate tone did not escape me. "And I, you."

For a fortnight Bonaparte mocked and belittled me, then swooned and begged my forgiveness. I weathered his tempestuous, cruel behavior and my dread grew stronger each day.

One evening at family supper, I did my best to ignore his agitated state.

"Josephine, you shouldn't be in that seat." He swigged claret from his goblet. "You're not master of this table."

His siblings regarded their brother with glee. They enjoyed seeing him take out his wrath on me.

"I always sit here."

"Sit somewhere else. Now." He threw down a chunk of bread.

He had to make a scene in front of his family? I wanted to wipe the smug looks from their faces.

"Very well." I set down my fork and moved to a new chair. A servant placed a fresh plate of food in front of me. But suddenly I was no longer hungry. I took a long draught of wine.

"Why did you wear that hideous dress to dinner?" Bonaparte demanded. "Had you nothing better to wear?"

"I had this dress made for you, Your Highness. It's blue French silk—your favorite. I thought you'd be pleased."

"I hate it. It's not flattering."

My stomach twisted into knots, but I pasted a pleasant smile on my face. "I'll give it to the poor."

"You've given enough as it is. You do nothing but spend my money. At this rate you'll bankrupt the empire."

Caroline chuckled.

Anger rose under my skin and I flushed. I met his eye. "Every empire ends. Yours may as well be known as one that gave to its citizens." I took another gulp of wine.

Joseph smirked and shoveled a piece of brisket in his mouth. He was enjoying the scene too much for my liking.

"Why don't you find another man to support your spending habits?" Bonaparte asked.

The blood drained from my face. There it was—his threat, the one he had longed to voice in these weeks since his return.

I folded my napkin and tossed it on my plate. "I'm quite finished here. Enjoy your meal, everyone."

I fled to my room to beat the tide of tears. I had scarcely closed the door when Bonaparte followed me in.

The sight of him fueled my rage. "What the devil has gotten into you? How dare you talk to me that way! You humiliate me and yet I've done nothing but what you ask of me!" My chest heaved and hot tears streamed down my face.

He hung his head in shame. When he looked up again, his own cheeks were streaked with tears. "I have something I need to say." He sat on the settee and ran a hand through his hair.

"Go on." I sat beside him.

"I've given this a lot of thought." His voice cracked. "For the country. For the empire . . . we must . . . It's not something I want to do, but I have no choice."

His words fell like stones in slow motion, as if in a dream.

"I'm so sorry, *amore mio*. I've been horrible to you these last few weeks, trying to assuage my guilt. You didn't deserve a moment of my ill behavior." He took my hand in his and kissed it.

My insides split apart. "Napoléon—"

"I can't even say this. . . . How am I to say this?" He groaned and rested his head in my lap.

An eternity passed. I sat in rigid silence, too numb to speak, to move.

At last he sat up and stroked my face. "My darling . . . we must divorce. I'm so sorry." He stroked my hair, my back. "I love you. I don't want to do this!"

My anger resurfaced. "You don't want to do this?" I lunged to my feet. "Then why do it?"

"You will always be my beloved Josephine." He reached for me.

"Don't touch me!" I held my sorrow close. It was all I had left.

"Please, can we talk about it? I love you. I will always—"

"Please leave me alone."

"Josephine—"

"Just go!"

He walked to the door and paused. "I need an heir. An emperor has no choice."

Tears blurred his image. "A man always has a choice—and an emperor more than any other!"

He hung his head and closed the door behind him.

The anger came.

I tore sheets from the bed, ripped drawers from the vanity and dumped their contents onto the floor. I kicked the pillows across the room and threw my writing tablets into the fire, watching them burn and fade to ash, to nothingness.

How could he abandon me? I had done his bidding, given him everything! Dismissed my friends, sold my daughter to his horrid brother! Sent my son to his wars!

I had saved him from himself.

I soaked my pillow with sorrow. I wept for our time together and our time apart, for his failings and for my own, for the loss of my crown, my people.

For the first time ever, I wept for the loss of myself.

Threshold

Palais des Tuileries, 1809

The divorce took place four weeks later—a public affair in the Throne Room of the Tuileries. The entire court attended in silver and gold lamé gowns, diamonds, and fine coats. Hundreds of candles blazed. Musicians poised to play as if at a fete, and it was—a celebration of my end.

Despite the crush of bodies, silence emanated through the hall.

The Bonapartes made the only sound. They gloated and clapped one another on the back. They had won. Soon they would be rid of la Beauharnais at last. Only Louis remained cordial. We had shared Hortense's darkest hour and he had not forgotten. Nor had I. We made eye contact and he quickly looked away.

I held my head high despite their triumphant looks, though my insides churned. I refused to cry in front of the gawking court, in front of my hateful in-laws. Eugène stood rigid at my left and Hortense held fast to my right hand.

How I longed for this to be over.

The provost called us to order. "Let us begin."

He read through the terms of the divorce. Bonaparte would pay my debts and grant me a generous yearly sum. I would keep my title and more important, Malmaison. But I could not live in Paris, lest my admirers refuse to accept the new empress. The thought cheered me. Perhaps my people would not like his new choice of wife.

"Hortense and Eugène Bonaparte shall retain their titles and properties," the provost concluded. "And now for the divorce decrees."

Bonaparte read his aloud first. "She has been a dutiful wife and loving mother, a patriot beyond compare. I have nothing but thanks to offer my well-beloved wife, with whom I shared thirteen years. You will not be forgotten, dear friend."

This could not be real. We were divorcing despite our love.

The provost nodded in my direction. "Empress."

I unfolded the damp note in my hand. "With my dear husband's permission, I offer the greatest proof of love, of my devotion. . . ." I paused. "I . . ." My voice quivered.

Eugène slipped his arm around my waist and Hortense squeezed my hand.

Caroline snickered.

The wolves would not have the pleasure of seeing me cry. Not today. I focused on my breathing and gave my speech to an aide, who read it promptly and without emotion.

Bonaparte stood. "I declare our divorce official and concluded." His voice shook and he wiped his eyes, his anguish plain.

My limbs went numb. It was done. I was divorced, dethroned, and cast off—but I was also free to go.

As my children and I turned to depart, my son, a war hero who had witnessed the last breath leave another man's body, had seen blood spurt from an enemy's wounds, fainted in his tracks.

A murmuring rippled through the crowd.

"Eugène!" I slipped my arm under his head.

"What a buffoon," Caroline piped. "They must always make a scene."

All the anger, sorrow, and disgust I had kept at bay for too many years rose to the surface. I released it into a single hateful glare. Caroline snapped her mouth shut and looked away.

"Shut up!" Bonaparte commanded. "All of you!" He ran to Eugène and knelt beside him.

No one dared speak, or even breathe.

A servant rushed over with salts.

Bonaparte waved them beneath Eugène's nose and tapped his cheek. "Dear boy."

Eugène's eyes opened slowly, filling with instant sorrow and then embarrassment as he realized what had happened.

"Let's take a walk," Bonaparte said, helping Eugène to his feet.

Eugène rubbed his head. "I cannot, Your Imperial Highness. I must go." His voice was hoarse. "Maman?" Eugène met my eyes. "I will return in the morning to escort you home."

Bonaparte's face crumpled in pain.

I was no longer home—I never had been. Malmaison. A sob stuck in my throat as I moved numbly toward the door.

I paused to look back at Bonaparte, to memorize his features. My greatest love, my greatest source of pain. Tears stained his cheeks. I turned to go, leaving him alone in the middle of his opulent court, surrounded by everyone and no one all at once.

My final evening in the Tuileries, servants whirled in and out of my rooms, preparing my things, leaving trays of food, and inquiring after my needs. I wept, then paced in agitation until I could take it no more. I threw my cloak over my shoulders and wandered through the haunted corridors and out into the garden one last time.

I turned my face to the moon. At last I was the maker of my own fate, sole mistress of Malmaison, my own beloved land upon which I could depend. The land I had salvaged from ruin and made my own. I had done my best by Bonaparte, but I would not sacrifice myself another moment. I had depended on others to fill my void for too long.

The cold night air bit my bared fingers and arms, but I did not shiver. I felt strangely alive. I took a cleansing breath and gazed at the eternal stars winking in the vast darkness.

The old sorceress's words echoed in my memory. "More than queen."

And I was—a daughter and mother, the mistress of France. A woman toiling for what was right, striving to do her part. The summation of all of my lifetimes: joy and pain, deeds and failings, and the lives I had touched.

Now I would create my own destiny, a livelihood and a happiness, without expectation or fear.

I wrapped my arms about my middle and strode toward the palace. When I returned to my room, I found a note that had been pushed under the door. I inhaled a sharp breath and opened it. A familiar script filled the small sheet.

I will not be here when you depart in the morning.

> Adieu, sweet Josephine.

> Bonaparte

He would not even say a proper good-bye. I tossed the note onto the floor and fell into bed for my final hours in the house of kings, the house of sorrows.

When the silver rays of dawn poured through the windows, I arose and splashed my face with water. I dressed slowly, without my ladies-in-waiting, without the help of anyone. I moved to the window. Rain came down in torrents and flooded the lawn. Servants loaded my belongings into a convoy of carriages, oblivious to the deluge. I sighed and opened the door of my boudoir for the final time.

As I walked toward the main hall, a guard stopped me. "Empress, forgive my impertinence, but he is a fool. He sends away his talisman, the only one who loves him. Forgive me for saying so, but it is true." I looked into his kind eyes. "Good luck, madame."

"Thank you, monsieur," I said, voice soft.

I joined Hortense, Eugène, and Mimi in the main hall. My family.

"Are you ready, Maman?" Eugène asked.

I nodded as a frantic servant approached. "Your Highness, we still have ten armoires of dresses to pack. Shall I send them later this afternoon?"

"Donate them to Penthémont and the other convents. I'm sure the ladies will be pleased to have them."

"But, Your Highness, they're priceless—"

"I have more than enough."

Her eyes widened in shock "As you wish." She curtsied and scurried away.

We dashed through the downpour and packed into our coach.

I held my breath as we pulled away from the imposing gray palace—my home and prison for more than a decade. I had always hated its drafty rooms and stuffy ambience, the rivalry of the court, the exhaustive days. It had suffocated my love and nearly suffocated me.

Hortense laid her head upon my shoulder. Eugène grasped my

hand in his. As we pulled through the palace gates, Parisians greeted us, sullen-faced, in the rain.

"Long live Empress Josephine!" they called.

"We love you, our Lady of Bounty!"

I waved as we rode through the boulevards; tears coursed down my cheeks. Eventually, they dried of their own accord. Hope budded in my chest. For the first time ever, I had no boundaries, no one to live up to or to persuade of my validity. My life and worth were my own. Bonaparte had provided the financial stability and I could provide the rest for myself. I could live in peace.

When we reached the drive of Malmaison—my solace, the land I loved—I looked out at my gardens, which lay fallow in the bleak weather. They would bloom anew with the spring sun.

I regarded my favorite maid and my children through misty eyes. Gratitude flooded my heart. I had everything I could ever need.

AUTHOR'S NOTE

Josephine led a rich and vivid life, almost melodramatic, some would say. So many details of her youth, her time during the Revolution, and especially her reign with Napoleon are documented in tireless detail. Yet despite the many factual accounts of Josephine's life, I found myself yearning to know her heart—her secret desires, the fear and desperation, the excitement or regret she felt as she began each new phase of her life. I became enthralled by her ability to adapt, her grace and generosity, and the fiery spirit beneath her perfectly lacquered veneer. She was a survivor, an ardent lover, and a mother to her children, her men, and her country. I hope I have communicated that in *Becoming Josephine*.

Though this novel is based largely in fact, it is ultimately a work of fiction. I made editorial decisions to preserve the momentum in the narrative or to highlight certain details for the sake of the story. Also, due to the thirty years spanned in the novel, I compressed periods of Josephine's history to emphasize the theme of her inner growth.

All letters have been fabricated (though based upon authentic letters), except for those attributed to Napoleon Bonaparte, which are excerpts from actual letters reproduced exactly as he wrote them in *Napoleon's Letters*, a collection edited by J. M. Thompson. The only exception is Napoleon's short farewell to Josephine near the end of the novel.

For more anecdotes about Josephine and the Bonapartes, and my own musings about these lives and times, visit HeatherWebb.net.

ACKNOWLEDGMENTS

When I began this process, I had no idea how many great minds would take part in shaping this novel! First and foremost, I must thank my lovely agent, Michelle Brower, whose warmth, market sense, and editing instincts (not to mention her baking recipes) are unparalleled. Denise Roy and the entire crew at Plume—thank you for sharing your wisdom and time on my great adventure. I am blessed to work with such a supportive and talented team.

To my family, the Webbs and DiVittorios, I can never thank you enough for your support, especially my parents, Jeff and Linda Webb, Chris, and Charlene—you keep me honest. I love you beyond words.

A special thanks to my best friend and sister, Jennifer Webb, who gets it. It's a hard road to follow our dreams.

To my in-laws, Pam and Richard Schreiber, who have cheered me on every step of the way, as well as Levi and Asa Petersen, and all the Petersens and Johnsons. I am utterly blessed to be a part of your loving fold. Also thank you, Joy Steed, for your warm support.

To my coven of women who have stood by me in the best of times and the worst, especially Angie Parkinson, Heather Tracy DeFosses, Christine Taylor, Kelly Loveday, Angela Burns, and Christina Mc-Crory. And to Rebecca Alexander Haeger—girl, no one should have to listen to so many conversations about the publishing industry. I'm not sure where I'd be without you all. I love you.

My novel would not have realized its full potential without the input of my beloved critique group, the SFWG. I cherish each one of you. Your insight and talent lift me up on a daily basis. I raise my glass to you: Susan Spann, Amanda Orr, Marci Jefferson, Julianne Douglas, Janet B. Taylor, DeAnn Smith, Candie Campbell, Lisa Janice Cohen, and Arabella Stokes.

A special thanks to my early readers and the never-ending support of many friends, including Jeffrey and Mary Withey, Christine Troup, Joe Anastasio, my book club, and all the fine folks at Bacon Academy and the Mansfield Community Center. Thank you!

To my tribe! From my childhood and college friends to my fellow teachers, students, and beyond; the fabulous group at Writer Unboxed; my friends at the Historical Novel Society; the Backspace community; and my hilarious, witty friends from Twitter and Facebook. You know who you are. Your daily cheer and thoughtful insight keep this party going.

Finally, the biggest gratitude there is to my babies, Kaia and Nicolas. There's no one on this planet who will ever love you more! And to my husband, Chris. You're the real deal, baby. You're the reason poetry was invented. I love you.